PRAISE FOR

" . . . Hickman masterfully balances tension with her whip-smart humor and addictive romance."

— BARBARA KLOSS, AUTHOR, THE GODS OF
MEN

"The perfect ending to a delightful trilogy. Tissues are a must."

— ELLE BEAUMONT, AUTHOR, THE DRAGON'S
BRIDE

"Oh my heart."

— NATALIE MURRAY, AUTHOR, EMMIE & THE
TUDOR KING

" . . . an addicting ride with characters who have started to feel like home."

— CANDACE ROBINSON, AUTHOR, LYRICS &
CURSES

"This entire series is by far one of the most unique, inventive, imaginative, compelling and entertaining series I've read."

— BRIANNE WIK, AUTHOR, ONE IRIDESCENT
NIGHT

The C.R.O.C.

Book 3 in The Pan Trilogy

JENNY HICKMAN

Midnight Tide
PUBLISHING

Published by Midnight Tide Publishing

www.midnighttidepublishing.com

Cover Design: www.milagraphicartist.com

Interior Formatting by Book Savvy Services

THE CROC/ Jenny Hickman. *– 1st ed.*

Paperback ISBN- 978-1-953238-29-0

Hardback ISBN- 978-1-953238-30-6

eBook ISBN- B08T8PT71Q

AUTHOR'S NOTE

This book has scenes depicting violence and captivity, discussions surrounding rape and suicide, and contains some sexual content. I have done my best to handle these elements sensitively, but if these issues could be considered triggering for you, please take note.

To the members of the PANdom. This one's for you.

ONE

The yellow liquid in the vial seemed to come alive in the palm of Vivienne's hand. She wasn't sure how long she'd sat on the edge of her bed staring at it, afraid to hope that the tiny glass bottle held the answers to her impending forgetfulness.

"I can't believe it was inside my mother's perfume all along." She had been toting around poison for over six months. It was a good thing TSA hadn't checked her bag on the way to London. That would've been super awkward.

Deacon took it from her, held it up to the lamplight, and peered through the glass. "I suppose this explains why HOOK torched your house."

Years ago, Vivienne's father had agreed to assist HOOK with their research in exchange for the poison. But she'd thought Dr. Hooke hadn't held up his end of the bargain. Knowing her father had succeeded gave her a little solace that her parents' death hadn't been completely in vain. Their sacrifice could save the PAN.

This was huge. Life-changingly big.

So big that—"We need to tell Peter right now." He would be thrilled. And after everything that had happened at the trial, Neverland could use some good news.

"As much as I love seeing you undressed," Deacon murmured, trailing his finger down her ribs and along her hip, "I don't think you should go rushing to the Wendy Bird in your knickers."

The idea of bursting through the door in her underwear made her laugh. "At least I wouldn't have trouble getting everyone's attention."

Deacon set the poison on the nightstand and pulled her between his knees. "Why do you need their attention when you have all of mine?" The kiss he pressed above her navel left her legs feeling like they were made of twigs, ready to snap and give out if he kept going.

"Let me go." There was no heat in her breathless command. "I need to . . . " What did she need to do? "Um . . . get dressed."

"No." His hold on her tightened.

"Deacon . . . we need . . . to . . . " His lips drifted south. "*Go!*" she squealed, wriggling out of his grasp.

Falling onto his back, Deacon scrubbed a hand down his face before twisting his wrist to check his watch. "It's four o'clock in the morning. Even if they're still there—which I'll admit is likely—they'll be drunk and useless."

Was it really that late? Vivienne narrowed her eyes at her own watch, but the hands wouldn't stay *still*. She should have gotten a digital one.

"Come to bed." He patted the mattress and gave her a crooked smile that made the fireflies in her stomach flit around. "I can think of a few ways to celebrate this discovery without leaving the room."

When he put it like that, how could she resist?

She laid down beside him, resting her head on his chest

and inhaling the spicy cologne where his neck met his shoulder.

"You've had a lot to drink," he said, pressing a kiss to her hair, "and I'm not exactly sober myself."

He was sober enough to make a good point.

"Why don't we both get some . . . rest?" he went on, shifting so he could nuzzle her neck. His warm breath tickled the shell of her ear, sending shivers across her bare skin. Vivienne let his wandering hands make an equally convincing argument.

Because she didn't *want* to leave this bed. Not really. She wanted to stay right here and forget about HOOK and Leadership and poison and everything except the guy kissing his way down her neck to her collarbone and . . .

"Tomorrow," she agreed, arching her back, giving Deacon access to the clasp on her bra. "We can talk to Peter tomorrow."

Deacon hummed as he smiled against her skin. "Tomorrow."

Vivienne peered through her lashes, afraid if she opened her eyes too quickly, the gray light drifting through a gap in the curtains would burn her retinas. Her mouth tasted awful. Why had she had so much to drink?

The water on the nightstand was only an arm's reach away, but her arms were too heavy, and her head felt like she'd slammed it against the wall repeatedly. How was it possible to feel hot and cold at the same time?

Deacon's groan gave her a bit of comfort; it was nice to know he probably felt as bad as she did. Not that she'd wish this monumental hangover on anyone, but she didn't want to be alone in her agony. They could be miserable together.

Memories mixed with dreams, making it hard to distinguish fantasy from reality. Had last night really happened? Had they really found HOOK's poison?

Everything looked the same as it had the night before. The armoire was still askew from the wall, her clothes abandoned next to Deacon's. The broom and dustpan were lying on the floor next to one of her shoes. And the vial of poison was right beside—

Gone.

It was gone.

She sat up too fast and had to brace herself against the headboard as the room started spinning and her stomach gurgled. *Oh crap.* She was going to be sick.

Water. She really needed water.

Vivienne grabbed the glass and took a large gulp. Then another.

"I'd make sure it doesn't want to come back up before you guzzle the whole thing," Deacon mumbled, his arm thrown across his eyes, one leg on top of the covers, one under. His black boxer briefs were still hanging over the footboard.

Vivienne set the glass back down and searched the floor for the vial. If she'd knocked it off in her sleep and it broke, she'd never forgive herself. It wasn't under the bed or behind the nightstand. Where the heck had it gone? Had she dreamt that part up?

No. It had definitely happened.

Twisting back to Deacon, she gave his leg a kick beneath the covers. "You didn't go to Peter's without me, did you?" If he had, she was going to kill him.

"I haven't budged since you took advantage of me last night." The way his lips curled upward told her that he hadn't minded one bit.

"Says the guy who refused to let me leave the bed."

His smile broadened. "I wasn't complaining, lovie. You can take advantage of me any time you want."

Lovie?

Where had that come from?

She'd never had a pet name before. She kinda liked it. A lot.

"Where is it, *lovie*?" she asked, poking him in the shoulder. It didn't sound as good when she said it.

"My sanity?" He caught her and pressed a kiss to the back of her hand. "As I've said before, you stole it."

Vivienne was too hungover for his charm to work. "You know I meant the poison."

"Oh, right." A chuckle. "Top drawer."

The vial rolled to the front of the drawer when she opened it, easing some of the tension in her shoulders. "When are we going to see Peter?"

"Give me a minute to wake up, woman." He grunted and rolled toward her, propping himself onto his elbow. His eyes caressed her exposed skin, then he frowned. "I distinctly remember taking this off." He snapped her bra strap at her shoulder. His hand slipped around her back and twisted. In one flick, her bra was unhooked again.

She caught the front before he could pull it off and throw it across the room. Deacon got a kick out of watching her wander around trying to find her clothes.

"I don't want to know how many bras you've undone to learn how to do that."

"No." A grin. "You don't."

Vivienne refastened the stupid thing before Deacon could convince her to postpone their trip to his grandad's house again. This was the only chance they would have to hand Peter Pan a vial of HOOK's poison, and as enticing as her fiancé looked all sleep-rumpled and bed-warmed, she wanted to get this over with.

Plus, she really, really needed to brush her teeth. They hadn't yet been together long enough to shatter *that* illusion.

"Get up." She shoved his arm, knocking him back onto

5

the bed. "I'll make breakfast." They didn't have much food in the apartment, but as long as there was bread, they'd survive. Hopefully some toast would soak up any remaining alcohol sloshing around in her stomach.

Deacon stretched his hands toward the ceiling and yawned. "I'd rather have you for breakfast."

Vivienne pulled her Ohio sweatshirt from the hook on the back of the door. Before she left the bedroom, she promised Deacon that he could have her for brunch.

Deacon's headache was just beginning to subside when the taxi stopped outside his grandad's cheerful yellow house. Vivienne's black top with an impossibly deep V at the neck peeked from beneath her jacket. Her tight jeans made him sorry they hadn't stayed in the flat a bit longer. He had done his best to try and convince her, but she was too stubborn for his own good. It wasn't like an extra hour would've made a difference. If anything, letting Peter sleep in would have been a good thing.

Deacon held open the wrought iron gate and kept his hand on her elbow as they walked up the tiled path and the stairs to the stoop. He really needed to stop thinking about the way she'd looked this morning, her cheeks flushed from his more arduous attempts to keep her in bed.

Rain. Think about the rain.

Or the house. It was a fine house. Could do with a lick of new paint though.

He lifted the cold knocker and let it fall. Once. Twice.

Vivienne smiled up at him, her dark hair a glorious mess of damp waves. God, he loved her. And for some reason, despite his less-than-chivalrous past, she loved him. With the trial behind them, they finally, *finally* had a chance to be together. And now that they'd found the poison, the lab could develop a cure for her forgetfulness. After the year they'd had, things were looking up at last.

"Donovan? Hello?" Deacon tried the knocker a third time. When no one answered, he twisted the knob to find it unlocked. "That's strange."

"What's strange?" Vivienne asked, gripping his arm and peering around him into the house. The patchwork tiles in the foyer gleamed like they'd been polished, and the smell of coffee and bacon wafted toward them.

Deacon's stomach rumbled. Bacon sounded really good right now.

"I can't remember ever arriving without Donovan meeting me at the door." Donovan was as much of a fixture at this house as the brass knocker.

"Maybe Peter gave him the morning off," she said with a shrug.

"Peter gives him every morning off. But Donovan insists on answering the door and making the tea and every other menial task he does."

"Why?"

"Because Peter saved his life."

Deacon went into the hall and checked the parlor. It was empty except for the hideous drapes and overly ornate furniture that belonged in a museum. There were a few modern pieces Deacon's mother had bought, like the armchair beside the fireplace and the colorful rug, but Peter refused to get rid of the other stuff because Angela had picked it out. Fifty years ago. And it was still "good."

Sometimes it was easy to forget Peter was an old man trapped inside a teenager's body—until Deacon saw his parlor. Who needed a parlor anyway? Seemed a waste of space considering there was another more comfortable sitting room in the converted conservatory at the back of the house.

"You can't leave me with that cliff-hanger." Vivienne

7

tugged his sleeve and followed him toward the staircase. "Deacon?"

"*Quiet.*"

There were voices coming from the hallway on the left. His grandad's office door was ajar, but the room beyond was black. It sounded like whoever was inside was arguing, but that made no sense. Peter rarely raised his voice, let alone—

A woman screamed.

Deacon's adrenaline skyrocketed.

Out. He had to get Vivienne out of here.

Deacon whirled around, caught Vivienne by the arm, and dragged her . . . *where*? Where were they going to go?

The street was busy and there was nowhere to hide in the yard and it was too bright out to fly and . . . *the parlor.* They could hide there until Extraction arrived. He hauled her into the room.

Drapes. Sideboard. Coffee table. Side tables. Sofa.

Sofa.

On the far side of the sofa, there was an alcove where he used to hide during hide-and-seek when he was little. He shoved Vivienne into the gap, and she tucked herself into a ball against the plaster.

"Who was that?" she asked, her words barely a whisper. Her rich brown eyes were wild and searching for answers.

"I don't know." Deacon kept his voice and head down, listening to the silence punctuated by the ticking grandfather clock in the far corner.

"Do you think Peter's okay?"

"I don't know."

"What do you think—"

"Vivienne? Lovie." He cradled her cheeks in his hands. How was her skin so soft? "I know as much as you do." Which was a whole pile of nothing.

She bit her lip and nodded.

The screaming had stopped. Which had to be a good thing.

Deacon needed to find his grandad, and the first place he had to look was the study. "If I'm not back in two minutes," he said, rubbing his thumb against the teeth marks on Vivienne's lower lip, "I want you to call Extraction."

"What? *No.*" Her nails dug into the skin at his wrist when she grabbed for him. "Don't leave me here."

He didn't want to, but what other choice did he have? "Two minutes." She didn't let go. "Please?"

Slowly, her grip eased, and she nodded.

Deacon's heart thrummed in his ears as he crept with his spine against the wall. The voices were back, but they seemed calmer. When he reached the door, he peered into the gap.

Peter was sitting on his chair, his face cast in a blue light from the computer screen. There was a man standing in front of the desk, his back to the entrance.

Reasonably certain he wasn't going to be killed, Deacon shoved the door aside.

Instead of a woman in distress, Deacon found only shelves and shelves of Peter's memorabilia, framed posters, and ridiculous cardboard cut-outs.

When the other man turned around, he narrowed his eyes at Deacon, and his lips twisted into a mocking smile.

The muscles in Deacon's stomach tensed, and he groaned. "What the hell is *he* doing here?"

TWO

Vivienne stared at the second hand on her watch as it went around once. Twice. Deacon still hadn't returned. But there also hadn't been sounds of a struggle or anything beyond that one scream, so that was a plus. Unless something terrible had happened to the woman and to Peter and now to Deacon—

She knew she was supposed to call Extraction, and she would—*after* she made sure Deacon was okay. The adrenaline igniting in her veins tried to steer her toward the front door, but she turned down the dark hallway instead.

The kitchen on the right was quiet and empty. Deep voices rumbled from Peter's study.

She tiptoed across the colorful tiles and listened.

"What the hell is *he* doing here?" *Deacon*. She'd be able to pick his voice out anywhere. He sounded more annoyed than worried, which she took as her cue to slip through the doorway.

Deacon was standing beside a stranger dressed in a pair

of black dress pants and a dark gray sweater. Vivienne tried to remember if the guy had been at the Leadership meeting yesterday but didn't think so.

The phone in Peter's hand clattered to the desk when he shot to his feet. "You both need to leave."

"There's no need to snap, Grandad. We have something important to tell you." Deacon slipped an arm around Vivienne's waist, tugging her close.

Her fingers wrapped around the cold vial in her jacket pocket, clinging to her only hope. Now that she had the cure for her condition, she could admit to herself that she was terrified of forgetting everything. Her memories made her who she was, and without them, she'd be no one. A stranger to even her closest friends. To Deacon.

"Whatever you have to say can wait until later," Peter ground out, his fists perched on his hips in the same pose as a cardboard figure behind him.

"No. It can't," Deacon insisted.

Groaning, Peter rubbed a hand down his face. His green eyes looked weary and shadowed. "Fine. Say your piece. *Then* leave."

Even after Deacon's funeral, Peter had been friendly. Why was he being so rude now? Had something happened at the Wendy Bird last night? And who the heck was this guy smirking at them?

Deacon stiffened. "Not until you tell us what's going on."

On the computer screen in front of Peter, there was a young woman, probably in her late teens, wearing a white nightgown that reached to her thin knees. She was in a gray-walled room with a hospital bed, a desk and chair, a toilet and sink.

"Is that who we heard screaming?" Vivienne asked, nodding toward the haunting image. It reminded her of something out of a horror movie. The woman's face was as

11

white as her nightgown, and there were dark smudges beneath her eyes. "Who is she?"

Deacon's head tilted as he squinted at the screen. "I haven't a clue."

That was no surprise. The time stamp at the bottom corner was over thirty years ago.

"We don't know who she is," Peter said quietly, sinking back to his chair and cradling his head between his hands, "but she's one of us."

Vivienne's stomach twisted. A PAN in a cage.

The room where Vivienne had been held at HOOK had looked similar. Not as stark, but a cage nonetheless. "Show me." When it looked like Peter was going to protest, she pulled away from Deacon and stepped closer to the desk. "*Please.* I need to see."

If this had something to do with HOOK—and she had a feeling it did—she needed to know what fate would have awaited her if she hadn't escaped.

The stranger's smirk disappeared as he crossed his arms and narrowed his eyes at her. Peter reached for his keyboard and pressed the space bar.

The woman's blond hair flowed wild about her shoulders as she flew around the room, making her look like a ghost. She clawed frantically at the door handle and beat on the walls.

Oh no.

No no no . . .

It was *worse* than a horror movie.

The blood dripping from her fists and splattering on her bare feet was real.

High-pitched wails of terror and desperation erupted from the woman's chest.

Peter muted the volume, but it was too late. The sound had already been scorched into Vivienne's brain.

In the video, an older man came in wearing a surgical

mask, cap, and gown, and dragged the woman kicking and screaming from the room. After fast forwarding a few hours, the man returned, pushing the woman in a wheelchair. Her head lolled to the side, her face pale and her eyes vacant.

The pattern of agitation and disappearing continued until one day, the woman stumbled out of the bed and fell to her knees in front of the toilet to vomit. As she knelt there, a red stain appeared beneath her, spreading into a wide puddle. Vivienne's stomach lurched.

There was *so* much blood.

"What's happening?" Vivienne covered her mouth with a shaking hand.

Eventually, someone in blue scrubs came in with a wheelchair to take the woman away.

Peter's answer was a whisper. "We believe she miscarried."

"*Shit.*" Deacon laced his fingers with Vivienne's. His lips pressed in a tight line as he stared at that screen.

The woman had been pregnant.

Tears washed Vivienne's cheeks as she watched the woman return to the room in a pristine white nightgown. How could anyone survive losing something as precious as a child, especially when she was alone in a cell, day in and day out, with no one to comfort her? No one to help her through it?

Peter skipped ahead six months.

The girl's stomach bulged beneath her nightgown; her thin legs looked like they would snap when she stood upright.

She was pregnant again. But how—

Oh god.

Bile burned the back of Vivienne's throat, and her skin started itching. Every part of her wanted to burst through the screen and save the woman from that room. From the evil monsters keeping her captive. How could anyone do something so unfathomable to another human being?

Instead of attempting to fly or escape, the woman sat at the desk all day, every day, writing furiously in a notebook she kept hidden beneath her pillow. She rubbed and cradled her distended stomach while she wrote, and she sang to her unborn baby when she curled into the bed at night. On the seventh of April, the man in the surgical mask and cap came back with a nurse in scrubs to wheel the woman out of the room.

Three days later, she returned . . . with a flat stomach.

Her eyes were wild as she beat on the door, scraped at the lock with her nails, and screamed.

And *screamed*.

But no one returned to check on her.

Deacon turned to Peter. "Where's the baby?" he asked, his voice breaking. Tears glistened in his wide eyes.

Peter raked his fingers through his hair. "We have a theory."

"And that is?"

"A discussion for another time," Peter said, his lips pressed tightly together.

Four days later, the girl fell asleep on the floor beside the door . . . and did not get up again.

Vivienne's eyes stung with tears and her head pounded and she wished there was some way to un-see everything she had seen. Some way to return to the blissful ignorance of waking up next to the man she loved, where her biggest problem was a hangover.

"Where'd you get this?" she asked, needing someone to confirm her suspicions.

Peter nodded toward the stranger. "Steve brought it to us as soon as he found it in the archives at HOOK."

Steve was short and blond, with a sparse patch of facial hair she supposed could be considered a mustache. He looked young enough, but too old to be a PAN—at least one with an active Nevergene. "They let you into their archives?" That didn't make sense.

Steve's head tilted as he studied her. "What HOOK doesn't know won't hurt me."

A detail mentioned at the trial yesterday sparked in her memory. "Does that mean you're the spy at HOOK?" Was he the one who had almost been killed in the fire?

"Spy, inside man, espionage extraordinaire," Steve drawled, his smile not reaching his eyes, "*and* a geneticist at The Humanitarian Organization for Order and Knowledge."

"I'm Vivienne."

"I know who you are."

"You do?"

His hazel eyes narrowed. "Yeah. *You're* the one that got away. The one that made Lawrence Hooke lose his shit." This time when he smiled, his face brightened.

"I thought you fell off the face of the planet, Steve," Deacon muttered.

Steve's smile turned vicious. "That'd suit you just fine, wouldn't it, bird boy?"

"Stop now or get out of my office," Peter barked. "There's enough happening at the minute without the two of you squabbling."

Deacon and Steve glared at each other but didn't say anything more.

Rubbing his temples, Peter closed his eyes and let out a heavy sigh. "Do you have any idea how they found her?" he asked, dropping back into his chair.

"Unfortunately, no. I located some old medical records and hospital admission forms for a woman named Sophia Tierney," Steve said, unzipping a backpack at his feet and withdrawing a stack of files, "but there's no way of knowing if this was her or if they had another girl captive around the same time." The files landed on Peter's desk with a *thud*.

Another girl?

Steve thought HOOK had done this to more people? Vivienne pressed a hand to her stomach, praying she wouldn't get sick in front of everyone. There was a trash can beside Peter's desk just in case.

"We've been so focused on maintaining what we have," Peter said, picking up a gold Charlie Bell from beside a photo frame, "that we've allowed our brothers and sisters to fend for themselves."

Deacon stepped forward, putting a hand on Peter's desk. "Grandad, you're doing your best."

"It's not enough!" Peter launched the clock against the wall. The glass shattered; the bell chimed when it clattered to the ground. "HOOK found this poor, defenseless girl. How do we know there weren't others? How do we know there won't be more?"

Vivienne was lucky the PAN had already known about her parents. But there had to be so many more who'd slipped through the cracks. Those whose Nevergenes had been active for a few days before going dormant again without the injection . . . and those who were found by HOOK.

"About that . . . " Steve dragged another folder out of his backpack and tapped it against his thigh. "The day before I left, I received a new set of tissue samples." He handed Peter the folder. Peter opened it and skimmed through the documents inside. To Vivienne, they looked like a bunch of nonsensical charts.

"They're from a deceased male with a Nevergene," Steve went on, "but I've checked *everywhere* and there are no cadavers on site."

No cadavers on site . . .

"Jasper told me the same thing," Vivienne said.

Three pairs of eyes locked on her.

"The night of the fire," she explained, letting go of

Deacon's hand and wiping her sweaty palms down her jeans. "Ethan thought they had Deacon because the body in Tennessee had gone missing from the morgue. Could those be from David?"

Saying his name aloud brought back the sickening feeling of guilt and shame. Peter had told her that David's death wasn't her fault, that someone had recognized her in the convenience store in Tennessee and called HOOK's tip line.

But if HOOK hadn't been looking for Vivienne, David would still be alive.

Deacon pulled her close to him and kissed her temple. It didn't make it better. Nothing could. But she leaned into him anyway, allowing his warmth to seep into her cold body.

"There's no way of knowing unless I have something to compare the samples to." Steve took the files back from Peter.

"If they do have him, then where are they keeping him?" Deacon asked, rubbing the back of his neck.

Vivienne wondered the same thing.

"I've combed the administrative offices from top to bottom. The main building is only framing at this point, and there's nothing in the prefabs." Steve dropped the files into his backpack. "If there's a second facility, Jasper doesn't know about it."

Deacon snorted. "And you believe him?"

"He's actually a pretty nice guy if you can get past the whole working-for-HOOK thing." Steve pointed to the haunting image on the screen. "He certainly doesn't know about this."

Jasper would've been a child when the woman was in captivity. But, as Peter had said, that didn't mean there weren't others. That they didn't have someone right now.

"You expect me to believe that Charles' own son doesn't know they've been keeping people in cells?" Deacon spat.

Jasper had known they had Vivienne.

He had allowed the blood tests. And if she hadn't switched the vials, he would've let her be neutralized. Ignorance didn't excuse his actions.

Steve's gaze cut to Peter, who closed his eyes and said, "Jasper isn't Charles' son."

Holy crap.

If Jasper wasn't related to Charles, he wasn't really a Hooke. "Then who is he?" Vivienne wondered aloud.

"I don't know. But I've done the SNP-based tests myself, and the two are not biologically related. I don't think Jasper knows. And I'm hoping that, when he finds out about all of *this*," Steve said, gesturing toward the screen, "he'll be willing to hand over the poison himself."

The poison. Vivienne had completely forgotten about the poison. "He doesn't need to give it to us." She reached into her pocket and withdrew the vial. When she held it toward them, the light from the computer made the yellow liquid inside look like it was glowing.

"*Bloody hell.*" Peter rose slowly, planting his hands on either side of his keyboard.

"Would you look at that?" Steve clapped. "I've been trying to get into HOOK's safe for months, and you had some all along."

Peter extended his hand toward Vivienne, and she dropped the vial into his palm. "Where did you get this?" His voice was mystified as he flicked on the Tiffany desk lamp and studied the liquid.

"It was inside my mother's perfume bottle."

"So you haven't kept it refrigerated?" Steve asked, his lips flat.

"Considering we only found out about it last night?" Deacon clipped. "No. It hasn't been refrigerated."

"Does that matter?" Vivienne asked, her hope shattering.

"It's fine. It's better than fine. It's brilliant." Peter's face broke into a smile. "We need to get this to Gwen in the lab right away." He pulled his coat from the back of his chair, knocking a stack of papers from his desk to the floor.

Vivienne and Deacon bent to help pick them up. Before she could hand him the pages she had collected, she froze. A black-and-white photo of a portly man with thinning dark hair and a wide bald spot on top of his head stared back at her. A man she recognized. "Why do you have a picture of Dr. Rhea?"

"Who?" Peter asked, his eyebrows coming together.

She straightened and showed him the photo. "Dr. Rhea. My pediatrician."

"Vivienne . . . " Deacon took the picture from her, his mouth flat and his brow furrowed. "That's Dr. Charles Hooke."

"No, it's not." She huffed a laugh. Her memory was going to fail her someday, but not today. "This is my doctor. I started seeing him after my parents—"

Crap.

After her parents had died.

Could it be true? Had Dr. Hooke been monitoring her all this time?

Deacon cursed.

This man—this *monster* had given Vivienne vaccinations, prescribed antibiotics when she was sick, had done her first pelvic examination and smear test. He'd offered to give her a prescription for birth control when she turned sixteen.

And he had killed her parents.

Her legs felt weak, and she couldn't hold herself upright.

"Vivienne?" Deacon's face was the last thing she saw before the world went dark.

THREE

D eacon watched the life leave Vivienne's eyes before they closed.

Shit.

She was going to pass out.

He lunged, catching her dead weight before she crashed to the floor. His knees cracked against the unforgiving tiles, leaving him cursing. Steve tried to help, but Deacon told him to go to hell.

It was irrational to blame the man for this disaster, but Deacon had to blame someone. If Steve hadn't been there, he and Vivienne could have given Peter the poison and left to enjoy the rest of their lives. The weight of what they had seen, what they now knew, was going to haunt them forever. Wasn't Vivienne's forgetfulness enough?

Deacon settled Vivienne onto the small sofa in his grandad's office. Her cheek was cold. Her forehead was clammy. Her pulse was weak.

What did he need to do? Why wasn't someone telling him what to do?

"Vivienne?" She was as pale as she'd been when she'd nearly drowned. *Dammit.* Deacon didn't need to think about that too. "Vivienne? Come back to me."

Her lashes fluttered open, and her cheeks flushed. "I can't believe I just did that." She covered her face with her hands and groaned. "How embarrassing."

The ache in Deacon's stomach eased a fraction. Everything was still shite, but at least Vivienne was all right. "To be fair, it's not the most mortifying thing you've done in front of me," he said, desperately trying to lighten the mood. "Do you remember that text you sent about my hot British mouth?"

Her eyes narrowed; her lips pressed into a disapproving line. Even irritated, she was beautiful. "I'm lying helpless, and you're making fun of me? Seriously, Deacon?"

He snorted even as relief coursed through his veins.

Behind him, Peter appeared with a glass of water. Deacon had been too focused on Vivienne to realize Peter and Steve had left the office.

"How are you feeling?" Peter asked, handing the glass to Vivienne.

"Okay." She reached for it with a shaky hand. "I'd like to lie down for a bit longer if you don't mind."

"I'm hardly going to kick you out," Peter said before returning to the hall to speak to Steve in low tones. The two of them kept glancing toward the sofa, but Deacon couldn't hear what they were saying. Their faces looked serious, so whatever it was, it didn't look good.

He'd figure it out later. Right now, he needed to take care of his fiancée.

Deacon dragged a throw from the back of the sofa, covered Vivienne, and asked if there was anything he could do to help her. First the video, then the revelation about Dr. Hooke . . . He felt so bloody useless.

"Stop fussing. I just need to close my eyes," she said quietly, handing him the empty glass.

"Deacon? Can I speak with you in private for a moment, please?" Peter called from the doorway.

That question usually meant Deacon was in some sort of trouble. And with the way today was going, he couldn't handle any more bad news.

"In a minute, Grandad." He wanted to make sure Vivienne wasn't going to pass out again. Was there a way to tell? At least she was lying down so she wouldn't hit her head.

"Go." Vivienne knocked him in the shoulder. "I'm fine."

Instead of speaking to Deacon in the hallway, Peter brought him to the kitchen. When Peter shut the door behind him, the sinking feeling in Deacon's stomach got worse.

Leaning his elbows on the stone countertops, Peter met Deacon's gaze. "I need to tell you something," he said, idly pressing buttons on his watch, "but you cannot tell Vivienne."

The idea of keeping something important from her didn't sit well—especially after the whole trial debacle. Still, Peter wouldn't ask him to keep a secret unless it was important. So Deacon nodded.

"Twelve years ago, HOOK nearly discovered Kensington. The details are irrelevant, but it was close. Too close. Then, after William and Anne were killed, it appeared as though HOOK stopped looking for us. We've had brushes with them, as you know, but most of those were because we got careless and flew too close. I've always wondered why. But now I know."

It took Deacon a second to process all the information. And when he did, his heart started pounding, filing his veins with adrenaline. HOOK didn't need to find the PAN because . . . "They had Vivienne."

A nod. "Dr. Hooke has been monitoring—and likely testing—Vivienne for almost twelve years."

Deacon had already figured that out.

"If they already have all of her information and DNA on file, they shouldn't need her anymore." And yet they had been dogged in their determination to get her back. No one else. Just Vivienne.

"I cannot believe I'm about to say this," Peter muttered, dashing his hand through his hair and cursing. "But what if they wanted her for something more than just her DNA?"

What could they possibly want other than—

Shit.

The video.

The woman.

The *baby.*

"You think they want to use her like they did that poor woman on the video?" Deacon choked.

No.

Not her.

Where was all the bloody air? His lungs refused to expand and his stomach was in knots and his heart was racing. If she hadn't escaped—no no *no.* He couldn't think about that right now. And he sure as hell couldn't think about what those bastards would do to the woman he loved if they got their hands on her again.

"Why would they need to find us if they could make their own test subjects?" Peter said to himself, pacing back and forth in front of the oven. "*Dammit.*" His fist cracked against the countertop. "We should have brought her to Neverland the day her parents died. What the hell was I thinking? Leaving her out there to fend for herself in the system."

"This isn't your fault, Grandad. You were following

procedure." And Vivienne's parents had said that they didn't want their daughter growing up in Neverland.

"Her parents were wrong. We were all wrong. But not you." Peter clutched Deacon's arms, his eyes wide. "If you had left her at the hospital like you were ordered, they would have her now. And with her levels of nGh, any children she has will probably end up with active genes."

The very idea of Vivienne being used that way made Deacon want to tear the entire organization apart with his bare hands.

"To ensure that, they'd need a father with a Nevergene as well." Deacon wasn't a genetics expert, but he had paid attention through the years. It wouldn't need to be active, just present. "They would need a male PAN."

Peter let him go with another curse. From his back pocket, he withdrew a folded piece of paper and slid it across the countertop.

Deacon's hand shook as he picked it up and opened it. What he saw made no sense. No matter how many times he read the test results, he couldn't believe them.

Groaning, Peter dropped his head into his hands. "HOOK already has one."

FOUR

"Hello?" Jasper looked up and down the dark, empty road before picking up a brown-paper-wrapped package that had been left on his doorstep. "What do you think this is, Pancake?" he asked the fluffy striped cat shedding brown fur over his socks. Pancake meowed her disinterest before returning to her favorite spot on the back of the couch.

Shrill screeching cut the silence. Jasper sprinted back to the kitchen to find smoke billowing from the pot of mac 'n cheese overflowing on his stovetop. Swearing, he threw the package onto the counter before turning down the burner and stirring the burnt orange gloop that was his dinner. He'd needed to go to the grocery store all week but hadn't had the time. With so many employees quitting, Jasper's workload had doubled.

After dumping the over-cooked pasta and "cheese" into a chipped bowl, he swore again at the blackness singed onto the bottom of the pan. Filling it with water and dish soap probably wouldn't help, but he did it anyway. He choked down dinner in front of the television, chasing it with a glass of white wine.

It had been another bad day in a string of bad weeks at the end of a particularly rotten month.

"My luck is bound to change soon, right?" He pulled a reluctant Pancake onto his lap and rubbed the curly, batter-colored fur covering her treat-loving belly. She closed her green eyes and, with her body vibrating with feline contentment, fell asleep.

Jasper stared at the news headlines for another ten minutes before joining her.

When he awoke, there was no sign of his furry hot-water bottle, and the television had switched itself off. With the empty calories from his dinner spent, he shuffled to the fridge. Milk. Butter. Strawberry jelly. And a container of chicken salad that should've been thrown out weeks ago. He pulled out the jelly and smeared it onto the only piece of bread he had left, a crusty brown heel.

The forgotten package was still on the counter where he'd left it. He carried his heel-sandwich over and slid his finger inside a gap in the brown paper. A terrible slicing pain lanced through his hand. Of course he got a paper cut. Of course he did. Because why not? Why the hell not?

He brought his sore finger to his mouth to keep blood from dripping on the counter.

Inside the box, beneath a mound of packing peanuts, was a DVD. Pancake jumped onto the counter so she could knock the foam bits onto the floor one at a time. Under the DVD was a gold alarm clock.

"I guess we know where this came from," he muttered to the cat.

Jasper brought the DVD to his bedroom, where his laptop sat open on the bed next to a bunch of files he wasn't supposed to have taken away from the lab. But if he didn't bring them home, he'd never get anything done. And if he didn't get anything done, Lawrence was liable to fire him.

The moment Jasper loaded the DVD into his laptop, the screen went black.

And then a woman screamed.

Everything in Jasper's father's office looked exactly the same as it did every other day: the certificates and degrees hanging next to framed photos of Dr. Hooke's philanthropic work, the aquarium quietly bubbling in the corner opposite the wide windows. But in Jasper's heart, he knew everything had changed.

"Who was my mother?" Jasper asked, trying his best not to shout.

Jasper's father didn't bother raising his eyes from the missive in his hand. The light glinted off the bald patch he no longer tried to hide. "Just once, I'd like you to come in here without sounding like the world is ending," he grumbled, flipping to the next page.

But the world *was* ending. At least the world that Jasper knew. The world where he was a good person who did good things for the good of humanity.

"Answer my question," he demanded. After seeing that video, he hadn't slept a wink. He had combed through every file on the VPN for answers, but there was no mention of a woman being held captive or the unspeakable things that had undoubtedly happened to her when she *wasn't* on camera.

"Stop pacing. You're giving me a headache."

Since 3 a.m., Jasper had downed an entire pot of coffee. Standing still wasn't an option. He was going to crash soon, but not until he had his answers. "Who. Was. My. Mother?"

His father dropped the papers and tented his fingers

beneath his double chin. "I distinctly remember having this conversation a few years ago," he said in a bored tone. "Your mother was some poor, unfortunate pregnant girl without any family or means to take care of herself—let alone a child."

Liar. His father—no, *Dr. Hooke*—was a lying bastard.

Jasper's hands flexed and trembled at his sides, adrenaline and caffeine surging inside of him. "So you *didn't* rape her and hold her in a cell until she gave birth to me?"

April 7th was Jasper's birthday. He hadn't wanted to believe it. Had hoped there was some other explanation. But from the deranged look on Dr. Hooke's red face, Jasper knew it was the truth.

"How dare you!" Dr. Hooke's fists cracked against the desk. "No one raped that woman. She signed a contract agreeing to the tests, artificial insemination, and to giving up the child when it was all over."

"Did she agree to being held against her will? Did she agree to be locked up like some sort of wild animal?"

"You didn't see her. She *was* a wild animal. Damn near took out your grandfather's eye."

Jasper didn't bother saying that he *had* seen her. That his grandfather had deserved to lose his damned eye—and worse.

Dr. Hooke picked up his mug of black coffee and took a long, slow sip. When he set it back down, he adjusted his weight on the chair. "Every scientific breakthrough has been made because someone was willing to push the boundaries of what society deemed reasonable."

"What society deems reasonable?" Jasper choked, pulling on the ends of his hair. "Contract or not, you kept a woman in a prison for months! We're talking about violating basic human rights, not to mention all the laws you broke."

"Take a deep breath and look at the bigger picture. All of this"—Dr. Hooke indicated the steel framing of HOOK's new headquarters lurking outside the window—"is the result of one small sacrifice."

Jasper could feel the fight leaking out of him, leaving his body shaking and unsteady. There was no point arguing with a monster. "It wasn't a small sacrifice for my mother." His mother had died—and for what? So HOOK could sell the key to the fountain of youth for a profit? A fountain drenched in the blood of an innocent woman.

Dammit.

Not just one woman. Vivienne had been telling the truth. How many PAN had been killed because of his family's greed?

"You're right." Dr. Hooke scratched his smooth chin. "It wasn't. So don't let her sacrifice be in vain."

Nausea rolled off of Jasper in waves. The first thing he'd done that morning was go into the lab and run tests on himself. His suspicions were confirmed when he learned he possessed the NG-1882 gene.

What would have happened to him if his gene had activated?

Would he be locked up in one of those cells?

"You make me sick," he spat, wishing there was some way to fix the past. Some way to atone for the sins he'd committed out of ignorance.

"You think *I'm* the villain here?" Dr. Hooke's eyes bulged. "If it wasn't for me, you'd be dead. You were six weeks premature and too sickly and weak to survive on your own. *I saved you.*"

"You only saved me because you thought I was one of them."

"You *are* one of them."

Jasper stared at the man responsible for his mother's death and waited. For what? He wasn't sure. It wasn't like an apology would make it any better. But it'd be something.

Dr. Hooke grumbled and picked up the document he'd

been reviewing before Jasper had burst through the door, not even bothering to dismiss him.

The moment Jasper left Dr. Hooke's office, Lawrence rounded the corner, a bag of BBQ potato chips in his hand.

His dark beard was freshly trimmed, making the gray at his temples stand out. "Why so glum, Lab Rat?" he asked, licking his fingers before wiping them on his pants and clapping Jasper on the shoulder.

Jasper stepped out of his grasp, not wanting to be close to the man in case he was a traitor as well. "Did you know?"

Lawrence held the bag of chips toward Jasper. "Did I know what?"

Jasper shoved it aside and shook his head. With all the caffeine and despair and horror he'd been exposed to over the last eight hours, his stomach was ready to revolt. "Did you know that I'm a PAN?"

"Uh, yeah. Dad used you as a pin cushion for the first half of your life." Lawrence snagged another chip and popped it into his mouth. "I can't believe it took you so long to figure it out."

Jasper was smart. Why *hadn't* he put two and two together before this? Oh, that's right. Because he was a good person who didn't expect to be working for murderous psychopaths. "I can't believe he told you and not me." The moment the statement left his mouth, Jasper realized that he *could* believe it. Dr. Hooke had admitted to torturing and killing Jasper's mother. He was capable of anything.

"Dad never actually told me. I overheard him and Edward discussing it before the old bastard keeled over."

"And it didn't cross your mind to pass on the information?"

"Come on, Jas." Lawrence tilted the bag into his upturned mouth. Crumbs spilled down his black dress shirt. "I've literally called you 'Lab Rat' for years."

True, but Jasper had always assumed it was because he

worked in a lab, not because his father had secretly used him to run tests.

"Are you done freaking out? Because I want to show you something." Lawrence wiped his hands on his pants again before dragging something from his pocket—a small black velvet-covered box with a glittering diamond ring inside.

"You're going to propose to Louise?" Jasper assumed. The two had been together for four years, so it shouldn't have been a shock. Still, Lawrence never struck him as the commitment type.

"I figure if she's put up with my sorry ass this long, she's probably a keeper."

"Can I give you some advice?"

"What's that?"

"When you ask her, come up with something a little better than that."

Lawrence chuckled. This time, when he clapped Jasper on the back, Jasper didn't shrug him off. "You worry too much, Rat. Knowing you're one of them doesn't change anything."

Jasper's gaze landed on the ominous black door at the end of the hall. The one he knew held answers he wasn't supposed to find.

Maybe nothing had changed for Lawrence, but for Jasper, nothing could ever be the same.

FIVE

W hy was Deacon nervous? He was going to talk to his mother. She had to love him no matter what, right? It wasn't that big of a deal that he hadn't told her about his engagement to Vivienne. She would understand. She would forgive him. After all, eternity was a long time to go without speaking to your only child.

He thought it would be best to visit without Vivienne, and she had agreed. But now that he was standing on his mother's stoop in the misty rain, he was beginning to regret the decision.

Perhaps he should come back next week and bring Vivienne with him. That way they could face Mary Ashford's wrath together. Was it cowardly? Yes, it was. But Deacon didn't care. This month had been shite enough without him bringing more problems onto his plate. His mother could wait.

He turned, jumped off the steps, and was halfway down

the footpath when he heard his name being called. Cursing under his breath, he twisted to face his mother.

Her eyes were wide, her mouth tight with disapproval. There wasn't a wrinkle on the pristine white top she wore tucked into a slim black pencil skirt. It looked like she was ready for a board meeting, but Deacon knew better. This was the closest thing to loungewear that his mother owned.

"How long have you been waiting out in the rain, Deacon?" Her voice rang with disapproval.

"A while," he confessed, pushing his damp hair back from his forehead.

Her perfect eyebrows arched toward her hairline. "And you were just going to leave without a word?"

"I . . . um . . . " *Shit.* "Yes. I was."

"This is ridiculous," she snapped, stepping aside and motioning him toward the dark hallway. "Come inside."

How bad would it look if he ran away?

He cursed silently. It would probably make matters worse.

He jogged back up the stairs and past his mother to the coat rack. This place had been his home forever, so why did he feel like a stranger today? It was the first time he had been over since they'd arrived in London, but he had been away longer before.

"Are you alone?" She glanced around the empty stoop, as if he had hidden Vivienne somewhere among the boxwood hedges.

"I thought it was best to speak with you privately."

Her expression shifted into a grimace, but she nodded. "Would you like some tea?"

"That would be great, thank you." Deacon settled his damp jacket on the rack and slid his shoes next to his mother's before following her stiff frame down the hall to the kitchen.

His mother had renovated the space a few years earlier,

replacing the outdated pine cabinets from his youth with sleek, glossy white ones. The room felt so clinical now, with under-cabinet lighting reflecting off white stone worktops and white marble floors.

Deacon hated it, but he supposed it suited his mother's personality since his father's passing.

Hard and cold.

She flicked a switch on the stainless steel kettle; the water inside immediately began to simmer. He settled himself onto one of the barstools at the island and tried to figure out what to say.

So much had happened the last few weeks, he wasn't sure where to start.

"I want to thank you." That seemed like a pretty good place.

His mother turned from where she was pulling two mugs from the cupboard, her eyebrows arched in silent question. "Thank me for what?"

"Your support during the trial." He wasn't entirely sure they would have won without it. "I know you don't like Vivienne—"

She slammed the mugs on the counter nearly hard enough to shatter them. "Do you, now?"

"Excuse me?"

"How do you know I don't like her? Because I have never said such a thing to you—or to anyone, for that matter."

"You didn't need to. It was fairly obvious by the way you told me to avoid her." She had warned him away from Vivienne the moment she had found out that he'd kissed her on New Year's Day last year.

A lifetime ago.

Sighing, his mother pinched the bridge of her nose and shook her head. Beside her, the kettle came to a boil. "That was because of HOOK. I was worried about you. And," she said, dropping her hand and fixing him with a pointed stare, "I was worried about her."

Worried about Vivienne? "Why?"

Rolling her eyes, she dropped two teabags into the mugs before adding water to each. "Who do you think reads every single complaint filed about you from the trail of broken hearts you've left behind?"

Surely she wasn't suggesting—

"Women have filed complaints against me?" Deacon had always been honest and upfront about what he wanted—or didn't want—from the women he knew. Formal complaints seemed like an overreaction to a mutual, casual relationship.

"Broken hearts have consequences," she sighed, collecting a carton of milk from the fridge.

"What did they say?" And why was he only hearing about this now? Had all of them filed complaints? Even Nicola? Gwen? What about April? Or Audrey? Or Lenka? Or —*shit*. He could go on all bloody day.

"Mostly, they wanted Leadership to know that you had willingly entered into a romantic relationship with another PAN despite the policy discouraging it." A smile. "But they were never filed by the woman whom you were . . . *dating* at the time."

Bollocks. "That's mortifying." Having his casual dalliances thrust in his mother's face must have been terrible. No wonder she was so disappointed in him. He knew people talked, that some of the women had gotten jealous, but he didn't think they would've run to his mother to tattle on him like schoolchildren.

"For you as well as for me," she grumbled, sliding onto the stool next to him. She added milk to her tea before handing him the carton. "The written complaints weren't nearly as bad as the calls."

Groaning, he dropped his head into his hands. Coming here had been a mistake.

JENNY HICKMAN

His mother's spoon clinked on the edge of her mug, punctuating the silence. "So, when I heard about you and Vivienne, I wrongly assumed that she was another complaint waiting to be filed."

How did he explain that what he had with Vivienne was different? He didn't give a toss that it sounded cliché. It was the truth.

"Deacon?" When he looked back at his mother, she was smiling. "I have never been happier about being wrong."

He was afraid to hope. Afraid that this was another one of those instances where he thought things were going well only to find they were actually shite. "You're happy for us? Truly?"

She clasped the mug between her fingers, bringing it closer so the steam curled around her chin. "I trust that you haven't made this decision lightly and that you understand the longevity of this kind of commitment. You're lucky to have fallen in love with another PAN, but it's not going to be easy. Especially given your history."

"I'm not going to run off with someone else," he assured her, adding too much milk to his cup. He snagged his mother's spoon from the counter to give the liquid a quick stir.

"That's not what I meant."

Heat slipped down his throat as he took a sip of milky tea. What did his history have to do with his relationship with Vivienne now? She knew everything about him and loved him anyway. Had agreed to marry him despite his past. And he sure as hell wasn't going to do anything to jeopardize what they had.

His mother brought the mug to her lips, but didn't drink. "Do you plan on going in front of Leadership any time soon?"

"I would have gone already, but Grandad told me to wait."

Her eyebrows flicked up in surprise. "You would get married that quickly?"

"I would have married Vivienne the day she accepted my proposal." And if there had been an officiant on the island, he probably would have suggested it. "But for some reason, Grandad doesn't think we'll be approved. Which is insane. I know Gwen and Aoibheann are likely to vote against us. And Alex, of course."

"Why Alex? I thought the two of you were friends."

They had never been friends—and now, thanks to Vivienne, they never would be. Alex had spent most of their youth trying to one-up Deacon, to prove how much smarter he was every chance he got. Of course he was smarter—Alex was a bloody doctor. Deacon had no interest in going to college or medical school or anything else.

Deacon wanted to recruit for Neverland.

But now that was over. Traditionally, recruiters were allowed to work until the ten-year mark—the cut-off point for when HOOK's poison ended up killing them. Then they transitioned into other, safer roles. Deacon's mother had been so worried when he'd gone into recruiting that the only way she had approved his application was if he promised to quit after eight years.

If he didn't have Vivienne to look after, he didn't know what he'd do to occupy his time now.

Actually, that wasn't completely true.

Without Vivienne, he would have been racking up complaints.

"Alex and Vivienne dated while I was in exile here in London." Thinking about them together brought his anger bubbling to the surface. He supposed it was karma for the way he'd treated women in the past, and that he deserved every sleepless night and jealous thought. But that didn't mean he had to accept it graciously.

"No wonder you were so adamant about going back to

Kensington." She shook her head, dark hair falling over her shoulders. "Well, I'd like to say the rest of Leadership would approve your request, but you have a lot to prove before they give you permission to marry Vivienne."

What could he possibly have to prove to them? His relationship was none of their business. He wouldn't even be asking for permission if he thought Vivienne would agree to marry him without it.

"Have they ever denied a request before?" He'd never heard of it happening. After all, couples knew that going to Leadership was asking for a life sentence. No one would take that lightly.

Her mouth pinched, and she winced. "They have."

"Whose?"

She shifted on the stool, stretching and flexing her hands on the mug. "They denied my first request."

"I thought everyone liked Da." At least that's the way it had seemed to Deacon. His father had been gone for almost a decade, but he had never heard a bad word said about Bruce Ashford.

"They did. He was the most likeable man on the planet," she said, her voice thickening with emotion. "But I'm not talking about your father. Before we met, I was engaged to Lee Somerfield."

Deacon had hoped that perhaps Maimie's forgetfulness at the trial had made her confused. That it had been some sort of misunderstanding.

"You and *Lee*?" He couldn't imagine them as a couple. Lee *hated* Leadership. And there was no love lost between himself and Peter. Was that because of Deacon's mother?

"We dated for a time before I met Bruce. Lee, Nicholas, and William were always hanging around together, and since Anne and William were dating, the five of us grew close." Deacon knew his mother and Vivienne's had been friendly, but had never realized they were more than casual acquaintances. "He was so charismatic and carefree and optimistic."

"Are you sure we're talking about Lee *Somerfield*?" Deacon could see the charisma; he was the leader of the resistance, after all. He had collected an impressive number of followers over the years, which wouldn't have happened if he'd been unapproachable. But carefree? And optimistic?

Not a hope.

"He was so different before Nicholas—before HOOK neutralized him. He had a vision for Neverland that I agreed with. Of course, Peter was never very keen on him, but perhaps that was part of the appeal." Her laugh was sad as she tucked her hair behind her ears. The wedding ring she still wore clinked against the mug. "Anyway, it was a long time ago. And as soon as Peter voted against us, the rest of Leadership followed suit. Only Maimie voted in our favor."

"What happened?"

"Nicholas was killed, and Lee started down a dark, destructive path that had no place for me." A shrug. "And then I met your father." She hid her face behind her mug and drank until it was empty. "Anyway, it's neither here nor there. But I think Peter is right. You should wait until you can be assured of a majority vote. Trying to sway people who've already made up their minds is nearly impossible."

Deacon stayed for another hour, sharing a second cup of tea and an entire sleeve of custard creams. On his way back to Harrow, he thought about what his mother had said. Not about Lee—he liked the man well enough now that they were on the same side, though that didn't mean Deacon wanted him near his mother. No, he stuffed the information he'd gleaned about their relationship as far down as it would go.

What he thought about was Leadership refusing his request to marry Vivienne. And how his previous indiscretions could interfere with their relationship. Hell, they already had. Aoibheann. Gwen. Even Nicola. It was a miracle Vivienne wanted to marry him in the first place.

He could wait.

He could prove to Vivienne—and to Leadership—that he was worth the risk.

And that he wasn't going to screw this up, no matter what.

SIX

P eter Pan drove like a maniac.

It didn't help that they were on the left side of the road and every roundabout made Vivienne feel queasy or that the speed limit on the highway was ridiculously high. Deacon had offered to let her sit up front on their trip to Scotland, but then she'd have had to make idle conversation with Peter. So she'd opted to sit in the back . . . with a life-size stuffed crocodile. Peter hadn't given a word of explanation when he'd picked them up in front of the gatehouse. He'd simply smiled and told her to hop in and mind the croc.

Deacon had said it was probably a gift for Tootles, since his birthday was the following week. She used it as a pillow when sitting upright made her too sick.

"Wake up." It was Deacon. "We're here."

Vivienne's eyes snapped open. It took a moment for her to adjust to the light and shove unsteadily to a seated position. Her stomach rumbled, but the queasiness had subsided. The crocodile's fur was matted where she had drooled on it.

In the distance, she saw a manor home in a valley surrounded by hills of muted greens and browns. And then she remembered: they had arrived at Áite Sítheil.

Scottish Gaelic for "peaceful place."

Áite Sítheil was sweeping and regal, four stories high and six windows across on either side. Two empty soccer goals sat facing each other in a field to the right. Piano music drifted from an open window, and curtains framing a set of French doors twisted in the damp breeze.

"All right. So, there are a few rules to keep in mind while you're here," Deacon said, offering her a hand to get out of the car once Peter shifted into park. Her back popped twice as she stretched her hands toward the gray sky. She didn't miss the way Deacon's gaze flicked to her chest before returning to her face.

"First," he said, clearing his throat, "you cannot fly. It's too open, and the last thing we need is some sightseer with a camera capturing one of us on camera."

Did he really think the reminder was necessary? It was daylight, and she knew the rules.

"How do you keep the . . . " What was the right word? "Patients" sounded too depressing. " . . . *residents* grounded?" They wouldn't follow rules they couldn't remember.

His mouth flattened. "Without memories, their 'happy thoughts' are few and far between. For those who still have some, they're put on adrenaline suppressants."

Vivienne's stomach twisted. Not only was she going to forget, she was going to be grounded too? The muscles in her back ached; she laced her fingers together over her head and stretched again. "What're the other rules?"

Again Deacon's gaze dropped. "Hmmm?"

Heat crept up her face and her body started to tingle, and if he didn't stop looking at her like that, they weren't even going to make it inside the freaking house. She smacked him on the arm.

His head snapped up, and he gave her a sheepish smile. "I really like your jumper."

"The *rules*?" she repeated

"Right. Rules. Um . . . " He blew out a breath. "Sorry. I don't remember. Just don't fly off on me and we should be good."

"You two finished over there?" Peter called, wrestling the crocodile from the back seat.

Vivienne had completely forgotten he was there. And from the way Deacon blushed, so had he. "We're ready," she said. "*Right*, Deacon?"

"I don't suppose I can convince you to take a stroll in the gardens with me first?" he said, low enough for only her to hear. "The Scottish birds are remarkable this time of year." He winked at her.

Peter whistled at them from halfway up the stone stairs.

"Yeah . . . I don't think your grandpa is going to let that happen."

Deacon grumbled under his breath as he laced his fingers with hers. They followed Peter—and the stuffed crocodile—up the stairs to a red door surrounded by stained-glass panels.

"How many people live here?" she asked, peering through the glass into a long hallway.

Deacon rang the bell since Peter's hands were full of reptile. "Fifteen PAN and seven members of staff."

"And the hardest part," Peter said, hauling the crocodile up the final step and accidentally whipping Vivienne with its long tail when he turned, "is keeping them from jumping into bed with one another."

"You're not serious."

Peter chuckled. "They may forget who they are, but their hormones certainly remember."

A middle-aged woman in green scrubs met them at the door. When she saw the crocodile, she snorted and told Peter he needed to stop bringing shite into the manor. He laughed and said it was payback for all the shite Tootles had bought him over the years.

After the introductions were made, the nurse escorted them down a long hallway with plaster coving and vaulted ceilings to what looked like a ballroom out of a period movie. Two crystal chandeliers sparkled like stars at either end of a ceiling painted to resemble the night sky.

Vivienne recognized Maimie bent over a piano, playing a whimsical tune that undulated like the wispy lace curtains around the open windows. All the chairs in the room faced the glass. The couches were placed in pairs throughout the space, facing each other.

Peter's smile broadened as he dragged the stuffed crocodile toward a teen with wild blond hair, sticking straight out of his scalp. "Hello, Tootles."

Tootles looked up from a table filled with gears and springs and bits of scrap metal. His light eyebrows came together over dull blue eyes. A pair of square-rimmed glasses slipped down the bridge of his slightly crooked nose. "Do I know you?"

"You used to." Peter settled the crocodile on one of the empty chairs and took the other free one before introducing himself, Vivienne, and Deacon.

"Peter . . . " Tootles scratched his head with the end of a screwdriver. "Sounds familiar. Did we go to school together?"

"Among other things."

"What brings you out in this terrible weather?"

Terrible weather? Vivienne glanced out the windows. It was gray outside but warm enough for this late in November.

Peter kicked his feet out and crossed them at the ankles

as he settled deeper into the chair. "I came to visit an old friend."

"What's with the big-ass crocodile?"

"Oh, this?" The croc's glassy black eyes wobbled when Peter put his arm around the gigantic stuffed animal. "I bought this guy for you. His name's Elvis."

"For me?" Frowning, Tootles poked the crocodile in the side with the screwdriver. "What the hell am I supposed to do with it?"

"I don't know. Scare the nurses? Sleep with it?"

Tootles twisted to look at Vivienne, his frown replaced by a crooked grin. "I'd rather sleep with *her*."

Deacon snorted.

"I don't think my fiancé would like that very much," Vivienne said with a laugh.

Tootles shrugged and looked back down at the gears. "I certainly won't tell him," he mumbled, picking up a spring and turning it over in his fingers.

"What are you working on?" Peter asked, clearly fighting a smile.

Tootles pulled what was left of a gold Charlie Bell from beneath the table. "My alarm clock stopped working."

Peter motioned toward it, and Tootles handed it over with obvious reluctance. "And you're trying to fix it?" Peter traced the clock's broken glass face.

"That was the plan. But I got a little carried away with surgery and can't remember where all these pieces go." Tootles held one of the gears so close to his nose that his eyes ended up crossed.

"Would you like some help?" Peter removed his coat, shoved his sleeves to his elbows, and grabbed a second screwdriver from the wreckage on the table.

"I'm sure you have more important things to do."

"Not at all. My day's wide open."

"What about the friend you're here visiting?"

Peter's smile remained in place, but the skin around his mouth tightened. "He won't mind."

Tears stung the back of Vivienne's eyes. Their exchange was too heartbreaking to continue watching.

Deacon said Peter did this every week? How did he survive it? How did he leave without breaking down? What kept him coming back when Tootles wouldn't know the difference?

That was going to be Vivienne, dissecting clocks for eternity. Or sitting on a chair beside a window, watching the lace curtains dance. Or wandering around the lawn, staring at the birds flitting across the clouds. What made her who she was would be gone.

Vivienne didn't want to hear Peter reminding his best friend of his own name. Tootles should remember. They'd had over a hundred years together. Surely some part of him knew who Peter was. What hope did Vivienne have if he didn't? She had only known Deacon for a little over a year. He would probably be the first person she forgot.

Her chest ached at the thought, and her lungs turned to stone.

She needed to get out of here. To escape to where she could breathe and pretend like this wasn't her fate. Without a word to anyone, she headed for the fresh air. When she reached the patio on the other side of the French doors, some of the tightness in her chest eased. The wind lifted her hair around her shoulders, and she longed to disappear into the clouds.

How could she condemn Deacon to this fate? How could she let him waste his never-ending life coming to see her when she wouldn't even know who he was?

"What's wrong?" Deacon asked when he caught up to her. His cold fingers wrapped around her wrist. "Did your newest admirer scare you off?"

How could Deacon be making a joke right now? Wasn't

he worried at all about this? "That's going to be me. I'm going to forget everything. Forget you." It had been easy to live in denial of her fate and pretend that her memory was going to last as long as she was. But being here, seeing this, reality slammed into her like a tidal wave. And she was drowning all over again.

Deacon smiled at her, but the look didn't reach his eyes. "They're going to find a cure."

"And if they don't? I can't do this to you. We should"— *Oh god*—"we should break up." He deserved better. He deserved more than she would be able to give him if she didn't know who he was. "It's for your own good."

"Not this again," he muttered, pinching the bridge of his nose. "As I told you before, this is my choice."

"What about *my* choice? Doesn't that matter?"

"Fine." He dropped her hand; the strained look on his face made it obvious he was brewing for a fight. "You want to break up with me *for my own good*? Go ahead. But I'll still be coming to visit you every single day when you don't remember who I am. Whether we get married or not, I will be here."

"Deacon—"

"Don't even start this martyr shit, Vivienne." His hands flexed at his sides as he drew in a ragged breath. "I'd *like* to have a life with you while I can. I'd *like* to have memories to hold when it's difficult. I know it's going to hurt like hell and kill me every time I have to reintroduce myself to you. But I don't care. I'm going to do it anyway because I love you. Now, if you still want to call this off, all you have to do is say the word. Is that what you want? Is that your *choice*?"

She pulled him close, burrowed her face into his warm chest, and held on. She was too selfish to let this go—to let *him* go. "I choose you." And she always would.

"Then stop talking bollocks about doing things for my

own good. *You're* what's good for me. Now, can we please go back inside? There's someone I'd like you to meet."

Deacon brought her back into the room and over to the piano, where they waited for Maimie to finish playing. She played with her eyes closed, no sheet music in sight.

"She's playing from memory," Vivienne whispered. Maimie was nearly as old as Peter. And if she could remember how to play the piano, maybe Vivienne really was being unnecessarily dramatic.

"See. I told you there's hope."

When Maimie's eyes opened, they locked onto Vivienne. "My goodness, girl. You look just like your Mum."

"You remember my mom?" The only time Vivienne had ever seen her great-grandmother was during the trial. They had never been introduced, so maybe Maimie was confusing her with someone else.

Maimie tilted her head. "Sure do. Anne was a little thing too. Had a big personality to make up for it though. Used to have all the fellas after her."

"She has more moments of clarity than the others," Deacon whispered, "but she's also at the beginning of her decline."

Maimie's lips lifted into a grin. "There's nothing wrong with my hearing, handsome."

Deacon's neck turned red under his collar. "Of course not, Maimie. My apologies."

"I'm Vivienne, and this is Deacon." Vivienne linked her arm with his. "My fiancé."

Maimie's gaze swept from Deacon's head to his shoes and back again. "Your fiancé has a great ass."

"Maimie!"

"What?" Maimie's slim shoulders lifted in a shrug. "Men say it to me all the time."

"I'm going to be honest with you, lovie," Deacon

murmured into Vivienne's ear, "I'm kind of looking forward to your hormones raging out of control."

Vivienne smacked him in the shoulder and sank next to Maimie on the bench. Deacon kissed her hair before going back to Peter and Tootles. Maimie was right. He did have a great ass.

"Will you tell me more about my mom?" Vivienne twisted to face her great-grandmother.

Maimie's head tilted to the side; her brown eyes narrowed. "Who's your Mum?"

"Anne. Anne Dunn."

"I don't know anyone called Anne. Are you sure you don't mean Alice? I know a few Alices. Pretty sure they don't have any children though. Oh, would you get a look at him." Maimie nodded toward a handsome teen with black hair curling around his ears, lounging by a window flipping through a book. "He's a fine one, isn't he?"

"He's very handsome," Vivienne agreed with a sigh. The last thing she had expected was to spend her afternoon checking out guys with her great-grandma, but it was better than being alone in the apartment, waiting for Deacon to come home.

SEVEN

Deacon found the piece Tootles was looking for and handed it over. Tootles mumbled his thanks and slipped the cog onto the spoke inside the back of his clock. There still seemed to be too many pieces to fit inside. Heaven only knew what else Tootles had dissected. He had always been a tinkerer, even when his memories were intact. Deacon supposed it was what made him who he was.

What parts of Vivienne would remain? She'd probably still hate spiders. And her laugh wouldn't change. He loved making her laugh. Most of the time it was because he said something inappropriate that earned him a slap or a shove afterwards, but it was worth it to see her smile.

He shifted his position, trying to get comfortable on the seat, but it was too rigid. He ended up knocking over the crocodile, nearly taking a nurse with it on its way to the floor. Deacon apologized and set it back on its chair, kicking its tail out of the way so he could stretch out his legs. A bit of late-afternoon sunlight drifted through the window, warming his left side.

Vivienne hadn't been sleeping well—which meant Deacon hadn't been sleeping well. If he closed his eyes for a moment, he'd feel better.

"Well, well, well. Look what the cat dragged in."

His eyes flashed open, and he found himself staring up at Gwen.

"Or should I say what the *croc* dragged in?" Gwen laughed, flicking the stuffed beast's snout. "For Tootles?"

"Who else?" Deacon glanced around the room, but he didn't see Peter or Tootles or Vivienne anywhere. His skin started tingling. He really, *really* wanted to fly away. "Are you working today, or just visiting?"

"Both." She dropped onto Tootles' vacant chair and picked up one of the gears. "Colleen called to say Mum's had a few lucid moments of late. I thought perhaps she'd remember me."

Gwen's mum had been in Scotland for as long as Deacon had known her. Tootles had been the first diagnosed, but his family had kept him at home until he became too hard to manage. Gwen's father had her mum brought to Scotland the moment she had shown signs of forgetfulness. Apparently, she had been violent. But the stunning blonde lounging on one of the couches flipping through a magazine certainly didn't look violent at the moment.

"And did she?" he asked, scooting closer to the crocodile.

Gwen shook her head, sending her platinum hair cascading down her shoulders. The blue top she wore clung to her shape like a second skin.

Where was Vivienne?

Deacon searched the ballroom again, catching a glimpse of her near the patio doors, still talking to Maimie. As if she knew he was watching, her dark eyes found his from across the room.

Deacon was about to excuse himself, to escape this conversation he did *not* feel like having . . . but then he stopped.

Gwen was a member of Leadership.

Which meant she had the potential to make or break a vote when it came time to ask for marriage approval. After what his mother had said about his past and the complaints, he and Vivienne would need every vote they could get.

Vivienne's eyes narrowed, and she turned her back on him.

Brilliant.

Now she was mad.

There wasn't anything he could do about it at the moment, so he focused on what Gwen was saying, trying to catch up—apparently, she'd been talking the entire time.

" . . . and I was so excited, but, like every other time I come to this wretched place, Mum didn't even know my name."

Her mother. Gwen was still talking about her mother.

"At least she's healthy—and she seems happy," Deacon said with a forced smile. There were worse things in life than being forgetful. Gwen's mum was still alive. He'd have taken a forgetful father over none at all any day.

Gwen spun one of the gears between her fingers over and over again. "What about you, Dash? I assume you're here with Peter?"

"And Vivienne."

Gwen's shoulders stiffened. "Isn't that *nice.*"

Deacon's teeth clenched, but he ignored the jibe. "She'd never been here, and I wanted her to meet Maimie."

"I forgot they were related." Gwen brushed a curl from her cheek before letting a heavy sigh escape her red lips. "I know I should tell you congratulations, but I'm not there yet."

"It's all right." He didn't need her congratulations. He

needed her vote. "How's work?" Work was a relatively safe subject, Deacon thought. "Have you had any luck with the poison?"

Peter had told him to stop asking and that he would give him any news he received the moment he heard. They had found the vial over two weeks ago and, to his knowledge, there had been no developments since.

"Not really." When she crossed her legs, her knees brushed against his.

Deacon shifted closer to the crocodile, wishing there was a way to put it between them. Gwen didn't seem to notice.

"Alex is having trouble identifying whatever sorcery HOOK used to create it," she went on. "But once he figures it out, I'm confident I'll be able to make it work for us."

And then good old Beardy McGee would take all the bloody credit for it. "You're one of the smartest women I know. If anyone can figure it out, it's you."

The gear she'd been spinning fell onto the table.

Shit.

Was that too much?

Gwen's lips pressed together.

It was too much.

Dammit.

Deacon should've run when he had the chance.

"I wish you wouldn't be sweet," she said, glancing at him through her lashes. "This would be easier if you were a wanker."

That made him chuckle. "We have eternity ahead of us, Gwen. I don't want to live with more enemies than necessary." Especially not in Leadership.

Tearful turquoise eyes met his. "I don't want to be your enemy."

That was good, right? That meant she wanted him to be happy. But did it mean that she would vote to approve his marriage?

Gwen picked up the brass cog that had fallen. "Want to help me put this back together?"

No, he didn't.

He wanted to go and find his fiancée.

Instead, he pasted on a smile and said, "Why not?"

They worked in relative silence for over an hour. By the time they finished, the clock was ticking away. As Deacon had suspected, there were still a bunch of parts littering the table.

"We make a pretty good team." She set the clock in front of the crocodile.

Deacon knew better than to comment. He stretched his hands toward the painted ceiling, hoping to free some of the tension in his shoulders. The staff was beginning to round up the patients and bring them up to their rooms.

Wait.

That couldn't be right.

It couldn't be that late.

Deacon twisted his wrist to check his watch. It was almost four o'clock. How had he allowed time to get away from him like that? He had only stayed past four once, and he'd vowed to never do it again.

"I'm sorry, Gwen. I need to find Vivienne." He shot to his feet and hurried to where Peter and Tootles were sitting beside the fireplace. "Grandad, have you seen Vivienne anywhere?"

Peter stood and straightened his dark jeans. "Last I saw her, she was with Maimie by the piano." When he caught sight of the clock on the mantle, his smile faded. His gaze met Deacon's. "We need to get her out of here before—"

Tootles started laughing, a high-pitched, maniacal sound. Then he shot out of his chair, his eyes wild and unfocused, and bent in half, clutching his stomach as he cackled. One of the nurses wearing scrubs dashed over, a pair of handcuffs jingling on her belt. Peter reached for

Tootles' arm, but he jerked away and started swearing viciously.

"Come on, mate. Just calm down, yeah?" Peter held his hands in front of him. "We need to get you up to bed."

"That bitch isn't coming near me," Tootles snarled, spitting at the nurse.

Deacon saw his opening—and took it. He wrapped his arms around Tootles' waist, knocking him to the ground. Tootles writhed and cursed and gnashed his teeth, catching Peter's shoulder as he wrestled to catch Tootles' arms. The nurse didn't seem fazed by any of it. With Tootles restrained, she dropped her knee onto his chest and jabbed a needle into his neck.

Tootles' eyes fell closed, and Deacon could feel the tension in his muscles ease as he passed out. Maimie had only been there for a few weeks, so she probably wouldn't be as bad. But still, he didn't want Vivienne to see what happened after dark. She had enough to worry about.

He rolled to his feet and hurtled toward the doors, hoping she hadn't wandered too far. Perhaps she wasn't with Maimie at all. She could have come outside for a bit of fresh air, or to enjoy the murky sunset over the burnished hills.

The patio was empty, as were the soccer pitch and the tennis court. Misty rain fell as he sprinted toward the walled gardens. Where the hell had she gone? The cloying scent from the high boxwood hedges choked him as he searched up and down the rows.

Crazed laughter lifted from somewhere on the other side of the gardens.

He shouted her name, his heart hammering inside his chest. The laughter was close, but where? Everything in the damn garden seemed to echo. If he didn't find her in one minute, he was going to fly—consequences be damned.

Koi pond or roses?

"Deacon!"

Koi pond. Her shout had come from the koi pond.

Deacon rounded the corner, but the area was clear except for a wrought iron bench and a serene, glimmering pool filled with golden fish and lily pads.

Vivienne called his name again, and he twisted down a stone aisle leading toward a line of rose trellises, praying she was all right.

Vivienne had never been big on flowers or gardens, but when Maimie had suggested they go for a walk, she had agreed, wanting to spend more time with her great-grandmother, even if she didn't know who the heck Vivienne was. Besides, Deacon had seemed to be in a pretty deep conversation with Gwen.

They looked so freaking perfect together, smiling and laughing and chatting like they hadn't a care in the world. Would he run to Gwen for comfort when Vivienne was stuck in this manor house? Gwen was probably biding her time before she could sink her claws back into him. And there was nothing Vivienne could do about it. She couldn't even blame Deacon. He deserved someone who could give him the life he deserved.

Someone who wouldn't forget him.

"Are you sure you don't remember anything about my mom?" Vivienne asked for the tenth time. Pressing the issue was pointless, but she needed some bit of hope that maybe things weren't as bad as they seemed.

Maimie had already apologized for not remembering. But only an hour earlier, she had said Vivienne had looked like Anne Dunn.

Was that how it happened?

One second you knew someone, and the next—*poof*—they were a stranger?

"Anything. Anything at all." Vivienne needed *something*.

"I'm afraid not." Maimie scratched her wrist where it poked out of her long sleeves. The loose dress she wore reminded Vivienne of something from the sixties. "I don't even have children. Are you sure you're not confusing me with someone else?"

Earlier that summer, Vivienne had gone back to the Records room in Kensington to check her family tree. Maimie had had two children, a daughter and a son. Her daughter's Nevergene had activated, but her son's hadn't.

"It's okay, Maimie. Forget I asked." Vivienne laughed at her joke, even though it wasn't the least bit funny.

Vivienne and Maimie turned down a stone path that led toward a fabulous pergola draped in blush-colored roses. It was whimsical and suited to the setting around them. She turned to find Maimie reaching to pick a rose.

Did she remember about the thorns? Was that something a person like Maimie would forget? "Watch out for the thorns," Vivienne warned, just in case.

Maimie yelped, then stuck her finger into her mouth. "Damned bloody flowers should come with a warning label."

Vivienne laughed as she reached for Maimie's hand. "Come on. Let's go back to the—"

"Don't touch me." Maimie knocked her away. "I'm not going with you."

Vivienne clutched her hand to her chest. Maimie had hit her so hard she wouldn't be surprised if it bruised. "I'm sorry. I just thought we should go back."

Maimie started laughing but there was something off about her eyes, like they weren't quite focused on Vivienne's face. Like Maimie was seeing through her.

A shrill shriek escaped Maimie's chest and she lunged, catching Vivienne by the sleeve.

"*Back*?" Maimie hissed, raking her nails down Vivienne's neck. Pain burst behind Vivienne's eyes, and she thrashed, trying to get free. "Do you know what they do to you in there? They bind you and tie you down and you can scream and scream and *scream* but no one comes. They never come. I'm not going back inside. I'm never going back."

Vivienne heard Deacon shout her name, which distracted Maimie long enough for Vivienne to get free and bolt for the house. If only she were allowed to fly. If only she didn't have to rely on her shaking legs. Why did she feel so weak?

Sharp footsteps, wild cackling, and low, inhuman growls followed Vivienne through the cascading flowers as Maimie closed the distance between them.

Gasping for breath, Vivienne shouted for Deacon. Around the corner, she pulled ahead and managed to slip between two tall bushes without being caught. Maimie stopped in front of her, twisting and turning before taking off toward a trail heading away from the house. Hunkered down, Vivienne's legs ached, but she didn't dare shout for Deacon again in case Maimie came back.

What the heck just happened?

Footsteps sounded in the gravel to her right, and she peered out from her hiding place to find a familiar pair of shoes. "Deacon!" Her voice shook as she crawled from under the bushes; her legs nearly gave out when she tried to stand.

Deacon gripped her elbow, drawing her against him. "We need to leave."

They may have needed to leave, but Vivienne needed answers more. "Maimie, she was . . . " How did she describe what had happened? "It was like she was possessed."

Deacon didn't respond as he brought her to the entrance

of the gardens. Peter burst through the front doors of the house and ran down the stairs.

"What's wrong with her?" Vivienne asked again.

Deacon's jaw ticked, but still he didn't say anything as he brought her across the driveway. Their feet crunched in the gravel. Misty rain fell softly around them, making her coat and sweater stick to her overheated skin. Every part of her was on fire with worry and fear and anger and jealousy, and she deserved a freaking answer.

Vivienne jerked out of his grasp. "Tell me right now or I'm done." She ripped the ring from her little finger and held it toward him. She deserved the truth.

And if Deacon wasn't going to give it to her, then Gwen could have him.

Cursing, Deacon scrubbed his hands down his cheeks. "This is what happens to the forgetful at night," he said, his voice as flat as his expression. His hair was damp and matted to his forehead.

The ring felt like a lead weight inside Vivienne's clenched fist as her hand fell to her side. "You're telling me this happens to everyone? That it's going to happen to me?"

Oh god.

Was she going to turn into a monster?

"It has to do with the time of day and hormonal imbalances." Shoving his hair off his forehead, he glanced at the manor, then back to her. "Look, the explanation doesn't matter. It's *not* going to happen to you because they're going to find a cure."

His words clanged through her head as he took her hand and brought her to the car. Peter was already inside with the engine running.

Deacon threw open the car door and helped Vivienne into the back seat. Instead of sitting in the front, he slid in next to her. Before he shut the door, a final bout of deranged laughter lifted in the background, echoing around the glen.

The peaceful place had turned into a cursed nightmare.

They're going to find a cure.

And if they didn't?

Then Vivienne was going to become one of the ghosts that haunted the gray stone mansion fading into the mist.

EIGHT

When Jasper heard a string of loud curses and a crash echoing down the hall, he dropped his laptop bag outside his door and ran for Lawrence's office, careful not to spill what was left of his coffee. The door was propped open with an office chair, and Lawrence was hunched over his desk, his head in his hands. His Newton's cradle was in the corner by the window, and the photo of Lawrence and Louise on their anniversary had been shattered against the wall.

"What's wrong?" Jasper asked.

"We just lost another one." Lawrence dragged a sheet of paper from his desk and held it toward Jasper, launching into another string of profanities. "This is the third notice this week."

"Who's leaving?" It didn't really matter. They had lost more employees this year than they had hired. Jasper was already working with a skeleton crew and being displaced to freezing pre-fabs hadn't helped morale.

"This one's from Marci."

"The lab assistant?" She hadn't even worked there for two months.

"Yes, the lab assistant," Lawrence snapped, crushing the paper in his fist and throwing it toward the wastebasket. It landed a foot away and disappeared beneath the bookcase. "There's only one Marci who works for you, isn't there?"

"There's no need to jump down my throat. This isn't my fault."

"I didn't say it was. It's those little flying assholes. I swear, when I get my hands on them, I'm going to make them wish they'd never been born."

"You really think they have nothing better to do than steal a lab assistant?" Jasper leaned his shoulder against the doorframe and took a sip of now-cold coffee. "When we lost Mark, I expected a few of his workers to go with him." Mark had been one of the senior lab managers. After his departure a few weeks ago, they had lost two lab techs and another lab assistant that used to work closely with him.

Lawrence's frown deepened. "I didn't think of that."

No, Lawrence wouldn't have thought about that, because he was terrible with people. He had a head for business, and he was ruthless when it came to budgets and spending, doing anything and everything he could to maximize profit. But he couldn't manage people worth a damn.

"Have you asked where they're going?"

"They keep giving me some bullshit about signing a non-disclosure agreement," Lawrence sneered, waving his hand toward the computer screen.

"Maybe you should have given them more money."

"Do I look like an idiot to you? I offered them a shitload of money, but they kept saying that they were getting more." Lawrence groaned, raking a hand down his beard.

"I warned you this was going to happen. We've been expecting our people to do the work of a staff twice the size without additional compensation." It had only been a matter of time before they found something better.

Jasper himself had spent last night surfing the job sites for something new. Working for heartless murderers wasn't something he wanted to do for the rest of his life. Unfortunately, one of the many problems he faced was that every application required him to include a list of references. His best references were his father and his brother.

And he couldn't let either of them know he was quitting before he was ready.

"Fine. Let's use some of the funds we're saving from everyone leaving to increase the rates for the remaining employees."

A small win, but a win nonetheless. Still, "That doesn't help with the workload."

"You know how long our system takes to vet new hires." Lawrence scratched his cheek; the lines on his forehead deepened as he frowned. "Even if I had people in the pipeline, it would be at least three months before they started training."

Because of the sensitive nature of their work—and his father's paranoia that the PAN had nothing better to do than spy on them—it took upwards of six months for new employees to come on board. The company paid well, but they lost a lot of potential hires because the wait time was so long. Most people wanted a job right away, and Lawrence wouldn't even hire a receptionist without the proper clearance.

"Is that something we could ease for a little while?"

"Dad won't like it," Lawrence said, massaging his temples, "but we may not have a choice."

When Jasper reached the lab, Steve was there waiting for him with a hot cup of coffee in the annex-turned-break room. "Morning, boss." His head tilted and his eyes narrowed. "Rough night?"

That was an understatement. Every time Jasper's eyes closed, he saw his mother flying around a concrete room, her white dress soaked in blood. "I haven't been sleeping well lately."

"Really?" Steve took a sip from his own mug. "Why's that?"

Jasper knew he couldn't tell Steve about the video. But for some reason, he wanted to. He felt like talking to a rational human. Someone who seemed to have a conscience.

"I saw something terrible and can't figure out what to do about it," Jasper confessed, wishing the heat from the mug could seep into his soul and replace the numbness that had settled there. He had too many bills to quit his job outright, and the market for his skill set was basically non-existent, especially this close to the holidays. Hopefully something would open up in the spring. At this point, he'd take a pay cut just to get out of this place.

"What kind of terrible are we talking about here? Like, body-in-the-woods terrible or puppy-kicking terrible?"

"Are those my only two options?" Jasper grimaced. Because that video was a lot closer to the first one.

"Nope." Steve held up his hand and started counting. "You also have seeing-a-waiter-spit-in-someone's-food terrible, screwing-your-brother's-wife terrible, punching-a-baby terrible, or—"

"Okay, okay," Jasper laughed. "You can stop any time." It felt good to laugh. Even if it was fleeting.

The men paused as Eliza came out of the lab to grab a bottle of water from the fridge. She didn't bother trying to talk to them as she scanned herself out of the building. Jasper had a feeling she would be the next to go; she had done nothing but complain since the main building burned down.

"Look, whatever it is, I'm sure you'll figure it out." Steve smiled at Jasper from over his mug. "It's not like you found out you're working for a bunch of murderers or anything."

Jasper's hand wobbled, spilling hot coffee all over his khaki pants. Swearing, he set the mug on the counter and grabbed a paper towel from the dispenser. The stain would wash out, but his washing machine wasn't working, so he'd have to take them to the laundromat. Another thing on the list of things he had no time for.

"What did you just say?"

"You heard me, boss." Steve handed him another paper towel before rinsing out his mug and setting it on the drying rack. "You seem like a decent guy. Don't let me down."

Don't let *him* down? What the hell did that mean? Steve turned, scanned his access card to the lab, and continued to his workstation beside Sarah's.

Dammit.

He knew.

Steve knew about the video.

Jasper threw the damp paper towels into the trash and stomped toward the door. His key card caught on the edge of his pocket, and it took him a second to free it. Mario, the security guard, watched him from his chair at the entrance, his black-on-black attire making him stand out among all the pristine white.

"Steve, can I speak with you for a moment, please?" Jasper said as calmly as he could manage.

"*Ohhh*, someone's in trouble," Sarah teased, nudging Steve's shoulder.

"It'll have to wait. I'm already a week behind, and I heard Marci just quit." Steve's smile was more of a smirk as he adjusted the knobs on the microscope he was staring into.

The five other lab techs spread around the room looked

up from their stations, their eyes wide. Then the murmuring started.

Not good. Not good at all.

The last thing Jasper needed was to tell his brother that he'd caused a mutiny in the lab.

"Everyone calm down," Jasper said as the murmuring got louder.

Screw it.

He didn't care if every single one of them quit. There were bigger things at stake here than his job. "Outside, Steve. *Now.*"

Steve stalked out the door and grabbed a red coat from the hook in the annex. Mario gave Jasper a look of concern, which Jasper returned with a strained smile. He didn't know why he bothered; the guy was going to call Lawrence the moment Jasper stepped out of the building.

When he made it outside, Steve was gone. *Dammit.* If Steve was gone, then—

Movement from the edge of the building calmed Jasper's frayed nerves. When he rounded the corner, Steve was waiting there in his puffy red coat, blowing air into his hands.

A chill snaked down Jasper's spine, but it had nothing to do with the flurries swirling in the air. "You know, don't you?"

Steve's eyebrows shot up. "Know what, boss?"

"Stop playing with me. Are you one of them?" He was too old. He couldn't be a PAN—at least not one with an active gene.

"Let's just say, I'm not one of you." Steve's smirk grew wider as he withdrew a hat and a pair of gloves from his jacket pocket. Instead of putting them on, he offered them to Jasper.

Jasper was cold enough to accept. The hat was scratchy against his forehead, but the gloves were a blessing. It felt like it had dropped ten degrees since he'd arrived that morning.

"Let me tell you a little story." Steve blew into his hands once more before tucking them beneath his armpits. "This story is about a boy who grew up on a pirate ship, being told he was the captain's son. He helped the pirates hunt and murder innocent people because he was an ignorant bastard who didn't know any better. But then he found out the truth. With me so far?"

Jasper could only nod, his heart sinking in his hollow chest.

"And despite knowing the truth, the guy kept swabbing the decks and dining with the captain, pretending nothing was wrong. Even though *everything* was wrong." Steve untucked his arms and kicked at a cluster of icicles that had impaled the drifting snow beneath the prefab's gutters.

"Now, I want you to tell me how the story ends, Jasper. Did the guy continue being a villain and raise the Jolly Roger, or did he have a conscience and jump ship with the rest of the crew?"

"You want me to quit?" Jasper considered it seriously for a moment. He could see if his student loans could be deferred. Sell his house and look for an opening out of state. But that didn't *fix* anything. Lawrence would just hire another lacky to take his place, someone as ignorant as Jasper had been.

"No, Jasper." Steve shook his head, sending blond hair falling into his eyes. He brushed it back from his forehead with a careless hand. "We don't want you to quit."

We.

Steve *was* a PAN. How had he passed through the vetting system? How had he made it through HOOK's rigorous background checks and the clearances? The PAN's network must be infinite.

Jasper wasn't a pirate or a villain or a murderer. And he was done being clueless. "What do you want from me?"

"Two things. First"—Steve held up a finger—"I want to know if I need to hightail it outta here, because I don't really feel like getting murdered today."

"I'm not going to tell anyone, if that's what you mean." He couldn't do anything to help his mother, but he could make sure the same thing didn't happen to Steve—or anyone else, for that matter.

Steve nodded. "That's what I was hoping you'd say. I mean, I'd hate for Lawrence to think you had something to do with all of the files that have gone missing from the records room."

Jasper stilled. There had been multiple security breaches in the administrative offices lately. If Dr. Hooke or Lawrence thought he was involved, he'd be out on his ass. "What's the second thing?"

Clapping him on the shoulder, Steve grinned and said, "We want you to get us some more poison."

NINE

After putting the finishing touches on her makeup and finger-combing her hair, Vivienne grabbed her phone from the nightstand and flicked off the light in her bedroom. Deacon had sent a text fifteen minutes ago asking where she was. They were supposed to meet Ethan at the Wendy Bird for a drink—the same thing they'd been doing every Friday night since the trial three weeks ago.

She sent him a text saying she was on her way.

The forgetful's crazed laughter and HOOK's captive's screams haunted her dreams. She wasn't getting any sleep at night. To make up for it, she'd been napping during the day. But in her exhausted state, she had set her alarm for 6:30 a.m. instead of 6:30 p.m.

Before leaving, she sent Emily a text saying that she missed her. They video-chatted every other day, but it wasn't the same. Emily and Lyle always seemed to be hanging out together, and Vivienne felt left out. If she was being honest, she was a little jealous of how close Emily and Lyle seemed to be getting.

Since the island, Lyle had responded to Vivienne's texts, but not once had he initiated a conversation. When she got home, they were going to have a talk about him being such a jerk.

Vivienne grabbed her raincoat from the stand and left the apartment. Outside the main door, the rain was pelting down in unrelenting sheets. She'd spent much of the last few weeks in tights and sweatshirts, but she had made an effort tonight, wearing a new black dress the Harrow shoppers had picked out. When Deacon saw the daring neckline, he was going to die. The thought made her grin.

Instead of going out in the rain, she went to the door that led to the secret tunnels beneath campus. Beside the door was a silver keypad like the one from her apartment back home. After typing in her code, the lock beeped and released.

Her black wedge heels clicked on the stone stairs as she descended into the dimly lit basement. The air was cold and musty, but there wasn't a cobweb in sight. A chill raced down her spine, leaving her bare arms covered in goose-bumps. Slipping into her raincoat, she continued until she reached the hollow passageway under Michael's Rest that led to what looked like a dead end.

There was a release lever hidden somewhere near the ceiling. She flicked on her phone's flashlight and flew into the shadows to examine the stones. One stone, about the size of her hand, protruded a few inches farther from the ceiling than the others around it. It took some effort, but she used her shoulder to shove it back into place. There was a scraping sound below her, and the secret door swung open. Motion lights flicked on when she stepped into the pentagon-shaped room. Behind her, the door slammed shut.

Now, which of the tunnels led to the Wendy Bird?

This was the first time she'd been down here on her own, and she couldn't quite remember which was right. The one straight across from her looked vaguely familiar. After following it for five minutes, she came to a mural of painted Mermaids that she'd never seen before.

She turned around, went back to the main room, and tried another one. The second tunnel was painted with a celestial masterpiece. Gorgeous, but wrong.

The third one had a fairy tree.

The fourth one had a . . . *wait.* She was back in the Mermaid tunnel.

How long had she been here? Deacon was going to start worrying. She should probably text him and let him know what was happening. Ever since he'd seen that video at Peter's, he'd been extra paranoid. When she pulled out her phone, she realized she had forgotten to turn off her flashlight and clicked it off before trying to text Deacon.

There was no service this far down. Maybe it would send when she got closer to the surface. She tried another tunnel, but instead of going up, it felt like it was going farther down; she saw the Mermaids again and wanted to scream.

The best thing she could think to do was go back to her apartment and brave the rain. She returned to the cavernous main room and flew into the darkness, searching for a rock to push or a lever or a freaking button so she could open the door. But every stone here looked the same as the others.

How had Deacon opened it the last time? She'd been at the bottom and hadn't seen.

She pulled out her phone in case being near the ceiling gave her a bar of service, but the screen was black.

Great. It was dead.

Hadn't she charged it? It had been plugged in, right? Oh well. It didn't matter now. The stupid thing was useless.

Think, Vivienne. Think.

There were cameras all around, so whoever was on duty in the security office had to know she was there and that she was lost. Assuming there was someone *in* the security office this late on a Friday night. Or was it Saturday?

She dropped to the ground and took a deep breath, trying to clear her head. Worst case scenario, she just had to wait a bit before someone came home from the Wendy Bird. It wasn't like she was going to die down here.

Maybe she should stay put. Or should she try the tunnel over there? The one she didn't think she'd tried before. This one had no mural, so it was a new tunnel. But her code didn't work on the keypad she found at the very end.

If only there was some way for her to mark the tunnels she'd taken. Then she'd find the one to the Wendy Bird.

There were only eight options. If she went back to the center room and kept going right, then she'd eventually find it. She gave that a try, and four tunnels later, she was back where she started and couldn't remember if she was supposed to go right or left. Left maybe. No, that was the tunnel with the Mermaids.

Man, she hated Mermaids.

And heels.

Why had she thought it was a good idea to wear heels tonight? She slipped out of her shoes and padded down the tunnel with the cold, dusty stones under her feet.

Left. She was going to keep going left and she'd find her way out.

Deacon checked his mobile again. Vivienne had sent a message saying she was on her way thirty minutes ago. Even if she was walking, it wouldn't have taken her thirty minutes to reach the pub. Something was wrong.

"Where do you think you're going?" Graham asked, setting three pints of amber cider on the table between them. Graham was Deacon's mate from the Limerick Neverland—and Caoilfhionn's brother. They both had mahogany hair, but that was where the resemblance ended, thankfully.

Caoilfhionn was a typical Mermaid: snippy and inherently evil.

Graham's sole purpose on this Earth was to have a good time. They'd gotten into a lot of trouble in their youth, before their genes activated. Deacon would never forget Graham's fifteenth birthday, when they'd stolen drinks from Graham's house and ended up passed out in a ditch between two cow pastures.

"I want to check on Vivienne," Deacon said, grabbing his jacket from the back of his stool.

Graham's dark eyebrows rose as he sipped from his pint. "Why? She said she was on her way, didn't she?"

"She should be here by now."

"Relax, lad. I'm pretty sure your little wifey can take care of herself."

Wifey. The thought of Vivienne being his wife made Deacon smile. Perhaps Graham was right. Vivienne had been complaining that Deacon was being too protective. That he needed to give her space. It wasn't like HOOK was going to find her here.

Deacon replaced his jacket and took a drink. He had always loved cider, but tonight, it tasted like youth and bad decisions. Bad decisions he refused to make now that he was engaged.

Ethan stumbled out of the WC and dropped onto the stool next to him. "What'd I miss?" he asked after gulping down half his drink.

"Only the three lovely outsiders ordering cocktails," Graham said with a sly smile.

Sure enough, three young women, early twenties and in

skimpy dresses, smiled at them from the bar. When had they arrived?

"But Dash was too busy pining over his wife to notice," Graham added.

"I see them. I just don't care." Rolling his eyes, Deacon took another drink. This was the same conversation they had every time they'd gone out. Graham and Ethan would spend the rest of the night spotting women, chatting them up, and trying to go home with them. It was a game Deacon had spent years mastering, never realizing how unfulfilling it was until he'd met Vivienne.

He glanced back at the bar, only to lock eyes with one of the women. Her dark hair was dyed pink at the ends, matching the bra straps peeking from beneath her black dress. Cursing, he drank some more. Where the hell was Vivienne?

Ethan laughed into his glass. "I liked you better when you were single, man. Settled Dash is *bor-ing* as hell."

"Settled Dash is *happy*," Deacon countered, dragging out his mobile to check for more messages. If Vivienne had decided not to come, she would have let him know. If she wasn't there by the time he finished this pint, he was going to go find her. He didn't care if it was overbearing.

"Hey there," a high feminine voice greeted. When Deacon looked up, he found himself face to face with the girl from the bar. "I saw you checking me out and thought you'd like a closer look." She dragged her lip ring through her teeth.

"Me? I wasn't checking you out."

His mates' laughter cut through his embarrassment.

"Yeah, okay," she snorted. "Can I get you a drink?"

"No, thank you. I'm leaving when I finish this."

"Leaving?" Ethan groaned. "What the hell, man? You said you'd stay out."

Deacon had promised to stay out, but only because Vivienne was supposed to be with him.

"Yeah, what the hell, man?" The girl grinned. "I just got here."

"Don't waste your time on him." Graham kicked Deacon's shoe off the rung at the bottom of the stool. "He's as good as married."

Ethan snagged Deacon's mobile, promising to give it back if he had one more pint. Deacon agreed reluctantly. When the full glass was set in front of him, he picked it up and drank until he thought it was going to come back up. The girl watched him with a smirk on her lips.

Ethan cursed under his breath.

What was his problem? It wasn't like he was alone. There was a woman all but sitting on his lap, and Graham would be out until the pub closed or the girl whispering in his ear invited him home with her—whichever came first.

Deacon made reluctant small talk with the pink-haired girl—Leah she told him, while leaning in uncomfortably close—until he choked down the last drop of cider.

"All right, Ethan, give me my damn mobile." Drinking that quickly was going to bite him in the ass, but if he hurried back to Harrow, he'd be in Vivienne's flat before the effects hit him.

Ethan grumbled but pulled Deacon's mobile from his back pocket and slapped it into Deacon's hand. There were no texts or calls from Vivienne, but a blocked number had tried calling him five times.

"Why didn't you tell me it was ringing?" Deacon growled, clicking on the voicemail icon.

Ethan muttered some excuse, but Deacon couldn't hear him.

"Hello, Deacon, it's Richard. I'm calling from the infirmary . . . "

Shit. Shit. Shit.

"We found Vivienne . . .

Richard said Vivienne's name again, but everyone was being so loud, Deacon couldn't hear properly. "Can you all shut the hell up for one bloody minute?"

His mates quieted.

"She's fine," Richard said, "just a little confused and won't stop asking for you. Please come as soon as you can."

Cursing, Deacon grabbed his jacket from the stool.

"What happened?" Ethan asked, eyebrows lifted over wide eyes.

"I told you something was wrong, didn't I? Vivienne got lost in the bloody tunnels. They've been trying to call me for the last twenty minutes."

"Lost? How the hell . . . " Ethan's words faded as realization crossed his face. "Shit, Dash. I'm sorry. Do you want me to come with you?"

"Your drunk ass has already done enough." He stalked toward the door, accidentally ramming into people and muttering apologies.

"What the hell, dude?" Ethan called, running after him. "Why are you jumping down my throat? This isn't my fault."

Alcohol and anger pulsed in Deacon's veins, and he couldn't hold back anymore. "Just because you screwed up your relationship by sleeping with Caoilfhionn doesn't mean you need to sabotage mine. For the first time in my life, I'm trying to have a serious relationship, and all you're doing is whining because I'm not trying to shag every girl that walks by. I didn't give you shit when you and Nicola were happy and I was bloody miserable. Grow the hell up, *dude*."

True, it wasn't Ethan's fault Vivienne had been in the tunnels. But if he'd been a better friend—if he'd cared about Vivienne at all—he wouldn't have insisted Deacon stay and get drunk with his sorry ass. And if Deacon weren't such a fool, he wouldn't have listened.

76

By the time Deacon reached the infirmary, he was soaked through and still raging, but also so worried he thought his chest was going to collapse.

Richard ran into him on his way out of the room, his bright red hair sticking out in every direction. "You look like shit, Deacon." His freckled nose wrinkled. "Are you *drunk*?"

"Not yet." Thankfully, the icy rain had kept him lucid on the way here. "Where's Vivienne? Is she all right?"

"She's fine, just a little shaken up." Richard tucked the clipboard he carried beneath his arm. "It was between shifts, so it took the security team a bit of time before they noticed her sitting down there."

Deacon's heart was pounding so loudly, he had trouble hearing. "How long?"

Richard winced. "An hour."

Vivienne had been lost for an entire hour? She must have been terrified.

"But, like I said, she's going to be fine. Although . . . she does seem to be quite thin. Is she eating properly?"

"She says she's not very hungry." Vivienne's appetite had been all over the place lately. Sometimes, she flat out refused to eat. "I'm trying to get her to eat more. And sometimes she forgets—" Deacon's mouth snapped shut.

Richard's eyes widened. "I *knew* there was something wrong. She asked me my name three different times. I didn't know she was forgetful . . . She's so young." His voice dropped as he shook his head.

"She doesn't want anyone to know about her diagnosis."

Richard's eyes narrowed as he tilted his head, studying Deacon with an unnerving intensity that left him taking a step back—and colliding with the wall.

"Go on in," Richard finally said with a nod. "She's waiting for you."

The infirmary resembled a small hospital ward: four beds along each wall with curtains between them. All the curtains were open except the set at the back of the room. When Deacon drew them aside, he found Vivienne sitting up in the bed, wearing a black dress that hugged every blessed inch of her. The front dipped in a deep V, leaving him staring at the swell of her chest beneath. His mouth went dry, and it had nothing to do with the alcohol.

A pair of heels had been discarded on a chair beside the bed; Deacon moved them and sank down beside her.

There were dark smudges beneath Vivienne's wide eyes; her hands were dirty, as were the bottoms of her black tights. Why had Deacon listened when she had forced him out the door earlier? Oh, right. Because she had threatened to murder him with her pillow if he didn't give her some breathing space.

He should have waited for her to wake up from her nap and gone with her. Then none of this would have happened.

Vivienne's sigh made her chest rise and fall in an exaggerated motion. "Whatever you're thinking, get it out of your head."

As if that was possible. "I shouldn't have left you on your own."

"This isn't your fault. I just got turned around in the tunnels." She spun her hand in the air. "It's not a big deal."

"Not a big deal?" Was she completely mad? If there hadn't been cameras, there was no telling how long it would have taken someone to find her. She could have been missing for hours. For *days*. She could have fallen down and hit her head and bled out and died.

"I knew someone would find me eventually."

Was that supposed to make him feel better? Because it didn't. "I don't want you going down there on your own."

Huffing a humorless laugh, she pressed her fingers to her closed eyes. Her shoulders slumped in on themselves, making her look even smaller. When she dropped her hands, her brown eyes were resigned. "Deacon? I'm fine. Please, don't worry."

Telling him not to worry was like telling the rain to stop falling.

She was forgetting already.

They didn't have time.

TEN

"Why don't we begin with the only topic today that shouldn't cause any arguments," Donovan said, adjusting his position on Peter's chair. The Leadership chamber was warm despite the winter winds howling outside. It had snowed that morning, which had put Vivienne in a great mood. Which meant Deacon was in a great mood . . . until he remembered what had happened in the tunnels this weekend.

They couldn't deny it any longer: Vivienne was getting worse.

When they got back to Kensington, she was going to Alex for treatment after the holidays. That meant the hairy bastard would have a chance to wiggle his way back into her life, but if it helped her, Deacon would suck it up with a smile.

He had tried convincing Vivienne to seek treatment while she was in Harrow, but that meant going to Gwen for help. She'd shot down that idea straight away.

He couldn't blame her.

"Hugh?" Donovan nodded toward the congregation. "The floor is yours."

"Thanks, Donovan." A teen with buzzed black hair stepped down from his place in the second row and situated himself in front of the arch of Leadership. Deacon had only met Hugh a handful of times before, mostly at the Wendy Bird. He was a few years older than Deacon's mother, though his active Nevergene made that fact irrelevant.

"The increase in drone technology is putting all of us at risk," Hugh said, crossing his arms as he paced back and forth across the open space. "Right now, there are only a handful of places we can fly in broad daylight without fear of being caught by unsuspecting eyes. But these drones threaten to expose us."

Deacon had always wanted a drone. Perhaps he'd buy himself one for Christmas.

Shit.

Christmas was in a little over a month. What was he supposed to get Vivienne? Last year had been easy after he'd taken a small replica of Peter's statue from his grandad. But he had only liked her then. Now he loved her, which meant he had to think of something really, *really* good. Perhaps he'd text Emily later and ask if she had any suggestions.

"And we have tech around each campus to jam the signals and scramble the footage," a woman in the third row said. Deacon thought her name was Cecelia, from the Limerick Neverland. He'd spent the least amount of time there. Perhaps he'd suggest traveling over for New Year's. Vivienne would love seeing Ireland.

Hugh's frown deepened. "That's true. But I'm afraid with the advances in technology, we will be in trouble soon enough."

Drones. They wanted to drone on about the bloody things. Deacon's joke made him snigger, drawing a warning glare from his mother. Stifling his smile, he attempted to focus.

He didn't need to think about drones or Christmas or Ireland or the way Aoibheann was glaring at him from her chair. Angry women were terrifying.

He closed his eyes, determined to focus on making his case to Leadership.

This was going to go well. It had to.

He needed a win.

After the tunnels, he had gone to Peter asking to be added to the meeting docket. He knew there was a risk Leadership would turn them down, but the timing was out of his hands.

Giving Vivienne a wedding and a marriage while she could still remember both was Deacon's top priority. All he needed were a few memorable events without any drama or depressing shite happening. Just pure, unadulterated happiness. Was that too much to ask?

"Does anyone have a solution they would like to submit, or should we table the discussion until we've had time for consideration?" Donovan asked, addressing the audience in general.

No one spoke up.

"I move to table the discussion," Curly said, flicking something from his sleeve. Instead of gelling his black hair today, he'd let it fall across his forehead. "Since September, we've acquired seven drones that were remotely disabled once they crossed the gates at Kensington. It is an issue, but not a pressing one with a clear solution."

Donovan nodded before asking if anyone seconded the motion.

When a bunch of hands raised in the air, Hugh gave a disappointed nod toward his fellow PAN.

"We will consider the problem and discuss more in depth

at our next meeting," Donovan said. "Thank you once again for bringing the issue to light, Hugh."

"That's the third time they've tabled the drones," Deacon's mother muttered, a smile playing on her lips. "If they do it again, Hugh's liable to explode."

The meeting went on for another hour, and they discussed everything from the upcoming holiday celebrations to the increase in video surveillance equipment around London's city center. Everyone knew they had to be careful flying in and around cities, so Deacon wasn't sure why it was even mentioned. Still, he sat and listened, with the damned wooden stool digging into his ass.

He checked his watch. How much longer was this going to take? It was getting late. He hoped Vivienne was taking a nap so she wouldn't be tired when he came back to tell her the good news.

Because he *was* going to have good news.

"I believe there has been one additional request added to today's meeting," Donovan said with a smile, nodding toward him. "Deacon, it's your turn."

This was it. The final hurdle between today and the rest of Deacon's never-ending life.

Deacon stood and straightened his jeans, wiping his clammy hands against his thighs. Why was he so nervous? He had been on trial in front of these people before, his fate in their hands, and hadn't cared nearly as much.

Then he realized it wasn't just his fate they were deciding.

It was Vivienne's as well.

He didn't want to let her down.

"Thank you, Donovan. I know everyone is anxious to head to the Wendy Bird, so I'll make this brief. As you know, Vivienne Dunn and I are engaged." He avoided looking at Gwen or Aoibheann, instead settling on Alex. He was going

83

to vote no anyway, so Deacon may as well piss him rightly off. "And we are seeking marriage approval."

"You've been engaged for a few weeks." Aoibheann crossed her legs and drummed her nails against the arm of the chair. "The two of you barely know each other."

Deacon bit back the retort on his tongue. Arguing with her in front of everyone would only end badly for him. Besides, she was always going to vote against this. He needed to appeal to the others—the ones who had hearts.

"I understand that, from the outside, it may look as though we're rushing into things. But I can assure you that we both understand the gravity of this decision."

"While I appreciate you following procedure for once," Slightly said with an unconcerned flick of his wrist, "I don't feel your situation deserves special treatment."

If Deacon broke the rules, he got shit. And now that he was trying to follow procedure, he was still getting shit. He was damned either way. For once, why couldn't Slightly be on his side?

"I'm not asking for special treatment." He managed to sound calm despite the anger building inside his chest. Yes, there was typically a time requirement for relationships. But he knew plenty of couples who'd had the waiting period waived. "I'm asking for approval of my marriage to the woman I love."

"With all due respect, Deacon," Curly said, his mouth turned down into a disapproving frown, "given your past . . . indiscretions, I think it is in everyone's best interest to wait."

Shit. Not Curly too. Gwen was an obvious no, as were Aoibheann and Alex. Slightly and Curly constituted a majority.

"I understand why you would think that." Deacon stuffed his hands into his pockets so they couldn't see his fists. *Dammit,* he wanted to hit something. "But after everything that has happened this past year, I think it's time to face facts: none of us are truly immortal. HOOK took Vivienne, and they shot me. Believing we own time, that it's not something precious, that it doesn't matter if we waste it, is foolish." And Deacon wasn't a fool anymore. Time was the one thing he knew he didn't have.

"Thank you for your speech." Donovan's eyes were sad as he closed his notebook. "I'm sure everyone can agree that it is refreshing to see someone so young speak so passionately about his future. I believe it's time for a vote. Those in favor of approving the union between Deacon Elias Ashford and Vivienne Renee Dunn, please raise your hands."

Two hands went up—Richard Two and Nibs.

Two bloody hands. Not even enough for Peter to weigh in and cast a deciding vote.

Deacon's fingers twitched as he glanced at his stool. He suddenly wanted to pick the thing up and splinter it into a thousand pieces against the cursed wall of this cursed chamber.

Deacon's mother put her cold hand on Deacon's elbow. "Don't," she warned in a low whisper.

He sank back down, ignoring the eyes boring into him from all sides, judging and smirking.

The session finished after that, but Deacon didn't follow the rest of them to the tunnels. The last thing he wanted was to spend time with the traitors. He stared at the painted trees, trying to figure out how he was going to break the news to Vivienne.

If only he could have told Leadership about her condition. There was no way they would have turned him down.

His mother shifted on the stool beside him; instead of standing, she put a reassuring hand on his knee. "I'm proud of you, son."

"I don't know why. They said no." If he had been a better person before, had fewer casual relationships, they would have taken him seriously. But he couldn't change that now. He could only accept that he'd made mistakes and move forward. Hell, that's what he was *trying* to do.

"You have to understand something." She clasped her hands together in her lap and twisted so she was facing him instead of the empty chairs at the front of the room. "These people see you once every few months. And the last time you were in front of them, they were trying you for a whole list of offenses. You haven't exactly put yourself in a position to be taken seriously. They see you as reckless and impulsive, and are painting your relationship with Vivienne in the same light."

"I'm not—"

She squeezed his knee. "Let me finish. I know you've changed. I can see it in the way you treat Vivienne. I can see it in the way you handled today's disappointment." She smiled, pride making her green eyes sparkle. "Give them a little time to see it as well."

That was easy for her to say. She wasn't racing against the clock. "And if I don't have time?" He kicked the stool in front of him. It made a satisfying *bang* as it toppled to the ground.

Her eyebrows came together. "What do you mean?"

Deacon's stomach ached from worrying; he really had planned on keeping Vivienne's secret. But when he looked at his mother, he couldn't stop the tears pricking the backs of his eyes. He turned his head, wiping them away before she noticed.

"What's wrong?" she asked, her voice laced with concern as she stroked her hand down his cheek.

Inhaling a deep breath, he attempted to get his emotions under control.

The thought of betraying Vivienne killed him, but holding all of this shite inside was getting too heavy.

Pretending that everything was going to be all right when he knew it was going to fall apart was too much.

"She's going to forget me, Mum."

Saying it out loud hadn't made it better.

It made it worse.

He wished he could take back the confession and erase the bitter taste the words left on his tongue. If he gave in to reality now, he'd never be able to dig himself out.

Deacon needed to stay positive, to keep the light of hope alive for as long as he could. That was the only way they were going to make it through this.

His mother sucked in a breath, but he kept his eyes trained on his shoes. "Oh, Deacon . . . " Her arms came around him. "Why didn't you tell Leadership? If you'd explained what's happening, they would have said yes."

"Vivienne begged me not to."

His mother sighed and pulled away, cupping his jaw between her hands the way she used to when he was little. "Talk to Vivienne. Explain that it may be the only way to sway the founding members."

Deacon left the Leadership Chamber through the tunnels and went back to Vivienne's flat, where he found her lounging on the sofa, curled up beneath the duvet she'd dragged in from the bedroom.

When she saw him, she paused the rerun of *Fawlty Towers* on the tele. "How'd it go?"

Discussing the meeting could wait. But addressing Vivienne's paleness and the dark circles beneath her eyes couldn't. It looked like she had lost weight in the few hours he'd been gone.

Deacon removed his jacket and threw it on the back of the sofa. "Have you eaten anything today?"

"I had some toast earlier," she said, rolling her eyes and nodding toward an empty plate on the table.

A plate that had been there since yesterday.

"Did the shoppers bring more bread?" He had meant to pick some up before the meeting, but hadn't had time.

"No. Why?"

Because they didn't have any bloody bread. Which meant she hadn't eaten any bloody toast. "Vivienne, you need to eat." He stomped to the kitchen to search the cupboards for something—anything. Even a bar of chocolate at this stage. "What sounds good?" Whatever she wanted, he would get for her.

"Nothing sounds good," she grumbled, pulling her hair into a messy knot at the top of her head, "that's the problem."

In the fridge was a pot of yogurt and a bit of leftover ham, and he found a granola bar at the bottom of one of the drawers. He opened all of them before putting them on a plate, knowing she was likely to slip them back into the drawers when he wasn't looking.

"Sit down and eat." He set the plate on the table and pulled a chair out for her.

"Okay, *Mom*." She kicked off the blankets, swaying slightly as she stood.

Deacon's stomach dropped. If he went to help her, she'd only tell him to back off.

Once she was seated, Deacon took the chair next to her. Vivienne stirred the yogurt, dipping the small spoon in and out. Instead of taking a bite, she abandoned the spoon and started pulling the ham into little pieces.

"Playing with your food isn't the same as eating it." And now that Deacon was thinking about it, he couldn't remember her having much of her dinner last night either. No wonder she looked like she was going to shatter with a gust of wind.

"Geez, you're grumpy," she muttered before shoveling in a massive bite of ham. "There. I ate some."

"Good. Now eat more."

Although she rolled her eyes, Vivienne began eating with more gusto. By the time she'd finished everything on her plate, some color had returned to her cheeks.

"I take it from the mood you're in that today didn't go well."

He was in a mood because his fiancée looked like death warmed over. But there was no point harping on and on about it. He would do better, be more vigilant. "They said no."

Vivienne nodded, wiping crumbs from the granola bar on her black leggings. "That's okay. They can't say no forever."

That was the problem. Leadership *could* say no forever. "I know how to get them to change their minds. At least the majority of them."

The knot on top of her head flopped from side to side as she shook her head. "Absolutely not."

"Vivienne, please." Leaning his elbows on the table, Deacon closed his eyes. He couldn't wait to go to bed and put this day behind him. "If we can help them understand our situation, that we don't have the luxury of time, then—"

"No. And don't ask me again."

When he opened his eyes, he found Vivienne leaning back in the chair, arms folded over her chest, glaring at him. Her lips pressed into a tight line, and he wished he could make her smile. But he couldn't let this go. She had the power to change the outcome of this whole disaster.

"Why are you being so damn stubborn about this? If you really wanted to marry me, you'd let me tell them." He was getting tired of fighting with everyone on all sides.

"Stop that crap right now, you big baby." She leaned forward until they were only a breath apart. He could smell the strawberry yogurt on her lips, and see the spark of anger in her narrowed eyes. "Do you think I want all of Neverland believing you're only marrying me because I'm forgetful?

This is my health we're talking about, and it's nobody's business. You may not know this because you've never been in an *actual* relationship, but they're supposed to be give and take." She jabbed her finger into his shoulder, hitting the spot where HOOK's bullet had gone through him. "I let you go to Leadership even though I thought it was too soon. That's me giving." Another poke. "When are you going to give something, Deacon?"

"I'm trying to give you everything, but you won't let me!"

She shoved away from the table. "Find another way to convince them, because this discussion is over."

Deacon groaned and dropped his head into his hands as he listened to her footsteps retreating toward the bedroom.

The only other way to convince Leadership was to prove that he was taking this relationship seriously.

But how long would that take?

Six months?

A year?

Ten?

Perhaps he could annoy it out of them. Deacon could attend every meeting and keep asking and asking and asking until he got the answer he wanted. They had to say yes eventually.

ELEVEN

I nstead of going for a walk as she had planned, Vivienne sank onto the edge of her unmade bed and kicked off her shoes. Now that the heating was fixed, her apartment in Harrow was warm and inviting—the exact opposite of the rain pelting the windows. As much as she didn't love the snow back at Kensington, she liked it a heck of a lot more than the dampness in England. Every time she left Michael's Rest, her feet got wet. Now she understood Deacon's thing about damp socks.

Socks made up the bulk of the dirty laundry piled next to the armoire. Doing laundry didn't require her to brave the rain, but if she didn't have the motivation to make the bed, there was no way she was going to wash all those clothes. If she hadn't napped earlier, she would have curled up and gone to sleep again.

Vivienne was ready to go back home. To her friends. To her apartment. To the familiar faces that smiled instead of glared. To the campus that wasn't built on top of a death maze. To a place where she didn't have to see Gwen-the-perfect every time she stepped out of the freaking building, or meet Aoibheann-the-devil every time she ventured into the cafeteria.

After the incident in the tunnels last weekend, Deacon had become a sexy tyrant. Any time she tried to leave the apartment, he wanted to know where she was going. Then he made sure she had TINK and her cell phone, and reminded her not to use the tunnels.

If she tried to leave campus, either Deacon or Ethan or Deacon's Irish friend Graham went with her as chaperones. Sometimes all three. Which she didn't mind nearly as much. She could sink into herself and enjoy their loud banter and pretend to smile and laugh with them.

But the truth was, she'd never felt less like smiling and laughing.

Vivienne was engaged to the man she loved. She lived in freaking Neverland. She had a credit card with no spending limit that she never had to pay for. She and Deacon went to West End shows and toured palaces and went sightseeing every other day. Her Instagram was filled with photos from places she never thought she'd get to see in person.

She could freaking *fly*.

She should have been the happiest woman ever.

Was there something wrong with her? Why wasn't she happy?

Instead of sitting in the bedroom wallowing, she dragged the covers from the bed and made her way down the narrow hallway to the couch. There were dishes in the sink that needed washed, but that required effort. And she couldn't drudge up the energy.

Vivienne dropped onto the couch and found the remote where she'd left it the night before, tucked beneath one of the throw pillows still dented from her head. Every stupid station was playing something British. Which had excited her when she had first arrived in England. Now, hearing the accent made her want to throw the TV out the window. Eventually, she found a channel showing re-runs of *I Love Lucy*. She and Lyle had used to watch old black and white TV shows late at night after Lynn had gone to bed because there was nothing else on.

Vivienne missed Lyle, even though he was being dumb right now. Maybe she should text him and ask him what was wrong. Except . . . her phone was *aaaall* the way in the bedroom. She'd text him later.

The door opened, but she didn't bother turning around. It would be Deacon, returning from whatever important *thing* he had to do. He had probably told her when he'd left earlier, but she hadn't really listened. And when he had invited her to come along, she had turned him down. Pretending to enjoy herself was going to take more energy than she had left.

"Oh good, you're awake." Deacon sounded breathless. He kicked the door shut and came around to where she was sitting. A black knitted hat was pulled low over his forehead, and his nose was red from the cold. But what most interested her was the massive black trash bag slung over his shoulder.

"Aren't you supposed to take trash *out* of the house?" she asked, nodding toward the bag.

Deacon's face split into a grin as he dropped the bag onto the coffee table with a soft *thud*. She almost felt like opening it to see what he'd lugged home, but only managed to pause the TV.

"This isn't rubbish. It's our next adventure." His green eyes glittered with mischief.

Unless it was a ticket back home, Vivienne wasn't interested. "I'm too tired for adventure."

He pulled the gloves from his fingers and sank onto the edge of the couch. His knees brushed against hers when he turned toward her. "Come on, Vivienne," he said, his smile tightening. "It'll be fun."

Deacon was trying. The least she could do was make a little effort. Vivienne unraveled herself from the covers and opened the top of the trash bag. She wasn't sure what she'd expected to find, but it wasn't a gigantic knitted sweater.

"I don't think this is going to fit me." She held the red wool against her chest. It was at least four times her size.

"They're not for you," Deacon snorted, grabbing a mammoth knitted hat with two holes on either side of the top.

"Are there giants in Neverland that I don't know about?"

The comment earned her a gruff chuckle. "They're for the statues." Deacon collected the two items and stuffed them back into the trash bag. "We're getting them ready for Christmas."

"What statues?" She had never seen any on campus.

"Come with me, and I'll show you." He held out his hand, reminding her of the first time they'd met, when he'd asked her to follow him to Neverland.

There was a small part of her that wondered if she'd feel better going with him. The fresh air could be good. And Deacon always ended up making her laugh. But it was still raining. And she would have to put her shoes back on. And find her coat. And deal with damp socks. "Maybe next time."

Deacon's smile disappeared, and his eyes narrowed. The longer he stared at her, the more his brow furrowed. She shifted on the cushion, wishing she had pretended to be asleep so she didn't have to disappoint him.

"What's wrong, Vivienne?"

"Nothing. I'm fine." Her smile felt strained. He was doing his best. This was taking its toll on him. Deacon had his own burdens to bear, and he didn't need her piling her worries and fears on top of him too.

"Don't lie to me." Deacon brushed her hair back from her face and pressed his forehead to hers. "You're not fine."

She didn't feel like denying it anymore, so she didn't.

When Deacon pulled away, his frown deepened. "Please come along tonight." He nudged her chin with his finger until she was looking at him. "I promise you'll have fun."

"I'm really tired."

His eyebrows came together again, creating a wrinkle between them as his eyes searched hers. "You slept all afternoon."

She shrugged. "Still tired."

He sighed as he stood and collected his gloves from where they'd fallen onto the rug. "Are you sure?" he asked, twisting the top of the trash bag and slinging it over his shoulder.

"I'm sure."

With a nod, he made his way to the door. "I love you."

Vivienne pressed play and snuggled deeper into the covers.

"Did you hear me?" Deacon called, hesitating in the doorway.

"What? Oh, yeah. Love you too."

"Are you sure? Because it sounded like it took a lot of effort for you to say that."

Loving Deacon didn't take any effort at all. It was like he was the only light in the increasingly dark world. But for some reason, when Vivienne told him she was sure, even she didn't sound convinced.

The weather that night was shite. Cold and windy and rainy. Good for pranks, because no one in their right mind wanted to be caught outside in it, but bad for Deacon's toes and fingers. He'd removed his soaked gloves an hour ago, convinced they were making his hands colder. And his socks were damp. He should have grabbed an extra pair when he'd been at the flat.

Taking one of the last scarves from the bag, he wrapped it around George IV's neck, hoping the wind wouldn't undo all their hard work.

"There's something wrong with Vivienne." Rain splattering on bronze muffled Deacon's confession. According to his fiancée, she was fine.

Fine. Fine. Fine.

If he heard the lie one more time, he was going to rip out his hair. It was so bleeding obvious that she wasn't fine, but he couldn't do anything to help if she refused to speak to him about it.

"Uh, yeah there is. She's depressed, dude." Ethan snagged an extra-large knitted hat for George's horse. The lions in Trafalgar square all wore scarves and hats like elves, and Lord Nelson had on a fabulous Santa suit that had taken a lot of time to get fastened.

Was Vivienne depressed?

The not eating . . .

The sleepless nights . . .

Deacon sank onto the back of the horse, looking out across the lights of the city but not really seeing anything. "Did she say something to you?"

Had she told him on their walk to the shop on Tuesday? The idea that Vivienne would confide in his best mate and not him made Deacon's heart ache.

"She didn't need to. My eyes work just fine. She's depressed as hell and wants to go home."

Deacon knew Vivienne missed Kensington—she talked about it constantly. And Emily, of course. And probably Lyle. Although for the life of him, he didn't know why anyone would miss that wanker.

But did Vivienne really miss Kensington enough to be

dragged into a depression? He didn't care where he lived so long as she was with him. He'd happily move to Peter's island with her and never speak to another soul and be perfectly content forever.

The idea that she may not feel the same didn't sit well. Was he not enough for her?

"You accused me of sabotaging your relationship, so let me make up for it by giving you some *good* advice for once." Ethan tossed him a scarf with long tassels on the end. "Take your girl back to Kensington ASAP."

Shit.

What if he *wasn't* enough?

What if Vivienne had realized it and didn't know how to tell him?

What if—

"You okay, man?"

Ethan was looking at him like he'd lost his mind. Perhaps he had. "Yeah. I'm all right. Just can't wait to get back and change my socks."

Ethan snorted. "You and your damn socks."

By the time Deacon returned to campus, the sun was beginning to appear over the horizon, glistening off the wet grass. It had taken an hour to get the Duke of York at The Mall and Captain James Cook winter-ready in knitted sweaters and matching caps. And another thirty minutes to get across the city and dress his grandad's statue in a neon green mankini, sunglasses, and leis. And then it had taken half the bloody night for Deacon to realize that he *wasn't* enough to make Vivienne happy. And that it was a *good* thing.

Vivienne needed more. Deserved more.

She had been right when she had accused him of taking from her without giving back.

But not anymore.

He wanted to give her everything—even if it meant giving her less of him and more of the other people she cared about. More of *her* life and less of his.

The unlocking door sounded like thunder in comparison to the silent hallway. Deacon stripped off his outer layers, untied his sopping laces, and peeled out of his soaked socks before tiptoeing to where Vivienne was curled up on the sofa with the duvet pulled up to her nose.

"Wake up," he whispered, kneeling in front of her and brushing her dark waves back from her neck. "Vivienne?" He pressed a kiss against the pulse at her throat, relishing the way her skin smelled like the new lilac perfume he'd bought her. "Wake up, lovie."

Her lips lifted into a sleepy smile as she leaned into him. "I don't want to."

"I'd like to give you your Christmas present a little early."

Groaning, she sat up and rubbed her eyes. "This had better be good. And I swear, if you take off your pants and have a big red bow on your boxers, I'm going to kill you."

That was a brilliant idea. He'd have to buy a bow for Christmas morning. "I like the way you think, but I'm not your gift—not this year, anyway."

"Okay then. What's my gift?" A yawn escaped as she closed her eyes and held out her hands.

He wrapped his fingers around her wrist and hauled her onto his lap. His internal spark ignited, sending jolts of fire and adrenaline coursing through his veins. He slipped his free hand beneath her sweatshirt, finding the soft heat of her skin beneath. If he was lucky, they'd have a little time to celebrate before their flight.

"Why are you so cold?" Vivienne yelped, trying to wiggle free. "Your hands are like ice."

"I was hoping you'd warm me up."

Her eyes narrowed even as her lips curled upward. "I'll decide if you deserve a warm up after you tell me what you got me."

Goosebumps lifted on her skin as his hand traced up and up, only to find she was wearing nothing beneath the hideous sweatshirt. "I bought plane tickets."

"Shut up." She knocked his hand away and sat back so she could see his face. Her eyes widened, and her mouth broke into the most breathtaking smile. "Are we going home?"

He nodded.

"Oh! Thank you, thank you, thank *youuu*!" She wrapped her arms around his neck and pulled him tight against her, dotting kisses from his jaw to his ear. His heart felt so full, it could practically burst. Instead of worrying about what could happen, he closed his eyes and committed her joy to memory.

"Wait. Are you okay with that?" She pulled back to search his eyes. "I know you usually spend Christmas here with your mom. Does she mind? Or are we coming back?"

"I thought we could make some new traditions." They were going to be married eventually. Things were going to change. "Perhaps alternate locations every other year?"

His response earned him more hugs and kisses. "That sounds perfect," Vivienne said. "Just perfect. What time's our flight?"

"Half ten."

She shot to her feet and collected the duvet. "I have to pack." She glanced toward the messy kitchen. "*Crap*. And clean. I don't remember where my passport is. Do you know what I did with it?" When she looked back at him, he couldn't help but smile.

"What are you smiling at?" Vivienne's eyebrows arched toward her hairline.

"I love it when you're frazzled." The spark was back in

her eyes. This was the most animated he had seen her since she got lost.

"I'm *frazzled* because we only have"—she checked her watch—"three hours to get this place cleaned up and get to the airport."

"We have plenty of time."

She rolled her eyes. "Get off your butt and help me."

"Help you what? Take off that sweatshirt? And those tights? And your knickers?"

Backing toward the bedroom, Vivienne said, "All three if you promise to wash the dishes."

TWELVE

Vivienne didn't realize how much she had missed the snow until she saw the Kensington campus draped in layers of glistening white. Zipping her coat to her chin, she jumped out of Deacon's toasty car. The breeze was so cold it stung her cheeks, but she welcomed the pain. They were *finally* home.

And Deacon had done this for her. She knew it had been hard for him to leave his mother for Christmas, but Vivienne swore to herself that she'd make this the best Christmas ever. And then next year, they could celebrate in London with his family.

Instead of using the glass door, Vivienne suggested taking the stairs. Emily had been living on her own for so long, there was no telling if she'd taken up walking around the apartment naked. When she explained her reasoning to Deacon, he chuckled and made a comment about wishing Vivienne would adopt the same habit, which earned him a punch in the arm.

Deacon had tried to convince her to stay at his place, but she couldn't wait to see Emily. She was ready to fall over from exhaustion but figured Emily would have enough energy for the both of them.

Deacon insisted on carrying her bags, so she stuffed her hands into her pockets and jogged up the stairs to the third floor. It wasn't until they reached the hall covered in picture frames that she realized she had left her keys at Deacon's house.

It was after two, so hopefully Emily was home. She could have called ahead, but where was the fun in that?

Vivienne knocked on the door and waited, her stomach fluttering with nerves. Why the heck was she nervous?

When the door jerked open, the nerves turned to excitement.

Emily was there, not a stray curl out of place, looking perfect as ever in a red sweater and pair of skinny jeans. "Am I dreaming right now?" Her grin was infectious. "I've gotta be dreaming."

"Nope, not dreaming." Vivienne's laughter was cut short by a hug so tight it squeezed all the air from her lungs.

"This is the best surprise ever. The *best!*" Emily squealed in Vivienne's ear, dragging her into the apartment. It looked like the number of snowflakes dangling from the ceiling had doubled since last year. And there was a new tree beside the door.

"Why didn't you tell me you were coming home, you little snake?"

"Because Deacon didn't tell me until this morning." Or had it been last night? Time zones made Vivienne's head spin—or it could have been the lack of sleep. If Emily hadn't been holding her, she'd probably already have fallen over.

Deacon set Vivienne's suitcase inside the door beside the new tree. "That's because it was a surprise."

His nose and cheeks were pink; he must have been

freezing in the light jacket he was wearing. She kicked herself for not noticing before now. Maybe she should have let him go home and change as he'd asked.

Emily let Vivienne go so abruptly, Vivienne had to steady herself against the wall. "You," she hissed, stalking toward where Deacon waited at the threshold. "I have something to say to you."

Deacon's eyes widened, and his gaze flashed to Vivienne. She shrugged. Heaven only knew what Emily was about to do.

"Don't look at her, look at me," Emily commanded. Deacon's gaze snapped back.

"This girl"—Emily snaked her arm around Vivienne's waist and dragged her close— "should have been home *weeks* ago. Next time you kidnap my best friend and hold her hostage until she's depressed beyond belief, I'm going to . . . " She leaned forward and whispered something into Deacon's ear. Something that left him flushed and retreating toward the door.

"You got it?" Emily snapped.

Deacon offered a tight nod. "Got it."

"Good. Now get out."

His brows flicked up in surprise. "Excuse me?"

"If you think I'm going to share my best friend right now, you're about to be disappointed. We have catching up to do." Emily let Vivienne go long enough to shoo Deacon out the door. "She'll see you tomorrow at Thanksgiving dinner."

He shot a pained look toward her. "Vivienne, I—"

The door slammed in his face.

"Don't you think that was a little harsh?" Vivienne asked with a laugh.

Emily's lips curled into a wicked smile. "For a guy who thinks he can keep my best friend hostage? Heck no."

"He didn't keep me hostage. I wanted to stay with him." Vivienne could have booked a ticket home right after the trial. But with everything that had happened, she felt like Deacon needed her in London. And she needed him too.

"So you say." Emily's pinched expression made it clear she had other opinions. "If me threatening his junk and kicking him out of our apartment is the worst that happens, then he got off lightly."

Emily was right. Deacon could weather a few threats.

Emily snapped the handle on Vivienne's suitcase and dragged it toward the bedrooms. "Come on. I want you to tell me everything."

Vivienne talked until she couldn't keep her eyes open, then she passed out on the bed.

It wasn't until she woke up a few hours later and had a shower that she truly felt human again. Now that she was thinking clearly, she sent Lyle a text asking if he wanted to come over, but she heard nothing back. Emily had ordered pizza, so they stuffed their faces with grease-soaked slices oozing cheese and covered in pepperoni.

By the time they finished, her stomach was so swollen it looked like she was going to have a food baby.

"Have you heard from Lyle today?" Vivienne asked, folding the pizza box in half and stuffing it into the already full trash can.

"Yeah. He called while you were asleep." Emily finished wiping the table with a dish cloth and rinsed the crumbs down the sink. "Why?"

Vivienne checked her phone again. Nothing. "I invited him over, but he hasn't responded."

Emily leaned back against the counter and pursed her lips. "Maybe you should go see him."

The pizza in Vivienne's stomach churned uneasily. "Why? Is he okay?" If there was something wrong, Lyle would have told her, right?

Emily's expression was guarded when she said, "That's something you need to ask Lyle."

Twenty minutes later, Vivienne was waiting on the stoop of Lyle's new home, a small brick rancher alarmingly close to Alex's house that had been gifted to him, rent-free, for as long as he wanted to live there. The scrap of paper Emily had given her, scribbled with his address, was crushed in her pocket. Vivienne had pressed Emily for more information, but Emily kept saying that it wasn't any of her business. Which made no sense. Emily thought everything was her business.

At her knock, a chain lock scraped on the other side of the door, and Vivienne adjusted the six-pack she'd brought as an early Christmas gift—and a potential peace offering. She couldn't remember doing anything wrong, but her memory wasn't very reliable these days.

When Lyle opened the door, he was wearing a pair of old sweatpants and an Ohio State T-shirt. He looked the same except for a hint of patchy stubble on his jaw—a jaw that was slack from shock.

"What do you want?" Instead of giving her one of his gap-toothed grins, he folded his arms over his chest.

Vivienne's stomach sank. "We haven't seen each other in a month and that's how you're going to greet me? Seriously, Lyle?" She had done everything to get him to Neverland. He was living in a free house because of her. Even if she had unknowingly offended him, the least he could do was pretend to be grateful.

Rolling his eyes, he turned back toward the living room. He didn't tell her to come inside but didn't tell her to get lost either. "I'm surprised your fiancé let you come over here alone," he grumbled, flopping onto a dark green couch.

"What's that supposed to mean?" Why would Deacon care if she went to see her brother?

Lyle's living room was small, but decorated with mid-century modern furniture and accents. The gold, peacock-shaped fireguard sitting in front of the stone fireplace screamed Emily. As did the massive Christmas tree in the corner and the tinsel over the door frames.

The can in Lyle's hand crunched before he lobbed it onto the coffee table. "Doesn't matter."

It mattered to her. This was their first Christmas together since Ohio, and Vivienne refused to let him ruin it by being a stupid jerk.

"It's pretty obvious you have something to say to me." She dropped onto the couch beside him and unhooked one of the beers. "I'm here now. You may as well let it out."

"I told you everything I needed to say on that damned island." He snagged a beer for himself. "But if you want me to repeat myself, here goes: I think you're an idiot. You're nineteen, Viv. *Nineteen*. This isn't the eighteenth century." He shoved back into the cushions and cursed. "You have no business getting married to someone you barely know when you haven't even *lived*."

Everyone thought that she was rushing into this. And she understood. But she had hoped Lyle would be different. That he knew her better than that.

"What makes you the expert on what I need?"

"I know guys like him." A muscle in Lyle's jaw feathered. "You deserve better."

"You don't know anything about my life." Lyle had only known Deacon for a couple of months—and most of that time he'd spent trying to irritate him.

"Because you don't tell me anything! I had to hear about Neverland from Peter-freakin'-Pan."

"I wasn't allowed to tell you!"

"That's bullshit, and you know it." He jabbed a finger toward her. "I didn't rat you out to those HOOK assholes. What makes you think I would've told anyone about Neverland?"

Vivienne had always known she could trust him, but she'd also had an obligation to keep her friends in Kensington safe. "I'm sorry, okay?"

"Yeah. Whatever. I'm over it."

He was such a liar. "Lyle, if I could go back and change things, I would tell you everything."

"Then why don't you tell me everything now?"

"You already know about Neverland."

"Not about Neverland," he groaned, raking a hand down his face. "Tell me why you're marrying that pretty-faced asshole. And don't give me some shit about being in love *blah blah blah*. Why are you rushing into this? You never used to be this way. I was the impulsive one. You always thought about your options and considered every angle. You expect me to believe that all of a sudden you're ready to just fly down the aisle with the first real boyfriend you've ever had?" His gaze dropped to her stomach. "You're not pregnant, are you?"

"No, I'm not pregnant!" She'd eaten a few extra slices of pizza and all of a sudden she was "pregnant." Vivienne should have slapped him for even suggesting it, but that would've made the situation worse.

"Then why, Viv?"

She had wanted to wait until after Christmas, to have one more normal holiday before everyone started treating her differently. But if she didn't tell Lyle, he was liable to miss the celebrations out of spite. Steeling her shoulders, she took a deep breath. "Because I'm going to forget everything and everyone, and I want to make as many memories with that *pretty faced asshole*—and all the other people I love—before I forget who they are."

"What the hell does that mean?"

Vivienne took another breath, praying she could get through this before the dam of emotions filling her chest broke free. She explained about the forgetful PAN, and her hormone levels, and all the inevitable things she had been trying to deny over the last few months.

Lyle's face paled, and he started shaking his head. Vivienne couldn't make out his expression from the tears in her eyes, but his voice shook when he said, "That can't be true."

"Yeah, well, it is." And denying it wouldn't stop forgetfulness from stealing everything from her. Vivienne needed to accept her fate—and take advantage of every waking moment until her memory was gone.

"My doctor told me it was inevitable. I thought I had more time, but little things are already slipping my mind." And big things too, sometimes. "So, excuse me for trying to have a life while I can. Yeah, if things were different, I wouldn't be engaged. Deacon and I would have forever to get to know one another, to have fun and take our time. But we don't. My mom started forgetting before she turned twenty-five, and my hormone levels are a lot higher than hers were."

Alex had told her she could have ten years before her memory started failing. But the whole Vivienne-can't-tell-directions incident in the tunnels had left her feeling like maybe he was wrong. Maybe she didn't have ten years. Maybe she didn't even have one year.

And she sure as heck wasn't going to waste a whole three hundred and sixty-five days not being with Deacon.

Lyle's arms came around her, and he muttered words that were probably meant to be comforting, but they only left her feeling helpless and empty.

"Does Smee—I mean, Deacon—know?"

"Of course he knows," she said, pushing away and scrubbing her burning eyes. The mascara she wore ended up smeared all over her knuckles. She probably looked like crap.

"Yeah. Sorry. I don't know why I even asked that." Wincing, he scratched his cheek. "Shit."

"You can say that again."

"Shit, shit, *shit.*"

He was so ridiculous. Still, she smiled.

"What the hell are we supposed to do now?" Lyle asked with a sigh.

Vivienne pulled out her phone and flicked on the camera. "Now," she said, holding the phone at arm's length and leaning her head on Lyle's shoulder, "we make some memories."

THIRTEEN

W as there anything better than a bacon cheeseburger? Vivienne didn't think so. She closed her eyes as she relished each bite, so incredibly thankful that she was back in America where bacon was bacon and grease tasted like heaven.

When she opened her eyes, there was a girl standing in front of her with dark, curly hair, watching her chew. "Do you mind if I sit down or are you wanting to be alone with that burger?" she asked with a smile, revealing a mouthful of perfectly straight teeth.

There were only seven other people in the entire Glass House. Why the heck did this girl want to sit with her?

"You can sit down if you want," Vivienne said, figuring it would be rude to tell her no. Maybe she was one of the new recruits. Vivienne had seen a few of them running around campus, the wonder still in their eyes. She remembered that feeling, the joy of magic and the promise of forever.

The girl dropped her purse onto the floor beside the

empty chair and slumped into the seat with a groan. "My feet are killing me." She slipped her feet free and set her shoes beside her purse. "What was I thinking, wearing heels to the mall? I'm going to have blisters for a week."

"They're really cute." Although Vivienne wouldn't be caught dead in heels. She could do with the few added inches of height but didn't think a broken ankle was worth it.

"Thanks. You can borrow them if you want."

Vivienne didn't want to borrow a stranger's shoes. "I'm good. Thanks, though."

"Suit yourself." She lifted her slim shoulders in a carefree shrug. "Oh, before I forget, you may want to go out the back door when you leave. There's a pretty epic snowball fight brewing on the green, and you don't want to get caught in the crossfire."

Vivienne glanced out the windows to where blurs of white were being launched back and forth. "Thanks for the heads up."

Reaching for the tablet at the center of the table, the girl asked Vivienne if there were any lunch specials.

"They have sweet potato soup today." It had sounded interesting, but Vivienne had skipped breakfast, so soup wasn't going to cut it.

The girl's nose wrinkled. "Nah. Doesn't sound good to me."

They chatted about nothing in particular until Vivienne finished her burger. The new recruit was funny, and Vivienne really liked her. She needed more girlfriends.

What was the protocol for asking for someone's number to hang out? Not wanting to sound awkward, she said, "We should do this again sometime."

The girl smiled. "Absolutely. I would love it."

"Can I get your number or whatever?"

"Ha-ha. Very funny."

Vivienne waited, but the girl didn't say anything else. Then she took the bag of chips right off of Vivienne's plate and started munching on them. What kind of person stole your chips without asking first? Maybe Vivienne didn't want to be her friend after all.

Slipping her arms into her coat, Vivienne collected her backpack from the back of her chair.

The girl dropped the empty bag onto Vivienne's plate and brushed her hands together to get rid of the crumbs. When Vivienne stood, the girl's delicately arched eyebrows came together in confusion. "Where are you going?"

"I need to get back home." She could really use a nap before she met Deacon later. They were supposed to go to the movies.

"Fine," the girl grumbled. "Give me a sec to get these devil heels back on and we can go together." She winced when she stuck her foot back into the high black heels.

"But . . . I don't know where you live?"

The girl's eyes narrowed, and her lips flattened. "I live with you."

Okay. This was officially getting weird. Vivienne had never seen this girl in her life. Just then, Ethan came in and waved. Vivienne felt so relieved that she nearly burst into tears as she ran to his side. "Don't ask questions, okay?" she whispered, grabbing his arm and turning him toward the entrance. Behind them, the girl shouted her name.

"*Ooookay?*" Ethan fell in step beside her.

"Don't look, but there's a girl trying to come home with me." And all she'd done was ask for her number.

When he started turning his head, Vivienne pinched him. "I said don't look!"

"Hey, Ethan! Wait up!" the girl called, catching up with them at the door. For someone in heels, she was really quick.

"Why are you running away from Emily?" He pushed open the door and let it fall in the girl's face.

Emily? Emily, Emily, *Emily* . . . That name sounded familiar. Why did Vivienne know that name? "Do I know that girl?"

Ethan snorted. "Ah, yeah. She's your best friend."

Vivienne stilled.

"Are you mad at me or something?" the girl—Emily—shouted, stomping across the snow-covered gravel. Her eyebrows were lowered over narrowed eyes.

"Mad at you? I don't even know who you are."

Something like hurt flashed across Emily's face. "Look, I know you're annoyed about me and Lyle hooking up, but I really like him. I thought you'd be happy for us."

"You're dating *Lyle*?" Why hadn't he told Vivienne himself?

The girl braced her hands on her hips and leaned forward. "Cut the act, Vivienne. You're freaking me out."

"How do you think I feel?" Lyle and this girl were dating? What the heck was happening?

Ethan pulled out his phone and typed a text before suggesting they go back to Vivienne's apartment.

"I think I'm just tired," she said, keeping her distance from the Emily girl. "I didn't sleep well last night, and my brain's a bit foggy."

Neither Ethan nor Emily looked convinced as they entered the building and jogged up the stairs to the third floor.

When they got to the apartment, Vivienne looked around, feeling a sense of safety and familiarity. Her dad's Ohio sweatshirt was on the chair where she had left it, along with the shorts she'd slept in last night. She grabbed them and muttered that she would be right back before escaping down the hall. Emily and Ethan were whispering as she closed the door to her room, but she didn't care as she turned the lock.

Let them talk about her all they wanted. She was tired and needed a nap.

After a long, luxurious stretch, Vivienne rolled over in bed and picked up her phone. She had two missed calls from Deacon and another from Lyle. Still feeling a bit groggy, she decided to hop in the shower to revive herself before calling them back.

The hot water scalding her back felt like it took a layer of skin with it. After scrubbing away the last of the tiredness, she got out and dressed in her dad's sweatshirt and a pair of tights. The waistband felt loose, which was strange. They had fit perfectly when Emily bought them for her last week.

"Hey, Emily?" Vivienne called, walking through the darkened hallway into the living room.

Emily was sitting on the couch between Ethan and Lyle. Deacon was pacing from the glass door to the TV and back. When she walked in, all of them stared at her like she'd forgotten to put on clothes or something.

Deacon rushed to her side and enveloped her in a hug so tight it hurt.

"You're squishing me," she mumbled against his chest.

"Sorry." His hold loosened, but he kept his arms around her. "I've been so worried about you. We all have."

She peered at her friends from around his shoulder, all of them pale and wide-eyed.

"Why are you worried about me? I was just taking a nap." She took naps all the time.

"Do you know who I am?" Emily's voice shook as she rubbed her hands down her skirt.

"That's a dumb question. Of course I know who you are. You're my best friend, Emily. And that's Ethan. And that's Lyle." What a strange day.

"Vivienne?" Deacon's low voice was laced with concern. "They know."

Her stomach sank. "Know what?"

"About your forgetfulness."

"You told them?" she hissed, shoving Deacon away. Betrayal washed over her like a shower of ice. "You promised you wouldn't! You promised I could tell them when I was ready!" And she wasn't ready. She wanted to have Christmas first. To celebrate New Year's. And start treatment with Alex before she let them know about her condition.

He shook his head and reached for her. "I didn't have a choice."

"That's a bunch of crap. I can't believe you would do this to me. It wasn't your story to tell. It was mine. And you took it away from me. You—"

"Stop it!" Emily roared, shooting to her feet and racing over. Tears cascaded down her cheeks as she braced her hands on her hips. "Deacon didn't want to say anything, but he didn't have a choice. You forgot who I was, Vivienne. You forgot *me*."

What she was saying couldn't be true. It couldn't. Emily was her best friend. "I could never forget you, Em."

"But you did. Today at lunch, you didn't even know my name."

"No . . . that's . . . that's not possible. I didn't even eat lunch today."

Lyle cursed and dropped his head into his hands.

"It's true, Vivienne," Ethan said quietly. "I met you on your way out of the Glass House, and you asked me who the crazy girl following you was."

"You think I'm crazy?" Emily whimpered, smearing mascara across her cheeks when she wiped her tears.

"I don't think you're crazy. I love you. I'm sorry. I just . . . I'm so sorry."

Vivienne wished she could be swallowed up by the carpet. Deacon moved to her side and laced their fingers together. "You and me."

Stealing his strength, she took a deep breath and said, "I'm going to forget everything."

FOURTEEN

Steve—if that was even his real name—was taking a huge risk coming in to work every day. Jasper wasn't going to turn him in, but that didn't mean Lawrence wouldn't figure out that Steve was a spy. He was already suspicious enough with all the employees quitting. One slip was all it would take. There was no telling what Lawrence would do to him if he did find out.

And Jasper had enough to worry about without adding Steve to the list. He had promised to get the PAN some of HOOK's serum—er, poison. It was *poison*—it had killed people. He needed to remember that.

Asking Lawrence for more vials wasn't an option. Jasper never had before, and he didn't want to look suspicious. Besides, there were procedures to follow and request forms to be filled out, and the last thing Jasper needed was a paper trail.

"Anything yet?" Steve asked, bent over a microscope. He

117

adjusted the knobs, then scribbled something into a note-book lying open on the desk.

Sinking onto a stool, Jasper nodded to Eliza as she passed. When she was gone, he whispered, "I have a plan."

Steve snorted.

Why was that so funny? Just because Jasper wasn't a spy didn't mean he couldn't have plans. "It's a really good one."

"I'm sure it is, boss." Steve's smirk remained as he doodled on the corner of the notebook.

Jasper wanted to wipe the look off his arrogant face. He was sick and tired of people underestimating him. "I don't think you're in a position to be an asshole, Steve."

Steve finally looked up, eyes narrowed and mouth pulled tight. "Are you planning on turning me in so they can torture and kill me?" He clicked the top of his pen once. Twice. A third time. "Because if you are, I'd like to know."

"No. Of course not."

"Then I'm gonna keep on being an asshole." Instead of putting his head back down, Steve waved Jasper closer. "Come and have a look at this."

Jasper pressed his eye to the microscope and rolled the knobs between his fingers. When the slide came into focus, he couldn't believe what he saw. "What have you done?"

"Even assholes can have breakthroughs." Steve chuckled at himself as he pointed to a section of doodles that Jasper realized weren't doodles at all. "If you splice in RNA, you can get the cell to produce nGh."

"We've tried that before, but it's never been enough to kickstart and old gene." And in terms of NG-1882, anything after age eighteen was old. Hormone therapy didn't work either; it just added the extra hormone instead of replacing hGh with the mutated nGh. As far as Jasper could tell, if there was any hGh present, the transition wouldn't happen.

Steve showed Jasper a small chart tucked away in the back of his notebook. All the data was the same, except instead of producing hGh, the cells were producing a significant amount of nGh. It wasn't enough to replace it entirely, but it was a start.

Jasper looked over it twice, his heart thrumming in his chest. "How?"

Steve pulled the chart from Jasper's fingers and slid it back into its hiding place. "I added a little magic."

If the results were correct—

If what he was saying was true—

Jasper could activate his dormant NG-1882.

He shouldn't get his hopes up. He should act blasé so that Steve didn't realize how excited he was about this discovery. He should—*screw it.* "Tell me *everything.*"

Twisting on his stool, Steve leaned his elbow on the edge of the desk, propped his chin on his closed fist, and grinned. "I'll show you mine if you show me yours."

Dammit.

Steve was right. Jasper had a job to do.

That night, Jasper brought four empty vials home from the lab and spent hours with a bottle of yellow food dye, trying to get the color right. The picture he'd taken of the actual poison was a bit blurry since the lighting in the lab was terrible, but Jasper thought the two looked similar enough.

After only three hours of sleep, Jasper rolled out of bed. Drinking an extra strong cup of coffee was the only way to keep his eyes open, but it also made him jittery.

By the time he reached the lab, his stomach was sick and his heart felt like it was going to explode. After a quick stop by the bathroom in the Administration building—where the heating actually worked—Jasper crossed the frozen grass to the lab, every unsteady exhale emerging in a white puff.

Steve and Eliza were already there. To avoid suspicion, he wanted a few more employees around to act as witnesses. Once Molly and Jack came in, Jasper used his key card to open the fridge where they kept the few samples Lawrence had released. It was nothing out of the ordinary; he was the only person with access to that case. But today, his hands were shaking. Instead of bringing the poison to the counter of beakers and petri dishes, he brought it to his desk. With his back to his employees, he swapped out the vials with the fake ones in his pocket.

The actual vials clinked quietly when he slipped them into his jacket pocket before setting it onto the back of his chair. No one seemed to be paying him any attention as he donned his white lab coat instead.

Breathing a sigh of relief, he picked up the tray and carried it to where Steve and Eliza were arguing over whose turn it was to use the thermocycler. The hardest part was over. All Jasper had to do now was bump into—

Steve stepped back, ramming into Jasper.

The tray in his hand clattered to the ground, shattering the vials and sending shards of glass and splatters of yellow liquid across the linoleum floor.

Jasper swore. "Look what you made me do!" Did it sound convincing? He hoped so.

Steve's eyes widened, and he shook his head. "It wasn't my fault. Eliza—"

"No way," Eliza hissed, smacking Steve in the shoulder. "You're not pinning this on me. I didn't touch him. This is all on you."

"I don't care who did it, just help me clean it up!" *That* was convincing. Jasper had to bite his lip to keep from smiling at Steve's bulging eyes.

Mario came running over, gun in hand. "What happened?"

Eliza squealed and ducked behind a chair. The rest of Jasper's employees dropped under their desks.

"Put that thing away," Jasper rushed, hoping the man wasn't as trigger happy as the last guards Lawrence had hired. "It's just a few broken vials of poiso—serum." *Dammit.* "The treatment serum."

Beside him, Steve stilled.

The guard's eyes narrowed as he holstered his firearm and grabbed his phone from the clip on his belt. "Lawrence? It's Mario. There's been an incident at the lab." Instead of continuing the conversation where Jasper could hear, he twisted and went into the annex.

Dammit.

Jasper had screwed up. *Really* screwed up. "You need to get out of here," he whispered, taking the sopping dishcloth from Steve's hand.

"Stop panicking," Steve said under his breath. "Everything's fine."

"Mr. Hooke?" the guard called from the doorway. "Your brother needs to see you in his office."

Everything was definitely *not* fine. "Give me a second. I need to clean this up."

"*Now*, Jasper."

Steve took back the rag and proceeded to wipe the glass into a pile. "Don't worry, boss. I've got this."

Steve may have thought he had things under control, but he didn't know Lawrence the way Jasper did. Lawrence didn't just get angry. He got even. If someone made a mistake, they paid dearly for it.

Jasper washed his hands before following the guard across to the Admin building. Lawrence was in his office, pacing back and forth between his desk and the window. "Get in here and close the damn door."

The quiet click of the door swinging into place sent Jasper's heart racing.

"What the hell, Jasper?"

Jasper knew better than to say anything incriminating.

"I expected this shit from one of the others," Lawrence went on, "but not from you."

"It was an accident."

"I know it was an accident." Lawrence threw his hand toward the window. "But you lost four vials of serum. That's half a million dollars down the damned drain."

Jasper's chest tightened. "How did you know there were four?" The guard hadn't been in the room. There was no way he could have told Lawrence.

Lawrence turned his monitor so that Jasper could see a bunch of different camera angles from the lab. He watched himself collide with Steve. It *had* looked convincing.

Lawrence believed it was an accident. So what was the problem?

Jasper's gaze slid to the video at the top of the screen and his heart stopped.

There was a camera aimed right at Jasper's desk.

If Lawrence ran it back a few moments earlier, he would see Jasper changing out the vials.

"When did you get the cameras installed?" Jasper choked, panic vibrating in his core.

Lawrence pressed the space bar on his keyboard, pausing the videos. "They've been in there since the cabins were brought in."

Biting his tongue, Jasper inhaled slowly, hoping the trembling in his body wouldn't seep into his voice. "I can handle my own staff, Lawrence. I don't need a babysitter."

"You sure about that? Because this"—Lawrence pointed to the frozen image of Jasper and Steve cleaning up the glass —"looks like a lawsuit waiting to happen. The last thing we need is some idiot cutting his finger on a piece of broken glass and suing us for worker's comp. Get your house in order, Jasper. The board is watching."

"It won't happen again," Jasper assured him, backing toward the door.

"Wait."

Dammit. Jasper didn't want to wait. He wanted to get the hell out of there.

Lawrence stalked over to his safe and typed in the code. "You'll need replacements, right?"

"Sorry. I don't know where my mind is." Jasper collected the vials and thanked his brother. When he got home, he was going to get drunk and pass out. He wasn't cut out for this espionage stuff.

"Don't worry, Rat. I'm not going to tell Dad. He'd lose his life over this shit." Lawrence rubbed a hand down his beard before clapping Jasper on the shoulder. "As a matter of fact, I'm going to have the tech guys scrub today's footage so your ass doesn't get fired."

That was by far the nicest thing Lawrence had ever offered to do for him. Jasper wasn't naive enough to think it wouldn't cost him, but whatever the price was, he'd gladly pay it. "Thanks, Lawrence."

Lawrence smiled and dropped his hand before falling into his rolling chair. "Yeah, yeah. I'm great. Now get to the lab and do something that'll make me happy that I saved your ass."

Back in the lab, all of Jasper's employees were working as though nothing had happened. The floor was clean, and a "slippery when wet" sign had been set where the accident had occurred.

Jasper placed the new vials of serum in the tray and returned them to the fridge. Steve met him at his desk with a clipboard in his hand.

"What's this?" Jasper asked, sinking onto his chair. The top page looked like an old expense report, but the rest of the papers beneath were blank.

"An excuse to talk to you." Steve pulled a pen from his lab coat pocket and handed it to Jasper. "All good?"

Nodding, Jasper accepted the pen and clicked the top. "Yes. But Lawrence has cameras all over this place." He signed one of the pages, wondering if his brother was watching him right now. Surely he had better things to do than sit around monitoring the lab all day every day.

"No shit, boss." Steve took back the clipboard and tucked it under his arm. "When do you think you'll have that twenty bucks you owe me?"

"I don't owe you—" Steve rolled his eyes. "Oh, right. Twenty dollars. Totally forgot." Jasper was a terrible spy. "Can I give it to you after work? I don't have any cash on me right now."

"I'm leaving early today. How about I swing by your house later?"

"Sure. Okay. Let me give you my address." Jasper pulled a Post-It from the top of the pile.

Chuckling, Steve shook his head. Under his breath, he muttered, "We know where you live."

"Jasper Hooke, I've gotta admit, I didn't think you had it in you," Steve said the moment Jasper opened the front door. He was wearing his poofy red jacket and the same hat he'd loaned Jasper a few weeks earlier. And there was a six-pack in his gloved hands. "We may make a spy out of you yet."

"I think I'll stick to the lab from now on." Jasper had been a ball of nerves all day. Any time a door slammed or someone coughed, he'd jumped out of his skin. If he wasn't so busy, he'd have taken a sick day tomorrow to give his heart a break. "Why'd you bring beer?"

"Because you, my friend, deserve a celebration." Steve pushed past him and kicked his shoes into the corner beside the door.

A celebration? Jasper didn't even celebrate his birthday. "You're *staying*?"

"I thought I might. That okay?" Steve unwrapped a black

scarf from around his neck and bit the end of his finger so he could slip off his glove.

"Yeah. I mean, I certainly don't care. But I'm kind of surprised you *want* to stay." Jasper never had people over. Lab. Home. Lab. Home. That was his life.

"Despite the fact that you're the adopted son of my mortal enemy, I think you're a decent guy. I figured, why not stop by and see what you're like when you're not in the office?" Steve turned and started down the hall. "This place is a lot nicer than it looks from the outside."

"Um . . . thanks?" Jasper closed the door and straightened Steve's shoes beside his own.

"You should probably have someone look at your roof this spring, though. Peter said you're missing a few shingles."

"Peter? As in . . . *Peter Pan?*"

Steve chuckled, dropping the beer and his hat and gloves onto the counter. His red coat ended up thrown over the back of Jasper's couch. "Yeah, Peter Pan. He said you need your gutters cleaned too."

No way. *No way.* Peter Pan had been to Jasper's house. If Lawrence or his father knew that, they'd lose their minds. "I'll have someone take a look when it gets a little warmer."

Steve nodded and continued surveying the room. If Jasper had realized he'd be coming in, he would have cleaned up. The place wasn't a mess, but there were dishes in the sink, and he needed to take out the trash.

"Got anything to eat? I'm starving." Instead of waiting for Jasper to respond, Steve opened the fridge.

"I think there's some leftover fried chicken in there."

Jasper didn't cook. If it didn't come in a box or a Styrofoam container, he didn't eat it. Lawrence kept onto him about his terrible diet, but so far, his waistline hadn't suffered. And his cholesterol was excellent.

When Steve turned around, he had a container of two-day-old chicken in his hand. "Are you having any?"

Jasper shrugged. "Sure." It wasn't like he had any other plans.

They shared the chicken, and Jasper threw some instant mashed potatoes into the microwave. Steve drank and chatted about his time in Neverland, never revealing anything specific. He'd grown up there; his father was PAN; he didn't have any brothers or sisters.

Jasper should have been trying to collect as much information as possible, but he wasn't. Because in that moment, he didn't care that Neverland had multiple locations or state-of-the-art labs or more research on NG-1882 than Jasper could gather in his lifetime.

Jasper wanted to know about flying. When he asked Steve, he half expected him to refuse to answer.

But Steve smiled and said, "My dad told me it feels as natural as breathing. That there's a sort of heat that builds inside"—he pressed a hand to his chest—"and your body feels lighter. He likened it to swimming, but instead of stroking and kicking in water, you're willing yourself through the air."

"I always wanted to be one of you," Jasper confessed. Ever since he'd seen that girl take off into the clouds, he'd wished and hoped and prayed that he could fly. When his brother wasn't around to make fun of him, he'd try jumping off of high things, thinking maybe his body would figure out how to do it naturally. It had taken a broken elbow and a shattered ankle to get him to stop.

"You *are* one of us," Steve said, clinking his bottle against Jasper's. "We just have to give our lazy genes a kick up the ass."

If only it were that easy.

"Is it really just luck of the draw for who gets an active gene?" Jasper understood the genetic aspects, but could never figure out what event sparked the activation. Whatever it was hadn't happened to him. When he was growing up, Dr. Hooke had constantly been running tests and taking blood and monitoring Jasper's health. But after he turned eighteen, Dr. Hooke had lost all interest in his existence until he said he wanted to go into the family business.

"Doesn't seem to be any rhyme or reason to it. Just nausea and dizziness from the increase in adrenaline and transition from hGh to nGh. We give an injection when the gene is activating to kickstart it."

Excitement stirred in Jasper's chest. "You do?"

Steve's eyebrows came together as he raised the bottle to his lips. "Figured you knew that."

"How the hell would I know that?"

Steve chuckled.

"What's in the injection?" Jasper pressed.

A grin. "Magic."

Okay, so they weren't there yet. But at least Jasper had learned something. Not that it was very helpful. Without a subject with an activating NG-1882, the knowledge would be useless. "And your *magic* doesn't work on inactive genes, right?"

Steve set his bottle on the counter and grabbed another one. "If they did, my ass wouldn't be walking around on the ground."

FIFTEEN

Deacon had believed he understood women. And then he met Vivienne, and everything he thought he knew went out the bloody window. If only he could see into her mind and figure out what the hell was going on in there.

"Absolutely not," Deacon clipped, trying his best to keep his temper in check. "You're not going anywhere without me. Tell Lyle you'll go out with him tomorrow." Yes, it was a Sunday night, but it wasn't like they had anything to do on Monday morning. Deacon was out of the field, Vivienne wasn't allowed to recruit anymore, and Lyle was a useless waste of space with absolutely no motivation to do anything besides irritate Deacon.

"Lyle can't go tomorrow," Vivienne insisted, propping her hip against the sofa in her living room. There was a blue dress draped over her crossed arms. "We're going out tonight."

Deacon didn't bother saying that he didn't think Vivienne should be drinking at all. She was a lightweight at the best of times, and he could only imagine alcohol would make her forgetfulness worse. Why did she need to go out with Lyle anyway? If she wanted to spend time with her foster brother, Lyle could visit her at her flat like he did every other day. Hell, she could even invite him over to Deacon's house if she wanted to. Going to a club in Worcester that she'd never been to with Lyle as her only chaperone wasn't going to happen.

He and Lyle were no longer at each other's throats, but that didn't mean Deacon trusted him to take care of her. "And I've already told you that I can't make it tonight. I'm heading over to Ethan's at half seven." They'd been planning this card game with Joel and Max since Christmas.

"You're not getting it." She closed her eyes and pinched the bridge of her nose. "You're. Not. Invited. I'm going out with my brother. Just me and him."

"*Foster* brother," he muttered under his breath.

Her eyes snapped open and narrowed on him. "Yes, my *foster* brother. The only family I have. Thanks for the reminder."

"You know I didn't mean it like that." When he reached for her, she stepped away from him.

He could play this one of two ways. From the stubborn lift to her jaw and her rigid stance, the likelihood that she was going to back down was slim. This was one of those instances where he needed to give.

Deacon dragged his mobile from his pocket and flicked to the messages app. Ethan's name was at the top.

"What are you doing?" Vivienne asked, raising to her tippy toes to see the screen.

"Canceling my plans." In the grand scheme of things, a card game didn't matter. They could reschedule for next week, or the week after. Hell, they had forever to play cards.

If Vivienne wanted to go out tonight, she was going to go out.

The mobile disappeared from his hands. Vivienne clicked the button, switching it off. "What part of 'you're not invited' don't you understand? I need a break from—" Biting her lip, she held his mobile toward him. "Never mind."

"A break from what?" Deacon's stomach sank. Was she saying she needed . . . "A break from *me*? That's just brilliant. We're not even married yet and you need a break. How do you think you're going to feel in another fifty years?"

"In fifty years, I won't even know who you are."

"Exactly! And you want to waste your time going out with bloody Lyle!"

Last week she had forgotten Emily, and yesterday she had had forgotten she had boiled noodles for spaghetti; the water had evaporated, ruining the pot and sending the smoke alarms in her flat screaming. He'd tried convincing her to move in with him, but she kept refusing. It wasn't that Emily couldn't handle Vivienne, but she wasn't Emily's responsibility.

She was Deacon's.

And now she wanted a break from him.

"I want to give you a break from worrying," Vivienne said, her eyes brimming with tears. "All you do is worry about me. And it has to be getting heavy. I want you to go over to Ethan's and play poker and have fun. I want you to forget about me and my problems."

Didn't she understand that not knowing where she was or if she was all right was only going to make him worry more?

"And I want to go out and feel like a normal teenager for the first time since I got to Neverland," she went on, tucking her arms around herself. "I want a break from this mess for one night. Is that too much to ask?"

"Nope. Not too much to ask. Take your break." Deacon shoved his mobile back into his pocket and twisted toward the door. "I hope Lyle can make you happy since I've been doing such a shite job lately."

If she wanted a break, he was going to give her one.

Vivienne called his name, but he didn't turn around.

Rejection wasn't something he had experienced very often, and when he did, he wanted to get as far away as possible.

Deacon drove straight to Ethan's house and pounded on the door.

"A little early, aren't you?" Ethan said after glancing at his watch. When he looked back at Deacon, his eyes narrowed into slits. "You're canceling aren't you? *Dammit*, Dash. You promised."

"I'm not canceling." Deacon tore off his jacket and threw it at the back of a dining room chair. It fell to the ground, but he didn't bother picking it up.

"What's wrong now?"

"Nothing."

"Right. Because you always pace and mutter and look like you want to punch someone."

Deacon stopped pacing and dropped to one of the leather armchairs in the sitting room. "Vivienne is going out with Lyle tonight."

"So?" Ethan disappeared into the kitchen and came back a moment later with two cans of beer.

"So, I don't trust him to take care of her."

The can made a loud *hiss* when Ethan opened it. "He's her brother, dude. Of course, he's going to take care of her."

"Why do people keep saying that? Lyle is her bloody foster brother."

"So *that's* what this is about." Ethan chuckled, slurping from the can. "She's not going to hook up with him."

"I know that." He did, didn't he? The two of them were so close, sometimes he did wonder if they'd ever been closer. But that wasn't what he meant. It was just . . . Lyle didn't strike him as the responsible type. And Vivienne needed someone to look out for her, not ply her with alcohol.

Ethan frowned as he tapped his nail against his can. "Do you want to go out with them? I can call Ricky and see if he wants to take your place."

Deacon flicked the tab on his beer, not bothering to open it. "Vivienne doesn't want me to go."

After a deep drink, Ethan grimaced. "Well, I'm not sure I want you here either. When you're in a mood, you're like a black hole. I don't want you sucking the fun outta tonight. Everything's been shit since Nicola broke up with me. I need this, man."

Brilliant. His best mate didn't want him around either. People had used to want Deacon around all the time. What the hell was happening? "I'll come out of it," he promised, considering the beer in front of him. If he drank, he'd forget his worries. But if the one he worried about needed him, he'd be utterly useless. But Vivienne had Lyle and wanted a break.

Deacon wrapped his fingers around the cold can and cracked the tab.

All of Vivienne's enthusiasm for her night had followed Deacon out the door. She wished he could see that she was doing this for him. For both of them. If she spent one more night in the apartment watching Netflix and worrying about what—or who—she was going to forget next, she going to go insane. And she could only imagine how bad Deacon must feel. His green eyes had looked dull lately, and she'd noticed the dark circles beneath, matching her own. The only difference was she could wear makeup and hide them.

He was constantly bailing on Ethan in favor of spending time with her. And she loved him for being so willing to sacrifice his plans and his happiness, but he deserved a break too.

And there was nothing to worry about. Lyle had promised to keep an eye on her. They were going to dance and have a few drinks and forget about their worries on purpose.

And on Monday, she was going to call Alex about starting treatment.

There was no telling what effect the hormone therapy would have on her body or her Nevergene, so she wanted to have a little fun before all the seriousness started.

"You look miserable, Viv," Lyle said, yanking on his seatbelt in the back of the cab. "And that's no way to start the night." He smelled like a mix of Emily's shampoo and Lynx.

"I'm just nervous about getting in."

A V formed between Lyle's eyebrows. "You have your fake ID, right?"

"Yeah. I do." But this was the first time she was going to use the thing. In Harrow, she hadn't needed it since the legal drinking age was eighteen.

"Then why are you nervous?"

She shrugged and pasted on a smile, hoping Deacon's night was going better than hers.

When the cab stopped outside of a line of bars, Vivienne grabbed the black purse she'd borrowed from Emily and paid the driver. She tried to keep her nerves at bay as they waited in line to get inside. Puffs of smoke lifted from the cigarettes the women in front of them were smoking. None of them were wearing coats.

After twenty minutes, they reached a stretch of red carpet blocked off by a velvet rope. Vivienne held her breath as the massive bouncer barely glanced at their IDs. When the man removed the barrier, she almost collapsed from relief.

Lyle paid extra for the girl taking money to keep their coats while Vivienne offered her right hand for a black stamp with a bunny on it. Strobe lights pulsed as they made their way from the upper-level entrance down metal stairs and into the heart of the club.

"What do you want to drink?" Lyle shouted too close to her ear.

Vivienne glanced around the room, her eyes eventually landing on a girl dressed in a tube top and black hot pants carrying a glowing tray of colorful shots.

"What about one of those?" She nodded toward the girl.

Lyle gave her a thumbs up and disappeared between packed high tables. Vivienne tugged the skirt of her dress down over her thighs, hoping she'd feel less awkward after a few drinks.

When Lyle came back, he was carrying four green shots. "They're two for one!"

Vivienne grimaced when she smelled sour apple but drank them anyway. Lyle took the empty plastic shot glasses from her and dropped them on a table at the edge of the sunken dance floor.

She pulled on her skirt again. If only she had asked for a different drink, something to keep her hands busy.

Her shoes stuck to the floor as they made their way to the bar. Colorful flashing lights reflected off the upside down liquor bottles hanging from a mirrored wall. Behind the bar, men and women dressed in all black raced from one customer to the next.

A bunch of shot glasses had been lined up where one of the bartenders was shaking a silver container. A moment later, he poured pink liquid from the container into the glasses, spilling a bunch of it onto the countertop.

"Do you want to dance?" Lyle asked. Had the DJ turned up the music? It was making Vivienne's head throb.

"Maybe another drink first."

"Yeah. Those shots don't have much alcohol in them. Two secs." Lyle twisted and ordered a couple of beers.

A drunk guy rammed into her, spilling whatever was in his martini glass down Vivienne's leg. He gave her a sloppy smile when he apologized.

Why did people come to places like this? The music was too loud and everyone was drunk and falling around the place. Lyle shoved a beer into her hand, and she thanked him. Vivienne had seen enough. After this drink, she was going to go home.

"I *love* it here!" Vivienne didn't care that she was drenched in sweat—or was that alcohol? It didn't matter. She loved every pulse-racing second of music and flashing lights and dancing.

Vivienne *loved* to dance.

Beside her, Lyle jumped around, his arms thrown over his head as he sang along with the rest of the crowd. Vivienne didn't know this song but she loved it anyway.

Nightclubs were magic.

Sweat dripped down her neck and chest. Someone she didn't know had his hands on her hips. Instead of turning to see who he was, she kept dancing.

She never wanted to stop.

Except she really had to pee.

"Hey!" She unhooked the mystery man's hands from her dress and grabbed Lyle's arm. "I'm going to pee."

He stopped jumping long enough to give her a thumbs up. Now, where the heck was the bathroom? Eventually, Vivienne found a hot pink neon sign shaped like a woman on the left side of the bar. Under the sign was a line of women disappearing into a dark hallway.

A pair of girls in front of her whispered and giggled as they stumbled forward. There was a couple making out next to a vending machine filled with condoms.

If Deacon were here, Vivienne could be making out with him right now.

He should be here.

She wanted him here.

And not just so she could kiss his beautiful mouth.

She wanted to share this experience with him. To be at a club together, letting loose. He was fun. They had fun together.

Was he a good dancer? He probably was. He was good at everything else. Or maybe dancing was the one thing he was bad at. She wished he were here so she could find out.

But if he were here, he would be spending the night watching her and worrying.

Hopefully he was having fun at Ethan's. She couldn't wait to see him tomorrow after her hangover wore off and tell him about her night. And she couldn't wait to hear about his. Was he any good at poker? She had never played. Maybe he could teach her.

Eventually, it was her turn. The pink light in the bathroom made her feel dizzy. The stall had no toilet seat and there was only a scrap of toilet paper left. She was pretty sure the girl in the stall beside her was puking. When she finished, she washed her hands under the freezing water.

"Hey. Can you help me?" a girl asked, her hand buried inside a black purse.

Vivienne looked around; there was no one else the girl could be talking to. "Sure?"

"Which one of these"—the girl pulled two lip glosses from her purse—"is the sexiest?"

If Emily had been with her, she would have known the right answer. Vivienne didn't have a clue, so she chose the bold red one.

"You're *soooo* right." The girl dropped the pink tube into her purse and unscrewed the lid. "This is so much sexier."

She smacked her lips together and pursed them as she studied her reflection. "Want some?"

Vivienne stared at her own reflection. The eyeliner Emily had painstakingly applied was a bit smudged, but overall, she still looked pretty good. "Sure. Why not?" Vivienne took the offered lip gloss and smeared it over her lips. It tasted like cherries.

Beside her, the girl finger-combed her short blond hair. Vivienne returned the lip gloss and tightened the straps on her push-up bra. It was too bad Deacon wasn't there.

"Come with me to get something to drink," the girl said, linking her arm with Vivienne's.

Vivienne was really thirsty.

"I'm Erica, by the way. What's your name?" Erica was a close talker who smelled like hairspray and cigarettes.

"Vivienne."

"Are you here on your own too?" Erica steered her straight through a group of girls grinding at the edge of the dance floor.

Vivienne's hair tickled her shoulders when she shook her head. "Nope. I came with my brother."

Erica's nose wrinkled when she grimaced. "Your *brother*? You're lucky I'm saving you then." She wiggled her way between two guys waiting at the bar and propped her elbows onto the counter. Vivienne smiled apologetically.

The guy to Erica's right returned her smile. He was tall, with dark hair and a black button-down shirt rolled to his elbows. It was hard to hear him over the pulsing music, but she thought he said, "Hey there."

Vivienne waved at him. "Hi."

"What're you drinking?" Erica asked, tugging her closer.

"I don't know. Beer I guess?"

"Seriously?" Erica fished around in the purse dangling from her arm and withdrew a credit card. "Yeah, I'm not buying you a beer."

137

Vivienne shrugged. She didn't really like beer that much, but the shots had been gross, and she couldn't think of anything else to order.

"I'll get you a cosmo."

"Sounds good to me."

"Do you like cosmos?" the guy next to Erica asked.

"I've never had one," Vivienne confessed. "I guess I'll find out."

When Erica handed her a pretty glass brimming with pink liquid, Vivienne thanked her and took a drink. At first it tasted good, like cranberries. Then the alcohol hit her throat, and she gagged.

The guy next to Erica sniggered as he lifted his beer bottle to his lips.

"Good, right?" Erica yelled at Vivienne from two inches away. Her mascara and eyeliner were so smeared, it looked like she had black eyes.

"*So* good." The moment Erica decided to be someone else's friend, Vivienne was going to abandon the glass and order a beer.

Vivienne smiled while Erica talked at her, not understanding half of what she said. She just nodded and sipped the terrible cocktail.

The guy from the bar motioned Vivienne forward, and she told Erica she would be right back. "You look like you needed help," he said with a laugh, handing her a bottle of beer.

The glass in her hand was empty. How had that happened? Had she spilled it? "That was very gentlemanly of you." The world could use more gentlemen.

"I'd hardly get your attention by being a jackass," he said with a smile.

She didn't bother telling him that he wouldn't get anything more than her attention. "Thanks for the beer. I can safely say that I do *not* like cosmos."

"I can tell." The guy picked up her empty glass and held it toward the lights flashing on the dance floor. "Must've been terrible."

Vivienne giggled. This guy, whoever he was, was funny.

"Do you even know that girl?"

"Who, Erica?" Vivienne found Erica with her tongue down some short guy's throat, her cosmo dangling precariously between her fingers, sloshing pink liquid onto a velvet couch behind her. "We met in the bathroom and became instant BFFs."

The guy laughed and shook his head. "I was wondering. She's here almost every night, and I've never seen you with her before."

"Does that mean you're here every night too?" Otherwise, how else would he know that?

"You caught me." He winced as he rubbed the back of his neck. "There's not much to do around here in the winter."

Another guy, wearing a black baseball cap, jogged over. "What's taking so long, Josh?" he asked, clapping the guy talking to Vivienne on the shoulder. When he caught Vivienne looking at him, his lips curled into a smile. "Oh, never mind. I see the problem."

"I'm a problem, am I?" Vivienne rolled her eyes and took a drink of her beer. It was cold and crisp on her tongue and a thousand times better than a cosmo.

"For this guy you are," hat guy said, knocking Josh so hard that he lost his footing and had to catch himself on the edge of the bar. "He has a thing for brunettes."

An arm snaked around Vivienne's elbow, and she found herself being pulled toward the bathrooms. Looking up, she saw Lyle scowling at her.

"Let me go!" She yanked free and stumbled backward. Her head spun, and the faces passing by were blurry. It took a second for everything around her to snap back into focus.

"Where've you been, Vivienne?" Lyle bit out. "I've been looking all over the place for you."

"I was getting a drink," she said, shaking the bottle in his annoying face.

"No, you were flirting with those guys." Lyle snagged the beer out of her hand. "Look, I don't like Deacon, but you shouldn't be doing stuff like that. I don't care how mad you are at him. If you two weren't engaged, I wouldn't say anything, but you are."

"I wasn't *flirting* with them." Vivienne was having a simple conversation with two attractive men. Was she not allowed to talk to people now? Deacon talked to girls all the freaking time. What was the big deal?

Before Lyle could annoy her even more, she whirled around and went back to the bar.

"Is that your boyfriend?" Josh asked, looking over her head to where Lyle was no doubt fuming. Josh reminded her of Deacon a little. Not nearly as good looking, but there was something about his smile that was nice.

"Who? Lyle?" The idea of the two of them together made her snort. "He's my brother, *not* my boyfriend."

"In that case," Josh said, leaning his elbow on the bar and motioning toward one of the bartenders, "let me buy you another beer."

SIXTEEN

Vivienne's head was pounding, and for some reason, her mouth tasted like a trash can. She had a vague, flickering memory of trying to smoke a cigarette. And she may have puked.

Rolling over, she expected to see her own desk covered in clothes and books, but was met by the sight of a nightstand with a glass of water on top.

Vivienne didn't own a nightstand.

And the wall should have been beige, not gray. And she didn't have blackout blinds or carpet or—

Crap.

Where the heck was she?

Slowly, she twisted on the softest sheets she'd ever felt and saw an unfamiliar dark head. The guy had his back to her and wasn't moving like he was still asleep and—

Oh god.

What had she done?

As much as she wanted a drink to clear her hungover

head, she didn't want to take the chance of waking up the stranger. It wasn't until she slipped from beneath the covers that she realized she wasn't wearing anything. At all. Where the heck were her clothes?

She found her dress hanging from the footboard and her shoes beside the closet, but her underwear was missing. She really had to pee. Hopefully there was a bathroom some-where outside of the guy's bedroom. Slipping into her dress, she hooked her fingers inside her shoes and tiptoed across the carpet to the door.

"Where are you running off to?"

Crap.

Vivienne stiffened and twisted to face the guy, hating herself but also hating him, because she had obviously not been in her right mind. Never in her life had she gone home with a random stranger.

"I need to go," she said, her throat scratchy and stomach churning.

He propped himself up on his elbow. The sheet around his waist slipped lower. "You're not staying for breakfast?"

"I don't think that's a good idea."

"Why? Are you sick?"

"Yeah. I am." Sick and tired and broken-hearted.

"Here." He leaned across the bed to grab the glass of water. The stupid sheet slipped lower. "Will I find you some painkillers?" he asked, holding the glass toward her.

Since the guy was already awake and Vivienne couldn't avoid this conversation, she brought her shoes back to the bed and took the glass. It wasn't cold, but it helped wash some of the grossness away.

"Give me a moment to get dressed and I'll bring you home." He threw the sheets aside.

He was completely naked.

She screwed her eyes shut. Her face felt like it was on fire. What had she been *thinking*?

"It's nothing you haven't seen before," he laughed. She could hear him moving around the room: the sound of a zipper being zipped, a dresser drawer being closed. "I believe these are yours."

When her eyes snapped open, the guy was holding her underwear.

An indignant noise escaped her chest as she snatched them from him and stuffed them into her purse. She was the worst human alive.

"You're going to freeze if you go outside like that."

"I don't know where my coat is." She must have left it in the nightclub. Or maybe Lyle had it.

Lyle.

When she saw him, she was going to kill him. It wasn't his fault she had gone home with a random stranger, but he could have at least tried to stop her.

The guy rolled his eyes and opened the closet door. Inside was her favorite mustard-colored sweater. "How did you get this?"

"You left it here last week. Are you sure you're all right, lovie?"

Lovie.

Deacon.

This was Deacon.

Her fiancé.

Oh, thank god. Hallelujah and amen.

This was amazing. This was . . .

Crap. This was bad. So, so bad.

She may not have cheated on Deacon, but she sure as heck hadn't remembered him. Was this a fluke or was it going to happen again?

"I think I'm still drunk," she said with a tense laugh, dropping her shoes and rushing to wrap her arms around Deacon's bare torso. His skin was warm against her cheek. He felt like comfort. He felt like home. How could she forget her home?

"I'm sorry about last night," he said, pressing a kiss to her hair. "I know I've been overbearing lately. When Lyle called me to collect you, I was so relieved that you wanted to stay here."

"Lyle called you?" Her brother really had looked after her.

"He did." Deacon ran his hand down her back. "I dropped his drunk ass home first, then you insisted I bring you here so I could ravish you."

"I didn't say that."

"You most certainly did." His mouth crooked into the sexiest grin. "You demanded it, actually. But after the third time you tried climbing on top of me—while I was driving, might I add—I figured you were a bit too intoxicated for a good ravishing."

Okay. Vivienne was officially never drinking again. She didn't remember any of that, and there was no way of knowing if it was her forgetfulness or the alcohol.

"It sounds like I was pretty obnoxious." The last thing she wanted was to annoy him.

"Not at all. I wish you'd climb on top of me making demands more often."

Despite the direness of their situation, Vivienne chuckled at Deacon's ridiculousness. "Give me two minutes and I'll be more than happy to." She rushed into the bathroom to pee and brush her teeth. But her hair smelled like smoke, and her skin felt gritty from dried sweat, so she stripped and turned on the shower.

She had to tell Deacon what had happened that morning but figured it could wait until after the ravishing.

Deacon lifted his hand to knock on the bathroom door, hesitated, and dropped it again. He was losing his bloody mind. Vivienne was in a room barely bigger than a closet. Nothing was wrong.

But there was something about the way she'd tried to sneak out of the room that didn't feel right. Like she'd been ashamed to be there.

He knew he'd been tyrannical yesterday but had texted to say he was sorry. That was why he hated typing words onto a screen: they always fell flat. When Lyle had called Deacon from Vivienne's phone, he thought perhaps Vivienne had been behind it.

Apparently, she'd been too drunk to remember.

At least he hoped it was the drink.

What if it wasn't?

What if it was her forgetfulness?

He glared at the doorknob, wishing someone would tell him what he was supposed to do. He never used to over-think inane things like opening the door to his own bloody toilet.

Women made life complicated.

There was a crash in the room that sounded like a bottle had fallen.

Not a big deal under normal circumstances.

Deacon knocked things over all the time in the shower.

But what if Vivienne had knocked it over because *she'd* fallen?

He knocked on the door.

No response, only the steady hum from the shower.

"Vivienne? Are you all right?" When she didn't answer, his worry grew exponentially.

He was going to go in.

No. He should wait.

Dammit.

His hand connected with the cold brass handle, twisted, and pushed the barrier aside.

Then he cursed himself. Hadn't he promised to stop being so overbearing? Still. What if something had happened? She could have slipped and banged her head or forgotten what she'd been doing or where she was and be confused or scared.

"I'm coming in." Steam filled the room, and he flicked on the exhaust fan to clear some of it.

Deacon tapped his knuckle against the foggy glass. "Do you need anything?"

"I'm okay," she said with a sigh. "Unless you'd like to ravish me now?"

Turning her down last night when she had been so insistent had been one of the hardest things he'd ever done. He'd thought he was going to burst out of his skin when her hand had dipped into his jeans in the middle of the bloody nightclub. And when they had gotten home, she had stripped out of that tiny blue dress and insisted on sleeping naked.

Once he knew she was asleep, he had pulled the duvet to her chin and stared at the shadowy light fixture above his head. He'd never bothered to study it before. It was nice, he supposed. Gold, with twisting arms and bulbs on the end. The curves reminded him of the naked woman beside him. *Aaaaand* then he was attracted to a bloody light fixture.

"Deacon? You still there?"

He shook his head, banishing his worry to the place where he stored such things. "I'm still here."

The glass door opened, and he caught a flash of skin before Vivienne dragged him into the shower by a belt loop.

Water cascaded down her body and scalded his back as she popped the button and unzipped his jeans.

"Couldn't even wait for me to get undressed." His blood rushed south as she peeled off his jeans.

"You were taking too long." All the unease he'd felt since

146

he'd woken up that morning washed down the drain when she closed her hand around him and slammed her lips against his.

Vivienne's tongue tasted like mint and stole every rational thought, but it wasn't enough. It would never be enough. The rest of the plastic bottles clattered to the ground as Deacon sank onto the tiled bench and pulled her so that she was straddling him. Shifting her hips, she took him in one excruciatingly slow movement. He buried his face into her neck, tasting and kissing and grabbing her hips to help her find a rhythm. And when she moved, her skin slipped against his, and nothing else mattered. It was just the two of them, finding their way to the top of a cliff before flying over the edge.

SEVENTEEN

Vivienne's phone buzzed on the nightstand for the tenth time in as many minutes. Snuggling closer to Deacon, she told herself to ignore it. But then it buzzed again.

And again.

"He's not going to stop until you respond," Deacon muttered, ripping the remote from his own nightstand to pause the movie. The screen cast half of his face in shadows. "Lyle needs to find a girlfriend and quit trying to steal mine."

The idea of Vivienne and Lyle ever being romantic made her snigger. Plus, he kind of had a girlfriend—although he'd never admit he was actually dating Emily. The two of them snuck around like it wasn't obvious they were together. He stayed over at least three nights a week, and she wasn't stupid enough to believe he actually slept on the freaking couch, even though he insisted on making a bed there every single time.

"I'll just put it on silent."

Lyle had been begging her to go back to Ohio with him this coming Friday.

Vivienne had spent most of yesterday hungover and worried after the nightclub debacle. Deacon had been in such a good mood all day, she couldn't bring herself to tell him about forgetting him. He deserved to know. But he also deserved one carefree weekend. There was no telling how many more of them they were going to have. This could be their last one.

When Lyle had brought up the idea of going back to Ohio, Vivienne had immediately shot him down.

But Lyle was as stubborn as she was.

Apparently, there was some massive party that one of Lyle's old friends was throwing. Vivienne told him that she didn't care because she was never drinking again. Then he told her that Lynn was having surgery the following week, getting a cyst on her wrist removed. Vivienne promised to call and wish her foster mother good luck, but it didn't warrant a trip.

Had Lyle accepted defeat?

Nope.

When she checked the messages, most of them were from her annoying brother. One was one from a blocked number, but was probably just a generic message from Kensington. That was how they usually came through.

After unlocking her phone, she clicked into the messages app.

"What does he want now?" Deacon grumbled. "Does he need you to tie his shoe? Or make him a bottle?"

The blocked number had sent her a picture message. It must have been a wrong number. While the image loaded, she reminded Deacon that Lyle wasn't a baby.

He snorted.

What the—

This picture definitely wasn't meant for her. Whoever it was had texted a photo of a girl with black hair, in her bra and underwear, with a shirtless, dark-haired guy burying his face in the girl's neck.

A shirtless dark-haired guy Vivienne recognized.

The phone slipped from her fingers, dropping onto the mattress.

Deacon picked it up before she could stop him.

His smile disappeared as he stared at the message.

If only there were some way to wipe the image from her brain. To keep it from being tattooed onto her memory. But there wasn't, and every time she blinked, she saw them. Together.

"Who is she?" Vivienne gasped, her head spinning and world tilting. This couldn't be happening. They were happy. They were *engaged*. They were going to get married.

"I . . . um . . . " Deacon winced, rubbing the back of his neck. "I'm sorry, but I don't actually remember."

How could he have been in that situation with a girl and not know who she was?

Oh god.

She was going to puke. Her stomach lurched and her head spun and she tried to steady herself against the headboard, but then she glanced at Deacon and it made everything worse.

"The two of you are naked together and you 'don't remember' who she is?"

Breathe.

Just breathe.

"Vivienne, I—"

"When was it taken?"

"If I don't know who she is, I obviously don't remember when it was taken," he ground out, the muscles in his jaw ticking.

Her mouth was dry, her heart racing. She felt like she was

stuck inside a glass room, screaming, but no one could hear her. *Oh god.* "Are you cheating on me?"

Deacon was cheating on her. There was no other explanation.

The ring on her finger was cutting off her circulation. No wonder he wanted to get married right away. He was afraid of getting caught.

"What? No!" He shook his head, his eyes wide with shock—or was it guilt? "Vivienne, you have to believe me. I would never do that to you."

"Give me my phone." She grabbed for it, but he held it out of her reach.

"Only if you promise to delete it."

"Why? What are you trying to hide?"

"I'm not hiding anything, *dammit.* I just don't want you staring at a picture of me in bed with someone else."

"Give. Me. My. Phone."

He jammed it into her hand with a curse. "Delete it. Now."

"You think you get to tell me what to do?" No way. No *freaking* way. She would delete it when she felt like it.

Vivienne shoved her phone into her pocket and stomped to the door.

"Where are you going?" He scrambled to his feet and followed her to the hallway.

"I'm leaving." She didn't want to see him.

Didn't want to talk to him.

And she sure as heck didn't want to be near him.

Vivienne was going home so she didn't have to see the regret in his green eyes.

"Vivienne, wait. Please." He clambered down the stairs after her, stumbling on the last one and stubbing his toe. "*Dammit!*" Clutching his foot, he cursed again.

"I just need . . . " What did she need? "I need some time

151

to process this. *Alone.*" And to ugly cry without hearing his worthless apologies.

"What's there to process?" He hobbled toward where she was slipping into her shoes. "It's obviously an old picture. I haven't been with anyone else since we met. I swear."

"Besides Gwen, right?" She dragged open the door. Wind and snow from the blizzard outside curled its way onto the welcome mat.

Groaning, he raked a hand through his disheveled hair. "I should have said that I haven't been with anyone since we started *dating.*"

His hair *had* looked different.

And his arms hadn't seemed as toned as they were now.

Maybe it had been an old picture.

Maybe he was telling the truth.

But that didn't change the fact that she had just seen him in bed with someone else.

It felt like someone had punched a hole in her chest and ripped out her heart.

"Please stay. Please."

"No."

"At least let me see the photo again." Deacon motioned toward her pocket. "Give me a chance to remember who she was? I'll tell you anything you want to know."

"Do you really think I want to watch you sit around reminiscing about all the girls you slept with?" Yeah, that wasn't happening.

Deacon ripped his keys from the bowl and grabbed for his jacket. "All right. Fine. At least let me drive you so you don't catch your death in this blizzard."

"I'd rather brave this weather than be near you for another second." The moment the words left her lips, Vivienne regretted them.

They were true. Sort of. But they also sounded final.

Deacon's eyes widened, and he opened his mouth like he

was going to respond. But then he clenched his jaw shut, dropped the keys back into the bowl with a clink, and turned to walk back up the stairs.

Vivienne shoved her arms into the coat sleeves, pulled the zipper to her chin, and slammed the door behind her.

There were cars on the road, so she had to wade through six inches of snow to the back of the house. By the time she was able to take off, her feet were soaked, and she was pretty sure she had frostbite.

What the heck was she doing?

Deacon loved her.

He wanted to marry her.

He would never cheat on her.

Except . . .

Could Vivienne really believe that she would be enough for someone who was used to having everything?

By the time she reached Kensington, she was no closer to an answer than she had been when she'd left. Her face and hands were numb, and the ends of her hair were frosty. Her nose was as red as the poinsettias on the wreath hanging on their door.

Draping her damp coat over one of the kitchen chairs, she waited for her hands to thaw so she could untie her sopping laces. Her phone dinged, and she felt herself sink lower.

Deacon had tried calling her on the way and had sent her three messages. *Please call me back. I love you. I know I was an asshole before, but I swear I would never do anything to hurt you.*

Not knowing how to respond, Vivienne closed his feed and clicked on the one from the blocked number.

Maybe it wasn't as bad she thought.

She reopened the picture.

Nope. *Nope.* Still bad.

So, so bad.

It was obvious why the girl was smiling, but why did

Deacon look so freaking happy? Surely he wouldn't look like that if it had been only a fling.

Maybe he was lying about not knowing the raven-haired beauty.

Or maybe he was just that good of an actor, making this girl believe she meant something to him when all he wanted was to get in, off, and out.

Men were such jerks, thinking with their—

"Hey, Vivienne. What're you—What's wrong?" Emily landed with a grunt on the chair beside her. "You look like you're going to cry or kill someone." She grabbed one of the candy canes left over from Christmas from the Rudolph bowl in the middle of the table.

As much as Vivienne wanted to hide the photo, she wanted a second opinion more. "How about both?" She handed the phone to Emily, feeling her chest rip open wider.

"*Wooooah*, girl." Emily squeezed her eyes shut and wrinkled her nose. "I don't want to see your homemade porn."

"Yeah, that's *not* me."

Emily's eyes snapped open. "It's not?" She spread her fingers across the screen, zooming in and frowning. "Then who is that with Deacon?"

By the time Vivienne finished explaining what had happened, the sick feeling in the pit of her stomach had turned to hollow numbness.

Emily set the phone on the table and leaned back in the chair. The candy cane crunched loudly when she bit into it. "Girl, that's insane."

Was it though? Deacon liked women. A lot. Was it that far-fetched to imagine him having one—or ten—on the side? "Do you think he's cheating on me?" Vivienne asked, her face burning with shame.

"No way. Absolutely not." Emily's curly ponytail swayed from side to side when she shook her head. "Deacon is *obsessed* with you."

"Yeah, but. I mean . . . come on. You've seen him. Do you really think he'd ever be happy with just one girl?" A girl who was going to lose her memory any day now.

"Vivienne, look at me." Emily leaned forward until they were nose to nose. "He *loves* you. He asked you to marry him for goodness' sake. He would *not* cheat on you."

"I know." Vivienne blinked back her tears. All of that was true, "But—"

"No 'but.' That's it. End of story. This person"—Emily slid the phone across the table—"is obviously trying to cause trouble. If you want my advice, you should delete it without giving them the satisfaction of knowing you even looked at the stupid thing."

Vivienne picked up her phone, took one last look at the photo because she was a masochist, and deleted it.

"Good for you." Emily smiled and handed her a candy cane.

⫘

Vivienne took the candy and pretended like she felt better, even though she felt worse.

Vivienne found herself glancing at her screen for what felt like the millionth time. Only instead of seeing a picture, she saw the text she had typed so many times over the past three days since the photo had come through.

Deacon had come to Vivienne's apartment every day, asking Emily to see her. And every day, Emily had told him Vivienne wasn't ready yet.

When he'd left last night, he had come to Vivienne's window.

After knocking and pleading, he'd gone away. But not before taping a note to the freezing pane.

Hiding in there won't fix this. Please come back to me.

With her finger hovering over the send button, she closed her eyes and let it fall.

Three seconds later, her phone was ringing.

She declined the call. It rang again, but the shrill tone was silenced when she switched off her phone. Turning to the bag she had packed for Ohio, Vivienne added a few more pairs of clean underwear and socks.

Once it was zipped, she dragged it to the living room where Lyle was waiting with Emily on the couch. Emily looked at her with pity in her eyes. And she hated it. That pity and the constant "Are you okay?" were part of the reason she wanted to escape.

Lyle gave her a goofy, gap-toothed grin. "All set?" he asked, jogging over and taking her suitcase. When he lifted it, he groaned. "Geez, Viv. How long do you plan on staying in Ohio?"

She rolled her eyes but found herself fighting her first smile in days. "Shut up, Lyle."

Emily stood and collected Vivienne in a tight hug. She smelled like the batch of cookies she'd baked that afternoon. "I'm really going to miss you."

"I'm leaving for the weekend, Em. Not forever."

"Yeah, but it's January. Nothing happens in January. And with you and Lyle gone, and Max in London, I'm going to be bored out of my mind."

"We'll make up for it next week. I promise." Vivienne squeezed a bit tighter before letting her best friend go.

"What do you want me to say when you-know-who shows up?" Emily whispered.

"He knows." Deacon was probably on his way at that very minute. But they'd be gone before he reached campus.

With a nod, Emily released her hold. "Oh! I almost forgot!" She bounced to the kitchen, returning with two baggies of peanut butter cookies, still warm from the oven. "Something for the road."

"Where's mine?" Lyle asked from the door.

"She has two bags, you idiot."

"Yeah, but you don't know how much she"—Lyle nodded his chin toward Vivienne—"loves peanut butter. She'll have those things eaten before we get to the airport."

Emily laughed even as she grabbed three more cookies and slipped them into a bag for Lyle. "You're so annoying."

"And you're a hideous troll," Lyle shot back.

Who did they think they were fooling?

Vivienne was too deep in self-pity to get into it. "Come on. Let's go." Their flight wasn't until three, but she wanted to be gone before Deacon showed up.

"Take care of my girl, okay?"

Lyle gave Emily a wink. "Always."

Turning toward the door, Vivienne pretended not to notice the kiss Lyle planted on Emily's cheek.

Bitter winter wind swirled around them as they left the apartment building. It wasn't snowing, but felt like it could start at any minute. The snow from the blizzard three days earlier was piled into white mounds on either side of the cleared path. Vivienne's feet crunched against the frozen stones as they passed the empty fountain and rounded the Hall.

There were a few other PAN rushing from one building to the next, none of them paying Vivienne or Lyle any attention.

The car Lyle had been given was still running in the driveway outside the Hall. He loaded her bag into the trunk next to his, and they sank into the heat inside.

"I'm surprised your bodyguard isn't here to see you off or curse me for taking you away," Lyle said, shifting into drive and starting down the crushed stone driveway toward the gates. The trees around them were dusted with snow, taking away some of the harshness of the naked branches.

Vivienne thought of the text she'd sent Deacon only a few minutes ago. The one telling him she was going to Ohio. She was such a coward.

"He's busy." In truth, he was probably in his car, driving at breakneck speed to get to Kensington. She had spoken to him once since that photo had come in, to assure him that she wasn't breaking up with him. But she also wasn't ready to see him yet. She still needed time and space to work through all the emotions she was feeling.

Fear. Anger. Jealousy. Betrayal.

Twisting the dials on the heat, she held her frozen fingers toward the air vents.

Lyle slowed the car when he reached the main gates. After a moment, the sensors kicked in, and they swung open. Turning toward Worcester, he stepped on the gas.

The closer they got to the airport, the more she relaxed.

Yes, Vivienne would have to hang out with her terrible foster sister, but she would also get to see Lynn. And, most importantly, she would be able to pretend everything was fine.

"Okay. Something is wrong." Lyle came to a jerking halt at a red light, and the car behind them laid on their horn. "You should be way more excited about hanging out with me two weekends in a row."

He was right. And the last thing she wanted was to spend the weekend in her own head. "I saw something terrible, and now I think maybe . . . "

Lyle nudged her with his elbow. "Maybe, what?"

"Maybe Deacon cheated on me."

He wouldn't do something so terrible.

He was one of the good guys.

Except he had a reputation for being one of the bad ones.

Lyle flicked the blinker and shot past a slow-moving minivan. "What'd you see?"

Twisting her engagement ring around her littlest finger, Vivienne explained what had happened with the photo.

Lyle listened without interrupting, giving nothing away with his blank expression. Eventually, he scratched his soft-stubbled chin and sighed. "I mean, I guess I see where you're coming from. But you said he's gone out with a lot of girls, so he could be telling the truth. And he didn't deny he was with this chick, just that it was before you guys were together."

"I know." How many times did she need to hear it to believe it? "But it was easier to be happy by imagining it was always just him and me instead of facing the reality of him and everyone else," she confessed, wrapping her hands in the hem of her top.

"Need me to kill him for you?" Lyle tossed an empty plastic bottle from the cupholder into the bottle graveyard in the back seat. "Because I would gladly do it. Like, you wouldn't even have to pay me. I'd do it for free."

The question loosened some of the tightness in Vivienne's chest, and she laughed for the first time since she had opened that stupid message "Maybe next time."

"Okay. Here's what we're going to do." Lyle twisted his grip on the steering wheel back and forth. "We're going to go to Ohio and gang up against Maren, get drunk with a few old friends from high school, and tell everyone how amazing our lives are. Because they are amazing. We live in *Neverland*. We know Peter-frickin-Pan."

"Lyle—"

"I know, I know. We have to tell people we're living in upstate New York, *blah blah blah*." A grin. "But that doesn't mean we can't *think* about it."

Lyle was right.

Despite everything, Vivienne's life *was* amazing.

EIGHTEEN

Jasper threw himself into his work for the next few weeks, waiting for Steve to give him whatever magic was needed to keep activating genes from returning to dormancy. Steve kept saying these things took time. That he needed approval before he was allowed to hand anything over.

Jasper decided to trust him—because he didn't have any other choice. If he was going to activate his dormant gene, he needed Steve's help.

The first Tuesday of the month, Lawrence cornered Jasper on his way out of the Admin building.

Lawrence's tie was loose around his neck, his face drawn and pale.

"You feeling okay? You're not getting sick, are you?" Jasper couldn't afford to miss work, so he kept a safe distance from his brother.

"I didn't sleep a wink last night," Lawrence confessed, rubbing his red-rimmed eyes. "The damn dog won't stop whining. I ended up spending the night on the couch with my hand in the kennel to shut it up."

With everything that had happened this winter, Jasper had forgotten that Lawrence's fiancée had adopted a little mutt. Lawrence hadn't wanted a dog, but Louise had convinced him to get one anyway.

"I'm sure once she gets used to the place, she'll quiet down." Jasper liked dogs, but they took way too much effort. That's why he had a cat instead. Pancake ignored him most of the time, except when she needed fed. And every once in a while she came around for a lazy cuddle. If only he could find someone who would be as content with his lack of attention as Pancake.

"If it doesn't, I'm bringing the thing back to the pound." Lawrence nodded to the cups in Jasper's hand. "Those both for you?"

They weren't. Jasper picked up two cups of coffee every morning—one for Steve and one for himself. But that was none of his brother's business. "Yeah. I need a little extra boost on these cold winter days." It had been the Januariest January on record, bleeding into the Februariest February. Jasper was counting down the days until March. If he ever moved, he was going somewhere warm.

"You're telling me. How're things in the lab?" Lawrence asked after a particularly drawn out yawn.

"They're fine." They could have been better. But they could have been worse.

"I need better than fine. The board is breathing down my neck, and I don't know how much longer I'll be able to hold them off. They want that injection you promised."

Jasper *had* told his brother that he had hoped to have an anti-aging injection ready by March, but that had been a year ago. Before Vivienne. Before the fire. Before the video.

"I'm not working on the injection anymore." Jasper took a sip of his coffee. It was still hot enough to burn his tongue.

"It's a dead end, anyway. If people don't possess the gene, then an injection isn't the way to get them to stay young." At least not using the research HOOK had been collecting for the last five decades.

Lawrence cursed and kicked at the wall, leaving a black mark on the white baseboard. "Then what the hell are you working on, Rat?"

Jasper could have sworn they'd had this conversation a week ago, when they'd met at Dr. Hooke's house for Sunday dinner. Jasper and the man he refused to call his father had spent half the night discussing it. Hadn't Lawrence been paying attention?

"Retroactive stimulation."

Lawrence groaned and scrubbed a hand across his beard. "How is that going to help the public?"

"Well, it won't. At least not directly. But it'll help us understand how the gene mutates and ensure activation for subjects with young genes." And old genes as well.

Lawrence's eyes narrowed, and he leaned forward until Jasper could smell the coffee on his breath. "Figure out how to fly on your own time, do you hear me? We want anti-aging. *That's* where the money is. Stop your selfish little side project and do something useful."

"Charles said—"

"I don't give a shit what he said," Lawrence roared, giving the baseboard another kick. "I want something to hand to the board by the end of the month." He jabbed Jasper in the shoulder. "And if you don't produce *something*, you're gone. Do you hear me? *Gone.*"

Jasper mumbled a response to placate him and escaped to the lab.

"Morning, boss." Steve replaced the coffee Jasper held toward him with a white paper bag that smelled like cinnamon and apples. Steve's apartment was near a great bakery that made the best apple fritters on the planet. So every morning, Jasper picked up the coffee and Steve organized breakfast. It was nice having a routine that didn't involve stale cereal or a granola bar.

Jasper thanked him and brought his things over to one of the small tables in the annex. His laptop bag landed with a *thunk* on the floor. Sarah waved as she passed and disappeared into the lab.

"Any news since yesterday?" Steve asked, taking the lid off his coffee and blowing on the top.

"Nothing noteworthy." Steve wouldn't care about Jasper's problems with Lawrence. He was only at HOOK to get poison and intel. It didn't matter that they'd bonded over beer and *Rocky I-III* this past weekend. The moment Steve got his orders to leave, he'd be out of Virginia, and they'd never see or speak to each other again.

Steve frowned as he sipped; his eyebrows came together slowly. "You sure about that?"

"I'm sure." Jasper tore off his winter coat and draped it across the back of the chair. "Thanks for this, by the way," he added as he opened the top of the bag. The pastry inside smelled like heaven.

"Yeah. No problem." Steve replaced the lid on his coffee and tapped his finger against the cardboard cup.

"Did you need something else?"

"Just wondering when you want to start working on our project."

"I'll be working on something different today. Why don't you help Eliza with whatever she's doing?"

Steve looked like he wanted to say something. Instead, he got up and walked rigidly to the lab door.

Jasper spent the day staring at the notes on his computer, trying to drum up some enthusiasm for taking away the public's wrinkles, but ended up wasting eight hours wishing he was doing something that would help himself. It wasn't as if they were solving world hunger or anything else really useful.

For once in his life, Jasper wanted to put himself first.

That night, Steve showed up with enough Chinese food to last a week.

"You're late." Jasper took the bag off of him and carried it into the kitchen. Steve was usually there by six thirty. It was almost a quarter past seven, and Jasper was starving.

"Still in a mood I see." Steve threw his jacket on the back of the couch. "I had things to do."

"Like what?" Steve was nearly as bad as Jasper when it came to work.

"Like take Sarah for a drink after work."

Jasper dropped the small white-and-red container of rice onto the counter. "Sarah-from-the-lab Sarah?" How long had this been going on? Why was he only hearing about it now?

Steve sniggered as he pulled what was left of his six-pack from this weekend from the fridge. "That's the one. You want red or white wine?"

"White." Jasper couldn't believe Steve was dating. Between office work and their after-work work and spying on HOOK, wasn't he busy enough?

Steve poured Jasper a glass before returning the bottle to the fridge. "I can't work all the time," he said with a lift of his shoulders. "Besides, the nights get lonely."

"You're *here* almost every night."

"Not all night," Steve said with a wink.

Jasper dragged two plates from the cabinet and dropped onto the stool. He couldn't remember the last time he had gone out with someone. It must have been at least five years ago.

"Can I offer you some unsolicited advice?" Steve dumped fried rice onto his plate, added a spoonful of sweet and sour chicken, and ripped open one of the packs of chopsticks.

"Does it matter if I say no?" Jasper muttered, drizzling soy sauce over his pork fried rice.

"Nope." Chuckling, Steve pinched a piece of battered chicken between the chopsticks. Thick red sauce dripped onto the plate. "If you don't take some time to have a life while you're young, you're going to regret it."

"Such sage advice from a guy barely out of diapers."

Steve grinned as he chewed. "I'm older than I look."

Jasper had never considered Steve's age. He was tall and slim with no wrinkles. He had obviously gone to college—or the PAN equivalent—so Jasper figured he had to be at least twenty-two. But that seemed low considering how intelligent Steve was. And surely the PAN wouldn't send twenty-two-year-olds on such dangerous missions. "Oh, I'm sorry. What are you, twenty-four? Twenty-five? Practically ancient."

"Double it, kid." Steve snagged one of the eggrolls. The crispy coating crunched when he took a bite.

Jasper's chopsticks dropped to the counter.

"No way." There was absolutely no way the guy sitting next to him was fifty years old. This was big. Bigger than big. This was monumental. "That means you've been able to isolate the genetic ingredients that keep the PAN young."

All Steve did was grin and take a sip of beer.

Excitement built in Jasper's chest. The PAN had actually done it. "You've gotta tell me how." If Steve could get Jasper on the right track, it could be enough to keep Lawrence at bay.

"Magic."

Not this again. "Enough of your magic BS. This is serious." He grabbed his chopsticks off the counter. "If I don't give Lawrence something by the end of the month, he's going to fire me."

Steve let out a low whistle between his teeth. "And that's a bad thing because . . . ?"

"Because then I'd be no good to anyone!"

Steve may be leaving, but the PAN could still need someone on the inside. Jasper didn't like playing spy—it stressed him out to no end—but at least he was doing something to help those he'd hurt.

If he got fired, he wouldn't have enough in his savings account to get himself through to summer. The job market for his skill set was basically non-existent.

He'd been working at HOOK since he had interned there in high school. Having only one place of employment on his resume—a company built on nepotism, no less—wasn't going to help his chances.

After finishing the bite he'd shoved into his mouth, Steve reached for his beer bottle. "Just come work for us."

Jasper couldn't leave HOOK and work for the PAN.

. . . could he?

"Like you would ever hire someone like me."

"I've already spoken to Peter. He said there's a job for you if you want it." Propping his elbow on the table, Steve picked at the label on the beer bottle. "We'll give you your own lab with real heating and plenty of space to move around so you don't run into anyone and break stuff." A grin. "And you've already worked with most of our team."

"I have?"

Steve rolled his eyes. "We've been poaching HOOK employees for the last six months, Jasper."

If the PAN had enough money to take all their people *and* keep them quiet, the possibilities were endless. Jasper had tried convincing Dr. Hooke and Lawrence to work with them forever, but they'd always refused.

Jasper and the PAN could accomplish a lot more together than he could on his own in a pre-fab lab with outdated, and often broken, equipment. He'd have access to people with active genes and whatever magical injections Steve was talking about and who knew what else.

Jasper finished his last bite of pork fried rice and cleaned up what he'd spilled on the counter before reaching for his wine.

"Is that why you were so stressed today? Because Lawrence the Terrible was on the war path?" Steve clinked his bottle against Jasper's wine glass.

Jasper nodded. Had it been that obvious?

"I tell you what. There's still a few more things I need to do before I finish up with HOOK."

Jasper wanted to ask what those things were, but figured Steve wouldn't tell him.

"In the meantime," Steve went on, "I want you to keep working on retroactive stimulation during office hours."

"But—"

Steve held up a finger. "And I'll get you something that'll blow Lawrence's mind before the end of the month. Then we'll both jump ship."

Jasper held out his hand. "You have yourself a deal."

NINETEEN

"You're going to have to explain this again." Ethan shifted on the sofa so he was facing Deacon. The fire in the hearth cut the chill from the storm raging outside. If the snow didn't stop soon, Vivienne would have trouble getting home. That was *if* she came home.

Biting his lower lip, Ethan shook his head slowly. "How could you *not know* someone was taking a picture of you with your pants around your ankles?"

Deacon cursed. They'd already been over it twice. "For the last time, it looked like I was a *little* preoccupied." And he certainly hadn't expected the girl he'd been with— whoever she was—to take a selfie. Didn't people live in the moment anymore?

"Dude." Ethan snorted. "We're not supposed to be in *any* photos. It is literally the *only* rule we follow."

A rule Deacon had followed until he'd learned about Vivienne's forgetfulness.

Or at least he thought he'd followed it.

"I know we mess around a lot," Ethan went on, "but this is serious shit. You don't even know where this person got the picture."

He said it like Deacon didn't already know how serious this was. His fiancée had left town without telling him and hadn't talked to him since. Hell, he didn't know if she still wanted to marry him.

"And you're sure the girl wasn't from Neverland?"

"Positive." Deacon could vaguely remember a girl—maybe, possibly—who looked like that when he'd gone to Ireland a few years ago. Then again, she could easily have been from somewhere near Worcester. But if she was from close by, he would have brought her back to his place. The floral wallpaper in the background of the photo hadn't been his.

"Then you shouldn't be focusing on the subject. You should be trying to find the sender."

"It was a blocked number." And Vivienne had promised that she had deleted the message. Could that kind of stuff be traced?

Deacon hadn't slept more than a few hours since Vivienne had received that damned message. The broken look on her face still haunted him. But it had been her faithless reaction, the fact that she believed so quickly that he'd do something like that to her, that had left him feeling more empty and alone than ever.

He'd made a lot of mistakes but had never lied about it. And he sure as hell hadn't cheated on anyone.

Vivienne may have been shocked, but his privacy had been violated.

"What're you gonna do?" Ethan asked, nudging Deacon's knee with his own.

"I haven't a clue." And now Vivienne was all the way in Ohio, with Lyle undoubtedly poisoning her mind and trying to convince her to call off the engagement. Not that any of that mattered if she got herself caught by HOOK again. How could she be so foolish as to go to the only place HOOK knew about?

Deacon had called Owen in Extraction to ask if he could send a team to keep an eye on her in case anything happened. *And bloody Lyle.* Deacon didn't need to think about that traitor. Lyle knew better than to suggest a trip back to his mother's house. If anything happened to Vivienne—

"I think you need a drink." Ethan nudged him again.

Did Deacon need a drink?

No.

That was an awful idea.

Ethan was full of awful ideas lately. Alcohol was at the root of this disaster. If Deacon hadn't been drinking, he would have remembered the girl, and wouldn't have sounded so pathetic and guilty when Vivienne had asked him who she was.

"I don't feel like going out." Deacon didn't feel like leaving the house. Unless it was to go to Ohio. He should go to the airport. That's what he should do.

"I don't care, Dash. You haven't left this place in forever. You need some social interaction."

Deacon didn't need anything but his fiancée. "I'm going to get Vivienne."

Ethan put a hand on his shoulder. "I know you're freaking out, but she wouldn't have run off to Ohio if she wanted to talk to you. And isn't she always saying she wants space? Give her the weekend and fix it when she gets back."

What if she never came back?

Shit.

It was going to be a long weekend, and if Deacon stayed inside, he'd go mad. Perhaps Ethan was right. Perhaps he should get out.

Ethan snatched their jackets from the stand and hauled Deacon to his feet. "Come on, man. I'm buying."

The weak smile on Vivienne's face was all Deacon needed to confirm that he should have spent the weekend groveling in Ohio instead of self-medicating in Massachusetts. He had very nearly purchased a plane ticket on Saturday at 3 a.m., but Ethan had stopped him again.

Deacon needed to find better friends.

"Hey," Vivienne said, brushing her hair back from her face. Her cheeks and nose were pink from the cold, but she hadn't bothered with a scarf or hat. Why had she knocked instead of using the key he'd given her?

The sun made the mounds of snow in his front lawn look like glitter. It was a beautiful day, but it was as icy as the feeling in Deacon's stomach as he opened the door wider and moved aside. "Come inside before you freeze to death."

She stomped the snow from her shoes before removing them and setting them on the mat beside his. That was a good sign, wasn't it? That she was going to stick around long enough to take off her shoes. A good sign. A very good—

"We need to talk."

A bad sign. A very bad sign. It was *never* good when a woman said that.

"All right." He walked numbly to the sofa and dropped onto the cushion. "Let's talk." If she was breaking up with him, he wanted to be sitting down.

Instead of sitting, Vivienne stood awkwardly in front of the fireplace, touching the bronze statue she'd given him on their first Christmas together.

Why wasn't she saying anything? Putting him out of his misery so he could get on a plane to somewhere far away?

"I'm sorry, Deacon."

Not nearly as sorry as he was. After all, this was his fault. If he hadn't been such a cad, none of this would have happened.

"I understand." How he managed to say those two words without breaking was a mystery.

Heaving a breath, she straightened her shoulders. "I shouldn't have gone to Ohio when things were so messed up between us. I should have stayed here and worked things out."

Wait. What?

He was afraid to hope. Afraid to breathe.

"It's just . . . that photo shattered some pretty strong illusions I'd had about you," she went on, twisting her hands together. "About us."

"What illusions?"

"That it's just you and me."

"It *is* just you and me. I told you, I haven't been with anyone else."

Closing the gap between them, Vivienne sank onto the sofa, tucking herself so that her knees pressed against his thigh. "That's just it. You were with *a lot* of other girls before me." Her lips flattened, and her eyebrows lifted. "And I knew I would have to face it at some point, but I didn't think I'd have to *see* it." Her words were barely a whisper as she stared down at her clasped hands.

"I'm sorry." It wasn't enough, but what else could he say? He'd always been honest with Vivienne and had never tried to hide his past from her. Of course, that didn't mean his past wasn't going to bite him in the ass. "I've done plenty I'm not particularly proud of. And I hate that you're hurting because of it."

When she raised her face to his, he could see tears glistening on her cheeks. Would he ever stop making her cry?

"Why me?" she whispered, using her sleeve to wipe her cheek.

"What do you mean?"

"I think this would all be easier to take if I knew why you changed for me. When you've been with girls like Gwen and Aoibheann . . . " Her words trailed off, and she shrugged her slim shoulders. "Just . . . why me?"

Why her?

There were so many reasons. She was beautiful and didn't realize it. She was kind and independent and didn't need him. The list went on and on. But all the reasons boiled down to one thing.

"Because of all of the women I've met, you were the only one to ever run away. And instead of letting you go, I have this overwhelming desire to chase after you."

She bit her lip as she watched him.

"You ditched me on that bus. You left me on Halloween night. You sprinted away before your genealogy meeting. And then you said you wanted to be my *friend*. Women don't want to be friends with me." The very idea had been so incredibly foreign. Sure, he and Nicola were friends now, but that wasn't how their relationship began.

While Deacon was laying his soul bare, he figured he may as well tell her everything. This was the woman he was going to marry—assuming she still wanted to go ahead with the wedding. "Last year, when I went to London and hooked up with Gwen, it felt . . . wrong. And it had never felt wrong before. And I couldn't stop thinking about you and how you would feel if you found out. For once in my life, I was more worried about someone else than about myself. And I know that makes me sound like an asshole, but . . . " But what? What more could he say? It was the truth.

Her hand came to rest on his. "I think it's time we both stop running away."

Vivienne was right. Instead of coming together to solve

problems, they went to their separate corners to fight on their own, then came back when they were feeling better, less broken. If they were going to get married, if they were going to spend forever together, they needed to run toward each other. To meet their problems as a team.

"All right. Let's stop running away." He opened his arms, knowing she may not want him to touch her yet.

She crashed into him, and his hands closed around her. Maybe, just maybe, everything really would be all right.

"I'm so sorry about this mess," he mumbled between kisses to her hair, her cheeks, her lips. "You know I'd never do anything to hurt you. You know that, right?"

"I know. I know." Her words were warm against his neck.

How did she smell so good all the time? Like lilacs after the rain. He wanted to bring her upstairs and—

No. No. He couldn't do that. That was what had gotten him into this mess in the first place.

Vivienne's phone dinged, and she pulled away, wiping her tear-stained cheeks. "Sorry. That's probably Emily wondering where I am."

"I have to share you with far too many people." Gathering her hair back from her shoulders, he kissed the spot between her collarbone and shoulder, knowing it would make her arch her back and sigh. "You should try being more unpleasant so you don't have as many friends."

Her body vibrated when she giggled. "Says Kensington's resident celebrity."

"*Celebrity?*" The thought was laughable. "There are only two people who text me, and you're one of them. And the other one I don't even like half the time."

Vivienne stiffened beneath him, and when he pulled back, her face was pale as she stared at the screen.

He peered over her shoulder to catch the last digit of her passcode and noticed a red notification beside her messages app. Without turning the screen away, she clicked the icon. Above the most recent text from Lyle saying something about Maren was a message from a blocked number. *There are no happily-ever-afters.*

Happily ever after? What was that supposed to mean?

Another message buzzed through.

A photo.

This time, Deacon recognized the woman he was in bed with.

It was Gwen.

For the next two weeks, every time Vivienne seemed to get over the most recent photo, there'd be another one waiting for her.

Deacon lying in someone's bed. Deacon dragging a girl into the storage closet at the Wendy Bird. Deacon making out with someone in the corner of some dingy bar.

Seriously. Did he *ever* keep it in his pants?

The only reason she hadn't thrown her engagement ring in his stupid handsome face and told him where he could shove it was because the photos had clearly been taken before she'd met him. Ever since he had saved her at the hospital, he'd had basically the same haircut. But in all the photos, his hair had been shorter and gelled.

Deacon hadn't stopped apologizing. Instead of running away like she always did, she had shown him every message. They'd talked about them—the ones he could remember, anyway. And even though it was easier to believe he was still doing those things, she knew in her heart it wasn't true.

When she got out of the shower on Friday morning, there was a message waiting for her. She wasn't going to check it though. She was going to delete it. That was the plan she and Deacon had come up with.

They weren't going to let this anonymous texter drive a wedge between them.

She slathered lotion onto her body and tried to ignore the phone staring at her from the desk. Once her hair was dry, she dragged on a pair of tights and her dad's sweatshirt for comfort.

Outside the window, the wind howled. Deacon had tried to get her to stay with him last night, but she had promised Emily that she'd be back to watch a movie.

The phone buzzed again.

There were two messages.

Deacon's asked if she was awake yet.

And the BLOCKED NUMBER had sent her another—

Crap.

It wasn't a photo.

It was a video.

Vivienne definitely shouldn't press the white triangle. Nothing good would come of it. The best thing would be to delete it immediately like she had planned.

Her finger tapped Play.

The video was black, but she recognized Aoibheann's voice—and Deacon's. It sounded like they were playing a sexy version of hide and seek. There was a bang, and Deacon cursed. Aoibheann giggled and squealed when he found her. Then the noises that followed, although muffled, were unmistakable.

Lips meeting.

Turn it off.

Heavy breathing.

Turn it off.

Soft whispers and moans.

Turn it off.

Another giggle. "I love you."

Tears fell, stinging Vivienne's cheeks.

Don't say it back.

Please, don't say it back.

"And I love you."

She hurled her phone against the wall and crumpled to the floor.

"What happened?" Deacon snatched his keys from the bowl next to the door and ran outside to his car. It was freezing, and he had forgotten his coat, but he refused to waste time going back inside to get it. He had been in the shower when Vivienne had tried calling him. And she'd been crying so hard the voicemail had been difficult to understand. She'd said she needed him to come over right away. When he rang her back, she hadn't answered. He'd called Emily two minutes later.

"I don't know," Emily said, her voice shaking. "I heard her crying, but she has the door locked and won't let me in."

"I'm on my way. I'll be there as soon as I can." Deacon threw his mobile into the passenger seat and started his car. The steering wheel was like ice, and the windscreen fogged up before he reached the stop sign at the end of his street. Even with the defrost on full blast, the cold air didn't clear a damned thing. He resorted to wiping the glass with his hand until the car warmed up.

He cursed the daylight for keeping him from flying, the blue hatchback in front of him for driving so damn slow, and the mysterious texter for torturing his fiancée for the last two weeks.

Of all the possible scenarios running through his mind, he knew beyond a shadow of a doubt that Vivienne was crying because she had received another photo.

He'd always prided himself on discretion. But apparently, the moment alcohol hit his system and a female slid onto his lap, he became oblivious to the paparazzi who must have been following him the last eight years.

After he'd seen the photo of himself with Gwen, he'd been convinced she was the culprit. But Vivienne had begged him not to say or do anything. To sit on his ass and wait for it to stop. But it hadn't stopped. And the next four photos had been taken in Worcester, when Gwen hadn't been in town, so it couldn't have been her.

Which meant it had to be someone else.

Someone with access to Neverland's case files since the photo yesterday had been from his first recruiting mission with Nicola.

Deacon turned toward the gates and rolled down the window to type his code into the icy keypad and scan his hand. By the time the gates had creaked open, he was already out of sight. He barely shifted to park before he tore out of the car.

Julie waved at him from the Hall stairs, her wild red hair bouncing in the bitter wind. The thick scarf she wore covered the bottom half of her face. "Just the guy I need to see—"

"Can't right now," he blurted before launching into the sky, up and over the Hall, and right to Vivienne's door on the third floor. Sunlight glinted off the silver keypad.

The door jerked open from the inside, and Emily waved him in.

"Is she still crying?" He ripped off his shoes and abandoned them beside the Christmas tree Emily refused to take down even though it was almost February.

"I'm not sure." Emily's eyebrows came together and she shook her head. "I haven't heard anything since I called you."

Deacon ran straight for Vivienne's bedroom door. There was another Christmas tree at the end of the hall; its colored lights blinked like tiny strobes. He pressed his ear against the wood. Silence. He knocked. No response. When he tried the handle, it was locked. "Do you have a paperclip?"

Emily hurried into her room, returning a moment later with a pink one. He straightened the metal and stuck the end into the pinpoint hole in the knob. After a few unsuccessful stabs, he connected with the mechanism and heard the lock on the other side *pop*.

"Good luck." Emily offered a sad, sympathetic smile before retreating back to the kitchen.

Vivienne was curled into the fetal position on the floor, her eyes closed. When he saw her mobile clutched in her hand, his heart ached.

Another photo.

It must have been bad to warrant this reaction.

Stepping over her dirty clothes, Deacon sank wordlessly to the floor and pulled her onto his lap. She didn't fight him, only snuggled deeper into his embrace and sobbed silently.

"You got another one." It wasn't a question.

She sniffled as she nodded.

He took her mobile and smoothed his thumb across the cracked screen. What he saw when he typed in her passcode made his heart race.

It took all of five seconds to recall when and where the video had been taken. And by whom.

Aoibheann.

Three summers ago, on Peter's island. His mother had gone to the mainland, and the damned Mermaid had shown up, and one thing led to another and—

Dammit. He'd been such an immature asshole, and now the woman he loved looked as broken as her screen.

"I swear I didn't know she was recording any of that." Like the confession made it any better. He sounded like a complete wanker.

Vivienne nodded, but a fresh wave of sobs wracked her body as she curled in on herself.

He sighed into her hair. "At least now we know who's been sending them." It had to be Aoibheann.

"You told her . . . you told her you loved her."

He'd thrown that word around a lot through the years. "I know it sounds cliché, but I didn't know what love was."

The skin beneath her closed eyes was so dark it looked bruised. He wiped her tears with his thumb, hating himself for being the reason behind them.

He bent his head to kiss her. Before their lips connected, Vivienne stiffened and turned her head away. "I can't stop thinking about you kissing *her*."

He knew the feeling. He had watched Vivienne crush her mouth against Alex's last New Year's and been privy to a pretty heavy make-out session when he'd returned from his trial in London. And it had nearly killed him. How would he handle learning her relationship with Alex had crossed other boundaries?

He had to put a stop to this. Had to do *something*. "I'm going to have a chat with Aoibheann."

"No!" Vivienne clutched his wrist, her eyes wide with panic. "Please don't."

He'd done things her way for two weeks. It was time for a different approach.

"This isn't just you they're harassing. It's me as well." He ran his thumbs along her cheeks. She looked as weary as he felt. "More importantly, it's us."

And Deacon knew one thing for certain: if the photos didn't stop, his relationship with Vivienne was as good as over.

"I'm begging you," he whispered, "let me do something about it."

TWENTY

Never in a million years did Deacon think he would be sitting in Paul Mitter's office, willingly watching the Head of External Affairs flick through pictures of him in various compromising positions with multiple women.

But for the first time in his life, it felt like the two of them were on the same side.

With his face burning from embarrassment, Deacon kept his eyes focused on Paul's yellow legal pad. At least Paul had only listened to the blacked-out video once.

"I didn't know anyone was taking photos," he confessed for what felt like the hundredth time. Beside him, Vivienne's hands balled into fists in her lap. She hadn't been happy with him for organizing the meeting, but enough was enough.

Paul's lips flattened into a disapproving line. Shaking his head, he swiped right on Vivienne's broken screen. Another shake. Another swipe. "You don't know who sent these?"

"At first I thought it may have been Gwen. But after the,

um . . . video . . . I think perhaps it was Aoibheann. But if it was her, then how did she get the other pictures?" *Shit*. This was a disaster. "Honestly? I haven't a clue."

Paul took off his glasses and threw them on the desk. Deacon was so glad he had deleted the picture of himself and Paul's daughter Nicola before the meeting.

"First things first." Paul set the mobile beside a stack of colorful folders. "We need to get Vivienne a new phone."

Vivienne nodded.

"And we should probably issue a new one to you as well," he said to Deacon, "in case you become a target."

Deacon dragged his mobile from his pocket and handed it over. The only person he wanted to talk to was by his side. And if anyone else needed him, they knew where he lived.

"I'll keep both of your numbers off the database. Don't give them to *anyone* else. As for the person responsible for this"—Paul leaned his chin on tented fingers and narrowed his eyes—"when we find them, they will be punished."

Muttering to himself, Deacon climbed the stairs to Ethan's front porch. The flowers Nicola had planted during the summer were nothing more than dried brown husks sticking out of the snow. Half of the shutters had been painted green; the other half were still a faded, chipping blue.

If Vivienne had stayed with Deacon last night, he would still be in bed with her instead of freezing his bollocks off at half six in the morning. But she had refused. Again. Which meant he'd been up all bloody night trying to sort shit out so they could move past this together.

There was no point wondering about the sender—as Paul had promised yesterday he would figure that out. What Deacon didn't understand was how the person had gotten so many photos of him in the first place.

The only explanation was that someone must have been following him.

He glanced over his shoulder, but there was only snow and silence and a miserable looking black cat huddling beneath Deacon's car.

One name kept popping up when he thought about the majority of incidents.

Deacon pounded on Ethan's door, praying he was wrong.

He had to knock three more times before the door jerked open. Ethan appeared on the other side, barefoot, hair sticking out, and wearing a pair of basketball shorts. "What the hell are you doing here so early?" he grumbled, leaving the door open and trudging toward the kitchen. An empty pizza box sat open on the coffee table.

"Did you do it?"

"My head's pounding, Dash. You're gonna have to be a little more specific." Ethan dragged two mugs down from the cupboard and fumbled with the buttons on the coffee maker. Empty beer cans littered the counter beside a bowl of blackened bananas.

"Did you take the photos?"

Ethan's shoulders stiffened. When he turned around, he glared at Deacon through bloodshot eyes. "Are you serious, dude? You think I'd take pictures of all the shit you've done?"

Ethan could be lying—he was an excellent liar. They all were. Lying had been bred into them since they were kids. But after a while, the lies got heavy. That was why Deacon made sure he was honest whenever possible.

"You were the only one with me." In the bars and the night clubs and the house parties. At Kensington or Harrow or some random town on assignment, they were almost always together.

The coffee maker beeped; Ethan swapped out the mugs

and pressed the buttons again. "Exactly. I was *with* you. Doing the same shit. If they have photos of you, they probably have photos of me too."

It was Deacon's turn to stiffen. "What do you mean 'they'?"

"Leadership. They're always watching. I've told you that a million times."

Deacon had never taken much notice of Ethan's conspiracy theories. He knew for a fact that Leadership had the means to track their mobiles. Did that mean they had access to information *on* their mobiles as well?

Shit. Had they seen the photos and videos he'd taken with Vivienne? Forget about the other girls, Deacon couldn't do anything about them. But there was no way he was going to stand for someone accessing private photos of his fiancée.

Ethan held a mug toward Deacon. He didn't really like coffee, but the lack of sleep was making his head spin. Or maybe it was the compounding sense of betrayal. Deacon dumped half of it into the sink, then added a bunch of creamer and two teaspoons of sugar.

His mother?

Peter?

Would they really do something like this to him?

Deacon couldn't rule out the possibility.

"Let's say you're right. They have photos of us. That means whoever's been sending Vivienne this shit must've gotten all the photos from the same place." Which meant it could be anyone in Neverland sending them to her. "But how would they have gotten pictures from mobiles not on our network?"

Ethan sipped his coffee slowly, his brow furrowed in concentration. "They'd have to know which girls to track, I suppose."

To know the girls, Leadership had to have *someone*

keeping an eye on Deacon. "And you're sure you didn't tell them?"

"Seriously?" Ethan slammed his mug on the counter. "I didn't tell them shit."

"If it wasn't you, then who was it?" No one else went out with them. It was always Ethan and Deacon and—

Shit.

Ethan's eyes locked with Deacon's. "You don't think . . . She wouldn't do that to you. No way."

There was no other explanation. There had only been one other person who had been out with them so often. "It had to be Nicola."

Nicola's house was a refurbished craftsman, painted gray-blue with white trim around the windows and doors. Ethan had tried convincing Deacon to let him come along. But bringing Ethan to his ex's house would almost definitely stir a whole lot of shit that he didn't need added to this disaster. The two of them weren't even on speaking terms after what had happened on the island. It was a wonder Nicola had bothered to show up for the trial in London.

When Nicola answered the door, something inside of Deacon died. It was only half past eight and she was already dressed and showered, her blond hair still damp around the roots.

They had been friends—or so he'd thought. And at one point, they had been more. Had any of it been real? "I need to speak with you."

"Okay?" She let him in, then shut the door. Compared to Ethan's house, Nicola's was immaculate. Which was no surprise. Ethan turned to alcohol when he was upset. Nicola cleaned.

Deacon hated that he knew that. He hated that he felt so close to her when she was nothing but a bloody spy.

"Do you want something to eat?" she asked, smoothing a hand over the folded decorative throw at the back of her sofa. "I was just getting ready to make some French toast."

"I'm not hungry." He wanted to get this over with, then go to the gym and run until his body shut down. And then he wanted to sleep.

She shrugged and went to the fridge for eggs. There was already a loaf of bread on the counter and a pan on the stovetop. "Well, I am. So you can just watch me eat."

He wouldn't be around long enough for that. "Why'd you do it, Nic?"

She cracked open an egg and added it to a bowl. "You already know why, Dash. Ethan screwed that fish. I know we weren't exclusive, but I couldn't handle his shit anymore." It looked like she was taking her frustration out on the egg as she beat it with a whisk. "And the drinking was getting out of control. I've tried to get him to see someone about it, but we all know how well that's worked out."

"I'm not talking about you and Ethan." They could work through their shite on their own time. "I want to know why you took the photos."

She froze. Then her head fell. "I was under orders."

Shit. Deacon had been right. He didn't want to be right. He didn't want Nicola to be the villain in this story. "How could you do that to me? To Vivienne?"

The whisk clattered to the counter. "*Me?*" she hissed, eyes flashing. "You think this is *my* fault? You know what? I'm not even surprised. You're just like Ethan. Never taking responsibility for your own mistakes. Always blaming someone else." She jabbed him in the shoulder, forcing him a step back against the counter. "Not this time, Dash. You did this to yourself. Every time you brought one of those girls to your house, you put our whole existence in jeopardy. Every single heart you broke was another liability."

"That's how you justify spying on me for the last eight years? Because I *deserved* it? Do you know how messed up that is? I thought we were friends. I *trusted* you."

Her lips lifted into a mocking smile. "That's the thing. I haven't had to spy on you at all. You did this right out in the open. Screwed girls in bathroom stalls. Brought them to your house so they knew where you lived. What if one of them was a psychopath who wanted to come find you? Who stalked you and got pictures of you flying home in the morning? Did you ever think about that?"

"*Psychopath stalker?*" Surely she saw the irony in that. "*You're* the psychopath stalker!"

"For the last time: I. Was. Following. *Orders.* All I did was take photos of you in the bars. You did the rest."

Broken hearts have consequences . . .

When Deacon's mother had said that, had she known about the photos? Had she *seen* them? "And the ones not in the bars?" The private ones from the bedroom. The thought of her spying on him in his own home made him feel like vomiting. Like he'd never known a moment of privacy in his entire life.

Nicola turned her back to him, withdrew a slice of bread, and dipped it in the egg. It sizzled when it hit the pan. "We had to steal their phones, Dash. They took pictures of you, and you didn't even know. If HOOK got hold of that kind of information, there's no telling what they'd do."

The smell of cinnamon filled the room.

Brilliant. His "friends" had been sneaking around, stealing phones from the women he'd slept with. *Bloody brilliant.* "What did you do with the photos?"

"They're in your file on the secured server," she said, flipping the toast.

A file already filled with complaints. No wonder Leadership didn't want Deacon marrying Vivienne. They were never going to give their approval.

This was worse than he could have imagined. But if it had just been his own privacy, he could have gotten over it. "How could you do this to Vivienne?" he asked, needing to know. "She's done nothing wrong."

"What are you talking about?" Nicola turned off the burner and transferred her breakfast to a plate. "I haven't done anything to Vivienne."

"You expect me to believe that you haven't been sending her pictures of me with other women? It's clear how you feel about me, but I'm not the person I used to be. I don't want her hurt because of what I've done. It has to stop." He'd beg if he had to. It wasn't as if he had any pride left to salvage.

"Hold on." She held up a hand. "You're telling me someone has been sending the photos to Vivienne?" The horror on Nicola's face seemed genuine. Bloody hell, this was a disaster.

If it wasn't her, then—"Who has access to personal files?"

"My dad, your mom . . . "

Shiiiit.

" . . . Peter, the higher-ups in Extraction, and Leadership, I suppose."

Leadership.

Gwen. Aoibheann. Alex.

It had to be one of them.

TWENTY-ONE

The pink sky beyond Deacon's bedroom window painted his bed in a soft, enchanting light.

When Deacon had called yesterday to explain what Nicola had done, Vivienne's heart had broken all over again. She understood that Nicola had been under orders, but there must have been some way around it. Nicola should have told Deacon what was going on, given him a chance to curb his actions, instead of spying on him for almost a decade.

Vivienne hadn't just been mad at Nicola, either. She'd been angry with Peter and the rest of Leadership too. How hard was it to have a freaking conversation?

Deacon wasn't innocent in this mess. It had been his carelessness that had gotten them into this situation in the first place. But surely he had deserved to know the consequences.

He'd been like a broken man when she'd gotten to his house, staring into the fireplace with a vacant expression on his face. It had taken an hour for him to give her more than one-word answers and broken apologies.

She had told him she loved him anyway. That despite it all, he *had* changed. On his own. Without threats or ultimatums. They had found their way to each other, and neither of them were letting go.

Paul had called later that afternoon to tell them he'd found the culprit.

It had been Aoibheann all along.

Vivienne wasn't surprised—the woman *had* tried to drown her a few months ago. Although, she didn't understand why. What had Aoibheann hoped to gain by sending those texts? Did she honestly think she would make them break up? Or had there been some other ulterior motive?

Deacon had wanted to call her and find out. Vivienne had begged him not to. What would be the point? It wouldn't help anything. She wanted to leave the whole ordeal in the past and move forward, even if that meant not having all the answers.

Deacon's fingers traced along Vivienne's bare hip, lighting her body on fire. Drawing her back to the present. A place she never wanted to leave.

"We should get married," he said, the heat from his breath sending shivers across her skin. She ran her fingers through his dark hair, loving the way it stuck up at the side in the morning.

"Is your memory faulty too?" she laughed. "You already asked me to marry you."

"I'm not talking about getting engaged." He caught her hand and kissed the gold band on her little finger. "Let's find a preacher or priest or rabbi or, hell, a captain of a ship, and get married."

Yes. She wanted this. Wanted him. Still . . . "We don't have permission."

He rolled off of her and settled himself onto his pillow, leaving her cold and aching. "Here's the thing, lovie," he said, walking his fingers from her navel to her breastbone, "I don't give a shit what they have to say anymore. I followed their procedures and asked—multiple times. It's not my fault they keep giving us the wrong answer." He curled his finger under her bra and slid it to the strap. "Actually, it *is* my fault." A grin. "But if you're ready, so am I."

He retraced his steps, only instead of his fingers, he used his lips.

"We're just going to get married in secret?" The idea was almost as appealing as what he was doing with his mouth.

"Why not?" he murmured.

Deacon was right. Why not? "Okay. Let's do it. Let's get married."

He glanced at her from beneath his dark lashes, his beautiful eyes glittering when he smiled. "When? Right now?"

"You need to give me at least a day to get my affairs in order."

"Affairs? You're not dying," he snorted.

"You know what I mean. First, we need to figure out if it's even possible. And I need to find a dress and get a dress for Emily and—" When she went to roll off the bed, his grip on her hips tightened.

"Where do you think you're going?" He pinned her to the mattress. "I'm not finished with you yet."

It was another hour before Deacon let Vivienne out of bed. And she hadn't protested. Those quiet, intimate moments together made up some of her favorite memories. The ones she would miss the most.

But she refused to think about that now. Today was for happy thoughts.

When Vivienne got back to her apartment, Emily was doing yoga in the living room.

"Hey, girl. Wanna join me?" Emily asked, reaching

toward her toes before dipping down into chaturanga. "I just started."

"Can't. Busy. Gotta get married in two days."

Holy. Crap.

Vivienne was getting married.

"What, what, what is this now?" Emily fell over in her rush to grab the remote for the TV. The instructor on the video froze in the middle of upward dog. "You're getting married? *In two days?*"

Vivienne smiled so wide her face hurt. "Sure am."

The idea of being married to Deacon forever made her stomach feel warm and fluttery. Not from nerves but from fireflies. After the photos, she wasn't sure they would ever return.

"*Yesssss!*" Emily fist-pumped the air and kicked her feet. "This is so *aaaamazing!* My best friend is getting married!" She jumped up, and Vivienne found herself body-slammed into the couch.

"Uh, Em?" Vivienne grunted.

"Sorry." Emily laughed and rolled off of her. "I can't believe this is happening. I always knew you guys were meant to be together. I called it from the beginning, didn't I?"

"You sure did." Emily had said they were going to get married on Vivienne and Deacon's first date. When was that? A year ago? So much had happened, it felt like a lifetime.

"I have a question to ask you," Vivienne began.

Emily's breathing hitched, and she grabbed Vivienne's arm. "*Yes.*"

"You don't even know what I was going to say."

"Doesn't matter." Emily's curly ponytail swished from side to side when she shook her head. "For you, the answer is always yes."

"So you do think I should ask Lyle to be my Man of

Honor? It's unconventional, but I figured he'd love to stand beside me."

Emily's expression went from excited to disappointed in a blink. "*Lyle*? Really?"

"Of course not," Vivienne snorted. "That's your job. If you want it?"

"You were this close to a slap," Emily said after her squealing stopped. "What am I going to wear?" Her eyes widened and she grabbed Vivienne by the shoulders. "What are *you* going to wear?"

"I have an idea, but I may need your help." Vivienne brought Emily to her bedroom and—*holy crap* did it need cleaned. Vivienne added that and laundry to her growing to-do-before-I-get-married-to-the-sexiest-man-alive checklist. She stepped over her discarded shoes and reached into the back of her closet. The long, white garment bag was right where she'd left it. When she unzipped it, Emily gasped.

"Where'd you get this?" Emily ran her fingers down the simple ivory silk bodice. "It's stunning."

"It was my mom's." Vivienne had collected it from the Kensington Records Keeper last year. "I'm not sure if it'll fit though." She had lost a lot of weight recently. She hadn't really noticed until she got back from London and tried on the clothes in her closet. None of them fit her anymore.

"I'm on it." Emily took the dress off the hanger and started for the door. "Meet me in my room in five minutes."

"Why?"

"Because we're going to plan your dream wedding."

Vivienne picked up all her dirty laundry, stuffed it into the hamper, and dragged it into the hall closet where the washer and dryer were hidden. After starting a load, she made her way into Emily's bedroom.

Emily was sitting at her desk, a notebook and cup of colorful pens at the ready and her laptop open. "Have a seat." She gestured toward the bed.

The quilt with tiny pink roses looked new. Which was no surprise. Emily changed her décor almost as often as she changed her outfits. Vivienne sank onto the bed and propped herself up against the piles of pillows in lacy pillowcases. Emily shoved a pint of ice cream and spoon into her hand.

"I've texted Clinton. He'll be over tonight at eight to take-in or up or out whatever you need for your dress."

"That was fast."

"I said I was on it, didn't I?" Emily selected a pink pen from the cup and clicked the top. "Okay, describe your dream wedding."

"I've never really thought about it," Vivienne confessed, freeing a gigantic piece of cookie dough from the center of the ice cream.

"You're joking, right?"

Vivienne shook her head. "Why? Have you?"

"Girl, I've been working on my wedding Pinterest board since I was fourteen." To prove her point, Emily turned the laptop screen so that Vivienne could see it. The board was called, *"When someone finally realizes how awesome I am."*

The title made Vivienne laugh.

"Come on. Give me something." Emily clicked her pen again. "What about a color scheme or theme?"

A wedding had always seemed like something that was so far in Vivienne's future that it wasn't worth thinking about. "I don't care about any of that stuff."

"Okay, then . . . " Emily set the pen down, hopped off the chair, and slid the closet door aside. "Why don't you pick out one of these dresses for me to wear."

There were five floor-length gowns hanging inside, all of them gorgeous. Vivienne scooped another spoonful of ice cream. A massive chocolate chip crunched between her teeth. "Which one do you like the best?"

"Which one do *you* like the best?" Emily countered with a groan.

Blush pink. Maroon. Royal Blue. Navy. Or black.

Eeny, meenie, miny moe . . .

"Since it's winter, why don't we go with one of the deeper ones?" Emily suggested, unhooking the maroon and navy dresses and laying them on the bed beside Vivienne.

"Sounds good to me."

Emily crossed her arms and tapped a red nail against her chin. "What do you want Deacon to wear?"

"I don't care as long as he shows up." Some small part of her kept waiting for him to freak out about how fast things were moving. But he still seemed calm.

Emily dropped onto the chair with a dramatic sigh. "I feel like you need higher standards."

"It's the truth," Vivienne told her, setting the ice cream container aside so she could warm her hands under her thighs. "None of the details matter to me. I'd like to wear my mom's dress if we can get it to fit. And I want Deacon, you, Lyle, and Ethan there."

Emily grabbed the ice cream and her own spoon and took a bite. "What if this was a perfect world and you could have anything you wanted? What if Leadership approved your marriage and you didn't have to have a wedding in secret? *Then* what would you want?"

Vivienne thought about it for a moment. What if . . .

"I guess I would have liked to get married at the chapel on campus." The courthouse was going to be great, but the chapel would have been better. Plus, those stained glass windows would've made for some pretty gorgeous photos.

"Keep going," Emily urged, handing back the ice cream in favor of her pink pen.

"I would have had the reception at The Glass House. And decorated it like it was at Thanksgiving, with all the lights and stuff. But no Christmas tree, obviously."

"Obviously," Emily agreed with a roll of her eyes.

The more Vivienne thought, the more ideas she had. She would have loved to have a string quartet playing instead of a Bluetooth speaker connected to someone's phone. And, it sounded dumb, but she had always loved ice sculptures. She wasn't sure why. They were just so fancy, and marrying Peter Pan's grandson seemed like it should have been a fancy occasion.

"And in a perfect world, Deacon's mom and Peter would be there." They were his only family, and she was worried that he would regret not inviting them. He had told her he didn't care, but that could have been the lingering betrayal talking.

"See! I knew you'd thought about it." Emily stopped writing long enough to steal another bite of ice cream.

Vivienne was sorry that she hadn't thought about it a little more. Still, in the grand scheme of things, the wedding didn't matter nearly as much as the marriage.

"What about you?" Vivienne asked, scraping her spoon around the softened edges. "Tell me about your dream wedding."

"Oh, girl." Emily laughed. "Get comfortable. This is gonna take a while."

TWENTY-TWO

The next morning was cold but clear, with sunlight glistening off the frost. Emily woke Vivienne early, shoved a cup of coffee and a granola bar into her hands, and prodded her into the bathroom for a shower. After she got ready, they went on a shopping spree that left Vivienne's head pounding by noon. They ordered flowers and bought hair products and makeup and a garter and sexy underthings that didn't look comfortable at all. They stored it all at Deacon's house—he'd offered to let them stay there for the night. Which was ideal since traipsing across campus in her wedding dress wasn't an option.

He was going to sleep over at Ethan's with Lyle. Ethan wasn't impressed about the lack of bachelor party, but he was thrilled about being a groomsman. Deacon had asked Lyle as well. They still weren't friends, but they seemed to have come to an understanding. That night, Vivienne and Emily stayed awake way too late, giggling and gushing and gorging on more ice cream.

"How mad would Deacon be if I told him you had to keep living with me?" Emily asked the morning of the wedding, wrapping a section of Vivienne's hair around her wide-barrel curling wand. The sink in the guest bathroom was littered with makeup, brushes, and bobby pins.

"He'd probably burn the apartment down so I didn't have a choice." The idea made her chuckle. Giving up her own space felt a little scary, but she was ready to start this next chapter with a partner.

"Ugh." Emily gave her an exaggerated pout in the mirror. "*Fiiiine*. But you can come over whenever you want. I mean it. My home will always be your home, and no stupid boy is going to change that."

Vivienne offered a watery "Thanks," and Emily yelled at her for screwing up her makeup.

Lyle arrived just as Emily was giving Vivienne's hair one final spritz with the hairspray. Emily promised the curls hanging over Vivienne's shoulders would fall, but it felt like her hair was never going to move again.

"Holy shit, Viv." Lyle slid a finger beneath the collar of his white dress shirt. At Emily's "request," he'd shaved and gotten a haircut. "You look beautiful."

"You don't look so bad either." Emily had gone back to the mall last night and "requested" he buy a navy three-piece suit.

"Em, you look like shit," Lyle said with a grin. "I hate your sexy dress, and your beautiful curly hair is so ugly."

Emily punched him in the arm, which earned her a peck on the cheek.

"Did you remember the flowers, jerk-face?" Emily asked, her face turning the same shade of deep red as her floor-length gown. "Because if you forgot, I'm going to kill you."

"Relax, witch. They're in the car."

Last month, Emily had told Lyle that she got bored with guys when they were too nice. So, Lyle wasn't nice. And Lyle had told Emily that he hated clingy girls, so the only time Emily seemed to touch him—at least in public—was to smack him. Their relationship was so weird—borderline dysfunctional. But they were laughing constantly, so Vivienne figured it was working for them.

"You girls want to head over, or am I driving a getaway car?" Lyle rubbed his hands together like a cartoon villain.

The only thing Vivienne wanted to escape from was inevitable, so she forced a smile and told Lyle she was ready.

Because she was.

So, *so* ready.

On the way to the courthouse, Vivienne committed everything to memory. The smell of Lyle's leather seats. The way Lyle kept stealing glances at Emily when she wasn't paying attention. The sunlight streaming through the glass and glistening off the freshly fallen snow. The softness of the petals in her bouquet of blush-colored roses. Even the fireflies buzzing around in her stomach.

When they reached the parking lot, Ethan was there waiting for them, his hands stuffed into his suit pockets. "Everything's ready," he said, helping Vivienne from the back seat and giving her a hug. "You look great, by the way."

"Thanks." Her cheeks flushed as she nodded toward the building. "Did he show up?"

Ethan snorted. "He's been here since they opened the doors."

Emily gathered the train on Vivienne's dress and lifted it so it didn't get dirty. Cold air slid up her legs, making her shiver. "Hey, Emily?" she said when they reached the top of the steps. Ethan and Lyle were holding the doors open for them. Beyond was a dark hallway filled with people bustling around. "Can you do me a favor?"

Emily gave her shoulder a reassuring squeeze. "Anything."

"Will you get this on video? I don't want to forget it."

Deacon's smile faltered as he waited for Vivienne in front of a thick mahogany desk. What if she changed her mind? He checked his mobile; there were no messages. Surely she would have told him if she didn't want to go through with it.

A moment later, there were voices outside in the hall—voices he recognized. And the nerves in his stomach calmed. Vivienne was snapping at Lyle for stepping on her dress, which made him chuckle. When the doors opened, there was music playing on what he assumed was Lyle's mobile.

Emily had threatened all of them that morning. Lyle was in charge of music. Ethan was in charge of the food afterward. And Deacon was in charge of showing up and making her best friend eternally happy. And if they didn't do as they were told, they'd have to face Emily's wrath. Deacon was glad Vivienne had such a bloodthirsty best friend looking out for her.

Emily and Ethan walked arm in arm past the three rows of hideous office chairs, stopping in the middle to snap a selfie. When they got to the front, Emily split off to the right, phone in hand and directed at the stunning creature in white waiting in the doorway.

That smile. Deacon silently vowed to keep it on those lips.

Those eyes. The only tears he wanted to see in them were tears of joy.

The only regret he had was that they had to get married in a courthouse. Not for him—he didn't give a toss one way or another. All that mattered to him was the woman gliding down the aisle.

But for Vivienne . . . He wished he could give her everything she'd ever dreamed of for her wedding day.

He'd have to give her everything from this day on.

Vivienne stopped when she reached him and took his hand. "You aren't going to fly away on me, are you?"

As if that was even an option. He was hers as much as she was his. "I'm not going anywhere."

A grin. "Good answer."

It wasn't the most romantic ceremony. There was a lot of paperwork and legal stuff they needed to get out of the way. But then the judge, a bald man with deep smile lines, said it was time for the vows.

Deacon took Vivienne's hands in his and smiled down at her. "Vivienne, I—"

The door burst open, slamming against the wall, rattling the plaques hanging there. Who the hell was—

Shit.

What was his grandad doing there?

From the irate expression on his red face, it was obvious this wasn't going to end well.

"*Everyone. Out!*" Peter roared, throwing a hand toward the closing doors.

Peter may have been in charge in Neverland, but they weren't *in* Neverland. "Don't listen to him," Deacon countered, turning to apologize to the wide-eyed judge. "Please, continue."

Peter stomped to where Ethan and Lyle blocked the aisle. When the two didn't move, he hopped on top of a chair and climbed over it. "This wedding cannot proceed."

Deacon loved his grandad, but at the moment, he really, really wanted to hit him. "Why the hell not?"

"You know why the hell not."

Was he referring to Leadership? After what they'd done, they no longer had a say in his relationship.

Without turning around, Peter told Emily, Lyle, and Ethan to get back to campus.

"Sir, you need to leave before I call security." The judge stood from his desk and planted his hands on either side of the unsigned marriage certificate.

Muttering under his breath, Peter pulled his wallet from his back pocket. "I'll give you a thousand dollars for five minutes alone with the bride and groom."

The judge's eyes widened, but he took the wad of cash and swept out of the room in a flurry of black robes.

"I'm so sorry," Emily said with a pained wince. "I had to."

Had to what? Deacon looked between Emily and Peter. Was this *her* fault?

Lyle threw them a worried look before linking his arm with Emily's and following Ethan out the door.

Vivienne's eyes were wide, and she looked like she was going to burst into tears. *Dammit.* If Peter made his wife cry on their wedding day, Deacon was going to hit him.

"We're getting married, Grandad."

"No, you're not."

"With all due respect, Leadership no longer has a say in this relationship." Leadership didn't have a say in his life now that he knew what they'd done. A small part of him understood. Every casual encounter he'd had was a liability. And he'd had *a lot* of liabilities. But why did they need to keep a bloody file on him? Those photos and videos should have been deleted the moment they were acquired.

After stuffing his wallet back into his pocket, Peter shoved a hand through his hair. "I cast the tie-breaking vote the moment I caught wind of this hair-brained plan of yours."

"Then why are you stopping us?"

"Really, Deacon?" Peter's eyes flared with anger. "You

can't think of *one reason* why I'd stop you from getting married in secret?"

Deacon shook his head. If they had permission, there shouldn't be an issue.

Peter cursed and pinched the bridge of his nose. "How do you think your mother is going to feel when she finds out her only son got married without telling her?"

Shit.

His mother.

Deacon had thought about inviting her, but figured that would put her in an awkward position between him and Leadership.

"She will never forgive you," Peter went on, propping his fists on his hips. "A wedding isn't meant to be a secretive, shameful event. It's meant to be shared with the ones you love."

Vivienne reached for Deacon's hand and squeezed. "He's right, you know."

The love shining in her rich brown eyes kept Deacon from snapping.

"If you insist on disregarding all the advice and orders you've been given, at least do it in the open. And for the love of all that is holy," Peter groaned, rolling his eyes heavenward, "invite your mother."

TWENTY-THREE

oly. Shit.

H Deacon was married.

This was no longer his girlfriend sitting in the car beside him messing with the heating. Or his fiancée. Vivienne was his wife.

Shit.

Deacon had a wife.

And he'd married her stone-cold sober.

By *choice*.

Even at the reception, he'd had only one glass of champagne for the ridiculous toasts Ethan insisted on giving. Vivienne had done the same. They both wanted to remember everything.

Peter had allowed Joel to record the ceremony at the chapel on campus and the good bits from the reception at The Glass House. The space had been covered in so many Christmas lights, it had lit up like a beacon. And there had even been an ice sculpture in the shape of a rooster. Deacon had no clue what it was all about, but when Vivienne had seen it, she had tackled Emily in a ferocious hug.

Emily had been snap-happy with her mobile the entire day. Deacon's face hurt from all the smiling. Although he wasn't a big fan of seeing photos of himself, he hadn't complained.

The photos and videos would have to stay locked up in Records, but that was a minor detail Deacon could always conveniently forget.

Vivienne wore the same dress from their almost-wedding a week earlier. Deacon's irritation at the unwelcome interruption had subsided the moment he'd seen his mother's face. Besides, the whole disaster made for a pretty good story. What was one more bout of drama in their lives?

He pulled into his driveway and turned off the ignition. Vivienne reached for the handle, but he told her not to move. Before she could protest, he jumped out of the car and ran to the front door. After unlocking it and leaving it open, he jogged back to where Vivienne waited, a wide smile on her lips.

"Welcome home, wife," he said, sweeping her into his arms. She felt too light and frail, but he couldn't focus on that right now. Tomorrow he could worry. Today was about joy.

He carried her over the threshold and kicked the door closed behind them.

"Oh, I see how it is," Vivienne giggled against his shirt as he headed straight for the stairs. "You're not even going to pretend like you want to make small talk first."

They'd been making small talk all day with everyone. What more was there to say?

"Lucky for you, I can multitask. How did you like the cake?"

She nestled her head beneath his chin and sighed. "It was delicious."

"Agreed. Best cake I've ever had."

Vivienne had said she didn't care what kind of cake they got as long as it was big. Deacon had always loved almond, so he chose the amaretto one. And they'd ordered the biggest one the bakery had ever made. They'd be eating cake for weeks.

"And the company was all right as well." He reached the landing at the top and pushed aside the bedroom door.

"It was the best company."

Vivienne had said she preferred to keep things small, not wanting to be the focal point in front of a big crowd. And he'd heartily agreed. The only ones at the ceremony were himself and Vivienne, his mother and Peter, Ethan, Max, Lyle, and Emily.

When they left Kensington, every person on campus— and a few from Harrow as well—were lined up along both sides of the drive holding sparklers and shouting well-wishes.

"Shall we discuss the dinner, or Emily's dress, or Ethan's toasts, or do I have your permission to cease small talk and commence ravishing?"

Another giggle. "You may commence ravishing, husband."

Holy. Shit.

Deacon was a husband.

He set Vivienne on the carpet beside the bed and kicked his shoes into the corner. A husband had husbandly duties to perform. Duties he'd been looking forward to all day.

Slipping out of her silver shoes, Vivienne nodded toward something behind him, her brow furrowed. "Did you get a new bed?"

Deacon had forgotten all about the bed. It wasn't exactly what he wanted to bring up on their wedding night, but since she'd asked, he didn't see any way around it.

"I . . . um . . . I wanted to have a bed that was just ours."

It didn't feel right sharing something with his wife that he had shared with others.

When Vivienne smiled, the tension in his stomach eased. "It's perfect. I love it."

"I was hoping you would." It was a bit feminine, but Emily had assured him the tufted gray headboard was classy. Deacon didn't give a toss so long as Vivienne was happy. "Is there anything else you'd like to discuss?" he asked, trying his hardest to keep his gaze from drifting toward her chest. "I bought a new set of sheets as well, and that lamp." He gestured to the bulbous lamp Emily had insisted he purchase because it went with the bed.

"It's a nice lamp."

"Is it?" Deacon couldn't remember what color it was at present. "I'm a little busy ogling my wife to notice."

Vivienne's grin remained as she gathered her dark hair and shifted the waves over her shoulder. "Would you like to discuss getting me out of this dress?"

Yes. Yes. YES.

She turned around and—

No. No. *Noooo.*

From her neck to her ass, there had to be at least a hundred buttons. And they weren't normal buttons. They were teeny tiny and slippery as all hell, held in place by loops of invisible thread. What kind of sadist put this many buttons on something that was supposed to come off?

"Deacon? You okay back there?"

"Why are there so many bloody buttons?" And why were his fingers so fat and bumbling? He tried—and failed—to release the first one. "How cross would you be if I ripped—"

"Don't you dare!" she squealed, jumping out of his reach and whirling around with narrowed eyes. "This is my mother's wedding dress. You're not going to ruin it."

"All right," he groaned, pulling her back by the wrist.

He could just lift her skirts and—

What was he thinking? This wasn't some nightclub bathroom stall.

This was their wedding night.

Deacon could be patient. He could do this.

One button. At. A. Time.

He kissed every inch of skin as he worked his way down until finally, FINALLY, he got to the last button, and the infernal garment of silk and lace slipped to the carpet with a sigh, and his wife was standing in front of him in a wispy lace contraption that looked even more complicated to remove than the buttoned garment from hell.

"Do you like it?" she asked, folding her arms across her chest.

"I do." Deacon tugged at her hands so that they couldn't cover her up. He hated that she still didn't feel comfortable with him, but figured that would come with time. "I like what's beneath even better."

Off. Off. *Off.*

All of it had to come off.

Except the garter.

She should definitely leave that on.

The moment his hand connected with the straps, Vivienne stopped him. "Are you just leaving your clothes on or what?"

His clothes? He'd forgotten what he was wearing.

Oh, right. A navy blue suit Emily had thrown at him the day before the first wedding.

Jacket: off.

Waistcoat: off.

More bloody buttons on his shirt . . . *aaaaaand* OFF.

Belt and trousers: off.

Vivienne's cold fingers trailed from his chest to the waistband on his pants, but it was his turn to stop her. There was no need to rush the rest.

"Get on the bed, wife."

She bounced onto the mattress. "I didn't realize getting married would make you so demanding."

"I'm demanding, am I?" Was that a good thing or a bad thing?

"*Sooooo* demanding."

When she laughed, he had his answer. He climbed onto the bed after her, kneeling between her knees. "And if I told you to lift your hips so I could take off your knickers, would that be demanding?"

Vivienne's smile was so beautiful, so carefree, it made his chest tighten. The way her dark hair spread across the white pillows made it look like she was floating in the air. "Not if you said please."

"Please."

"That's a good husband." She gave him a pat on the head before bracing herself on her heels and allowing him to slip the thin scrap of lace down her thighs to her ankles and off off *off*.

Deacon grazed his lips up her thigh, snapping the garter with his teeth on his way up up up and—"I should probably stop now. I don't want to be too demanding."

"If you stop, I swear I'm going to divorce you in the morning."

He muttered, "Demanding wife," before doing as he was told.

He didn't stop until her legs were shaking and it felt like she was going to rip his hair from his head, and she tensed, then relaxed with a sigh. Then it was his turn.

He kissed his way up to her neck as she ground her hips against him.

She felt so damn good, and he was on fire and—

Shit. He wasn't going to last very long.

He needed to focus on something else besides the way her body felt slipping against his chest or her thighs gripping his hips as he moved, bringing him back to her every time and . . .

He was better than this. *Limerick. Tipperary. Waterford. Wexford.*

Hiding her face in his neck, Vivienne whispered, "You feel so good."

And that was it.

This woman, who took a chance on him even though he'd done nothing to deserve her, was his undoing. He knew people thought they wouldn't last together, but they were going to prove everyone wrong.

Even if he had to move to Scotland and introduce himself every single day for the rest of his life, make her fall in love with him again and again, he would do it.

Vivienne was his purpose, his love, his life.

Vivienne was his wife.

TWENTY-FOUR

V ivienne's legs were going numb from crouching on the hotel roof. She shifted her position, dropping a knee onto the gritty concrete. There was no way anyone could see them up this high late at night, but she wasn't taking any chances.

"Let me get this straight," Vivienne whispered, pulling the black backpack she'd been assigned closer. "You want us to stretch this stuff across the gaps the entire way along the street?"

The strands glistening from inside the backpack looked like a bunch of string. Deacon had assured her it was biodegradable, not harmful to animals, and dissolved in water. And since it was supposed to rain in the morning, no outsiders would get hurt trying to remove the thousands of feet of silver whatever-it-was. Apparently, someone had accidentally created it in the lab, and they had been about to throw it out.

One PAN's trash was another PAN's prank.

"I want us to weave it." Deacon's grin was a flash of white in the darkness. "Like a giant spiderweb."

"Like a spiderweb," Vivienne repeated. Spiders. *Gross.* Shivers crept down her spine.

"Yeah. A spiderweb," Ethan said, making his hand "crawl" toward Emily.

"Can we stop talking about spiderwebs and get this over with?" Emily smacked Ethan away and tucked her hands beneath her arms. "I'm freezing and I want to go home."

"Stop whining," Ethan shot back, handing her a backpack of not-string. "You're the one who said you wanted an invite the next time we were playing a prank."

"That was on the island. Where it was warm. And I was hungover, so I obviously wasn't thinking straight."

"You didn't have to come." Ethan slung one bag across his back and a second over his front.

"Stop it, you two." Vivienne shoved her black mask toward her hairline. The stupid thing was so itchy she wanted to rip it off, but there was no way she was going to get caught without one after the whole HOOK debacle. "Let's get this done so we can get back home." When Deacon had said they were playing a prank, she hadn't realized how stressed out she'd be. Her skin was itchy and tingly, adrenaline pumping through her veins, and they hadn't even done anything yet.

Ethan and Emily took off toward the other end of the street. They were to work in pairs, crisscrossing and weaving from one side to the other until they met in the middle.

Vivienne went to pick up her bag, but Deacon nudged it aside with his toe. "I thought they'd never leave." He slipped his cold hands beneath her shirt and drew her in for a soft, teasing kiss. "You know what I think we should do first?"

She figured he was thinking the same thing he was always thinking. "No, what?"

"We should probably see if there are any birds up here."

"We can't go birdwatching on every rooftop we visit."

Deacon's lips turned down into the sexiest frown. "Why not?"

She couldn't think of a reason, so she gripped him by the back of the neck and dragged his mouth to hers.

"*Soooo* is that a yes?" he asked when she let him go.

She gave him a flirtatious smile. "Hurry up. I don't want our friends getting suspicious."

He had her back against the rooftop access wall before the words were out of her mouth. She couldn't get enough of him. She loved the way he felt moving inside of her. The way he made her feel like the most irresistible woman who had ever existed. When he shuddered and whispered that he loved her, she smiled against his neck.

Being Mrs. Ashford was awesome.

After some adjustments to their wardrobe, Vivienne collected the backpack. "How are we going to do this?" she asked, pulling her mask back down to cover her face.

"Let's start at that gray building over there." Throwing his own backpack over his shoulder, Deacon turned to her and grinned. "Last one finished has to do the dishes for a week."

Vivienne *hated* doing the dishes. "You're on."

"On your mark . . . get set . . . " He swatted her butt and took off running.

"You're such a cheater!" she hissed, taking off after him.

His laughter lifted into the darkness as he dove over the edge. Vivienne's adrenaline stirred to life, and she had so many happy thoughts in her head that she didn't need to focus on one. But as she vaulted off the roof, the fire electrifying her veins was more of a hum than an explosion.

And instead of flying . . .

Vivienne fell.

A scream of terror pierced the night.

Deacon jerked around and—

Shit. Vivienne was plummeting toward the empty street.

He changed directions as quickly as he could. Panic choked the air from his lungs. He reached toward her, grabbing for her outstretched hand. Her fingers slipped through.

They were almost to the ground.

He lunged, stretching against the stiffness in his shoulder, cursing and praying until he clasped a hand around Vivienne's wrist.

Another bloodcurdling scream ripped from Vivienne's throat when her arm snapped taut. A split second later, they slammed into the ground. If he hadn't broken a rib, he'd sure as hell bruised one. If he breathed too deeply, it hurt like someone was jamming a knife into his lung.

Then Vivienne moaned, and he forgot all about his own pain.

"Are you all right?" he croaked, cradling his wife in his lap and throwing her mask onto the ground. Her face beneath was covered in a layer of sweat. "What happened?"

"I don't know," she gasped between tears. He shifted her weight and her hand flew to her right shoulder. "My arm's killing me."

Ethan and Emily landed, eyes bulging beneath their masks. "What happened?" Ethan dropped to his knee beside them and shoved his mask to his hairline. "We heard screaming."

"She fell."

"Did you forget how to fly?" Emily asked, her voice shaking as she knelt beside Vivienne.

Vivienne shook her head. "No. It just didn't work."

It didn't work? What did that mean? Flying should have been ingrained for her by now.

Deacon couldn't focus on the why. He needed to help his wife. Touching the top of her shoulder, Deacon cursed when he felt a tell-tale bump. "I think it's dislocated. You need to go to the hospital."

"No. No hospital. Take me home."

"Vivienne—"

"The fire wasn't there, Deacon. Bring me home and call Dr. Carey. We need to figure out"—she winced—"why this happened."

"Will you make it? It's two hours." What had he been thinking, bringing Vivienne to do something so stupid? She had begged to come along, but he should have told her no. Hell, he should have turned Ethan down when he had suggested it.

Tears streamed down Vivienne's cheeks even as she promised she was fine. Deacon knew she was lying, but she was right; they needed to speak to Dr. Carey.

He flew home with Vivienne trembling in his arms. At one point, she fell asleep. She needed rest. But what if she had hit her head when they landed and he hadn't noticed? What if she had a concussion and never woke up again?

"Vivienne? I need you to stay with me, lovie."

"It hurts too bad," she whimpered, fresh tears rolling from between her closed lashes.

Dammit. He knew they should have gone straight to the hospital. They could have called Dr. Carey after her shoulder was fixed. "I know it does. I know. But I'm bored and need someone to talk to."

That brought a pained smile to her lips. "You're such a baby."

"Do you remember last Halloween, when you were dressed as a fairy?"

"I was a witch, Deacon."

Brilliant. She remembered.

"Were you?" He pretended to think about it. "Oh, that's

right. You *were* a witch. And for some unknown reason, you covered your beautiful face with green paint." He had been so angry with Nicola and Ethan for making them late. The moment he'd stepped out of that car and seen Vivienne, he'd forgotten everything else. "I wanted to kiss you so badly, but didn't think a mouth of green paint went with my costume."

Her laugh was a puff of warm air against his neck. "When you told me that, I thought of washing it off with puddle water."

"It's probably best you didn't. If I had started kissing you, I wouldn't have wanted to stop."

Deacon had wasted so much time with her. Was the inability to fly a side effect of her condition? He knew the forgetful in Scotland were on meds to decrease adrenaline and keep them grounded. But what if that was just a precaution? *Dammit.* He should have told her to start treatment the moment they returned to Kensington. But he hadn't wanted her hanging around Alex, so he hadn't pushed when she said she wanted to enjoy the holidays and wait until January. And with all the harassment and the almost-wedding, then the actual wedding and the honeymoon—

Excuses. All of them. Deacon had failed her, simple as that.

He pressed the button in his ear, and TINK's cheerful voice cut through the night. "Hello, *Deacon.*"

"TINK, I need you to call Dr. Carey for me."

"Calling . . . *Hilary Carey.*"

Vivienne whimpered, and Deacon apologized again for hurting her.

"This is Dr. Carey."

"Hey, Dr. Blue Eyes."

"Deacon Elias Ashford." There was a smile in the young doctor's sleepy greeting. "To what do I owe the unexpected pleasure at four o'clock in the morning?"

"I need you to come to my house right away."

Silence. "You didn't get shot again, did you?"

A chuckle forced its way through his lips. "It's not me this time. It's Vivienne."

"Someone shot Vivienne?" Dr. Carey gasped. A drawer slammed on her end of the line.

"Thankfully, no. But I'm afraid she may have dislocated her shoulder."

"Bring her to the ER."

"I wanted to, but she refused. We need someone who understands our situation." The trees surrounding his back garden came into view. Dr. Carey told him she'd be there in ten minutes and ended the call.

"She's on her way," he assured Vivienne. Her eyes were closed, and her lips were as pale as her cheeks. "You'll be feeling right as rain in no time."

Deacon managed to get her into the house and up to their room without jostling her too much. He was convinced she was asleep until she started groaning. "I think I'm going to be sick."

Being in that much pain, it was a wonder she hadn't gotten sick sooner.

Deacon guided her to the en-suite. She eased herself onto her knees in front of the toilet and told him to get out.

Like that was going to happen.

He grabbed a hair tie from a basket on the sink and gathered her hair into a terrible ponytail.

Instead of protesting, she emptied the contents of her stomach.

He found a clean cloth from beneath the sink and wetted it before handing it to her. Then he ran downstairs to collect a bottle of water and a can of soda from the fridge in case she wanted to rinse her mouth out with something flavored.

"Are you finished?" he asked from the doorway, placing a tentative hand on his sore ribs. She was trembling and so bloody green when she nodded.

By the time he had her settled in their bed again, there was a knock at the front door.

Instead of leaving Vivienne, he threw open the window. "It's unlocked," he called down to where Dr. Carey waited on the stoop. "Come straight up. It's the last door on the left."

Vivienne waved weakly from the bed when the doctor came in, her wild red hair collected in the usual clip on top of her head. "Hey, Hilary."

"How're you feeling?" Dr. Carey asked, setting a black bag on the bedside locker.

"Not so great."

"I can see that. Want to tell me what happened?" She rubbed her hands together before reaching for Vivienne's shoulder.

Deacon gave her a quick rundown of events. If he had been a second later, Vivienne would have—No, he couldn't think about that. "I caught her, but the force of it damaged her shoulder."

"You were right. It's dislocated," Dr. Carey said with a frown.

"What does that mean?" Vivienne asked, wincing when Dr. Carey touched her again.

"It means we need to put it back where it belongs." She rolled up the sleeves on her white shirt and instructed Vivienne on how she needed to set her shoulder. Deacon offered his hand for her to hold, but closed his eyes against his wife's scream.

After a sickening crack, Dr. Carey said simply, "All done."

"What now?" He sank onto the bed and cradled Vivienne against his chest. Should she be shaking so badly? It felt like she was vibrating against him.

Withdrawing an orange pill bottle from her bag, Dr. Carey explained that Vivienne was to take two pills three times a day—with food—to help with the pain and bring down inflammation. "She'll need to wear this sling for a few weeks," she added, withdrawing a navy sling like the one Deacon had worn in autumn. "I'll be back to check on her tomorrow, but you can call me sooner if you need me."

Deacon thanked her but knew their problems didn't end there. When would things stop going wrong? "We need to figure out why she fell."

Dr. Carey frowned as she nodded. "Has anything like this ever happened before?" she asked Vivienne.

"Not since I graduated from Aviation."

Deacon thought of the time he'd rushed her final exam—and had nearly killed her. "Did you feel any difference when you took off? An inkling that things weren't right?"

"I had plenty of adrenaline after we . . . um . . . " Vivienne blushed and bit her lip. Deacon tried to hide his smile in her hair when Dr. Carey's eyes narrowed on him.

"Let's just say I had a lot of it," Vivienne rushed, her color still high. "And happy thoughts weren't a problem either. The fire was there when I jumped, but it wasn't as . . . big? I don't know how else to explain it."

"Have you been feeling unwell at all lately?" Dr. Carey asked, tapping her finger against her chin.

"Just a bit lightheaded this last week or so."

"I'll check your blood pressure, just to be on the safe side." Dr. Carey rummaged around in her black bag for the monitor. When she found it, she undid the Velcro and slid the cuff over Vivienne's arm. Was it just him or did her arm look a lot thinner? The thing beeped and made a quiet hissing sound as the air released

Dr. Carey hummed as she stared down at the screen. It didn't sound like a positive hum.

"What's wrong?" Deacon read the numbers as though he knew what they meant.

"It's quite low. Are you sure you've been feeling okay,

Vivienne?" Dr. Carey removed the cuff and replaced it in her bag.

"I've felt fine."

Fine fine fine. Vivienne *wasn't* fine. It was so bloody obvious. Why did she insist on lying? "That's not true. You got sick right before Dr. Carey arrived."

Vivienne dismissed his concern with a wave. "That was because of the pain."

"Maybe not." Dr. Carey lifted her bag. "Excuse us for a minute, Deacon. Vivienne, come with me." She helped Vivienne to her feet, bringing her to the en-suite and closing the door.

Deacon paced the floor outside, leaving marks in the carpet. What were they doing that was taking so long? He could hear them whispering to each other, but couldn't make out what they were saying.

Ten minutes later, Dr. Carey opened the door and gave him an unreadable look. Behind her, Vivienne was sitting on the closed toilet, her face ashen.

He rushed to her side, dropping to his knees in front of her. "What's wrong? Look at me, lovie. Tell me what's happening."

Vivienne didn't raise her gaze from her feet. Why wouldn't she look at him? Why wouldn't she speak to him? He twisted back to catch Dr. Carey studying them from the bedroom.

"Will someone tell me something?" he demanded, his stomach sinking lower with every second of silence stretching like a chasm between them.

Vivienne sniffled, and he realized she was crying.

Shit. This was bad. So bad, neither woman would tell him.

He dragged a tissue from a box beside the sink and offered it to his sobbing wife. Whatever it was, no matter how bad it seemed, they'd get through it together. When she took the tissue, he noticed she was holding something in her closed fist.

A white stick with a blue cap.

"What's that?" he asked, his heart beating so hard it felt like it was going to burst.

"It's a pregnancy test," she confessed between sobs.

"You're *pregnant*?" Vivienne refused to meet his eyes. "But . . . " His mind raced too fast to form a coherent sentence.

"Looks like you've been busy, Casanova," Dr. Carey muttered as she packed her things. The orange bottle disappeared into her black bag.

"I thought you were leaving the medicine," he said, pulling himself out of his stupor.

"Vivienne can't take these if she's pregnant." Dr. Carey replaced the orange bottle on the bedside locker with a smaller white one. "I'm afraid it's good old-fashioned Tylenol for the next few months."

"But home tests aren't always accurate." It had to be wrong. Tests were wrong all the time, right?

"Oh, they're pretty accurate."

"There has to be some other explanation. It takes years for two PAN to reproduce." The majority of couples couldn't even have children. Nevergenes were good for a lot of things but bad for baby making.

"Then you're the exception to the rule."

"Stop arguing with her, Deacon," Vivienne mumbled, staring at the two lines on the test in her hand. When she looked up, she looked past him to Dr. Carey. "Does my inability to fly mean the baby won't have the Nevergene?"

The pills in the bottle rattled like a maraca when Dr. Carey tapped it against the heel of her hand. "You're going to have to ask someone who knows a bit more about your situation that question."

"How far along is she?" They'd had wine with dinner

last week, and she had gone to Ohio with Lyle last month, and that night at the club—*shit*. What if there was something wrong with their baby? Was there a way to tell?

Deacon tried to see her stomach, but the way she hunched over made it impossible.

"Vivienne?" Dr. Carey stepped around him. "When was the first day of your last period?"

"The *first* day?" Vivienne closed her eyes and rubbed her temples. "I don't even know. My cycle is so irregular, I never give it that much thought."

"It was the day we got back from our honeymoon." Deacon remembered because she didn't want him to touch her.

Vivienne's blush put some life back into her face. "That sounds right."

"Instead of guessing, why don't you both get some rest and come by the hospital tomorrow afternoon? Then I'll be able to give you some real answers." Dr. Carey said good-bye, and Deacon offered to walk her down.

He still had questions.

And when he started asking them, he couldn't stop.

"Deacon?" Dr. Carey put her hands on his shoulders, stemming the flow of words pouring out of him. "I know you're worried, but so is Vivienne. Go upstairs and be with your wife."

TWENTY-FIVE

W hat did a girl do when she found out she was going to be a mother?

Vivienne was married to the man she loved, so she had it easier than a lot of girls would in this kind of situation. But there was still so much to worry about . . .

Was the baby okay? How big was it? *Crap.* She'd had wine last week. What if she'd poisoned the little person? *Oh god.* If she had done anything to harm her baby, she would never forgive herself.

What if she was a bad mother? She had never considered having children, figuring she and Deacon would have decades to discuss the possibility of creating a family. But now they didn't have decades. They only had a handful of months.

When Deacon didn't come back right away, she started worrying about him too. He had never said anything about kids. Was he mad at her? She had started birth control a few weeks ago but wasn't very good at remembering to take it.

She had to put a reminder in her phone so she didn't forget. Would the pills hurt their baby?

Vivienne left the test on the bathroom sink and curled onto the mattress, careful with her aching shoulder. She considered taking the painkillers Dr. Carey had left, but really didn't want to jeopardize the baby. Pressing her unbound hand to her stomach, she decided to stop worrying and start praying.

Would it be a boy or a girl? She had a feeling that she'd have a boy. A beautiful boy with Deacon's eyes. And his smile. Actually, she'd be thrilled if he looked exactly like Deacon.

There was movement from the doorway, and she looked up to find her husband watching her from the hallway, his shoulder propped against the doorframe.

Fighting back tears, Vivienne offered him a weak smile. "Hey."

"Hey."

"So . . . um . . . this is crazy, right?"

"Not really, considering I can't seem to keep my hands off of you." He raked a hand through his hair, coming into the room and sinking onto the edge of the mattress. "It's all your fault though." Her stomach sank until he grinned. "You're too damn irresistible."

The idea of her being irresistible made her laugh. Vivienne's mouth tasted gross; her skin was gritty from sweat. Had her stomach always looked so bloated?

"We're breaking rules all over the place," he said, settling onto the pillow beside her. His hand fell on top of hers, his thumb rubbing reassuring circles against her knuckles.

"What does that mean?"

"You're supposed to apply for permission to procreate."

That was insane. Leadership wanted to control every aspect of their life. She really liked Peter, but couldn't bring herself to agree with it all. "I don't see how it's any of their business."

Deacon snorted. "It's not, but Neverland doesn't seem to care."

"You have said you like breaking the rules."

"For you, I'd break every single rule." He lifted Vivienne's shirt and laid his cheek against her belly button. "I'll break the rules for you too," he whispered, pressing a kiss to her skin.

She smiled down at her husband. "I don't think he—"

He glanced at her from beneath his lashes. "Or she."

"Or *she* can hear you."

"My dearest wife, you have so much to learn. First and foremost, my child has supersonic hearing."

"Of course he—"

"She."

"He *or* she does. But what are we going to do if our baby isn't one of us?"

His eyebrows came together as he stared at her stomach. "We're both PAN, so she'll have a Nevergene."

"But what would life be like knowing our child's life has an expiration date? How could we go on living after—"

"Shhh. Don't think like that, lovie. Please. Not tonight. Tomorrow we can worry. Tonight, let's just be happy."

"So you are happy then? You're not mad at me?"

"How can you even ask me that?" He scooted until he could press his forehead against hers. "I am beyond thrilled. Terrified as well." He chuckled. "Beyond terrified, actually." A sour look crossed his features, and he fell back onto the pillow with a groan.

When she asked what was wrong, he sighed and said, "Ethan is going to give me so much shit about this. He already thinks I'm boring as hell. As soon as he finds out I'm going to be a father, there's no telling what he'll do."

"Emily's going to scream." Whenever she dragged Vivienne to the mall, she always insisted on looking at the baby clothes for Vivienne's non-existent British babies. Now that she had a reason to buy them, there wasn't enough closet space to handle the amount of crap Emily was going to pick out.

"Me and you," Deacon said, pressing a kiss to her temple and closing his eyes. His hand fell to her stomach. "And you."

According to the ultrasound, Vivienne was seven weeks pregnant. And their baby had a heartbeat. She could barely see Deacon through the tears in her eyes as she watched the screen and listened to the most glorious sound she'd ever heard. He asked questions the entire time. At one point, she had to tell him to shut up. Dr. Carey told them everything looked fine a hundred times. He needed to stop asking.

When they left the hospital that afternoon, it was already getting dark. Vivienne was exhausted, but there was one more stop they had to make.

Deacon wanted to tell his mother.

They went to her apartment at Leadership House, thankfully meeting no one on their way there. They had decided not to tell anyone the good news until they figured out how Leadership would respond. Once Mary and Peter knew, they would tell Lyle, Emily, and Ethan.

Vivienne needed to see Alex about treatment, so she'd have to tell him too. That was a conversation she wasn't looking forward to. What would he say?

Deacon knocked on the door and, like the coward she was, Vivienne hid behind him. She'd suggested he visit his mother on his own, but he was a coward too.

They were stronger together.

The door opened, and his mother answered in a crisp

white button-down shirt and a pair of dark skinny jeans. Her dark hair was pinned back from her flushed face.

"Deacon? What are you doing here?" Instead of smiling, her mouth turned down.

Deacon threw his shoulders back. "We need to speak with you."

"We?"

When Deacon stepped aside, Vivienne offered his mother a weak smile and a little wave. "Hello, Mary."

"Vivienne." Mary bobbed her head in greeting. "Can this wait until tomorrow? I was just sitting down to . . . ah . . . dinner."

"That's all right. We won't stay long," Deacon promised.

Still Mary didn't move. Which was weird. Like she didn't want them coming inside. "Mother? Are you going to invite us in or not?"

"Everything okay, Mary?"

Holy crap.

That was a *man's* voice. Deacon's mom had a guy in there —and it wasn't Peter. Deacon shoved his way inside and cursed. Vivienne apologized as she followed him, too curious to be polite.

Lee Somerfield was lounging at the dining table. His eyes went wide when he saw them. The table was set for two, with candles and a bottle of wine in the middle. Whatever Mary had cooked smelled amazing.

"What the hell is he doing here?" Deacon snarled, his hands clenched at his sides.

Vivienne hid her smile behind her hand. If he didn't go nuts now, he was going to lose it the minute they left. She wasn't sure why she found that so funny. Mary and Lee deserved happiness. And what was happier than rekindling an old romance?

"Well, Deacon, if you must know," Lee drawled, offering

227

a sardonic smile as he twisted the stem of his wine glass between his fingers, "your mother and I—"

"It's none of your business." Mary slammed the door and planted her hands on her hips. "And if you're going to cause trouble, you can leave now." Turning to Vivienne, she offered a tight-lipped smile. "Would you like a glass of wine or some pork chops?"

"We're not staying for dinner." Deacon reached for Vivienne's elbow.

"Speak for yourself." She shook free and told Mary that she'd love some pork chops. They smelled delicious. And some mashed potatoes. *Ohhhh* was that apple pie? Since she was eating for two, did that mean she could have two slices?

Deacon looked at her like she had lost her mind already. "You're going to eat?"

"Yeah. I'm starving." Who knew growing a human was such hungry work?

Instead of protesting further, Deacon helped Vivienne into one of the empty chairs, drawing stares from Lee and Mary. He needed to stop fussing. Otherwise, she'd end up killing him before the nine months was up. But snapping at him in front of his mother would only make things worse, so Vivienne put it on the back burner until they got home.

Mary made Vivienne a plate, and when she asked Deacon if he wanted any, he grumbled but agreed. He was never one to turn down food.

Watching him sit in the spare chair beside Lee left Vivienne stifling her laughter. The two glared at each other, but no one spoke. She tried to take off the heavy sweater she'd worn as a coat, but had some trouble. Deacon pushed back from the table and helped her out of it.

When Mary saw the sling, she sucked in a breath. "What happened to your arm, dear?"

"I fell." Vivienne stared down at the pork chop. How the

heck was she supposed to cut it up with only one good hand?

As if he heard her thoughts, Deacon grabbed up her knife and fork and started cutting the meat for her.

"You don't have to do that," she muttered, her face burning with embarrassment.

"Would you prefer to pick it up and gnaw the meat off the bone like a neanderthal?"

If they hadn't had an audience, she would have done it to annoy him. But the candles and general ambiance in the room didn't really allow for pettiness. "Thank you, *Deacon*."

"You're welcome, *Vivienne*." When he finished, he went back to his own dinner.

The sounds of cutlery scraping on plates cut through the thick silence. Deacon went to reach for the pepper grinder; Lee picked it up and held it toward him. Instead of taking it, Deacon narrowed his eyes at Lee and turned back to his dinner without the pepper. Lee slammed the shaker onto the table, which drew a glare from Mary.

Vivienne tried not to laugh as she shoveled food into her mouth. The meat was tender, the mashed potatoes were smooth and buttery. And the entertainment was better than watching re-runs on TV.

"Did you fall down the stairs?" Mary asked, her voice tight and shoulders rigid as she turned toward Vivienne.

"Out of the sky, actually." Vivienne reached for the glass of wine Mary had poured for her.

Deacon's eyes widened as he watched her bring the glass to her lips. Why didn't he mind his own—*crap*. She couldn't drink wine.

"Vivienne? Would you like some water instead?" Deacon set his fork and knife on his plate.

"That'd be great. Thanks."

Mary's eyebrows lifted as she drank from her own glass.

And drank. And drank. At the other end of the table, Lee started laughing.

"What's so funny?" Deacon's knuckles turned white as he gripped the glass of water he'd poured from the silver pitcher on the table.

Lee tried to hide his smile beneath his cloth napkin, but his rumbling laughter was hard to ignore.

Mary groaned and dropped her head into her hands. "Vivienne's pregnant, isn't she?"

How could Mary possibly have known that?

"Um . . . well . . . " Deacon drank some of his own wine.

"Grandma Mary," Lee sniggered. "Has a nice ring to it, don't you think."

Mary jabbed her steak knife in the air between them. "Don't you *dare* start."

"What? I think it's kind of hot that I'm dating a grandma."

Deacon choked. "The two of you are dating again? Since when?"

"Since none-of-your-business," Mary shot back. "We're not talking about me. We're talking about the two of you."

Dr. Carey hadn't had a lot of answers about the Nevergene aspect of her pregnancy, so Vivienne figured she'd take advantage of Mary's experience. "Does me falling mean the baby doesn't have the Nevergene?"

"Not necessarily," Mary said, topping up her glass. "The pregnancy hormones take precedence over everything else happening in your body. You should still be able to fly most days until you're further along. Although there will be times the fire may die out unexpectedly. Most pregnant PAN don't take the risk."

Not being able to fly would suck, but Vivienne had walked for eighteen years. She could wait a few months if it meant her baby would be safe. The last thing she wanted was another dislocated shoulder. That crap really hurt.

"What do you think Leadership is going to say?" Deacon asked, finishing his last bite of mashed potatoes.

"Leadership isn't going to do a thing," Lee muttered. When Deacon narrowed his eyes at him, Lee smiled. He looked so much younger than when Vivienne had first met him. It helped that he'd shaved off his beard. "What? You're hardly the first couple to have a baby without Leadership's consent."

Deacon turned toward his mother. "Is that true?"

"We're immortal teenagers with a lot of time on our hands." Mary shrugged. "It's not something they like to advertise, but Lee's right. You don't have to worry about them."

"That's a relief." Vivienne reached for more gravy to smother what was left of her pork chop. "I don't think I could handle being put on trial again."

"Same here." Deacon withdrew a stack of small photos from his wallet and handed them to his mother with an infectious grin.

The fireflies in Vivienne's stomach started dancing.

What if they weren't fireflies? What if it was her baby saying hello? He had been dancing and wiggling around during the ultrasound, but Dr. Carey said it was too soon to feel anything. Vivienne pretended she could anyway. Their little firefly.

"This is the best news." Mary flipped through the photos, her smile growing with each one. "I couldn't be happier for the two of you." She turned tear-filled eyes toward Vivienne. "Are you feeling all right?"

"A little sick and lightheaded, but Dr. Carey said that's normal. Other than that, I feel great."

"Can I see?" Lee asked quietly, giving Deacon an unreadable expression. Vivienne thought he was going to say no, but he took the photos from his mother and gave them to Lee.

"And the doctor said everything looks good?" Lee asked, returning the photos before reaching for his wine.

Deacon launched into a recap of everything the doctor had told them. Vivienne sat back and watched how animated he was when he spoke, falling in love a little more every minute.

He'd assured her he was as terrified as she was, but he didn't look terrified, or even nervous. Then again, Deacon didn't have to push a baby out of his body. Men got the good part with none of the pain. How was that fair?

Vivienne finished every bite of her dinner and accepted the slice of apple pie Mary offered her with a heartfelt thank you.

If Deacon wanted her to eat, all he had to do was buy her pie.

Vivienne never turned down pie.

She looked up from her slice, catching Deacon smiling at her from across the table. The light had returned to his eyes, and for the first time in a long time, he looked like he used to —like he hadn't a care in the world.

TWENTY-SIX

Jasper dropped onto the stool next to Steve, ignoring the odd looks from Eliza when he told her that he liked her haircut. She had always worn it long and tied back, but now it dusted her shoulders.

It looked nice.

He told her.

No big deal.

Now she was gawking at him like he'd offended her. He should have kept his mouth shut. A sexual harassment suit was the last thing he needed.

"What's wrong?" Steve asked.

"Eliza keeps giving me strange looks." Jasper glanced over and caught her staring at him from the ancient CRISPR-chip they'd sourced after the fire.

"That's because she thinks you're hot."

Huh? That couldn't be right.

"You're not serious." Jasper smoothed a hand over the

curls that were starting to come back. The last barber he'd gone to had skinned him alive.

He sneaked a peek at Eliza. She didn't seem to be paying him any attention. Eliza had a pretty face, he supposed. And a nice smile when she decided to use it. But Jasper could never be romantically interested in someone he worked with. First, he was the boss. Second, when things went south—and they always did—he'd have to see the woman every single day. There was enough pressure as it was.

"You've gotta be the most oblivious human on this planet."

"I'm just focused." There was no point starting a relationship when he was going to be gone in two weeks. Steve had been given permission to hand over the ageless injection next Friday. They were going to work another week after that because Steve had something else he needed to do for Peter, and then they were both going to jump ship.

"Speaking of focused, I have a question for you about the treatment serum." Jasper wouldn't make the mistake of calling it poison again within earshot of his employees. "I need to know exactly what happens when someone with an active NG-1882 is injected."

He could have conducted experiments with the PAN tissue samples they had on hand. But he refused to take the chance with Lawrence spying on them. What excuse would he use if he got caught? The product had been approved decades ago.

A muscle in Steve's jaw ticked as his mouth flattened. "The *serum* inhibits nGh production. If the individual is young enough, their body produces a sort of hybrid nGh-hGh that allows them to survive, but they begin ageing like everyone else." His Adam's apple bobbed when he swallowed. "But if they have a gene that has been active for too long, it inhibits nGh production altogether. Their cells can't handle the deprivation. That shit literally sucks the life right out of them."

The faraway look in Steve's eyes as he stared out the window made Jasper uneasy. "Have you . . . Have you seen it happen?" he asked, keeping his voice low.

Steve nodded, dropping his gaze to where he gripped his coffee cup with white knuckles. "I saw my best friend neutralized."

"I'm so sorry." It wasn't enough, but there was nothing Jasper could say or do to make it better.

Steve shrugged, his eyes glittering with tears. "Yeah, well. Shit happens."

Jasper couldn't help Steve's friend, but he could do something for the living PAN.

The affinity of the nGh to the receptor was lower than the wildtype version. It could only bind if there was little to no hGh present in a PAN's body. But how did it happen exactly? Without understanding more about the event that sparked the conversion, there was no way of artificially re-creating it to activate a dormant gene. Steve had to give him more.

"What do you give to individuals with activating genes?"

The steam from the mug curled around Steve's furrowed brow as he took a sip.

"You have to trust me," Jasper went on. "If we're going to figure this out, I need to know everything."

"I can't tell you."

"Why not?" Hadn't Jasper proven himself? Hadn't he betrayed his brother and given the PAN the poison they'd so desperately needed? "I've done everything you've asked."

"They still haven't made a decision."

Jasper's chest started aching. "A decision about what?"

Steve grimaced. "Don't get mad, okay? I may have been a bit too quick to offer you a position."

"*What?*"

Eliza and Sarah glanced over at them, their eyebrows pulled together in silent question. Jasper tried to tamp down his worry and anger.

"Keep it down," Steve hissed, dragging on Jasper's lab coat sleeve. "Everyone's looking."

Jasper didn't care if people were looking. His world was falling apart. "Were you going to tell me? Or were you just going to slink through the next two weeks without saying anything and disappear?"

Steve scrubbed a hand down his cheek. "I'm doing my best, okay?"

"You told me Peter has a position for me."

"He did. He does." Steve set the coffee on top of his notebook. "Peter isn't the one who needs convincing. It's a lot to ask people to trust you. Give them a little time. The other leaders are starting to come around, but they're slow as molasses when it comes to making big decisions. The downside of dealing with immortals."

The thought of being stuck at HOOK after next week made Jasper's heart sink. If only he had known he needed a contingency plan for his contingency plan.

"There's a way you can convince them though."

"What's that?"

Steve glanced around the lab before rolling his stool closer. "If you can get us the information from HOOK's secured server, there's no way they'd say no."

There were only three people with access to the secured VPN: Jasper, Lawrence, and Dr. Hooke. Every time one of them logged on, there was a record of what files and documents were opened and any changes made. It was possible to copy the information onto a hard drive, but if Jasper did it, there would be no way to cover it up.

"I can't do that."

Steve scooted away, his eyes wide. "Why not? It's not like you want to stay here."

Didn't Steve get it? Without the promise of Neverland, Jasper didn't have any other choices. He was in debt up to his eyeballs and he needed a job.

He'd thought this was a done deal, and now they were taking back the offer?

What sort of guarantee could they give him that if Jasper handed over the information, he'd be kept safe? That they wouldn't change their minds again?

They could hire him as easily as they could say, "Thanks for the info, but there's no way in hell you're working for us."

And then where would he be?

The moment Lawrence found out, he'd fire him and bring a lawsuit down on his head. A lawsuit Jasper couldn't hope to win. He could end up in prison.

Or Lawrence could save himself the trouble and cost and just kill him.

"No."

"Jasper. Listen to me—"

"I said no." Jasper pushed to his feet, crossed to his desk, and tore his jacket from the back of the chair. Mario asked him if everything was okay on his way out the door. Jasper ignored him and didn't stop until he was outside.

Cool air hit his overheated face, and he forced himself to take a deep breath.

How could Steve ask him to do this?

Jasper had already gotten the PAN four vials of poison. And another two he'd managed to swipe in a notably less dramatic fashion. And he had loaned Steve his own restricted-level key card to use—twice.

All Steve had given him in return were empty promises.

Was he even going to hand over the anti-aging injection he'd been promising? Or was Steve going to leave him high and dry?

"Jasper, I need you to listen to me—"

237

Jasper whipped around to glare at Steve. He had exchanged his own lab coat for his poofy red jacket.

"I'm done listening," Jasper ground out. "It's time you came through on at least one of your promises."

"There's a disease affecting PAN with high levels of nGh," Steve said, continuing as if Jasper hadn't spoken. "They're forgetting everything. One minute they're fine, the next"—he snapped his fingers—"they're gone."

Forgetfulness *had* been listed as one of the side effects to look out for when dealing with individuals with an active NG-1882.

"The body isn't affected. Just the mind. They suffer from personality changes at night. Violent tendencies. And have no recollection whatsoever."

If Steve had still been set on taking him to Neverland, Jasper would've gladly done what he could to help. But since that wasn't happening, "I don't see what this has to do with me."

"Peter's closest friends and family are suffering from this disease. There are some who believe your poison holds the answer to getting the cells to produce acceptable levels without neutralizing them. But we have to know how the poison is synthesized. And that information is on the VPN. If you give them access, you're as good as in."

Jasper's life was too much to risk for a chance. "I can't."

Steve's eyes narrowed. "Then I guess there's nothing more for us to discuss." He dragged his knitted hat from his pocket and pulled it over his blond hair.

Jasper glanced toward the building to find all of his employees lined up at the windows, staring at the two of them. There was a lot more to discuss, but this wasn't the time or the place. "I want you to hold up your end of the bargain."

Getting Lawrence off his back would buy Jasper some

time to find another job—something he could have been doing this whole time.

Stuffing his hand into the pocket of his red jacket, Steve sneered and said, "I don't bargain with murderers."

The following day, Jasper brought an extra-large coffee as a peace offering. Steve's desk was empty.

"Sarah?" Jasper searched the lab in case he'd missed Steve the first time. Everyone seemed to be there except Steve.

Sarah looked up from her computer and smiled at him. "What's up?"

"Have you seen Steve anywhere?" Jasper checked his watch. It was nearly ten o'clock. Steve was usually the first to arrive.

"He was here earlier." Sarah frowned as she glanced around the room. "Not sure when he left though."

Jasper thanked her, then went to his desk to get his phone and send a quick text to check in. When Steve didn't respond right away, an uneasy feeling settled into the pit of his stomach. Steve's phone was practically an extension of his arm. He *always* had it on him. Which meant he was probably ignoring Jasper.

All people ever did was take, take, *take* from him.

Jasper was finished giving.

Instead of spending the day getting reacquainted with the work he'd done on anti-aging as planned, he ended up staring at his notes, his phone, and Steve's empty desk. What if Steve never came back? Surely he wouldn't abandon Jasper like that.

The next day, Jasper arrived early. Apparently, Steve had come in after everyone had left and worked through the night. The only reason Jasper knew that was because the night guard had told him. Steve had said he had permission—and an upgraded key card "issued" by Jasper. Which was a lie.

Jasper stayed late, hoping to catch Steve when he arrived. At nine o'clock, sitting in the empty lab, the sound of machine motors humming round him, Jasper decided enough was enough.

He was wasting precious time. Time he didn't have.

Jasper wouldn't make any headway without access to the information the PAN refused to hand over. But if he gave Steve the data he wanted, he would come back to work, and they could get on with their mission, at least until Lawrence found out or Steve left for good.

Jasper found the thumb drive he had stuck into his laptop bag and inserted it into his computer, conscious of where his chair was the entire time. With the angle of the camera, Lawrence shouldn't be able to see anything besides Jasper's back.

He had to override all the security protocols in place and authorize the file transfers with his personal access code. If it bit him in the ass, he'd deal with the consequences. Lines had been drawn, and when this was all over, he didn't want to be known as the bad guy, even if it landed him in jail. Or dead.

It was risky, but he left the thumb drive under Steve's notebook, hoping he'd find it when he got to work that night. With Steve ignoring Jasper's calls and messages, he didn't have much of a choice. And Steve only had a few days left at HOOK.

TWENTY-SEVEN

D eacon was having the best dream. He knew it wasn't real because he never would've been allowed to dive off the Empire State Building in the middle of rush hour. But it had been something he'd always dreamed of doing. He wanted to watch the outsiders' faces as he hurtled toward the ground, to see the worry in their eyes—and then the wonder when he pulled up at the last second and soared over the crowds like a bloody superhero.

He supposed most men felt the same way. Especially the ones that never grew up.

Deacon rolled over and reached for Vivienne, but her spot on the bed was cold. The room was still dark, and the door to the hall was ajar.

He kicked aside the duvet rolled out of bed. Perhaps she had gone downstairs for some food. One of the perks of pregnancy was that she seemed to be eating a lot more. It had been a week since they told his mother about the baby, and Vivienne hadn't stopped eating since.

Last night, she'd sent him to the shop for pomegranates. It had been freezing out, but he hadn't complained. If his wife wanted pomegranates, she was going to feast on pomegranates. No one told him how much of a pain in the ass they were to open up; there had been red juice all over his counter by the time he finished, and he'd ruined his favorite white shirt. But seeing Vivienne's eyes light up when he returned to bed with a bowl of plump red seeds made it all worthwhile.

A groan from the en-suite stopped him mid-stride. There were downsides to pregnancy too. Like morning sickness. Who the hell had come up with the term 'morning sickness' anyway? It lasted all bloody day.

When Vivienne groaned again, he hurried over, only to stop when there was another noise.

It was low and guttural, and sounded like a . . . a growl?

"Lovie? Are you all right? What do you need?"

A dark blur shot out of the bathroom, colliding with his torso. He fell under its crushing weight—under *her* crushing weight. *Vivienne.* She slashed at him with her nails and pummeled his chest with her fists and laughed like a creature out of a horror movie.

Slicing pain radiated from his face. Something warm and wet dripped down his cheek. He managed to catch her wrists; she tried to bite his shoulder.

"Stop. Vivienne, stop. It's me. It's me. I'm right here."

How was she so strong with only one good arm? She was half his size, and he could barely keep a hold on her as she thrashed and growled and groaned and—

Shiiit.

She kneed him in the bloody groin.

Cursing, Deacon let her go. She shoved off of him, escaping toward the bed. Something crashed to the floor— probably the lamp—but he couldn't move from where he was curled on the carpet, clutching his stomach and waiting for the nausea to pass.

Vivienne laughed again, the sound piercing the silence.

And Deacon just laid there praying until the room grew silent.

It was too soon.

Alex had told Vivienne that she had years.

It was too bloody soon.

As the sky outside lightened, he could see shards from the new lamp on the other side of the bed, along with all the pillows. But he still couldn't move. Didn't want to. He wanted to lie on the ground and pretend nothing had happened. That everything was fine.

Vivienne giggled and murmured his name.

Instead of making him feel warm inside, the sound made him shudder. At 6 a.m., he got up the nerve to sit up.

Vivienne was asleep in a tangle of sheets, her dark hair spread in a riot of waves across the mattress. Her face was pale, the skin beneath her thick lashes dark. How did her face look so gaunt when she'd been eating so much? Her cheeks were sunken, almost hollow. And the bones along her shoulders protruded at unnaturally sharp angles. *Dammit.*

Afraid of waking her but too worried to leave her alone, Deacon collected a pillow and duvet from the spare room and made a bed on the floor. He could do this. He knew he could. But . . .

What if he couldn't?

Vivienne had been having the best dream. She and Deacon were back on the island—alone. No chaperones, and definitely no Mermaids. And he had suggested they bring the blankets and sheets to the beach so they could sleep there. Only they didn't sleep. The thought made her skin tingle, and she rolled over only to find Deacon's spot empty and cold.

Sunlight streamed through the windows. It was going to be a beautiful morning. Maybe they could go for a walk.

"Deacon?" She sat up and glanced toward the bathroom. The light was off. Maybe he had gone downstairs to make breakfast. He wasn't very good at it; usually burned the eggs, but he could make a mean slice of toast. And ever since she'd found out she was pregnant, she had been ravenous. Even his eggs a la char sounded appetizing.

"I'm down here," he groaned.

Deacon was curled up near the closet, using the bedding from one of the spare bedrooms.

"What in the world are you doing on the floor?" She laughed as she stretched her hands toward the ceiling. "Did you fall out of bed?"

When he rolled over, she gasped. There were nasty red gouges across his left cheek.

"What happened to your face?"

"I scratched myself." He turned his face away from her and rested his forearms on his knees. His head dropped as his shoulders slumped inward.

"They look really bad." She untangled the sheets from her legs and crossed the cold floor to where he was sitting. "Let me see."

When she reached a hand toward his reddened cheek, he flinched. "Sorry."

Why was he sorry? Vivienne sat back on her heels and noticed the pieces of broken lamp on the floor. "What happened to the lamp?" Had he knocked it off when he fell? And if he had fallen, why did he have the blankets from the spare bed?

"I'm sorry. I should have cleaned it up last night."

"You didn't answer my question." Why was he avoiding her eyes?

Deacon dropped his head into his hands and cursed. "I knocked it over, all right?"

"But it's on my side of the bed."

A flash of memory lit inside her brain like a firework: the satisfying sound of the ceramic body shattering against the wall. "Did . . . Did I break the lamp?"

Deacon kept his head down.

"Deacon, look at me. Please."

When he did, his green eyes were filled with tears.

Her hand trembled when she reached to touch his cheek. This time, he didn't pull away. But then she saw blood beneath her nails and she was the one who jerked back.

"Oh god. Did I—" *Oh god.* She had hurt him. She had scratched his beautiful face and broken the lamp and couldn't remember anything. "I did that to you, didn't I?"

Deacon winced. "It was an accident. You were having a nightmare, and I got in the way."

She shook her head, retreating until her back collided with the bed. "It's happening, isn't it?" Her hand flew to her forehead. She didn't remember having a nightmare. "It's too soon. It has to be too soon."

"We'll figure it out," he assured her, cupping her cheeks. "I'll call Dr. Carey—"

Dr. Carey couldn't help them anymore. "You need to call Alex."

"What?" Deacon's eyes widened and he shook his head. "No. Absolutely not. I don't want him near you."

"He's the only one who understands my case and knows about the forgetful PAN." She could tell from Deacon's defiant expression that he wanted to protest, but they were out of options. And it wasn't just her they needed to look after. "Please. He's the best chance we have of saving me."

In the end, Deacon agreed. Vivienne curled onto the bed while he paced the floor, waiting for the call to the lab to connect.

"Hey, Robert, it's Deacon." He offered Vivienne a tight smile. "Can you put me through to Alex?" He murmured a few "all rights" and one "I understand" before hanging up.

"What'd he say?"

"Alex won't be in until this afternoon." Deacon slid his phone into his pocket. "We've done everything we can for now. Why don't you rest?"

As tired as she was, the last thing she wanted was to go to sleep again. What if she woke up and didn't remember anything?

Vivienne picked up her phone and found Alex's cell number.

"Vivienne, please. Just wait."

She pressed the button before Deacon could say anything else.

It only rang once before Alex answered. "Vivienne?"

Hearing Alex's voice filled her stomach with dread. "Hey, Alex."

Silence.

"I, um . . . I'm sorry to be calling you this early. We tried the lab, but they said you weren't going to be in until later, and I really need to talk to you now." She was blubbering like her brain was too muddled to handle the emotions bubbling to the surface.

"Where are you?" Alex clipped.

"I'm at my house. At, um, Deacon's house, I mean."

"Are you okay?"

She was as far from okay as a person could be. At this rate, she wasn't going to be able to remember her twentieth birthday. "No. I'm not okay."

Twenty minutes later, Alex was in the house, kicking Deacon out of their bedroom. "What happened?" Alex's blue eyes widened as he touched the sling. "Did that bastard hurt you? I swear, I'm going to—"

Vivienne caught Alex's shirt sleeve. "Deacon didn't do any of this. It was all me."

The mattress dipped when Alex sat down. "You broke the lamp? And you hurt your own shoulder?"

Vivienne nodded, unable to find her voice. Explaining what had happened the night she had fallen was pointless. They had already figured out what had gone wrong. "I had an . . . episode last night." Was that the right word? "And I can't . . . I can't remember any of it."

What if she had the baby and didn't remember her own child? What if this was it? What if these terrifying moments were the last ones she ever experienced?

Alex wrapped his arm around her waist and pulled her close. "It'll be okay. Don't cry. We'll figure something out."

She shook her head. "You don't understand. I attacked him. I hurt him. And then I woke up happy like none of it had happened. I'm turning into a monster," she sobbed, pressing the heels of her hands to her eyes. Deacon had probably been too worried about hurting her to defend himself. When would it happen again? Tonight? Tomorrow?

"It's not you. It's the disease." He brushed her hair back from her forehead and pressed a kiss to her temple. "Come by the lab tomorrow. I'll check your levels and start treatment right away."

Treatment. She remembered him saying that it wouldn't help in the long term, but maybe it would keep the episodes at bay. At this point, she'd take anything. "I know you must hate me, but I really appreciate this."

"I don't hate you." Alex's lips lifted into a sad smile as he glanced at the door. "I hate *him*. But never you."

"Thank you, Alex."

"Why don't you lie down and rest?" He drew down the covers. "You look like you're ready to collapse."

"I'm afraid it'll happen again."

"That's not the way it works. But I'll stay here until you fall asleep if you want."

Vivienne shouldn't want him to. But Deacon had already been through enough. He probably didn't even want to look at her. She settled her head on the pillows, closed her eyes, and tried to think happy thoughts.

Alex was in the bedroom with Vivienne. Alone. The wanker had kicked Deacon out of his own room the moment he had burst through the door, like he was the bloody hero. And they had been in there for over an hour. What could they possibly have to discuss that took so long? Vivienne was forgetting. Alex needed to give her something to fix it. End of story.

The door to the room opened, and Alex came out, his face grim. When he saw Deacon waiting in the hallway, his eyes narrowed.

Deacon opened his mouth to ask what the hell took so long.

"Not here," Alex snapped in a harsh whisper. "She's asleep, and I don't want you waking her up."

Vivienne had fallen asleep with Alex? Jealousy twisted in his stomach, but Deacon managed to tamp it down. Instead of telling the bearded bastard exactly what he thought of being ordered around his own home, Deacon turned and stomped down the stairs. He didn't stop until he was in the kitchen.

Alex made himself at home on one of the bar stools, like he planned on staying after Deacon heard what he needed to hear. He would be disappointed to find himself on his ass in the front lawn.

"How long has Vivienne been exhibiting signs of forgetfulness?" Alex asked, folding his hands together and speaking in that condescending tone he used when he was trying to sound intelligent.

Damn, he was insufferable. "I don't know when it started," Deacon said, knowing the sooner he got this over with, the sooner he could kick Alex out. "I mean, she'd forget little things here and there. But everyone does that."

"Yes, we all forget sometimes. But the difference is that *we* forget because we're absentminded. Vivienne has a medical condition, so every single instance should have been recorded."

Don't hit him.

Do not hit him.

"The first time I noticed her forget anything was when we were at Peter's island."

Alex's eyes widened. "*Before* the trial?"

"Yes. She forgot her swimming costume."

"That was months ago!"

"She told me it wasn't a big deal."

"Vivienne isn't a doctor. She doesn't have a clue." Alex raked his fingers through his hair and dropped his head into his hands. "I asked her to tell me if she had trouble sleeping, or if she's forgotten anything, or if her appetite disappeared."

Shit.

Vivienne hadn't told him those were the additional side effects.

Why hadn't Deacon pushed her? Why hadn't he sucked up his pride and asked Alex himself?

As much as it killed him to do it, Deacon told Alex that Vivienne hadn't been sleeping well and about her lack of appetite. "And Emily mentioned that Vivienne had been having trouble with her PIN code this summer. They thought the door was faulty, but every time maintenance came to check it, they couldn't find an issue. Do you think . . . I mean, could she have been forgetting her code?"

Alex's pale, panicked expression was the only confirmation Deacon needed. "This summer?" he choked.

Deacon nodded.

Alex cursed and kicked the island. "Why didn't she tell me?"

"Now you know how I feel."

Alex's eyes narrowed; a muscle in his jaw feathered. "You get everything you want. So, no, I don't know how you feel."

"What's that supposed to mean?"

Alex's hands flexed on the countertop. It looked like Deacon wasn't the only one who wanted to hit something. "I didn't come over to get into this with you. Vivienne needs to start treatment right away."

Right. Treatment. That sounded positive. And Deacon *really* needed positive. "What kind of treatment are we talking about?"

"Hormone suppressants mostly, something to counteract Vivienne's high levels of nGh. She'll need to refrain from flying until we see how they interact with her system, but there are no other options."

Vivienne had said she wasn't going to fly again until after the baby was born. Deacon wished he could make the sacrifice for her. She was already giving up her body for their child; all he was doing was buying her pomegranates. "I don't think Vivienne can take anything like that."

"Why not?"

This wasn't how they'd wanted people to find out. This wasn't in the plan. Still. What choice did he have? "She's pregnant."

Alex's face drained of color.

Then his fist connected with Deacon's jaw.

Pain shot through Deacon's face, and blood leaked from

his split lip onto the counter. "What the hell was that for?" he shouted, cupping his sore jaw.

"You've screwed enough women to know how to put on a condom, you selfish asshole!" Alex shoved him into the counter. The bowl of pomegranates fell, shattering and sending fruit rolling across the floor.

Deacon knocked Alex into the island. The bastard was a lot stronger than he looked. "What we do in our bedroom is none of your damned business."

"She's *my* patient."

"Yeah, well, she's my wife."

"A wife you've failed because you were too interested in screwing her to protect her!"

"Get the hell out of my house."

Alex stalked to the front door, slamming it behind him.

"Deacon?" Vivienne was standing on the stairs with wide eyes. Her plaid pyjama pants hung off of her hips.

Alex was right. Deacon *was* a selfish asshole. He should have been thinking about Vivienne and not himself. He should have taken the hit he deserved and kept quiet instead of roaring and shouting and waking his pregnant wife. "I'm sorry we woke you."

"It's okay. I was hungry anyway." Her smile was sad. "Would you make me breakfast?"

"Yes. Of course. Anything you want."

"Eggs and toast would be great."

He turned to grab butter, milk, and eggs from the fridge. "Do you want juice as well?"

"Please."

This was good. Perhaps the situation wasn't as dire as he thought.

"You may want to clean your face first. I don't want blood in my eggs."

When he smiled, the new cut in his lip split wider, leaving him wincing. "No blood in your eggs. Got it."

The eggs were kind of burnt, but the toast was perfect. The best part was that Vivienne ate everything but the crust. When she finished, the color had returned to her cheeks.

Deacon popped the crusts into his mouth and loaded everything into the dishwasher, determined to turn this day around.

TWENTY-EIGHT

The stool beneath Vivienne squeaked as she twisted back and forth, waiting for Alex to say something. Deacon had told her that coming today would be pointless, but she wanted to hear the bad news from Alex himself. There was no way either of them had been thinking clearly yesterday after their fight at the house. Was it possible that Alex had kept some information to himself out of spite?

It was hard to believe he would be so petty; he was a medical professional after all. But Deacon's split lip told another story.

"I'm afraid there's not a whole lot we can do since you're . . . " Alex's words drifted into an incoherent whisper.

Vivienne crossed her arms and fixed him with a hard stare. "The word you're avoiding is *pregnant*." His gaze slipped to her stomach before returning to her face—and he wasn't admiring her sweatshirt.

Alex's mouth pulled into a tight line. "Yes. Pregnant."

"Well, there's nothing I can do about it now, is there? So

let's figure out how to keep these episodes at bay until after the baby is born." Then she could worry about the rest.

"That's what I'm trying to tell you. By then, it'll be too late."

Alex had been wrong before—like when he said her memory should be fine for another ten years. He could be wrong about this too.

"If we had started treatment sooner," he went on, knocking his heel off the stool, "there's a slim chance we would have been able to bring your levels down for a few years. But six months from now?" Alex shook his head. "I know this isn't what you want to hear."

"You're right. It's not." Vivienne bit the inside of her cheek to keep from crying. All these pregnancy hormones were making her feel like a crazy person. Earlier that morning, she had bawled because of a car commercial. A freaking *car commercial*. "I don't understand why it matters. It's only six more months."

"Let me show you." Alex tore a piece of paper from a spiral notebook and slid a laptop out of his way so he could write. After clicking the top on a pen from his lab coat pocket, he drew a circle and wrote nGh inside. "The Never-gene produces never-growth hormone, or nGh. It's a mutated version of hGh. If there is too much hGh present in a person's system, then the nGh can't do its job."

"I remember." High levels of nGh were the reason Vivienne was in this mess.

"As long as you're pregnant"—Alex drew a smaller circle inside the larger one and wrote hGh inside—"your hGh levels will continue to rise because the baby's levels are rising. That's why it becomes dangerous for expectant mothers to fly further into their pregnancies. Something you've already experienced."

Vivienne didn't want to think about the blind panic she'd felt falling out of the sky.

Alex drew the smaller hGh circle bigger and bigger and bigger.

"Okay, you've made your point." Deacon's mom had explained this to her at dinner a few weeks ago. "But why can't we fix it once the baby is born?"

Alex pushed his glasses onto his forehead and rubbed his eyes. "Because the Nevergene doesn't act like a normal gene when it comes to hormone production. If you had an overactive thyroid, I'd give you medication to reduce your levels. We'd have to keep testing you every six months to make sure the dosage remains correct, but you'd eventually have normal levels."

Vivienne didn't need a lesson in endocrinology. She needed answers. Instead of snapping and telling him to get to the point, she nodded dutifully and waited as Alex doodled some more on the paper.

"Imagine nGh levels are on a scale from one to ten." He wrote the numbers onto the page. "I have a Nevergene, but it's not actively producing enough nGh to do anything helpful, so I would be a one. Most PAN hover between four and five." He drew a line between those two numbers. "Your levels are at a nine. Your body is used to nine. It wants to stay at nine. It loves nine."

"Got it. My body loves nine."

Alex huffed a laugh. "Yeah, well . . . The hGh from"—he gestured to her stomach—"what's happening *in there* cancels out the nGh. So as baby gets bigger, the levels of hGh in your system are going to rise. And since your body likes nine so much, it's going to do everything in its power to keep you at nine."

"So my body is producing more nGh to try and fix it."

"Exactly. Which means, once the baby is born, your body will be used to producing so much nGh that there will be no way to stop it."

"Does this happen to every female PAN who gets pregnant?" Had it happened to her mother?

Nodding, Alex dropped his pen onto the notebook. "For most women, it only raises their levels a little. But because you started out so high, you were already at risk." He leaned his elbows on the desk and dropped his head into his hands. "I should have warned you. I should have told you what would happen if you got pregnant. I just didn't think—"

"This isn't your fault." Even as the words slipped from her lips, she couldn't help shifting away from Alex. If he had told her, she could have taken precautions with birth control, or Deacon could have bought a lifetime supply of condoms, or they could have been more careful.

But then they wouldn't have this baby.

Her hand fell to her stomach.

Even if it cost her everything, they had been given this child for a reason.

"But it is," Alex said quietly, turning to face her. "Yesterday, I told Deacon it was his fault. But it wasn't true. This was on me. I'm your doctor and I should have insisted you start treatment as soon as your tests came back. I just got so caught up in you, and us, and then losing you to *him*." A wince. "I'm so sorry."

With the world slipping through her fingers, Vivienne didn't have it in her to comfort him. "So, that's it. Even if I took the medicine now, it couldn't save me."

"I'm afraid not."

Tears burned the backs of her eyes as she nodded. "Well, I guess that's that." How was she going to tell Deacon?

"There is one solution." Alex's shoulders slumped when he sighed and slipped off his glasses. "But you're not going to like it."

Vivienne reached for his hand. "Tell me what it is." His blue eyes met hers, then he looked away.

"Please," she begged. "I'll do anything."

When Vivienne got back to their house, she found Deacon in the kitchen, bent over a chopping board, cutting an eggplant into thin slices. From the garlic and onion and tomato paste on the counter, she assumed he was trying his hand at eggplant parmesan. If he was a good cook, she'd be looking forward to it. But there was a ninety percent chance they'd end up ordering take out.

The scratches on his cheek were scabbing over, but they still looked painful. Thankfully, the swelling on his lip had gone down after she forced him to sit with a pack of frozen peas pressed against his face yesterday.

He glanced up at her from the chopping board, his green eyes narrowed. "How was your date with Beardy McGee?"

"It was great. We made out the whole time."

The knife fell onto the counter. "That's not funny."

Deacon was right. None of this was funny. "It was obviously a joke." She slid onto a stool at the island and grabbed one of the pomegranates Deacon had bought for her. "We only made out *half* the time."

A piece of eggplant smacked her in the cheek.

"Say it again and see what happens." Deacon picked up the jar of red sauce. The muscles in his arms flexed as he twisted off the lid. The seal broke with a *pop*.

"You wouldn't dare."

A grin. "Try me."

Vivienne laughed despite everything. It was either that or burst into tears. Deacon set the jar back onto the counter and picked up the knife.

"I'm sorry."

His dark eyebrows disappeared beneath the hair falling over his forehead. "Did you actually make out with Alex?"

"No, of course not."

"Then what on earth do you have to be sorry for?"

How could he ask that question? "For this whole stupid mess." Sighing, she rested her chin on her hands. "I knew I had been forgetting things and didn't want to accept what was happening. We shouldn't have gotten married. I should have let you go."

The entire drive back to the house, she had gone around and around about how different life would be if she had done things the right way.

"I hate to tell you this, lovie," Deacon said, layering the eggplant into a baking dish, "but that whole '*if you love someone, let them go*' mantra is a crock of shite." He picked up a dishtowel from the counter and cleaned his hands. "If you love someone, you fight for them."

That was great when there was an enemy to fight against. But what about when the fight was invisible? When the enemy was invincible?

"It's always been me against the world. And now I'm dragging you—and our child—down with me."

Deacon slid the baking dish into the oven and slammed it shut. "Well, when we get to the bottom, at least there'll be nowhere to go but up."

Deacon didn't get it. Once Vivienne got to the bottom, she was going to stay there. She tried explaining to him what Alex had said about the hormones and nGh, but all Deacon did was shake his head and tell her that Alex was a wanker who didn't know anything.

"You can shake your head all you want. That's not going to change the facts." Vivienne's head was throbbing. She really needed a nap.

"They're going to find a cure," he insisted for what felt like the millionth time.

Vivienne could resign herself to that slim possibility or she could take matters into her own hands. An hour ago, Alex had given her a solution that had sounded like the worst idea in the entire history of ideas. But the more she thought about it, the more she considered that maybe he was right.

Vivienne couldn't control her memory loss or her hormone levels.

But that didn't mean she was powerless.

"Deacon." She reached for his hand and waited for their gazes to connect. "I've made a decision."

His eyes narrowed as his brow furrowed and lips flattened. "What's that?"

"Once I have the baby," she said, fighting back tears, "I'm going to be voluntarily neutralized." She would endure whatever she must between now and the birth and then she was taking back control of her life.

Deacon jerked his hand free, and his face turned the same shade of white as the marble counter. "You're not doing that. I won't let you."

Once the idea settled in and Deacon had time to think about it, he would realize she was right. "Yeah, well, it's not your choice. It's mine."

"*Choice*? It's not a bloody choice!" He raked a hand through his hair. "It's suicide, that's what it is!"

"Living a normal life is suicide?" She took a deep breath, praying for patience. "Do you hear yourself right now?"

"It's the truth." He gripped the edge of the marble counter and hung his head. His chest heaved as he sucked in ragged breaths.

"Alex suggested—"

"Of course he did." Deacon exhaled a humorless chuckle. "The bloody snake filled your head with nonsense. Once you get that injection, that's it. It's over."

The eggs Vivienne had eaten earlier turned sour in her stomach. "You'd leave me?"

Of all the things Vivienne had imagined Deacon saying, she hadn't expected him to want to end their relationship.

"That's not what I meant." He sank onto the stool next to

her. "What I'm saying is, if you do this, there's no way to reverse it. You can't change your mind."

"I know." Vivienne wasn't going to change her mind. Deacon had told her that Jasper had handed over some poison to help with developing a cure. Surely there would be some left for her. And if not, she'd go to HOOK herself. She'd have to make sure it was safe, maybe even ask for a police escort, but one way or another, she was going to get that injection.

Cursing, Deacon rested his head in his hands and stared down at the counter.

Instead of focusing on the tears glistening in his green eyes, she stared at the marks she'd left on his cheek, more determined than ever to stop this.

"It's not the end of the world," she told him. "It'll be like I'm an outsider. Robert can give me the ageless injection so I don't gross you out when I'm old and wrinkly, and we can live out the rest of our lives making memories."

The muscles in his jaw ticked.

Silence stretched between them, making her wish she had kept all of this to herself. "Don't you have anything to say?"

"You have everything figured out. I don't see why you need my input."

"Why are you acting like this? I thought you'd be happy." Or at the very least understanding.

"My wife wants to kill herself. What part of that should make me happy?"

Vivienne didn't *want* to die. But one lifetime of memories was better than an eternity in darkness. "Your mother married an outsider and—"

He shot off the stool and skirted away, knocking into the corner of the counter with his hip. "Don't you dare bring my father into this. Your parents died together. You don't have a clue what it was like for her or for me, being left alone."

"So *that's* what this is about." Why hadn't she seen it before? He had accused her of having abandonment issues, but he was the one with the issues. "You would honestly rather I waste away in Scotland like a mindless zombie than have memories of our child growing up? Memories of our life together? You would take all of that away from me so that you aren't alone in sixty or seventy years?"

"The forgetful aren't zombies."

"They're shells of humans, Deacon. And that's so much worse." She left him there and ran to their bedroom. The pillows smelled like Deacon's shampoo. His cologne drifted from the sheets.

Those were the tiny details he wanted to steal from her.

Curling onto her side, she cradled her stomach and allowed her tears to fall. This was the right decision. She knew it was. She hoped it didn't take Deacon long to see it.

What did you do when the person you loved most in the world wanted to give up? Deacon knew he was being dramatic and irrational and a whole host of other things, but he couldn't get past the fact that his wife was willing to give up hope and end everything.

The last time he had spoken to Peter, his grandad had said there had been no new developments. Still, he had faith that the PAN working tirelessly in the lab would figure this out.

The promise of forever was worth more than what they were going through right now. All they had to do was endure. It was going to happen. He knew it. Yes, it was going to be hell for a little while, but if they went through it together, didn't that count for something?

Deacon sat on the stool and stared at the orange light

from the oven until the timer went off. For once in his life, he hadn't burned dinner.

And it smelled amazing.

But he didn't feel like eating.

He should try to comfort Vivienne.

He made it to the third step, turned around, and retreated to the living room. How could he go upstairs when he didn't know what he was going to say?

Instead, he threw himself onto the sofa and stared at the coffered ceiling. There were some cobwebs in the shadowed corners. Vivienne would freak out when she saw them. If he hadn't been spiraling, he would've gotten the brush from the closet to clean them.

If only there was someone he could speak to. Someone who knew what he was going through . . .

He dragged his mobile from his pocket and called Peter.

Deacon managed to explain the situation without cursing or breaking down. When he finished, the line was silent.

"Let me ask you something," Peter said eventually. "Do you trust your wife?"

"Of course I do." Deacon never would have married Vivienne otherwise. He trusted her implicitly.

"And do you think that she would make this decision lightly?"

"No. She wouldn't." But knowing Vivienne had considered the consequences didn't make a blind bit of difference to the outcome. Had she considered him at all?

"Then it sounds to me like you need to respect your wife's choice."

That wasn't what Deacon wanted to hear. "Even if she's wrong?"

Peter's chuckle was without humor. "Would your opinion change if I told you there would never be a cure? That there was no hope? That this is your only chance to have a life together?"

Deacon kicked his feet off the cushion and sat upright. "Is that what's happening?" His stomach twisted. His heart thudded. Was the lab giving up? Were they moving on to something else? Were they abandoning every lost soul stuck in Scotland?

"Answer the question."

Deacon dropped his head into his hands. "I don't want to."

"Deacon . . .

"All right. Fine. Yes, it would change. Is that what you wanted to hear?" If there was no hope, then neutralization was the obvious choice.

"Don't bite my head off. You're the one who called me."

"I just . . . I just want her to get better."

"I know it's not the same thing. But look at Tootles. There's no doubt in my mind that if he had the choice, he'd take HOOK's poison without batting an eye. This isn't a life I'd wish on my worst enemy. What's the point in living forever if you're going to do it on your own, looking after someone who doesn't even know your name?"

Deacon let the words sink in, then mumbled his thanks and fell back onto the cushions.

He'd always been an optimist. But perhaps it was time to think about the worst-case scenario. If what Alex said was true—and he still had his doubts—then Vivienne's memory would be gone in six months. Deacon would be left to raise their child on his own. Could he trust her to be around their baby with her violent episodes? The thought of keeping her away broke his bleeding heart.

He had two choices.

He could spend the next six months trying to change her mind or he could accept her decision.

During the trial, he had been willing to give up everything for her. What had changed?

Sure, Leadership was no longer threatening his wife. But

the outcome was still the same. Vivienne was making a decision about treatment for a disease that currently had no cure.

With his battered heart close to failing, he trudged up the stairs. Inside their bedroom, Vivienne was curled up on top of the duvet, her hands tucked protectively around her abdomen. He slid in behind her, forming his body around hers.

A sigh escaped her lips as his arms closed around her and he pulled her close. If outsiders could face death with smiles on their faces, then Deacon could do the same.

When Vivienne was neutralized, Deacon was going to be neutralized with her.

He was never flying alone again.

TWENTY-NINE

J asper pressed the button above him, switching on the light so he could read the address he'd scribbled on a scrap of paper before leaving work. He wasn't supposed to snoop through employee files. But after everything else he'd done the last few months, an invasion of privacy was the least of his sins.

Eighties music played softly on the radio. He glanced toward Steve's BMW sitting outside the brick apartment complex where he lived. Orange light from a streetlamp reflected off the shiny black surface.

The tall building looked new, with patchy grass and a bunch of construction equipment parked in the vacant lot beside it.

All the apartments in the block had lights on except 302.

Jasper turned off the engine and unbuckled his seat belt. Pulling the collar on his jacket around his face to keep out the evening chill, he crossed the pristine sidewalk to Steve's green door. After a swift knock, he waited and watched the closed blinds for signs of movement.

Nothing.

He knocked again, but still no one answered.

The door to the neighboring apartment opened, and a middle-aged woman in scrubs popped her head out. When she saw Jasper, her eyes narrowed. "You looking for Steve too?"

Too? Did that mean someone else had stopped by?

"Yeah, I am." Jasper hopped off the step and crossed to stand in the light from the woman's porch. "Have you seen him today?"

She shook her head. A little girl, about four years old, came barrelling out the door. Her mother caught her by the sleeve before her foot hit the pavement. "Get back into the house, Josie!" The little girl screeched in protest but did as she was told.

"Sorry about that." The woman blocked the entrance with her arm, deterring another escape attempt. "What do you need with Steve?"

What *didn't* he need from Steve?

Tomorrow was the first of the month. He owed Jasper that injection.

"We work together at The Humanitarian Organization for Order and Knowledge. I haven't heard from him in a couple of days and wanted to make sure everything was okay."

She pursed her lips as she considered him. And then she sighed. "I'll tell you what I told the guy who came by last night. I haven't seen Steve since Tuesday. He always smiles and waves, but keeps to himself, ya know?" She shoved her curly black hair from her flushed face. "Tuesday was my day off, and a delivery driver dropped off a box for Steve. There's been trouble with people's packages being stolen lately. Don't figure it's anything serious. Just kids havin' fun.

Still, I didn't want anyone taking the thing, so I brought it in. Left a note under Steve's door. I've checked a few times since, and the note is still there."

Steve hadn't been home since Tuesday? Jasper's stomach sank lower. "Thanks for letting me know. If you see him, can you tell him Jasper Hooke was asking for him?"

The woman smiled and nodded. "No problem."

Jasper turned to go to his car, worry tightening his chest.

If Steve was gone for good, why had he left his car?

What was in the package?

And who in the world had stopped by last night?

The woman's door closed, and the porch light turned off.

Jasper whirled around and jogged back to her porch. When he knocked, the door opened right away. "I'm sorry to bother you again," he rushed when he saw the confusion on the woman's face. "This is going to sound strange, but can you tell me what the other man asking for Steve looked like?"

She tapped her lips with an unpainted nail as she thought. "He was young, eighteen or nineteen maybe? Black hair, dark eyes. Friendly enough. Very polite. Nothing like the hellions I'm raising."

Could it have been one of the PAN?

No, that didn't make sense. They would know Steve's whereabouts.

Jasper thanked the woman again before jogging to his car. For some reason, he watched Steve's dark apartment for another ten minutes. He tried calling Steve, but it went straight to voicemail. He couldn't shake the feeling that something was wrong.

267

The following morning, Jasper cornered Sarah by the coffee maker. "Hey. Do you have a second? I have a question to ask you."

Her eyebrows came together, and her lips pressed into a flat line. "*Ooookay?*"

Behind him, Eliza slammed her coffee mug on the counter.

Jasper didn't spare her a second glance. "Have you heard from Steve this week?"

"Nope." She added a packet of sugar to her coffee and reached for one of the wooden stirrers in the caddy. "We were supposed to go for drinks two nights ago, but the jerk stood me up."

"Did you try texting him?"

"Uh, yeah." She rolled her eyes. "I've been texting him all week. Radio silence."

If Steve had left for Neverland, he would have at least said goodbye to Sarah, right? He didn't seem like the kind of guy to treat a woman so poorly.

But then again, what did Jasper know?

Jasper was a notoriously poor judge of character.

He brought his coffee to his desk and sank onto his chair. It was official. Steve had disappeared. At first, he'd felt betrayed for being abandoned. Now he was worried. *Really* worried. Things weren't adding up.

Should he call the police? How would they even help? If only there was some way to contact the PAN and make sure Steve was okay.

What was he saying? Steve was fine. He had probably taken the thumb drive Jasper had left and gone straight back to Neverland. If only he had kept his promise and brought Jasper with him.

The phone at his desk rang, pulling him from his misery. "This is Jasper Hooke."

"I need to speak with you in my office."

It was Lawrence. Jasper's gaze flicked to the date on his desk calendar.

It was time to face his fate.

Either his brother had learned about the security breach or he was going to ask for the non-existent anti-aging injection.

Either way, Jasper was going to be fired.

Instead of spending the last week scrambling, Jasper had scoured old research in hopes of a breakthrough.

All this nonsense with Steve had reminded him that the only person he could rely on was himself. And if he was going to activate his NG-1882, he was going to have to do it on his own. He had been slowly "acquiring" lab equipment. A beaker here. A hot plate there. An old microscope he'd claimed needed fixed. An extra centrifuge that had been stuck in the back of a cabinet and forgotten. The spare room in his house had become a makeshift lab. He wouldn't have access to any of the large equipment, like the CRISPR machine, or mass spectrometer, or thermocycler, but when he found a new job in a genetics lab, he'd have access to all of them.

That was *if* he got a job.

Jasper didn't bother changing out of his lab coat. He dropped his cell phone into his pocket and nodded to a stone-faced Mario on his way out. The walk between buildings was cool. The monstrous new complex was coming along quickly now that it had been closed in from the elements. Every day, construction workers in hard hats and yellow vests bustled in and out of the building, leaving the formerly pristine lawns a muddy mess.

Jasper used his key card to unlock the main door at the Admin building. He wiped the mud from his shoes onto the dark rug at the entrance and waved toward Priscilla, HOOK's receptionist. The middle-aged woman returned the wave before turning back to her computer.

The door to Lawrence's office was ajar, but Jasper knocked anyway.

Anything to delay the inevitable.

"Come in."

Jasper found his brother leaning over his bookshelf, his back to the room. "You wanted to see me?" He tucked his clammy hands into his lab coat pockets.

"We need to discuss your progress," Lawrence said, not bothering to turn around.

So, Lawrence hadn't found out about the files he'd stolen. *Yet.* "About that." Jasper cleared his throat and shifted his weight from one foot to the other. "I'm running behind, but if you give me a bit more time, I promise you'll get something that'll—"

"Jasper Hooke. You're a genius."

There must have been something wrong with Jasper's hearing. He couldn't think of one time in thirty years that Lawrence had given him a genuine compliment.

Lawrence twisted around, a grin on his face.

Only it wasn't the Lawrence Jasper had seen yesterday.

It was Lawrence from ten years ago, a fresh, youthful glow on his unlined face. Even the grays at his temple were gone.

"What happened to you?" Jasper rubbed his eyes. He had to be seeing things.

"This shit," Lawrence said, holding a black pot filled with clear cream toward Jasper, "is going to make us *billions.*"

No way. Steve had actually come through.

"Where did you find that?" Jasper choked, dread tainting his relief.

"In your desk drawer, you sneaky bastard." A grin. "How long have you had it ready?"

"Why were you rummaging through my drawers?" Had he found the notes Jasper had been keeping about activating his dormant gene? Were they still there, or had Lawrence confiscated them too?

"Routine security check." Lawrence propped himself against the front of his desk, knocking over the newly framed photo of himself and Louise from the night they'd gotten engaged. "Why the hell didn't you store it in my safe?"

Jasper's gaze flicked to the ominous black box behind his brother's desk. "The lab is secure enough."

"How can you be that naïve? People would kill for this." He lifted the cream to examine it more closely. "We've had a lot of shit go missing lately. And just the other day, there was a major security breach."

Dammit.

Jasper's heart pounded, sweat beading on his upper lip. Lawrence knew about the files. Did he know Jasper had been the one to take them? "What kind of breach?" His voice cracked on the last word.

Lawrence waved his question away. "Nothing to concern yourself with, Rat." His finger tapped against the cream. "When can you have more of this?"

"It'll be a while. It's . . . um . . . it's not tested. You really shouldn't have put it on your face. We'll have to go for FDA approval, so it could take years before the product is commercially available." That sounded believable enough, right?

"You dragged your feet for so long, I didn't think you were going to do it. I have to admit, I was kinda looking forward to firing your ass," Lawrence laughed.

At least this "discovery" would buy him time to gather more information and find another job. It wouldn't be in Neverland, but any place had to be better than HOOK.

"Actually, it wasn't me at all. One of the guys in the lab came up with it."

Lawrence's smile disappeared. "Was his name Steve?"

"Yeah. How did you know?"

Lawrence swore and ripped a paper from his desk. Beneath it was a red restricted access key card. He shoved the paper into Jasper's hands.

To Whom It May Concern:
Please consider this my formal resignation . . .

Jasper read it over twice, wishing things hadn't ended like this. Some small part of him had hoped that Steve would show up today and make good on his promise to take Jasper with him. But Steve had quit.

Lawrence was right. Jasper was naïve.

Steve wasn't in trouble.

He had taken the information and left Jasper to fend for himself.

He'd thought they were friends.

He'd thought they were the same.

But they weren't the same.

Steve had his family, friends, and an entire community of people supporting him.

Jasper had no one.

THIRTY

Deacon burst through their front door, then cursed. Vivienne jerked upright from where she'd been lounging on the sofa, scrolling through Instagram and texting Emily about bringing over some ice cream later.

"I'm so sorry, I didn't realize you were asleep." His face was flushed, and his jacket was unzipped, revealing a fitted black T-shirt beneath. The dark, hole-ridden jeans he wore hung low on his hips, revealing a sliver of the waistband on his boxer briefs.

If she'd known how hot he'd looked when he went to meet Ethan for lunch at Kensington, she wouldn't have let him leave the bedroom.

"I was awake." She yawned, rubbing the tiredness from her eyes. "Just being lazy."

It had been a week since Deacon had told her that he was going to get neutralized when she did—and she hadn't slept right since. There was nothing she could do to stop him, he'd made that much clear. But knowing he was going to give up everything he'd once lived for . . . it didn't seem fair.

A small, selfish part of her was relieved that they would be grounded together. Not that she wanted him to die. But knowing he wasn't going to end up with someone else after she was gone made her inexplicably happy.

She blamed it on her hormones.

Deacon's smile was wide and giddy as he dropped his keys into the bowl on the entry table and shed his coat onto the floor. It had been a long time since she had seen him look like that. And he *never* left his clothes in a heap. That was her thing.

"Why do you look like you just got away with some ridiculous prank?" she asked.

A wave of fresh air breezed over her as he rushed to her side. "They found it."

"Found what?"

"A vaccine."

Vaccine? What the heck was he talking about? A vaccine for what?

"Do you know what this means?" Deacon dropped to his knees and collected her hands in his.

Vivienne shook her head, afraid to admit she didn't have a clue what he was talking about.

Deacon's lips were soft as they grazed her knuckles. "Apparently, the lab in Harrow figured out how to create a vaccine for HOOK's poison."

"That's great." At least her fellow PAN would be safe from HOOK—as long as they didn't get shot.

Deacon squeezed her fingers and adjusted his stance. "Not only does it make the poison ineffective, but it can *fix forgetfulness.*"

Did he just say . . .

Hope sparked inside Vivienne's chest, chaotic heat building and building and building until she felt like she could fly again. Not that she'd take a chance and try. But her dormant fire was definitely back. "Are you serious?"

Deacon nodded. "I told you, didn't I? I *told* you."

When he pressed a hard kiss to her lips, she could taste his relief. His fingers tangled in her hair as he held her against him. Their tongues met with a sense of urgency. As interested as she was in where this was leading, Vivienne cupped his strong jaw and pulled away. "Tell me everything."

"Right. Sorry." His lopsided grin tugged at her heart. Deacon's arms came around her waist, and he pulled her close, fitting his hips between her knees. "Steve got access to HOOK's VPN. Gwen and her team were able to use the info to create an alternative injection that should take away the lethal effects of the poison. I don't understand the science behind it, but essentially, they'll be able to bring down levels of nGh artificially, with only a few mild side effects."

"I don't believe it." The next time she saw Steve, she was going to give him the biggest hug ever.

"Believe it, lovie. The injection still needs to go through a few rounds of testing, but Peter said everything looks promising. He wants us to come to Harrow right away."

Vivienne held on to that hope in her core, letting it warm her and spread through her veins. "What time's our flight?"

Being back in the Leadership Chamber felt surreal. Instead of being somber and serious, the PAN were chatting and laughing. Energy vibrated around the room of stained glass rainbows, making them seem brighter, almost magical.

Gwen stood in front of a whiteboard, pointing at equations and numbers that looked like a bunch of toddler scribbles. Deacon mumbled something about the stool hurting his butt, and Vivienne smiled. They were really uncomfortable.

But that was probably a good thing. After being stuck on a plane all night, she was beyond exhausted. If they had been soft, she'd definitely be asleep. And she didn't want to sleep through this.

Alex was sitting in the front with the rest of Leadership. He'd greeted her with a hug when they had first arrived. Deacon hadn't said a word, but his jaw had been ticking. Thankfully, he had kept his fists to himself.

Vivienne focused on Gwen, but what she was saying didn't make any sense. She was talking about splicing RNA and hormone suppression and adrenaline and measles and a bunch of terms that went right over Vivienne's head.

Then Gwen said the sweetest words that had ever come out of her evil mouth: "We think we also stumbled upon a cure for forgetfulness."

A cure. Even if Vivienne had to wait until after the baby was born, her forgetfulness wouldn't be forever. There was a light at the end of this dark tunnel.

"First, if we're right, this would neutralize the effects of HOOK's poison. Meaning if you're injected, it won't deactivate your Nevergene," Gwen explained, shining a laser pointer on a bunch of letters and numbers on the bottom corner of the board. "The only downside is that our serum will restart the ageing process."

That brought about a new round of concerned whispers.

"It won't be rapid," Gwen assured them, tucking the laser pointer into her lab coat pocket. "We estimate a six-month age progression for every decade you've been alive. But this would essentially take away our immortality."

The PAN around Vivienne exchanged worried glances, and the muttering got louder. Behind her, someone whispered, "What's the point then?"

The point was that HOOK couldn't hurt them anymore. Not with their poison anyway. And the plague of forgetfulness would be over.

"And there's another problem," Gwen went on, her lips pursing into a perfect red pout.

Beside Vivienne, she felt Deacon stiffen. His hold on her hand tightened.

Gwen moved to where vials of blue liquid were displayed on a rolling tray lined with medical supplies and plucked one from the stand. "We don't have any way of testing it. The patients in Scotland don't have the faculties to give their consent, and we'll need volunteers."

"I'll do it."

Everyone turned to where Peter lounged, draped across the stairs, his feet three steps higher than his head. He'd been laying like that for almost the entire presentation, pressing buttons on his watch every so often and bouncing his heels off the steps.

"Are you mad? We're not letting you risk your life for this," Slightly snapped.

"*Letting me?*" Peter twisted so he was in a seated position. His head cocked to the side and his eyes narrowed. "You think you have a say in what I decide to do with my life?"

"That's not what I meant." Slightly averted his gaze and tugged on the ends of his waistcoat. "It's just that you're our leader, and without you, we're nothing."

If something happened to Peter, the Neverlands would descend into chaos.

"That's utter nonsense," Peter snorted, waving away Slightly's concern with a flick of his wrist. "I'm an old man trapped in a teenager's body. I've experienced more love than most people hope for in a lifetime. I've seen my children and grandchildren grow, which is more than many of our brothers and sisters can say."

"And if something goes wrong?" Mary asked from her seat in front of Deacon. "If it kills you?"

The toast Vivienne had eaten earlier felt like it was about to come back up. She pressed a hand to her tiny bump. She

277

had come to hear about a solution, not to watch Peter Pan die.

"Then you can say 'I told you so,'" Peter said with a grin, standing and straightening his jeans. "It's a risk I'm prepared to take in order to make our family a little bit safer. In order to give my best mate a chance to annoy me for another century." He rolled up his sleeve and flew down to where Gwen waited with wide, worried eyes.

"I'm not . . . I can't do it right now." Gwen scooted the rolling tray behind her. "We need to monitor your vitals. We need to take blood and check that you're healthy."

"Gwen?" Peter's eyebrows lifted. "Give me the injection. That's an order."

Frantic whispers buzzed around the chamber as the other PAN exchanged horrified glances.

Gwen finished pushing Peter's sleeve over his bicep and pulled an antiseptic wipe from a pack. After cleaning the area, Gwen stuck the needle into Peter's arm. Peter didn't so much as wince as the blue liquid disappeared. After replacing the needle with a cotton ball, Gwen secured it with surgical tape.

"That wasn't so hard, now was it? And look. I feel just—" Peter's eyes widened. His hand flew to his chest. Stumbling back, he collapsed onto the tiles.

Deacon shot to his feet. Mary whimpered as she flew to Peter's side. Gasps and wails and curses lifted around the room.

Then there was silence.

Peter couldn't be dead. He just couldn't.

A single bark of laughter echoed.

Then another.

And then Peter started laughing so hard he was wheezing.

"I'm sorry. I'm so sorry. Please forgive me," Peter managed through fits of laughter, sitting up and clutching his stomach. "It's just . . . How often will I get to scare the shite out of an entire room of people?" Peter wiped at the tears in his eyes, his face turning red as he continued laughing. "Oh, Mary. You should've seen your . . . your *face!*"

And Peter lost it again.

Deacon fell back onto his seat, smiling and shaking his head.

"I hate you so much right now," Mary spat, punching Peter in the arm.

"Dammit. You don't have to hit me." Peter winced, rubbing his shoulder. "I did just get an injection, you know."

Gwen dropped to her knees beside Deacon. Vivienne felt like pushing her out of the way. "How are you feeling, Peter?"

"Besides a bit of a sore arm thanks to my brute of a daughter, I feel fine. A bit tingly, maybe. But it's not uncomfortable."

"Grandad," Deacon whispered, his eyes widening, "your face . . . "

Peter's face was ageing right before their eyes. He didn't look old, maybe late twenties. But there was no mistaking the shadow of stubble on his strong jaw.

Holy crap.

Peter Pan with stubble was hot.

Gross. That was her husband's grandfather.

Gross!

"Hell. Yes," Ethan muttered from his seat behind Vivienne. When she turned around, she saw him rubbing his smooth cheek. "Do me next, Gwen!"

Everyone started laughing, and Vivienne found herself giggling too.

Gwen rolled her eyes and told Ethan to shut up.

"How will we know if HOOK's poison will hurt him?" Mary asked, clutching Peter's shoulder as she pulled his chin from side to side to examine him.

Peter started rolling up his other sleeve. "Give me some and we'll find out."

"I swear, Da. If you don't stop offering to let people inject you, I'm going to stab you myself."

"Mary's right. Let's see how this settles first, yeah?" Gwen said with a smile.

"Can you still fly?" Richard Two asked, rising from his chair between Nibs and Curly.

Peter grinned as he stretched his hands toward the ceiling. "There's only one way to find out."

THIRTY-ONE

The ballroom at Áite Sítheil was as silent as a bloody tomb despite the crowd of people waiting for the first forgetful PAN to be injected. Deacon shifted his weight from one foot to the other. His fingers ached from Vivienne's death grip.

He tore his gaze from the nurse attaching a needle to a vial of blue liquid.

The chandelier reflected in Vivienne's wide eyes as she chewed her lip. Deacon gave her hand a reassuring squeeze.

The core members of Leadership had signed up to receive the vaccine, feeling it was their duty as the oldest PAN to volunteer as test subjects. A few younger PAN had volunteered as well—including Ethan, Gwen, and a number of lab workers. Apparently, to Ethan, facial hair was more important than immortality.

So far, everything had gone well. The only side effect appeared to be slight, sudden ageing. They still had a long way to go before testing it against HOOK's poison, but at least it was a start.

Peter's hands flexed as he fidgeted with the buttons on his watch. His knees bounced beneath the table separating him from his best mate.

It had been a week, and Deacon still couldn't get used to seeing his grandad with a stubbled jaw. The laugh lines around his mouth and tiny wrinkles at the corners of his eyes were well earned. But so, *so* odd.

Tootles sat across from Peter, looking as confused as ever. It had nothing to do with Peter's change in appearance. Tootles didn't even know Peter's name.

Tootles' glasses were tucked into the pocket of his white button-down shirt. His gold alarm clock was in pieces again, spread across the table like a shiny puzzle.

"What's this injection for?" Tootles asked, frowning at the nurse in green scrubs cleaning his upper arm with an alcohol wipe.

"It's something to help you remember," Peter said for the fourth time in as many minutes, not a hint of frustration in his tone.

He had the patience of a bloody saint.

Tootles' light eyebrows came together over searching blue eyes. "Remember what?"

Peter just shook his head.

Vivienne squeezed Deacon's hand harder as the nurse injected Tootles.

"There now, pet," she said in a thick Irish accent. "I'm all done with ye." She put a plaster over the injection site and rolled the silver cart over to the window.

It seemed like everyone watching let out a collective breath.

Tootles scowled at his plaster like he didn't remember where it had come from.

This had to work. It *had* to.

Deacon prayed to whoever was listening. He'd made more mistakes than he could ever count, so he didn't deserve anything good. But with everything that had gone wrong lately, something *had* to go right.

Seconds ticked by, and still they waited.

The rest of the forgetful would be injected if this worked.

Dammit. It had to work.

Tootles' face began ageing; the lines around his mouth were faint, but they were there. Deacon's adrenaline stirred.

It was working . . .

But would it fix Tootles' memory?

Peter's knees stopped bouncing as he leaned forward, resting his elbows on the clock-strewn table. "Tootles?"

Still staring at the plaster, Tootles muttered, "I hate bloomin' needles."

Peter huffed a laugh. Deacon could feel his grandad's resignation as his shoulders fell. "Tell me someone who doesn't."

Vivienne closed her eyes and pressed her forehead against Deacon's arm; silent tears rolled down her cheeks.

It *had* to work.

It just *had* to—

Tootles' head snapped up. Tilted. The fog seemed to leave his blue eyes as they narrowed on Deacon's grandad.

"*Peter?*"

Deacon rolled over in bed and checked his watch where he'd discarded it on the bedside locker. They had one hour to kill until the next Leadership meeting. Vivienne slipped her cold hands across his bare stomach, tucking them into the waist-band of his pants. For some reason, the woman was always cold.

"Did you sleep?" she asked, her voice thick and husky

from the nap she'd taken. Deacon already had trouble sleeping at night, so he wasn't very fond of napping. But when his wife had asked him to come to bed with her two hours ago, he couldn't resist.

"I passed out right after you started snoring." He'd been exhausted after their joyful trip to Scotland the day before. His uncle Tootles' memory was slow in returning, but he'd been forgetful for so long, it was no wonder. All that mattered was that he knew Peter's name.

Maimie had remembered Vivienne almost immediately, and spent the entire afternoon regaling her with tales of Vivienne's mother's youth.

Which meant even if Vivienne's memory failed during her pregnancy, it would come back. All they had to do was endure the next few months. Then they would have the rest of their lives together. This whole neutralization nonsense she'd planned wouldn't be necessary.

Vivienne pinched his arm. "I don't snore."

"You snore so loud, I had to put a pillow over my head to drown out the awful sound."

That earned him another pinch. "*I'll* put a pillow over your head, you jerk."

Deacon caught her hand and locked his fingers around her wrist. She squirmed and tried to get away, but he trapped her legs with his and pinned her to the bed. "You're feisty when you wake up. I kind of like it." Her lilac-scented skin tasted like sugar on his lips as he kissed his way down her neck.

"Let me go."

"Not until you promise to love me forever."

"Like I have a choice," Vivienne laughed, twisting so he got her shoulder instead of her collarbone.

Ah, well. He'd take what he could get. "Are you happy?"

"The only thing that would make me happier is if you got the injection."

Back to this again. He wished she'd let it go.

Deacon released his hold on her and fell onto his back with a groan. "You first."

"I can't get it until I have the baby."

"And that's when I'll get mine."

Vivienne glared at him from her pillow. If she thought that was going to sway him, she was going to be disappointed. All it did was make him want to kiss her pouty lips.

"Are you really that anxious for me to grow facial hair?" he asked, touching her smooth cheek.

Vivienne rolled her eyes. "I'm *anxious* for you to be safe from HOOK's poison."

"Tell you what. Why don't we compromise?" She was always preaching about give and take. "I'll get the injection if you agree to let me grow a soul patch."

Every time Deacon saw Ethan, his best mate had a different style of facial hair.

Full-beard. Goatee. Mustache. Fu Manchu. And finally, a soul patch.

Deacon had lied and told him that the soul patch was brilliant. It had been a week, and Ethan still hadn't shaved it off. How long would it take him to realize that patch of hair was the reason women were avoiding him?

Vivienne's eyes widened, and she shook her head. "No deal. If you grow one, it's grounds for divorce. You're allowed a five o'clock shadow and that's it."

"Then I'm afraid you'll have to wait until our little potato is finished cooking."

Deacon had started calling their baby that at the last ultrasound. The little one had been in Vivienne's stomach, flailing her arms and legs like she was dancing. Deacon had told Vivienne that all babies looked like potatoes. It was kind of true. The babies he'd seen had the same squished-face, old-mannish features.

Vivienne and the ultrasound tech had been appalled.

"We'll get injected together," he said. "It can be our first post-potato date night."

If any side effects showed up between now and then, or if it didn't work 100%, he had no doubt that Vivienne wouldn't hesitate to let them neutralize her instead of taking the vaccine. And if he'd already been vaccinated, he'd be immune to neutralization.

Whatever happened, they were going to do it together.

Deacon smoothed the wrinkle forming between her eyebrows. Before she could argue, his fingertips grazed her upper lip. "You're going to look so sexy with a mustache."

Like a switch had been flipped, her dark eyes narrowed. "I'm going to make you pay for that comment."

His blood stirred with the heat of desire. "Now?"

Vivienne rolled on top of him; her dark hair fell in a curtain around their faces as she leaned closer and whispered against his ear, "Right now."

"Today, we welcome our newest member of Leadership, Lee Somerfield." The noise level from the congregation lifted with applause.

Deacon couldn't help the grin spreading across his face. He'd spoken to Lee himself about the nomination. Lee wasn't thrilled, because it meant he had to play by the rules, but Deacon figured that was why he had been chosen to replace Aoibheann on the committee.

She was there though, sitting in the back with Caoilfhionn and Muireann. Three angry Mermaids. Deacon tried keeping his eyes forward but they kept drifting to her. What had compelled her to send Vivienne those photos? What could she have hoped to gain? The only life she had ruined was her own. Why bother?

Nicola was there too, sitting next to Graham. She'd tried waving to him, but Deacon had ignored her.

Lee sat down next to Slightly, looking more like his father than someone half Slightly's age. They had formed an unlikely friendship over the last few months. Lee had been making routine trips to Harrow in preparation for his appointment. According to Peter, Lee and Slightly had ended up tucked into the corner of the Wendy Bird, locked in serious discussions after every meeting. They were two sides of the aisle coming together, the old ways and the new.

The members of Leadership looked strange with their newly-stubbled faces.

Donovan called the meeting to order, his booming voice causing the crowd to stop their chatter and turn toward the members of Leadership sitting at the front of the chamber. "Lee, you have the floor."

"Thank you, Donovan." Lee smoothed a hand down his dark waistcoat before moving to stand between the rest of Leadership and the congregation. "Today, I would like to propose something that would change our world as we know it. I have been an advocate for going public ever since I first came to Neverland. There are those of you who have agreed with me"—his gaze cut to Deacon's mother—"and those of you who cannot see the merits.

"But before you discount the idea entirely, I want to share with you my vision for Neverland." Lee undid the buttons on his cuffs and rolled his sleeves to his elbows, exposing his blackened veins. The congregation stirred uncomfortably on their stools. "Imagine what it would be like to fly in broad daylight. How it would feel to meet new people and tell them proudly that you're a PAN. Imagine how many more PAN we could find if outsiders knew about the Nevergene. We're hiding away in secret while HOOK thrives in the open." He threw a hand toward the ceiling. *"They're* the

287

villains in this story. We should be the ones flying in the light."

"The state of this world is tragic," Slightly said, though not unkindly. "I'm not sure I want my children or grandchildren or great-grandchildren to be part of it."

"They're part of it whether you like it or not." Lee folded his arms across his chest and shook his head. His lips pressed together as he frowned. "Just because we're hiding away in our Neverlands doesn't mean we're living in a bubble. Our people interact with outsiders every day. In the supermarkets, at the gas station, the mall, on the bus or train, in restaurants. And because PAN look like teenagers, they're treated like children." Lee turned toward the congregation. "How many of you have been dismissed because you're 'only a kid'?"

Every one of the PAN raised their hands. It was one of the downsides of being eternally eighteen. Deacon hated how outsiders spoke down to him, like he couldn't possibly know as much as they did. He could only imagine how infuriating it was for those who were even older.

"See?" Lee stepped closer to Slightly. "You already face prejudice every day. The color of your skin, your religion, your sexual orientation, your age, your active Nevergene—it doesn't matter. The world finds fault in difference. But what if we could show them that there is *magic* in diversity?"

"Prejudice has been around since the dawn of time. We're hardly going to change their minds."

"Why do you assume this is going to create more division instead of bringing about more unity?" Lee directed his question toward Slightly before twisting to face the congregation. "Going public can help us show a disillusioned society that *magic exists*. That they could be part of something so much bigger than themselves."

It wasn't until that moment that Deacon saw why his mother had fallen for Lee Somerfield. Unlike most of the cynical Leadership panel, Lee was an idealist. If what HOOK had done to him and his brother hadn't turned him so bitter, there's no telling what would have happened.

Deacon scanned the crowd, trying to gauge their mixed reactions. Again, his gaze landed on Aoibheann. When he found her scowling at him, his stomach twisted. He couldn't let it go. He had to know what he'd done to deserve her hatred.

The vote ended split down the middle, with Peter refusing to weigh in either way. But it had opened a dialogue, and from the chatter afterwards, Deacon knew the discussions in the Wendy Bird would be about nothing else.

The thought of coming into the open went against everything he'd been taught for the last twenty-six years. But Neverland was due for a change. And he didn't want his child growing up having to lie about her very existence. He wanted her to be able to fly to school in the mornings. To date whomever she wished without worrying about them finding out who she was. He wanted her to grow up in the light instead of hiding in the shadows.

Most of the congregation headed toward the tunnels, but the Mermaids stood and started for the stairs. Deacon told Ethan he'd meet him at the pub and followed Aoibheann up and out into the fading day.

Caoilfhionn and Muireann were chatting, Aoibheann a few steps behind. Her shoulders were rigid, and her long, greenish-blond hair swayed as she walked. Deacon called for her, but instead of stopping, she picked up her pace. Caoilfhionn and Muireann twisted toward him, both wearing the same wide-eyed looks of surprise. He bypassed them and eventually caught up to Aoibheann outside of Harrow Hall.

"Aoibheann, wait up. Please."

She whirled on him, blue eyes narrowed and full of hate. "Leave me alone, Dash."

The venom in her voice sent him back a step, into the shadows cast by one of the Hall's tall chimneys. "Look, whatever I did, I'm sorry."

"You're sorry?" She huffed a mirthless laugh. "*You* are *sorry.*" Shaking her head, her lips twisted into a mocking smile. "Take your worthless apology and shove it up your ass. It means *nothing*. Do you hear me? *Nothing*."

"Tell me what I did to deserve this." Those messages may have been sent to Vivienne, but they had been an attack on him. On his relationship. On his happiness.

"You said you'd never get married. Do you remember that?" She stalked forward until she was within arm's reach. "Said you didn't 'believe' in it. That you didn't want to settle down with just one woman. And I was fine with that." Aoibheann crossed her arms over her heaving chest, her cheeks red and eyes blazing with fury. "But you only said those things because you didn't want to be with *me*."

He had said those things—and more. "They were true at the time—"

"Bullshit." She shoved his chest, sending him back another step. "I let you treat me like I wasn't enough for you. For anyone. And that's on me. But your little *fiancée* deserved to know the truth about you before she made the biggest mistake of her life."

Deacon had changed. It didn't matter if Aoibheann couldn't see it. "I'm sorry I made you feel that way. I was an immature asshole and I treated you poorly. You deserved better."

Her mouth opened . . . then closed. A V formed between her eyebrows as she searched his face. He shifted uncomfortably under the force of her scrutiny. But there was nothing more for him to say. He had taken ownership of his actions and apologized. Whether or not she forgave him was on her.

"I do deserve better," she said finally, lifting her chin and twirling toward the serpentine drive.

THIRTY-TWO

The Wendy Bird was packed. Ethan waved at him from a table in the back beneath an old Guinness poster. Deacon dropped onto the stool beside him with a sigh. He had considered heading back to the flat after his confrontation with Aoibheann, but figured he'd be better off getting rid of some of his adrenaline before telling Vivienne what had happened.

"What are you drinking?" Deacon asked, nodding toward the glass of clear liquid in Ethan's hand. He had only ever seen Ethan drink three things: beer, cider, or bourbon.

Ethan leaned closer and whispered, "Water."

"You're drinking w—"

Ethan's hand connected with Deacon's mouth, smothering his words. "Don't advertise it, man." When he removed his hand, his gaze darted around the room. "I don't want people knowing."

"Why not?"

A shrug. "I don't know. I guess I just don't want to answer their questions."

Deacon understood. He didn't like when others poked their noses into his business either. "Good for you, mate." Deacon clinked his glass of soda against Ethan's. He had decided to stop drinking until the baby was born. If Vivienne needed him, he would need all his faculties. The last thing they wanted was another tunnel disaster.

"This place isn't nearly as fun sober."

Deacon looked around the room at his fellow PAN mixing with a handful of oblivious outsiders. "Can you imagine what it'd be like if the outsiders knew about us?"

Ethan's head tilted as he considered. "It'd be awesome. Think of all the girls we'd—I mean, *I'd* get."

Deacon hid his smile in his drink. Ethan wasn't getting any women until he shaved off that bit of fluff taking over his chin. "You do realize this is so much bigger than that, right? We'd be changing the world."

Ethan shoved his shoulder so hard it nearly knocked him off the stool. "Preaching to the choir, man. I've been on board with Lee's ideas from day one. You're the one who's late to the party."

"They're going to do it." Deacon felt it in his bones. Neverland was changing. One day—and soon—his dream of flying in the middle of Times Square was going to become a reality. "It's just a matter of when."

He hoped that Lee would be alive to see it.

Lee was leaning against the bar, speaking to Peter, sitting on a stool next to him. Deacon's mother was with them, chiming in every once in a while, a smile on her face. What would happen to her as Lee got older? When he died?

The thought of watching her lose another person she loved made his stomach ache.

"All we need is one more vote." Ethan sipped his water, then made a face.

It would take a lot more than that. "Then they'll have to vote on how to do it. And when. And where. And you know everyone will have different opinions. Do you remember how long it took for them to decide on crest colors?"

It had taken them seven years to choose gold.

Gold.

Ethan groaned. "I totally forgot about that."

Perhaps that was why the PAN held their traditions and rules so close; changing them took ages.

When Deacon looked up from his drink, he found himself staring into Nicola's blue eyes.

"Hey, Dash." Her smile was strained as she fiddled with the zipper on her black leather jacket. "Can we talk?"

Deacon set his drink aside and lifted his jacket from the back of the stool. "Not now. I was just leaving."

"Come on. Give me five minutes. Please?"

"It's just five minutes." Ethan offered Nicola a smile. "Surely she deserves that."

Deacon thought Nicola deserved to be exiled in Limerick along with Aoibheann for what she'd done, orders or not, but he kept his mouth shut. "Whose side are you on?"

Ethan shrugged. "I'm a sucker for a beautiful woman in need."

So *that* was what this was about. Ethan was trying to get back into his ex's good graces.

Deacon stuffed his arms into the sleeves of his jacket and zipped it halfway. Aoibheann had listened to him; perhaps he could extend the same courtesy to his former friend. "I'll give you three." After saying goodbye to Ethan, Deacon pushed his way past Curly and Nibs, skirted around a table of outsiders, and opened the door to the dark night. Instead of waiting for Nicola, he continued until he reached the shed at the back of the pub that concealed the entrance to the tunnels.

When he turned around, Nicola was behind him, her face

draped in shadows. It never ceased to amaze him the way everyone working in Extraction moved like ghosts. "All right. Go."

"First, I want to apologize," Nicola said, picking at her nails. "I shouldn't have taken the assignment. I was just so mad at you when you said you didn't want to see me anymore."

Bloody hell. That had been eight years ago. They'd hooked up during their mission, and when they got back, the magic had worn off—at least for him. "And that warranted spying on me for almost a decade?"

"No. It didn't. But I was the only one from Extraction you were close to." A sigh. "And no one else wanted the job."

That was because they had souls. "You could have said something."

Her eyebrows arched toward her hairline. "Would it have helped?"

Probably not. Although Deacon would've tried to be a bit more discreet. Still, "It wouldn't have hurt."

Dropping her chin, Nicola nodded. "Do you think you'll ever forgive me?"

Deacon could either carry it around, allowing his anger to weigh him down, or he could let it go. "I'm sure I will." He was on his way to forgiving Aoibheann, and she had been the one to start this mess. "But I'm not there yet."

She nodded again, but this time, she offered him a tentative smile.

"You guys done?" a voice called from the darkness. Ethan came around the whitewashed building and waved.

Deacon wouldn't put it past the two of them to have planned this whole thing. "Yes. We're finished."

"Good. You heading home?"

Deacon nodded. "The wife is waiting for me." He wanted to get back before it got too late in case it was another bad night.

Chuckling, Nicola shook her head. "I still can't believe you have a wife."

"Whatever about the wife." Ethan tucked his hands into his pockets and kicked at a clump of daffodils growing along the path. "I can't believe he's going to have a little potato—and is happy about it."

"Me either." Deacon had always assumed that if he had children, it would either be a terrible accident or when he was at least a hundred years old.

"Potato?" Nicola's eyebrows came together as she glanced between the two of them. "Do I even want to know what that means?"

It was only a matter of time before everyone found out. "Vivienne's pregnant," Deacon told her. They'd known for weeks, and it still felt strange saying it aloud. "She's due at the end of September."

Nicola launched herself at him, wrapping her arms around his neck. "*Ahhh!* I'm so excited for you guys."

Deacon stiffened. Since getting married, he'd felt awkward around women. What was he supposed to do with his hands? He'd never had a problem figuring it out before. After a moment, he relaxed and patted Nicola on the back.

"How's she been feeling lately?" Ethan asked Deacon, his eyes following Nicola's every move. "Any more flare-ups?"

Deacon had told Ethan about the night Vivienne had attacked him. But instead of using the word "attack," which made his beautiful wife sound like a violent maniac, he'd decided to refer to the incident as a "flare-up."

Nights were getting harder and harder to endure. They were lucky to go two days without an incident. But that was between himself and Vivienne.

"She's still forgetting little things here and there." The other night, she'd forgotten to turn off the water in the bathtub and had flooded the entire bathroom. It hadn't been entirely her fault though. Deacon had dragged her into the bedroom the moment her jumper had hit the ground. She'd been a little too distracted to remember.

Nicola cursed. "The rumors are true then?"

Deacon knew people talked. And the PAN loved nothing more than a bit of juicy gossip. He saw no point in denying it, especially now that there was a cure. "I'm afraid so. She can't get the injection until she has the baby."

Ethan clapped Deacon on the shoulder and gave him a rattling shake. "Only a few more months to go, poppa."

"I'm sorry." Nicola held up an hand and turned to Ethan with narrowed eyes. "This has been killing me all night. What is that *thing* on your face?"

Ethan crooked a smile as he stroked the patch of hair on his chin. "Do you like it?"

"Absolutely not." She planted her hands on her hips. "It's gross. You should get rid of it."

Deacon hid his snigger behind his hand.

Ethan's eyes narrowed into slits as he twisted toward Deacon. "What the hell, man? You told me it looked good!"

THIRTY-THREE

"What was I going to do?" Vivienne looked around their bedroom for a clue. She had gotten out of bed to do *something*. There were no clothes on the floor, so she wasn't going to clean up. None in the hamper, so she wasn't going to do laundry. She didn't have to pee either—which was a miracle. It seemed like she always had to pee.

Ever since they'd gotten back to Kensington two days earlier, she had been in a fog. And it wasn't all jet lag.

Deacon settled himself against the pillows. The covers slipped down to his waist, revealing his glorious upper half. "I believe you were about to take off your top."

The giddy fireflies living in her belly woke up. "I was?"

She glanced down at her Ohio sweatshirt. That didn't sound right.

"Do you think I'd lie to you?" He covered his mouth with his hand but couldn't hide his growing smile.

"You jerk!" Vivienne stomped back to the bed and slammed a pillow into his smug face. He didn't bother dodging it. "Don't you dare use my condition to your advantage."

"I'd make it to your advantage as well," he crooned, peering from beneath, a slow grin curling his lips.

"I'm serious, Deacon."

He lunged forward, catching her wrist and pulling her on top of him. "So am I, *Vivienne.*"

Her baby bump jiggled like Santa Claus's belly when she laughed. "This isn't funny."

"Then stop laughing."

He had to know that she was getting worse. She couldn't remember half of what she needed to do and *she* knew it was getting worse. Despite it all, Deacon managed to make her smile and laugh and feel like she was still attractive, even though she was bloated all the time and getting plumper by the day.

"I think I was going to go downstairs and get breakfast." She hadn't eaten yet, had she? Asking Deacon would only upset him.

"I like my idea better," he murmured, tugging on the hem of her sweatshirt.

"Me too," she giggled, pulling her shirt up and off.

Every step Deacon took as he descended toward the underground lab at Kensington made his stomach twist. Tomorrow was the first of April, and he couldn't put this off any longer. He ducked into the small room at the end of the dark hall and pulled the cord on the exposed bulb. When the blue screen appeared, he bent to scan his eyes. The light from the machine temporarily blinded him, making him see spots in the darkness. There was a mechanical whine, and the wall to his left disappeared.

The lab was bustling with workers. Some waved to him, but most kept their focus on whatever brilliant discovery or invention they were about to make. Robert caught up to Deacon before he reached the frosted windows at the back. His lab coat looked too small for his broad shoulders. He and Deacon had used to work out together, but since this autumn, Deacon had been too busy to go to the gym regularly.

"Hey, Dash. Is there anything I can help ya with?" Robert's smile was a flash of straight white teeth.

Deacon didn't have time for chitchat. He wanted to get this over with and get back home. "I need to speak to Alex. Is he in?"

Robert's mouth pressed into a tight line. "You're not here to cause trouble, are ya?"

"Of course not." Although he owed Alex a sucker punch. "It's about Vivienne."

Recognition lit Robert's dark eyes, and he winced. "How's she doin'?"

"She could be better." He had spent the majority of last night holding her down between fits so she didn't injure herself. The muscles in his arms still ached.

Robert nodded as he reached for the screen beside the door and scanned his hand. "If you need anything, you'll let me know, won't ya?"

"I will." But there was nothing Robert could do to help. There was nothing anyone could do now.

The microbiology sector at Kensington had always reminded Deacon of the set of a sci-fi movie, with beeping machines and workers in lab coats and goggles bent over microscopes and vials and computers.

He searched the space for Alex but couldn't see him. Then he heard a familiar voice cursing from the area at the rear of the room, near a counter with blue lights above it. Deacon found his bearded nemesis on his back beneath one of the pentagon-shaped tables, messing with a bunch of electrical cords.

When Alex saw Deacon, his eyes narrowed into slits.

Besides seeing one another at the Leadership meeting, this was the only other time Deacon had met Alex since their altercation at his house.

"I need to speak with you," Deacon said, hating that he needed this asshole's help.

Alex didn't bother getting up. "I'm busy. Come back later."

Deacon didn't give a shit how busy Alex was. "It's important."

Alex crawled out from beneath the table and stood with his arms crossed, a defiant tilt to his jaw. A jaw Deacon really, really, wanted to break.

"What is it?"

"Vivienne is getting worse."

Alex muttered as he scrubbed his hand down his cheek. "It was only a matter of time."

Deacon knew that, but he hadn't expected her to get so bad so quickly. Vivienne wandered around the house leaving the fridge and freezer open, taking everything out of the cupboards and piling it all on the counter, then walking away. Not a big deal in and of itself. But she had been trashing their room nearly every night as well recently.

Deacon tugged his sleeves to his wrists to conceal the bruises on his arms and cuts from the light fixture she'd shattered.

"Is there anything I can do to help her?" There had to be something he hadn't thought of.

There was nothing breakable left in the room. What Vivienne hadn't destroyed was hidden in the hall closet. And Deacon had installed extra locks on the doors after he found her sitting in the back garden in her knickers, staring vacantly at the starry sky.

"Not until she can get the injection." Alex adjusted the square-rimmed glasses on the bridge of his nose. "If you can't handle her, the best course of action would be to move her to Scotland."

Deacon bit back the smart retort on his tongue. He had known that would be Alex's answer but had hoped there was some alternative.

"All right." His shoulders fell in resignation. It was time to accept that this wasn't a fight he could win on his own.

Nodding, Alex started for a desk at the front of the room. "I'll take care of everything," he said, exchanging his lab coat for a denim jacket. "I'm going over in two days and can escort her myself."

Surely he wasn't serious. There was no way Deacon was going to let Alex bring his wife to Scotland without him. "I appreciate the offer," Deacon lied, stuffing his hands into his pockets so that his fist didn't "accidently" find its way to Alex's face, "but I'll handle it myself."

He and Vivienne could fly out on Sunday. That gave Deacon time to pack and get Vivienne used to the idea. He'd call Colleen at Áite Sítheil and have her reserve two rooms together. The nurses and staff could monitor his wife, and Deacon was going to monitor all of them.

Alex's eyebrows flicked up. "Is she safe at your house?"

"What's that supposed to mean?"

"I'm simply asking if she's becoming more violent at night. Because if she is, she will need to be contained." Alex removed his glasses and tossed them onto the desk. "Otherwise, there's no telling what she'll do."

How could he be so matter-of-fact about this? Didn't he care about Vivienne at all?

Deacon couldn't bring himself to admit how bad it was. "What does 'containing' her entail?"

When Alex explained, Deacon was sorry he asked.

That afternoon, a bed was delivered to their house.

At least it was *supposed* to be a bed.

It had leather bindings connected by straps that looped under the bedframe. The two in the middle were for Vivienne's wrists, and the two at the bottom were for her ankles. There was a third strap that was supposed to fasten across her midsection.

When Vivienne saw it, she sank onto the edge of the blue "mattress" and told him it looked comfortable.

Comfortable? It looked like a torture device out of a bloody nightmare.

"You're not sleeping on *that*," Deacon choked, reaching for her. They were going to shut the door to the spare room and pretend the horrific thing wasn't there. And if the staff in Scotland thought for one minute that he was going to let them tie up his wife, they had another thing coming.

"If I scarred your face, you wouldn't be nearly as hand-some." Vivienne laced their fingers together. "And then I probably wouldn't love you anymore."

Deacon chuckled reluctantly as he touched a leather binding. Every day there seemed to be less and less to laugh about.

"Besides, it's only for a few months. A few months compared to eternity isn't so bad, is it?" Vivienne wrapped her arms around his waist and laid her head against his chest.

"I should be the one comforting you."

"We comfort each other."

Deacon wasn't sure how long they stood like that, but eventually, Vivienne drew away, leaving his arms empty— and his heart emptier.

"It'll be dark soon," she said after checking her watch. "Maybe I should go to bed?"

Deacon tugged on one of the straps and forced a smile to his lips. "Want to put these to the test first?"

Vivienne giggled. "Only if you let me strap you down."

That night, Vivienne screamed so long, her voice was hoarse the next morning. She'd offered Deacon a smile and asked what was for breakfast as he unhooked her. The dullness of her hair and eyes was easier to ignore than the red marks on her wrists.

The second night was worse.

Vivienne sobbed for hours.

But the third night broke him. The third night she shouted his name.

Deacon stared at the missing light fixture above the bed the same way he had the last three bloody nights, wincing every time he heard his wife grunting as she strained against the bonds.

"Deacon, please. Please let me out. I'm here. I'm still here tonight. Please," Vivienne cried. *"Let me out."*

Did that happen? Could she have lucid nights? It was 2 a.m., so it was too late to call anyone in the States. But it was seven in the morning in London. Deacon grabbed his mobile and dialed his grandad's number.

Peter answered on the second ring. "What's wrong? Is it Vivienne? The baby?"

Deacon explained what was happening as Vivienne shouted for him in the other room.

"I know it's hard," Peter said with a frustrated sigh, "but you need to trust this is what's best for Vivienne. She may be fine right now, but in an hour, it could be another story. She'll be in Scotland in a few days, and they'll know what to do with her."

Deacon knew what they'd "do with her."

They would strap Vivienne down and ignore every strained plea that fell from her perfect lips. The same way he was right now.

"I wish I had better news. But you're strong," Peter went on. "You'll get through this. You both will."

That was the thing. Deacon *wasn't* strong. Not when it

came to hearing the woman he loved crying in the next room. He stabbed the red button on the screen and dragged a pillow over his head to drown out the terrible sounds.

Dammit. The pillowcase smelled like Vivienne's shampoo.

"Deacon! Get your butt in here and untie me or I swear I'm going to let Emily kill you!"

Vivienne remembered Emily? She hadn't remembered her in weeks. Lyle and Emily came over every other day, usually with ice cream or pie. Vivienne always remembered Lyle, but Emily was like a stranger to her.

Deacon shot out of bed and ran straight for the spare room.

"Oh, thank goodness," she whimpered when she saw him; her voice was so jagged it sounded painful. Her eyes were wide and wild in the moonlight seeping through the lone window. "Let me out. I'm still here, and I miss you. I just want to sleep with you one more night. Please."

Deacon was unfastening her bonds before the last word left her lips. Even in the dim light, he could see blood seeping from the sores on her wrists.

"I'm sorry. I'm so, so sorry." Tears clouded his vision as he pulled her into his arms and sank against the wall, cradling her in his lap. "I don't know what the hell I'm doing. All I know is that everything feels so bloody wrong."

As much as it killed him to think of bringing her to Scotland, it couldn't be any worse than this.

"I know. It's okay. Just hold me tonight."

He kissed away her tears and brought her to their bed, turning the three locks on the door behind him, just in case. She could scar his entire body, leave him in bloody ribbons. Deacon was never tying her up ever again.

"I love you." When she kissed him, her lips felt dry and cracked, and she was so small in his arms and—*dammit.* Six months. That was all. Then the baby would be here, and he would get his wife back.

Vivienne's heart sank with the sun falling behind the trees. The cool evening air smelled like the dying charcoals in the grill. It didn't matter that it had been too chilly for a back-yard barbeque. The moment Vivienne had said she wanted a burger on the grill, Deacon had organized everything.

Empty plates, cans, and condiments littered the picnic table. Deacon's best friend Ethan, her brother Lyle, and his girlfriend Emily had left an hour ago. Three o'clock had been too early for dinner, but there was no telling what time her episodes would start. The other day, it had been before five.

Deacon had invited everyone over because he and Vivienne were going on a trip. She couldn't remember where. She would ask him, except he'd stress over how bad she was getting. As long as Deacon was at the final destination with her, it would be fine.

Living in the constant state of not knowing was the worst part of this hell. Having other people tell her what she'd done. What she needed. What she liked. It was terrifying and infuriating. But Vivienne wasn't alone. All she had to do was glance at the tiny bump that made her look like she'd had a really big dinner to make herself feel better.

Her little firefly didn't have any memories either.

"We should probably go upstairs now," Vivienne said, snuggling deeper into Deacon's warm shoulder. The arm on the folding lawn chair dug into her ribs.

When she thought of the bed waiting for her in the guest room, the blistered sores around her wrists started pulsing. Every night, she told herself not to fight. To think happy thoughts as she drifted off to sleep and then wake up and pretend it was all a dream. And every morning, despite feeling exhausted, she thought that was what had happened. But the haunted look in Deacon's vacant green eyes told a different story. She'd stopped asking how bad it was after the first morning. His face was all the confirmation she needed.

"I'm not chaining you up." Deacon squeezed her closer and pressed a hard kiss against her temple. "You were fine last night. You'll be fine tonight."

"We don't know that." Vivienne drew away so she could see his face. A face she never wanted to forget. She didn't want to go back to that awful bed. But . . . "If I hurt you again, I'd never forgive myself."

Deacon's arms were bruised; his chest was covered in scratches.

His eyes narrowed as the muscles in his jaw ticked. "Hearing you in that room fighting and screaming hurts me more than anything you could ever do to me physically. Give me one more night."

It was only one more night. Vivienne could do this. She was so exhausted, she could close her eyes and go right to sleep. "Okay."

Vivienne helped Deacon clean up and then they went up to their bedroom hand-in-hand. Deacon told her that he would love her forever. She never wanted to forget the way his mouth shaped every promise he made to her that night.

Six more months.

Then they would have their forever.

THIRTY-FOUR

V ivienne flew through the stars and clouds, searching
for something. It was important. But for the life of her,
she couldn't remember what it was.

When she turned over, she found herself staring at the
photos from junior prom on her desk. Rolling onto her back,
she stretched her hands toward the ceiling.

Why were her arms and legs so sore? It felt like she had
just finished running a marathon. Not that she knew from
firsthand experience. She didn't really like running.

Yawning, she pushed herself upright. If she weren't so
hungry, she would've gone back to sleep. What time was it
anyway?

Her cell phone wasn't on the nightstand or tucked under
her pillow. Hopefully she hadn't lost it. She didn't have the
money to buy a new one.

The room felt different, but she couldn't put her finger
on why.

Maybe after breakfast she'd figure it out.

Her robe was where she always left it—on the hook at the back of her door. Maren was screeching in the shower. Lyle's bedroom door was closed. He was probably still asleep. He wasn't a morning person.

Vivienne had to grip the bannister to keep from falling forward. Why did she feel so woozy? Every step took too much effort.

Lynn was talking with a man who sounded vaguely familiar. His voice was deep, low, and serious, but also oddly soothing. The boards squeaked when Vivienne crossed the wooden floor.

Lynn was sitting at the kitchen table, her hair gathered in a leopard print scrunchie on top of her head. A man sat next to her, his back to the door.

When Lynn saw Vivienne, she shot to her feet and rushed over in a cloud of perfume and stale cigarettes. "Thank god you're awake." Her neon pink nails dug into Vivienne's arm as she escorted her to the table. "I've been so worried about you."

Vivienne couldn't remember the last time Lynn had been worried about something other than bingo or her job.

"What's Dr. Rhea doing here?" Vivienne asked, dropping onto a chair. He'd never made house calls before.

Dr. Rhea shifted on his chair, adjusting his hulking bulk. For a doctor, he seemed really unhealthy. At least he had shaved the few remaining hairs on his head instead of combing them across the shiny bald patch like he used to.

"You don't remember?" Lynn gasped, pressing a hand to her chest.

"Remember what?" Vivienne reached for a box of generic granola cereal and poured some into one of the chipped bowls on the table. When she grabbed for the carton of milk, she caught sight of bloody blisters on her wrist.

They hadn't been there when she'd gone to sleep, had they?

Come to think of it, Vivienne couldn't remember falling asleep.

"Oh, honey. You showed up a few hours ago, barefoot and covered in blood," Lynn cried, ripping off a paper towel from the roll and wiping the corners of her eyes. "I didn't know what to do. You were so out of it. I thought you were drunk, but I couldn't smell any alcohol. So I cleaned you up and called Dr. Rhea as soon as I got you to bed. He's really worried about you too."

"Maybe Lyle knows what happened." If Vivienne had gotten into trouble, it was probably his fault. "Just ask him."

Lynn's eyes widened. "Lyle doesn't live here anymore. He lives with you in New York."

What they heck was she talking about? "I've never been to New York." Vivienne had never even left Ohio. But when she graduated from high school, she was going to get out of this state and move somewhere warm, like Florida.

Tears glistened in Lynn's eyes, trailing eyeliner and mascara in black streaks down her cheeks. Scrubbing at them with the paper towel only made them worse.

"It'll be okay, Mrs. Foley." Dr. Rhea gave Lynn a reassuring pat on the shoulder. "We'll take care of her."

There was movement in the hallway, and Vivienne looked up to find two guys standing near the front door. The older of the two had dark hair and a dark beard. The other had short, strawberry-blond curls, glasses, and red Converse. Neither of them were smiling.

"Vivienne, you're going to come with us so we can run a few tests," Dr. Rhea said, rising and offering her his hand.

As much as she didn't want to go with him, there was definitely something wrong with her. And if it was serious, the safest place to be was with a doctor.

"Can I finish my breakfast first?" she asked, taking a huge bite. The granola was a little stale but still crunchy. "And I should probably put on something besides a robe."

"Of course, of course." Dr. Rhea didn't smile when he sat back down. He and Lynn made small talk about the weather and the economy and a bunch of other stuff Vivienne didn't really care about. When she finished, she loaded her bowl into the dishwasher and went upstairs to change.

The stairs behind her squeaked; she whirled around to find the guy with the beard following her. "I can get dressed on my own," she told him.

He offered her a tight smile. "I'm just making sure you're not going to run off."

Run off? She was on the third floor of the house. Where did he expect her to go? "It's not like I'm going to jump out the window."

The guy stiffened, which was weird.

"It was a joke," she assured him. The last thing she needed was a broken arm or leg to add to this bizarre situation.

He continued up the stairs but didn't say anything when she slammed her bedroom door in his face. Today was so weird.

She changed into her yellow sweatshirt and tights. Not sure how long the tests would take, she packed a small overnight bag. Where was her brother's sweatshirt? It wasn't in the closet. Her drawers were completely empty, and there was nothing but a pair of tights and a black sweatshirt in her hamper. If Maren had taken it, Vivienne was going to kill her.

When she came back out, the guy was waiting for her. He offered to take her bag, but she didn't want him touching her stuff. She wasn't sure why, but he gave her the creeps.

They descended the stairs in silence.

Lynn gave her a hug and told her that she'd be there as soon as she got off work. Why was she acting so clingy? She usually didn't take any notice of Vivienne. Maren was out of the shower now too. When she hugged Vivienne, her sense of unease grew. Maren hated her.

"Where are we going?" she asked Dr. Rhea as he held open the door for her.

"Unfortunately, we need to go to our medical facility in Virginia."

If they were bringing her out of state, then whatever was wrong with her must be serious. Besides a little dizziness and the achiness—and the unexplainable marks on her arms and ankles—she felt fine.

There was an ambulance waiting for her next to Ms. Melkova's beat-up red car. The blond guy helped her onto the trolley in the back and settled on a bench to her right. "Do you know who I am?" he whispered, his bright blue eyes wide with concern.

"No? Should I?" There was something about his shoes that seemed vaguely familiar, but she shrugged it off.

"Vivienne, listen to me—"

"Dad wants me to ride back here with you, Jasper," the dark-haired guy said with a friendly smile, clapping the other guy, Jasper, on the back.

Jasper. Jasper. Jasper.

Should that ring a bell? Vivienne felt like there was something just out of reach. Something important.

Jasper and the other guy, who said his name was Lawrence, strapped her onto the trolley.

"Dad said you need to give her the injection," Lawrence said.

Unease buzzed beneath Vivienne's skin. It felt like she had caught on fire. "What injection?"

"It's only something to help you sleep. It's a long drive to Virginia, and you're understandably exhausted." Lawrence patted her shoulder before reaching into one of the cabinets above his head.

Jasper's eyes widened, and he started shaking his head. "I think we should wait until we get to Virginia."

"Why is that, little brother?" Lawrence's nostrils flared like he was trying to keep his temper in check.

Jasper's gaze flicked to Vivienne's and then back to Lawrence. "Because I'm pretty sure she's pregnant."

"I'm *not* pregnant," Vivienne snorted. She had never even had sex. Not that it was any of their business. Leave it to guys to think a girl who may be carrying a little bit of weight around her midsection was pregnant. Maybe Vivienne just liked pie. *Mmmm . . .* pie. That sounded really good right now. When was the last time she had eaten?

Lawrence's eyes widened as he stared at Vivienne's stomach. If she hadn't been strapped down, she would have covered herself. "Holy shit. That bastard got her pregnant. Dad!" Lawrence banged against the side of the ambulance.

Vivienne heard a curse from the front, then the vehicle stopped. Lawrence opened a window and started talking fast about Vivienne being pregnant and shadows and mosquitoes and a bunch of nonsense that made no sense whatsoever.

"Get back to the house, Lawrence, and wait for them to show up," Dr. Rhea commanded. Lawrence adjusted his coat, and she caught sight of a gun at his hip. Since when did doctors need guns? Lawrence hurried to the door and threw it open. It closed again a moment later with a *bang*. The ambulance lurched forward.

"Jasper? It is Jasper, isn't it?" The guy gave her a tight nod. "I need you to tell me what's going on."

"Jasper?" Dr. Rhea called. "Give our guest a sedative so she can get some rest. It's going to be a long drive."

Jasper's mouth pulled into a tight line as he rummaged around in a cabinet behind him and found a vial and sterilizing packet. The smell of rubbing alcohol reminded her of all the times she'd given blood. The wipe was cold against her shoulder.

"I'm sorry, Vivienne."

She averted her gaze, staring at his red shoes and wishing she could remember why they made her want to run away. The needle pinched as it pierced her muscle, then her eyes fell closed. Instead of feeling heavy, she felt light. Like she was going to float away into the sky like a bubble. She was flying among the clouds and the birds, and she wasn't alone. There was a gorgeous dark-haired guy with sparkling green eyes flying next to her.

Jasper's head thumped against the window, jarring him awake. The lights from the oncoming cars on the other side of the highway were blinding. He had fallen asleep shortly after they crossed into Pennsylvania. It took a minute for his brain to register everything that had happened.

Dr. Hooke had called him in the middle of the night, telling him that they needed to go to Ohio right away. When he collected Jasper in an old ambulance, Jasper had been full of questions. Questions Dr. Hooke and Lawrence had both refused to answer.

Vivienne had returned to her foster home looking worse for wear. There was a bruise on her cheek and red marks on her wrists and ankles. His first thought was that she had been the victim of some terrible crime or abuse.

But the way she'd looked at Jasper, like she had no clue who he was, left him with a different theory. Vivienne was either a very good actress or she was one of the forgetful that Steve had told him about. The moment he could get a blood sample, he would check her hormone levels. They had been particularly high when she'd been at HOOK the first time.

And he'd check her hCG levels as well.

Jasper was almost positive Vivienne was pregnant.

When he had seen her in Nashville, she'd been wearing a tight black T-shirt that highlighted her petite frame. She was still thin, but the bump on her stomach when she laid flat on the trolley looked like more than extra weight.

Jasper read the road signs as they passed, the sun rising in the distance, painting the horizon in brilliant shades of orange.

"Did you miss the exit?" he asked, glancing at Dr. Hooke's somber expression.

"We're not bringing her to the main facility."

"Where are we going then?"

"You'll see."

Two exits later, they left the highway. Eventually, they pulled into a parking lot at the end of an abandoned strip mall.

Jasper's chest tightened. "We can't take Vivienne in there." The windows in the office next door were smashed out. And the far end looked like it had sustained significant fire damage.

"Where would you suggest we bring her?" Dr. Hooke turned off the ignition and released his seat belt.

"The lab—"

"That's the first place they'll look." He threw open the door and was outside before Jasper could ask him anything else.

Vivienne was still unconscious in the back. Jasper checked her pulse, hoping the dose of sedative hadn't been too high. After they unloaded the trolley, Dr. Hooke wheeled it over the jagged pavement to the door.

Dr. Hooke pulled out his wallet, located a black key card behind his credit cards, and swiped it in the lock. The old HOOK offices never used to have such a sophisticated security system. Why would they invest in one now if this building was abandoned?

The waiting room looked the same as Jasper remembered —right down to the dusty ficus and sagging poster. But the camera in the corner with a steady red light was new. After unlocking the door to the back hallway with the same key card, Dr. Hooke wheeled Vivienne to an elevator located next to the stairwell.

"Do you want to go home?" Dr. Hooke asked.

"What? No. Why?"

"You've always been soft. I need to know that you're with us. That you understand sacrifices are necessary to make the world a better place."

Jasper's gaze dropped to Vivienne's pale features. If he left now, there was no telling what would happen to her. He didn't owe the PAN anything. He didn't owe HOOK anything either.

But he owed Vivienne.

She could have let him die in that fire at the lab. She probably should have.

But she hadn't.

Dr. Hooke was right. Sacrifices *were* necessary.

Jasper straightened and took a deep breath. "I understand."

The elevator dinged, and the steel doors opened. Dr. Hooke wheeled the trolley inside and pressed -2 on the keypad.

Jasper's heart began racing as the doors closed.

THIRTY-FIVE

Something was wrong. Really, *really* wrong. Vivienne's eyelids felt like they weighed a thousand pounds. She would have pried them open with her fingers, but she couldn't move. There was a strange metallic taste in her mouth, and she was freezing—she realized suddenly that she wasn't wearing any pants. She could have sworn she had pants on this morning.

When she managed a blink, her vision was blurry. As her eyes finally focused, she wished she could go back to sleep. The room was made entirely of concrete. Concrete floors: okay. Walls? She'd seen them before in basements. But concrete ceilings? That didn't seem safe. This didn't look like a doctor's office. It looked like a freaking bunker.

The worst part was that she couldn't move. At all. Someone—she assumed Dr. Rhea—had bound her ankles with leather straps at the bottom of the . . . whatever-you-call-it she was laying on. It was bed-ish, but the mattress was so thin she could feel every seam and bolt holding the thing together. And her arms had been strapped outstretched across a T-bar, like a cross. Someone had replaced her clothes with one of those uncomfortable, open-back hospital gowns.

"Hello?" Her voice cracked.

There didn't seem to be anything else in the room besides the bed. Something rattled behind her. The bonds were too tight to check what it was. Since she couldn't see one in front of her, she assumed that it was the sound of a door.

"Good morning, Miss Dunn." The dark-haired guy from earlier, Lawrence, wore a pair of scrubs and surgical mask as he rounded the top of the bed. "You've been asleep for so long, you gave us a scare. So much has happened since we last spoke." His voice sounded delighted.

"Where's Lynn?" She was supposed to be there. That much Vivienne remembered.

"Let's get you in the other room so we can begin," he said, continuing as if Vivienne hadn't spoken.

"I want to talk to Lynn."

"I'm sure you do."

What the heck did that mean? Was Lynn in the other room?

He kicked the release on the bed-thing's brakes and wheeled her through a concrete tunnel with flickering lights hanging from the ceiling. At the end of the corridor was a red exit sign.

Why was she so freaking itchy? If her hands had been free, she would have scratched her skin off. "Can you untie my hands? My arms are really starting to itch."

That made Lawrence laugh for some reason. "Excellent."

He didn't untie her hands.

The itching got so bad that it felt like she was on fire. When she tried to pull free, the wounds on her wrists burned, bringing tears to her eyes. Stopping at a black door, Lawrence came around to where Vivienne could see him and knocked.

"Come in." It was Dr. Rhea.

The blinding light inside the white room left her squinting; the stench of bleach stung her nostrils. The entire length of the far wall was a wide, reflective window that looked like it could be a two-way mirror. That's where Lynn must be. Some of the medical equipment Vivienne recognized, like the IVs and heart monitors. She didn't get a good look at the rest because Lawrence pivoted and positioned her under a light on an adjustable arm.

Beside her was a wide steel table lined with trays, vials of yellow liquid, and surgical instruments.

On the other side of the table, Dr. Rhea was bent over someone lying on a second bed. If this was a sterile room, she shouldn't be in there with someone else, right?

When he stepped aside to throw his rubber gloves into a biohazard waste bin, she sucked in a breath.

On the other bed was a teen with a swollen, bruised face, his bottom lip split and bleeding. Dark hair fell limp over his forehead. They had strapped him down the same way, with arms outstretched. From the way his head lolled to the side, she assumed he was unconscious.

"What happened to him?" she asked, fear curdling in her stomach. It was a good thing these people were doctors. That guy needed serious medical attention.

"There's no need to concern yourself with this one," Dr. Rhea muttered, scribbling on a clipboard before tossing it onto the steel table. After washing his hands in the corner sink, Dr. Rhea grabbed another pair of gloves.

"Let's talk about you, Vivienne." He dropped onto a rolling stool and scooted until he was next to her. He was wearing scrubs, but his surgical mask hung around his neck. His dark eyes felt comforting and familiar. "It appears as though you've been a very busy girl since you left Ohio."

"What do you mean?" Vivienne hadn't left Ohio. Why did people keep saying that?

"Still playing at the amnesia, are we? That's fine. There are other ways to make you talk." He picked up a needle from a tray and attached a vial to the other end.

The door burst open. Vivienne recognized the other guy, Jasper, from the ambulance by his red shoes. "She's not playing," he said from behind a surgical mask, eyes trained on another clipboard. "Her levels of nGh are off the charts. I've never seen numbers this high." The pages rattled as he flipped through them.

Dr. Rhea's eyes narrowed as he examined her. "You're telling me this one can't remember a thing?"

Jasper looked up from the clipboard and shook his head. "I didn't realize it could happen this fast. I suspect in the next few weeks, she'll forget everything."

Forget *everything*? Vivienne's memory was great. Well, maybe not great. She didn't remember how she hurt her wrists and ankles. But average, at least.

Dr. Rhea cursed and kicked the bed, making Vivienne's heartrate spike. Then his lips curled into a strange smile, and his eyes glazed over like he was drunk. "This could work in our favor." Dr. Rhea wet his thin lips. "How often will her memory reset?"

Jasper flipped to the back of the clipboard, his mouth moving as he read. "According to Edward's notes, her mother's memory reset every four hours."

Why were they talking about Christine? There had been nothing wrong with Christine's memory. At least nothing Vivienne could remember. She glanced back at the lifeless guy across the room. There was something about him . . .

"Wonderful." Dr. Rhea clapped and turned back to her. "You don't happen to remember who the father of your child is, do you?" He nodded toward the guy with the bloody face. "Was it this one over here?"

Vivienne knew she'd remember if she'd slept with the unconscious teen. Even bruised and bleeding, he was the hottest guy she'd ever seen. "I already told you that I'm not pregnant."

Another laugh. "Lawrence, roll that ultrasound machine over here."

Okay. This was going too far.

Dr. Rhea tugged up her hospital gown, exposing her underwear and very swollen stomach.

"What are you doing?" Vivienne shrieked, her face burning in embarrassment. "Cover me up!" If she could have moved her arms, she would have yanked the gown back down. She didn't want them seeing her without her freaking clothes on.

"It's okay, Vivienne." Dr. Rhea reached for a white tube on the table. "We're all medical professionals."

A red-faced Jasper pulled a sheet around her ankles to cover her bottom half.

Dr. Rhea squeezed a pile of clear goop onto the end of the wand. Then he brought the cold gel to her stomach and started moving it around, pressing hard enough to be uncomfortable. How far were they going to push this sick joke? She wasn't—

Holy. Crap.

There was a baby. *Inside. Her. Body.*

It was tiny, but there was no mistaking its little arms and legs flailing around.

"Heartbeat looks good. I'd say you're about eighteen weeks. Almost halfway there."

Vivienne didn't know *how* she'd gotten pregnant. But there was no denying it now.

"Looks like someone should have taken the prescription for birth control when I offered it to her," Dr. Rhea sniggered, wiping the gel off her stomach before turning back to clean the machine's wand.

Jasper pulled Vivienne's gown back down and settled the covers up to her chest. "Thanks."

"Don't thank me." Jasper twisted away and moved to stand next to the table and trays.

"Can we get this show on the road?" Lawrence drawled, twisting a gold watch around his wrist. "Louise and I have dinner plans, and I really don't want to be late." He grabbed a vial of yellow liquid and a different needle in a sterilized packet. After assembling them, he held the sharp needle toward the light and squirted some of the liquid into the air.

"You can't give her that," Jasper hissed, knocking the needle out of his hand. It clattered onto the tray next to the other unused injection.

Lawrence shoved Jasper into the wall. "What the hell did you do that for, *Rat*?"

"He's right, Lawrence." Dr. Rhea continued writing on the clipboard. "If we give it to her, it could hurt the baby."

"What do you want me to do with it then?" Lawrence picked up the syringe again. "We can't waste it."

"Give it to that one." Dr. Rhea nodded toward the unconscious guy. "He's been a pain in my ass for years."

Years? The guy didn't look any older than Vivienne. What kind of trouble could he have possibly given a doctor?

A sneer twisted on Lawrence's mouth as he stepped over to the teen and injected him with whatever the yellow stuff was. Vivienne watched the young man's face turn a sickly shade of gray. The skin around his eyes and mouth wrinkled like he was smiling. But he wasn't smiling.

"What are you doing to him?" *Oh god.* The guy started convulsing so hard that the bed shook. "Stop! You're hurting him!"

"That, my dear, is the point." Lawrence laughed, making no move to assist the poor guy. "If you two have this under control, I'm going to head out. Louise and I have reservations at seven."

Dr. Rhea waved him away and told him to come back first thing in the morning. The guy agreed, threw the needle, along with his mask and cap, into a biohazard waste bin, and swept out the door, whistling a happy tune.

The guy they had injected went still. Vivienne watched his chest for signs that he was breathing, but she couldn't tell. What if he was dead? What if Lawrence had killed him?

Oh god.

What if they were going to kill her?

She tried to pull her hands free, but they were bound too tightly. How was she going to get out?

"Jasper? I need you to take some tissue samples." Dr. Rhea nudged a tray of petri dishes toward him. "The more we have, the better."

Jasper washed his hands before slipping on a pair of gloves. He cleaned the guy's arm with an antiseptic wipe, then went to grab a different tube that looked almost like the one with the ultrasound gel.

"There's no need to waste anesthetic," Dr. Rhea told him.

Jasper's eyes narrowed. Instead of protesting, he picked up an instrument that looked like a pen with a silver ring on the end and pressed it to the guy's upper arm. Vivienne winced when the guy flinched and groaned, happy he wasn't dead but hoping he wasn't conscious enough to feel the pea-sized hole oozing blood.

Vivienne's stomach turned. *Oh no.* She was going to puke.

She screwed her eyes shut. The bleachy smell made her nausea worse as she inhaled short, shaky breaths through her nose and exhaled through her mouth.

Jasper took three more samples, placed them in separate petri dishes, and labeled them. "Will you close him up, or shall I?"

"Don't bother."

The samples slammed onto the tray. Jasper stalked to where Dr. Rhea was collecting another tool that looked like the one Jasper had used. "It would do no good to have the wounds get infected. If you plan on keeping him here for more samples and blood tests, I *suggest* closing the wounds."

"I don't plan on keeping him."

Vivienne's breath caught in her throat. What did that mean? If they weren't going to keep him, what were they going to do with him?

"Do you understand how much information I could get from a live PAN?" Jasper shot back, throwing his hand toward the unconscious guy.

PAN.

There was something about that word that resonated within Vivienne.

"You have a live one right here." The alcohol wipe was cold against Vivienne's upper arm.

"She's pregnant. Her numbers are skewed."

"Then we'll have to wait until she has a lucid moment and ask her where the rest of the filthy bastards are hiding. If that one survives the serum"—Dr. Rhea nodded to her fellow captive—"he's not leaving this place alive."

Vivienne's heart raced, which made the itchiness worse. They were going to kill him. She had to do something. Had to say something. "Don't hurt him. Please. I'm begging you."

"After the trouble you've caused, you have the gall to ask for mercy?" Dr. Rhea's dark eyes narrowed. "All you had to do was stay in the hospital. But you chose to run. We could have worked together. Helped each other. But you chose the wrong side of this fight." Dr. Rhea threw the wipe onto the tray but didn't reach for the anaesthetic gel. Surely he wasn't going to—

The end of the contraption pressed against her arm, and a searing pain shot through her. Vivienne screamed as blood oozed from the deep wound.

"Scream all you want, my dear," Dr. Rhea said with a malicious smile. "No one can hear you down here."

THIRTY-SIX

The moment Jasper left the operating suite, he fell back against the cold cement wall. Mario came around the corner wearing his usual black-on-black attire. The flickering lights glinted off the weapon holstered at his hip. Jasper nodded as Mario passed, unable to force a smile. There was nothing to smile about anymore. If he didn't do something, people were going to die.

What would happen to the baby when it was born? What would happen to Vivienne?

And the other PAN . . .

Lawrence had injected that poor bastard without batting an eye.

And Jasper had stood by and let him do it.

Jasper hadn't *wanted* to help Dr. Hooke. He hadn't wanted to do anything that evil man had ordered him to do. But he had, because if he'd refused, there was no telling what would have happened to him—or to Vivienne. So he had kept his mouth shut and followed orders. Waiting.

Biding his time until he could do something that would help instead of hurt.

But the longer he stayed, the more apparent it was that he may not be able to help at all.

The light above his head buzzed like a mosquito. His hand fell to the pocket of his lab coat out of habit. Dr. Hooke had confiscated his cell phone the minute they got into the elevator. He would have protested, but when they got out, Mario and another giant security guard had been waiting on the lowest level.

His phone had to be around here somewhere. If he found it, he could call in an anonymous tip. Then the police could handle this. Jasper had barely survived stealing a few vials of poison. He was in way over his head, and there was no way he could bring Dr. Hooke down on his own.

There were three doors between Jasper and the red exit sign illuminating the end of the hall. The first one was a storage closet with an old mop and bucket, a "slippery when wet" sign, and a broom with a broken handle. The second was the locker room where he and Dr. Hooke had changed after arriving. Was Jasper's phone in one of the lockers? He slinked into the empty space. The first locker was empty. The second one had a bunch of white towels folded at the bottom. The third one had a poofy red coat.

It could have been Mario's. Or the other guard's.

Although, Jasper couldn't imagine either of them wearing anything but black.

His heartrate spiked as he checked the pockets . . . and found a pair of black gloves and a matching hat stuffed into one pocket.

And a cell phone. It was turned off, but he already knew whose it was before he turned it on. When the screen lit up, there was a photo of Sarah and Steve smiling.

A thousand different scenarios flitted through Jasper's mind—and none of them ended well.

The door flew open, slamming against the far wall.

Jasper dropped Steve's cell phone into his pocket and forced the locker closed. When he turned around, the guard he didn't know was glaring at him.

"What're you doin' in here?" the man growled, his hand falling to the gun at his hip.

"I—I had to use the bathroom."

The guard grunted and told him to get the hell out. Jasper kept his eyes on his shoes as he crossed to the exit. Maybe Steve had left his coat at work, and Lawrence had confiscated it during one of his "routine security checks."

Maybe Steve had found the facility, stored it in there while he snooped around, and forgotten it.

Stomping footsteps echoed from the far end of the corridor. Jasper didn't want to know who was on the other side of the bend.

If he went back to Vivienne, Dr. Hooke would get suspicious. And he couldn't just loiter until the guard came out. The digital display above the steel elevator doors counted down slowly. And dinged.

Jasper ducked into the room beside the stairwell.

It was pitch black and at least ten degrees colder than it had been in the hallway. A sickly sweet odor hung in the air. It was so strong, he had to tuck his nose into the neck of his shirt to keep from gagging. There were low voices outside, but whatever the men were saying was muffled. He waited in darkness for the voices to subside. A few moments later, he was surrounded by silence. Jasper slid his hand along the cement beside the doorframe to find the light switch.

Fluorescent bulbs clicked when he flipped it. The ceiling was so low, Jasper could touch the concrete. When he turned around, what he saw left his heart hammering against his ribs.

In the center of the room was a steel table with raised edges. An old surgical lamp on an adjustable arm loomed above it. To the right were shelves with metal bins, an x-ray machine, and hanging scales beside a large sink with hoses dangling over the edge.

Jasper had watched enough true crime shows to recognize the row of steel body coolers on the far wall.

His footsteps echoed as he crossed to the first door. With a shaky hand, he reached for the handle. It released with a *woosh*.

Empty.

And the next one, and the next. Every empty cooler he opened eased the tearing pain in his chest.

When he reached the second to last one, it wasn't empty.

The stench of formalin left him gagging as he stared at a foot sticking out from beneath a white sheet. With everything inside of him screaming to run away, Jasper slid the body free.

He lifted the sheet.

It was the teen from Tennessee, his skin a ghostly greenish-gray. Jasper had hoped he had survived the gunshot wounds.

Dammit.

If only he had refused the assignment when his brother had told him to get Vivienne.

Sliding the boy back into his metal coffin, Jasper's heart felt like it was going to explode.

He didn't want to check the last one.

But he had no choice.

Sure enough, there was a body inside.

Jasper lifted the sheet. Bile rose to his throat.

He'd found Steve.

THIRTY-SEVEN

"Hey!" Vivienne whisper-shouted to the unconscious guy across from her. "*Pssst*. Hey. Wake up."

The guy groaned.

"*Wake. Up.*"

His lashes fluttered open, revealing eyes so piercing and green and—

Vivienne knew him.

She knew him as intimately as she knew herself. Flashes of memories blinked through her mind. A rooftop. An open window. An exotic island in the middle of a turquoise sea. And this guy . . . this guy had been there for all of it.

Her stomach fluttered and her core pulsed. Heavy breathing. Skin searing skin. Lips on her neck.

And those eyes.

"I know you." This guy . . .

This guy was part of her.

"I'm so sorry," he croaked, his voice like a siren's song.

She knew his voice. Had felt it vibrate against her neck, whisper in her ear. She knew his laugh and his smile. She *knew* him.

"I was too late. I'm so sorry."

There were more important things than asking him what he meant by that. "They're going to kill you."

His lips lifted into a resigned half-smile. "I know."

"You have to escape. You have to try."

Blood flowed bright and red down his arm when he strained against the bonds holding him to the bed. "I can't do a bloody thing." He cursed. "Why do I feel as weak as a kitten?"

"They took a lot of blood. And they gave you a shot."

His eyes were wide when they trained on her. "What color was it?"

What color had it been? "I think it was yellow."

He cursed and banged the back of his head against the mattress. "That's it for me." When he turned back toward Vivienne, his wide eyes glittered. "Did they give it to you?"

She shook her head.

"Good. You can still escape."

If he couldn't break out of the bonds, what chance did she have? "And how do you suggest I do that?"

"Fly away."

Fly away? That shot must've made him loopy. "Did you hit your head or something? People can't fly."

"You can."

"No, I can't."

"Vivienne, listen to me." He jerked on the bonds again, but they didn't budge. "You *can* fly. You can fly and you can escape."

Even if he wasn't crazy . . . Even if she *could* fly, "I'm chained to a bed."

His eyes ran from her head to her toes, making her

insides feel warm and tingly. When they locked with hers again, he grinned. "Then take the bloody bed with you."

Of course. Why hadn't she thought of that?

It sounded simple enough.

Except the bed was heavy.

AND SHE COULDN'T FREAKING FLY.

"You'll need adrenaline," he gasped, wincing as he struggled to free himself. The bed he was on scraped against the concrete floor. "You have to get your adrenaline pumping."

Her heart was already racing. "Adrenaline isn't a problem." She wished her hands weren't bound so she could scratch her skin off. "I itch so bad."

"That's a good thing. Lean into it. Are you feeling warm?"

"I don't know. Maybe a little?"

"Brilliant. You're doing brilliant. Focus on the fire in your chest. Let it spread to your limbs. You can do this. You're one of the most brilliant fliers I've ever met."

His praise made her flush, and she could feel a fire igniting and building in her core. Spreading and tingling and burning. *Holy crap.* She felt it. She felt the fire. "Now what?"

"Think happy thoughts."

Happy thoughts? She was being held captive in a basement by a bunch of insane doctors. She had no happy thoughts.

"They need to make you feel lighter. The kind of memories that can banish even the darkest sorrows. The kind of happiness that can destroy nightmares and make dreams come true."

"I can't—" *Come on. Come on. COME. ON.* "I can't think of anything. My mind is blank."

"What about the time I kissed you in my back garden? When I proposed to you on Peter Pan's island? The day we got married, surrounded by our friends? The night we found out about our child? All the times we've made love? Every single memory I have shared with you is a happy one. Try to remember, Vivienne."

They were *married*?

Why couldn't she remember any of it?

She was staring at a black wall between herself and her memories. She pummelled it with her fists, trying to break through. But the wall didn't budge or shake or dent. It was as impenetrable as the concrete walls caging them in.

"I don't remember." Tears streamed down her cheeks, and she tried and tried, but the fire inside of her was dying out. "I'm sorry. I don't even know your name."

The guy's lips lifted into a slow, cocky smile that made her stomach feel like it was full of butterflies.

No, not butterflies. There was a light, a warmth.

Fireflies.

She felt like she had swallowed a bunch of fireflies.

"My name is Deacon Elias Ashford."

The spark ignited, and she felt like she'd burst into flames. Her body lifted, taking the whole bed with her. *Holy crap.* Vivienne *could* fly.

Deacon's head fell back against the bed, and he started laughing. She knocked the ultrasound machine over on her way to him, arms still spread wide. Her fingers ached as she angled herself so she could reach for the bonds keeping him on the bed.

"There's no time." Deacon shook his head even as he fought to free his hand.

The strap slipped through Vivienne's fingers. If only she could twist her wrist a little more . . .

"Vivienne, look at me."

She didn't want to look at him. If she looked at him, he was going to say something she didn't want to hear. The stupid strap was just too short. She couldn't get a good enough grip on it.

Come on. Come on. *Come ON.*

"You have to get out of here. They could come back any minute. Leave me."

Was he crazy? She couldn't just leave him there. Still, there was no point freeing him if they couldn't get out of the room. She abandoned the straps to try the handle on the door.

"It's locked."

Think, Vivienne. Think.

When she looked back at Deacon, she caught her reflection in the two-way mirror that stretched the length of the back wall. If she could get enough momentum, maybe. Just maybe.

Using the side of her bed, she scooted Deacon's bed against the wall. "I need you to close your eyes." If this worked, there'd be glass everywhere.

She flew until her nose was pressed against the door. Then, closing her eyes, she took a deep breath, imagining the oxygen fanning the flames in her chest.

She held onto the ghosts of her memories, willing the flames to engulf her body . . .

And shot toward the window.

There was a sharp, ear-piercing crash of shattering glass.

The room on the other side was black, with only a handful of chairs facing the jagged gap where the mirror had been.

Vivienne flew to the door past the chairs.

The handle twisted and released.

The hallway was clear, but she could hear voices.

Closing the door, she flew back to Deacon.

Chairs clanged against the ground.

Sharp, searing pain sliced through her thigh. Blood dribbled from beneath the hospital gown where she had caught herself on a shard still clinging to the mirror's frame.

"Why aren't you coming with me?" she asked, her voice trembling.

"I can't fly. Not anymore. You need to get out of here. Don't worry about me. I'm too stubborn to die."

He was lying. If she left, they were going to kill him. "I'm not leaving you."

"If you stay here, they're going to hurt you and our baby. Get out."

There had to be some other way. She reached for the strap again. "No, I—"

"Get out! Get out, Vivienne!" Deacon thrashed and shouted, his face turning red, his green eyes wild. "Get the hell out of here. I mean it. I'll never forgive you if you don't get out."

"I'll come back for you." The second she found a phone, she would call the police.

Deacon stopped fighting and dropped his head. "I know you will, lovie."

A high-pitched alarm sounded from the ceiling. Red lights in the corners of both rooms flashed. Vivienne flew back through the gap and threw the door aside. Right or left? Which way had they brought her?

There. At the end of the hall.

A red exit sign.

Vivienne flew toward that sign, praying she'd make it. Praying they would *both* make it.

Jasper burst through a door to her right. He stumbled into the wall. His face was covered in sweat, his eyes bulging. "Take the stairs." He nodded to the door beside the one he'd come from. "Go up two floors, then take a right. You'll need a key card to get out." He dragged a black card from his back pocket and reached for her bonds, untying one hand.

Blood dripped down her leg and onto the floor. It could be a trap. He could be leading her into another concrete cell. "Why are you helping me?"

Jasper dropped his hand and stepped back. "Because when this is over, I want to be on the right side of history."

The shouting behind them got louder. His gaze landed on whoever was coming for them. "Come at me hard as you can and bowl me over."

"I'll hurt you."

"It doesn't matter."

Vivienne hadn't come this far to get caught. She flew backward a few feet, then rammed into him with the side of the bed. Jasper collapsed into a heap on the ground. She made it to the door and got the top half of the bed into the narrow stairwell before the sound of gunfire erupted behind her. No matter how she twisted, she couldn't get the bottom around the corner. The wheel caught on the door, and she tried maneuvering it, but with the bullets flying she couldn't get it at the right angle and there was so much chaos from behind her she couldn't—

There. She got through the door and jolted up the stairs, emerging into another hall, taking a right, and flying through the first door she saw. It opened to some kind of old waiting room.

And the key card was gone.

With the main door locked, the only way out was through the window. But it was too small to fit the bed. Vivienne struggled with the straps around her other wrist, her fingers clumsy and weak. Once she managed to get free, she undid the bonds around her ankles. Footsteps pounded from the stairwell.

There was no time to think.

She dragged the bed to the receptionist's desk and hurtled forward.

The glass cracked.

She hauled back and tried again.

The glass exploded at the same time the stairwell door slammed against the wall. Two men burst into the room. Gunshots echoed as Vivienne flew through the gap and escaped into the starry sky.

THIRTY-EIGHT

R ed lights flashed in slow motion from the ceiling. *On. Off. On. Off.* Deacon tugged on the bonds keeping his arms outstretched. It could have been his imagination, but he thought the one Vivienne had messed with felt a little looser. He wrenched. Pulled. Twisted. Yanked. Wiggled. Nothing got his damn hand through the gap.

Sharp pain shot through every nerve as he inhaled a shaking breath. Deacon had landed in the back garden at Lynn's house and made it halfway up the stairs before Lawrence had jumped him, tackling him to the ground. He'd fought to get the larger man off, but the last thing he remembered was the butt of Lawrence's pistol coming toward his head.

The unmistakable *pop-pop* of gunfire reverberated off the menacing gray walls. Deacon fought memories of that balmy night in Tennessee. Even broken and bleeding from a gunshot wound, he'd had hope. For survival. For the future.

The only hope he had now was that Vivienne would escape.

Please be okay. Please, please be okay.

Men were shouting. The more vicious their cursing grew, the more his heart swelled. If Deacon hadn't been neutralized, he would've been with her. If only he hadn't been a fool and agreed to take the bloody vaccine.

Ah, well. Hindsight and all that.

There was no point focusing on everything he had done wrong.

Death was enough to face on its own.

He yanked his hand again, twisting. The leather slipped.

Just a little bit more . . .

Dr. Hooke barrelled into the room, red-faced and drenched in sweat. His eyes bulged as he gasped for air. When his gaze landed on Deacon, his eyes narrowed into slits.

There was only one reason for the old bastard to look so murderous: Vivienne must've escaped. The shite thing was that he wouldn't be able to congratulate his wife on her brilliance.

That he wouldn't be able to meet his daughter.

Vivienne kept saying they could be having a son, but he knew it was a girl. And she would look like her mother. He hoped she had something of him in her. Perhaps his eyes. But if not, that'd be all right too.

They were going to be fine without him. Vivienne had Peter and his mother. And her friends. And even bloody Lyle. And knowing her memory would be returned to her eventually gave him a bit of solace. All the memories they had made would give her something to hold on to. Something to share with their little potato.

It wasn't enough for Deacon. He'd wanted to give her more. Give her everything.

But it wasn't meant to be.

"You," Dr. Hooke snarled. "I'm going to dissect you and keep you alive long enough to watch me do it."

"Such ambitious plans for a man with very little time left." One way or another, this would be the end of HOOK. Peter wouldn't let Deacon's death go unpunished a second time.

"You think you're in a position to threaten me?"

"I'm not the one you need to worry about." He huffed a laugh, then winced. "They're coming for you."

Dr. Hooke's thin lips pulled back in a sneer. "You're bluffing."

"Am I?" Deacon wasn't sure why he was egging him on. He probably should have been trying *not* to get killed. But begging wasn't his style. Not when it came to HOOK. He'd rather spend his last few minutes on earth annoying the shite out of them.

If only he'd brought a Charlie Bell. But he had been in a bit of a hurry. The moment he'd woken up and realized Vivienne had escaped out the window, he had known in his heart that this was over.

She'd left her phone and TINK on the bedside locker, so there had been no way to track her. He'd wasted too much time searching Kensington when he should have caught a plane straight to Ohio.

Then Lawrence had attacked him, and he'd woken up here.

Strapped to a cross and neutralized.

Dr. Hooke stumbled forward and bent to pick something off the floor. The flashing lights glinted off a scalpel.

Deacon's adrenaline surged, but there was no fire. Only blind panic.

If he could get a hand free, he'd have a chance.

Again he tried. Again he failed.

Jasper Hooke fell through the open door, blood trickling from a gash near his temple. So much for the traitor being trustworthy. Steve had been missing for over a week. Were they keeping him down here too?

"She's gone. She made it out." Jasper may have been talking to his father, but he was looking at Deacon.

At least he could die in peace knowing his wife was safe.

Dr. Hooke didn't react as he continued searching the floor. "Find the petri dishes. We need more samples."

"You can't be serious." Jasper grabbed his father's arm. "It's over. We need to get out of here."

"This bastard isn't going to live to tell the tale. Grab the tray." Dr. Hooke jerked free and kicked aside the rest of the surgical instruments scattered across the floor. "We're taking as much of him as we can get."

The leather cut into Deacon's wrists as he tried and tried and tried to get free but . . .

Shit.

This was it.

"Any last words?" Dr. Hooke snarled in Deacon's ear. The heat from his breath left him gagging. A trickle of blood rolled down Deacon's neck as the scalpel pressed against his throat.

"Yeah." Deacon grinned toward the flashing lights. "Tick tock."

THIRTY-NINE

"Any last words?" Dr. Hooke adjusted his hold on the scalpel pressed against the teen's jugular.

The boy's lips curled into a wicked smile. "Tick tock."

If this had been a movie, Jasper would've laughed at his audacity. But this wasn't a movie.

An indignant growl erupted from Dr. Hooke's chest. The red flashing light reflected off of the heavy steel tray discarded on the floor.

Without thinking, Jasper took it in both hands, lifted it over his head, and smashed it over Dr. Hooke's bald head.

Dr. Hooke slumped. His hand slipped.

Blood spurted into the air, splattering the ceiling. A strangled gurgle escaped the teen's lips.

Jasper searched frantically for something to staunch the flow of blood. Pressure was the only thing that would save this guy's life. And even then, it may not be enough. He dragged Steve's cell phone from his pocket, ripped off his lab coat, rolled it into a ball, and pressed it to the wound.

"Stop fighting. It'll be okay. It'll be okay," Jasper repeated like a prayer.

Was the artery cut through or just nicked? *Dammit.* There was too much blood . . .

Color leached from the teen's face.

Blood smeared over the screen as Jasper pressed the button on the phone. There were no bars of service, but the screen said, "Emergency calls only." He pressed *Emergency* at the bottom and typed in 9-1-1.

"9-1-1, what's your emergency?" The woman's voice was faint and full of static.

"I'm with a guy who's had his neck cut. He's bleeding, and I don't know what to do." This boy was going to die, and it was all Jasper's fault. Why hadn't he called the police the moment he found Steve's body? "Please send someone. Please help him."

"Sir, I need you to calm down. Do you have anything there to apply pressure to the wound?"

"I did that already, but I don't know if it's working."

"Are you at 204 Elm?"

"I think so." That was the address, wasn't it? "I'm at the end of the strip mall. In the basement. The doors have security locks on them. There are armed guards."

"Did you say *armed* guards?"

"Yes." Jasper glanced toward the doorway. It was only a matter of time before Mario and his hulking partner found him.

"Emergency services are on their way. Can you tell if the victim is breathing?"

"I don't know." If the teen's chest was moving, it was too shallow for Jasper to see.

There was a loud crash from the hallway and shouting and bullets and *dammit.*

The phone slipped from Jasper's hand, bounced off his shoe, and slid under the metal bedframe.

"Sir? Sir, can you hear me? Are you still there?" The woman's muffled voice was hard to hear above the ruckus outside.

Dr. Hooke groaned. His hand went to his head as he struggled into a seated position.

A black blur charged through the door, pistol drawn. At first, Jasper thought it was Mario. But this guy was thinner and wearing a black bulletproof vest, helmet, cargo pants, and top. Two more officers in similar gear followed him in.

The one in front gestured toward Dr. Hooke. The other two nodded and stalked to where the doctor was scooting toward the corner, begging them not to hurt him. The shorter one zip-tied his wrists behind his back.

The leader raised his visor. Piercing green eyes peered through the gap. "Lift your hands slowly and back away from him," he ordered Jasper in a posh British accent, the barrel of his gun aimed at Jasper's chest.

"If I do, he'll die." Jasper prayed the teen wasn't dead already. "Please don't shoot me. Please."

The man cautiously sidestepped to the foot of the bed. "Bloody hell . . . " His eyes widened, then flicked to Jasper. "*Did you do this?*" The gun shook in his hand.

"I didn't. I swear. It was *him*."

"That's not true," Dr. Hooke cried from the floor. "Jasper tried to kill the kid. I saw him. I saw him slit his throat. I *saw* him!"

"I'm the one who called the police, you lying bastard! I'm the one trying to save him."

The leader's gaze bounced between Jasper and Dr. Hooke. "Nic. Get over here and check him out."

The shorter officer took off his helmet—

Her helmet. It was a woman. And a gorgeous one at that. She nudged Jasper aside and peered beneath the blood-soaked lab coat. "It doesn't look good." Blue eyes met Jasper's. "How long has he been bleeding?"

"I . . . I don't know. A few minutes? I put pressure on the wound right after it happened. I should have acted sooner. I should have stopped him."

"Don't believe a word out of his mouth," Dr. Hooke sneered.

"Hooke, Hooke, Hooke," the leader muttered, removing his helmet and running a hand through his dark, matted hair. He was younger than Jasper had been expecting. And there was something familiar about him.

Jasper's chest tightened when the guy withdrew a gold alarm clock from the pouch at his thigh.

It was them.

It was the PAN.

The clock clanged against the concrete when the guy threw it at Dr. Hooke. "I know better than to believe a bloody codfish."

Dr. Hooke's eyes bulged as he shook his head. "No. No. How did you find us? No one knows about this place. *No one.*"

The guy bent to pick something up off the floor. Steve's cell phone. "You probably should have destroyed this when you had the chance."

"I swear—"

"Hey, Owen? Can you shut him up?"

The guy kneeling behind Dr. Hooke raised his pistol and brought it down on his head. Dr. Hooke slumped to the ground once more.

Two more officers ran through the door. One of them was carrying an armful of clothing. "The cops will be here any minute. We need to go."

The leader nodded, then turned and pressed a button on the walkie-talkie attached to his vest. "Everyone clear out. Police are on their way." Instead of leaving, the young man started removing his gear.

"You can't stay," the girl beside Jasper scolded.

The guy handed over his gun and helmet before undoing the belt at his waist. "I'll not let him die alone."

"Peter—"

Peter? As in Peter Pan? Jasper couldn't believe it. He couldn't be. He looked too old to have an active NG-1882. He had a stubbled jaw and wrinkles at the corners of his eyes. The PAN never had wrinkles.

"Jasper, I want you to go with them." Peter gestured toward the officers as they filed out of the room. "They'll give you an alibi."

Alibi? Why were they helping him? "I don't deserve to escape." He deserved to be taken into custody with Dr. Hooke.

Peter's smile was sad as he nudged Jasper out of the way and took over with the blood-soaked coat. "Everyone deserves a second chance."

It felt like Jasper was moving underwater as he followed the PAN up and out of the basement. Shards of glass glittered on the waiting room tiles. The woman who had been downstairs replaced her helmet. Sirens echoed in the distance.

"We're bringing you home, okay?" She linked her arm with Jasper's left. Another officer took his right.

"What's the point? Once the police see the security footage, they'll know I was there."

"There is no security footage." Her grip tightened. "Not anymore. You ready?"

Jasper nodded.

Next thing he knew, he was being carried into the clouds.

FOURTY

S hifting on the stiff plastic mattress, Vivienne picked at the tape holding the needle to the back of her hand. The colorful bouquets on the bedside table made the hospital room smell like a funeral home. The bandage around her thigh was too tight, but the nurse she'd complained to had refused to do anything about it.

It had been three days since she had been admitted. The first day she'd spent mostly unconscious with an IV pumping fluids and medicine into her body. The second day she'd spent suffering through question after question from the police.

The problem was that she couldn't really remember what had happened. And the details she did remember didn't make any sense.

Outside the door, there were people talking. Lyle had told her there were news vans and cameras everywhere. Apparently, she was famous.

Vivienne didn't want to be famous.

She wanted to go back to Ohio and pretend this had never happened.

"I never would have called them if I had known. I'm so sorry, Vivienne." Lynn sniffled from the chair beside the bed, dabbing at her swollen eyes with a tissue. "This was all my fault."

"It was Dr. Rhea's fault. Not yours." Vivienne offered Lynn a reassuring smile. No matter how many times she told her foster mother that it was okay, Lynn wouldn't stop apologizing.

The door opened, and the green curtain around her fluttered. Between the gaps, Vivienne saw a bed being wheeled in.

"He should be awake soon."

Vivienne recognized the nurse's voice.

"Thank you for all your help," said a man with a British accent. "You've been brilliant, Barbara."

"Just doing my job." The nurse giggled. "If you need me, buzz."

Lynn's mouth pinched in disapproval, highlighting her too-dark lipliner. "They said we would have a private room," she muttered in a harsh whisper.

"It's not a big deal." If Vivienne had to share for one night, she'd live with it.

"Yes, it is. I'm going to speak with someone about this." Lynn dropped her purse beside the chair and breezed through the curtains. The door clicked closed.

"How are you feeling, Vivienne?"

The question had come from the British man on the other side. How did he know her name?

Not wanting to be rude, she told him she was okay.

When he came through the gap, she sucked in a breath. "You're the one who saved me." She recognized his face from the news. This guy had been searching for his younger brother and had found him in the basement of HOOK's old office complex. The details were fuzzy, but she remembered him unhooking her from a bed and carrying her to the ambulance.

"Something like that." His green eyes sparkled when he smiled.

Wow. He was hot. A bit too old for her, but that didn't mean she couldn't appreciate his tall, lean build. Or his tanned, toned arms. Or the way his black T-shirt fit.

Okay. She needed to stop drooling or he'd think she was a weirdo. "How's your brother?"

The man's smile faltered. "He'll live."

"I'm glad."

"Me too." His eyes narrowed as they combed her body. "How's the baby?"

Her hands fell onto her swollen stomach. She still couldn't believe she was pregnant. "Fine."

"Good."

A groan from the man's brother left her hero retreating to the other side of the curtain.

Vivienne spent the afternoon chatting with the guy, who said his name was Peter, and Lynn, who suddenly didn't seem to mind the fact that Vivienne had to share her room. When visiting hours were over, she had trouble sleeping. Curiosity eventually got the better of her, and she slid out of the bed. Wheeling the IV along behind her, she hobbled to the dividing curtain.

Moonlight fell softly on a young man's sleeping form.

His face was dotted with cuts and stitches. A black-and-blue bruise surrounded his left eye, and his neck was wrapped in surgical dressings.

But the most surprising thing of all was how absolutely gorgeous he was despite it all. Maybe even hotter than his brother.

His eyes flashed open—and landed on her.

Crap. It was too late to hide. "I didn't mean to wake you

up." Like that mattered. What had she been thinking? This guy obviously needed to rest.

The corner of his mouth lifted into a half-smile. "It's all right," he said in the softest whisper.

"I couldn't sleep. And I was curious about you after what I heard on the news." Why was she telling him that? It made her sound like a creep. "How are you?"

"I've been better."

"Sorry. That was a stupid question."

Now he was full-on smiling. "How are you?"

"Still pretty confused. And pregnant. So *that's* been interesting."

He huffed a laugh, then groaned and clutched his side.

"Do you need anything? Should I call the nurse?"

He nodded.

Vivienne found the remote attached to his bed and pressed the red call button. When the night nurse came in, she scolded Vivienne for being out of bed and kicked her back to her side of the room.

It took a while, but eventually, Vivienne managed to sleep. When she woke the next morning, Lynn was already there.

"They're releasing us first thing." Lynn patted Vivienne's hand. "I brought you clothes. Once they unhook your IV, you can go ahead and get dressed."

The nurse came in a short time later to discharge her. Lynn left to sign final paperwork and give Vivienne some time to change. The jeans Lynn had brought for her were too tight around her waist to button. Luckily, her oversized yellow sweatshirt covered everything. Before she left, she went over to where Peter was sitting, speaking quietly with his brother.

"I wanted to thank you again for what you did for me," she told him. If he hadn't helped her escape that basement, she could have been killed.

Peter's head tilted as he smiled at her. "There's no need. But you're welcome."

To the guy in the bed, she said, "I hope you get out of here soon."

"Thank you." His smile was tight as his gaze flicked to Peter. "Do you mind giving us a moment alone?"

Peter hopped off the bed and disappeared through the curtain.

"I know this is going to sound strange," he said in a voice barely above a whisper, "but do you mind if I touch your stomach?"

Lynn had warned Vivienne that random strangers would try to touch her belly. At least this guy had asked first. "I guess not." She moved to the head of the bed. He struggled to prop himself on his elbow.

He leaned in and pressed his cheek to her sweatshirt. The crazy thing was that it didn't feel strange. It felt nice. "Hello, little girl. You have the strongest, most brilliant mum in the whole world. I—I mean, *she* can't wait to meet you."

Vivienne thought it best not to tell him she didn't know if the baby was a boy or girl.

There were tears in his eyes when he let her go.

She said goodbye and met Lynn at the nurse's station in the hallway.

Vivienne left the hospital feeling lighter than she could remember.

Almost as if she could fly.

FOURTY-ONE

Six Months Later

Deacon paced up and down the hospital waiting area. The bouquet of roses in his hand banged against his thigh. If only he had been allowed in the bloody room. Being excluded from the most significant event in his life was shit, but the worst part was not knowing. Vivienne's screams had abated forty minutes ago. If something was wrong, surely someone would have told him.

"Sit down, man," Lyle grumbled from one of the chairs. The magazine in his hand rustled as he turned the pages. "You're making me dizzy."

"Shove off." Deacon would sit when he was good and ready.

Emily kicked Lyle's shoe. "Leave him alone." A massive teddy bear sat next to her, three foil balloons tied to its hand.

The PAN had purchased a house in Columbus a few doors down from Lynn's, where Deacon, Lyle, and Emily had been living for the last six months.

He saw Vivienne every day.

And every day he had to reintroduce himself multiple times. Every day except the 15th of May, the 10th and 28th of June, the 23rd of July and the 24th of August.

On those days, Vivienne had remembered who he was—and what had happened to them. They had tried fitting six months of life into that short span of time.

The door to Vivienne's room opened, freezing Deacon in place. Lynn came out, her face flushed and eyes brimming with tears.

"What's happened?" Deacon ran toward her. "Is Vivienne all right?"

"Everyone's fine." Lynn's nicotine-stained teeth flashed when she smiled. "It's a girl." Withdrawing a crumpled tissue from the pocket of her too-tight jeans, she wiped the corners of her eyes.

Deacon had known they were having a girl. Still, hearing Lynn speak the words aloud left him steadying himself against the wall. "When can I see her?"

"The doctor said she'd come get you when it's time." Lynn gave him an awkward pat on the shoulder and continued to where Lyle and Emily waited. Lynn now knew there were problems with Vivienne's memory. And that Deacon was the father. But that was it. Lyle had wanted to tell his mother more, but until Leadership voted again—or Peter made a decision about going public—he wasn't allowed.

The door to the room opened again. This time, it was Dr. Carey. Most of her hair had escaped the clip at the top of her head. "There's the proud poppa." She beamed. "You have a healthy baby girl."

"I know." He raked a hand through his hair. "Lynn already told me."

"Vivienne was asking for you."

His heart constricted in his chest. "She was?"

A nod. "By name."

Rose petals spilled onto the pristine white tiles as he sprinted for his wife's room. After throwing open the door, he approached the blue curtain with more caution. Inhaling a deep breath, he drew the thin material aside. Vivienne was lying on her side, her back to him. As he rounded the foot of the bed, he found her smiling down at an impossibly small pink blanket.

He didn't know what to do. So he just stood there, staring like a fool.

The smile remained on her lips when her gaze met his. "Aren't you going to come meet your daughter?"

Did she actually remember, or had Dr. Carey told her who he was?

Deacon took a halting step forward to peer into the blanket. Wide green eyes stared back at him. A shock of dark, fluffy hair stuck up like a mohawk.

"Isn't she beautiful?" Vivienne stroked their daughter's impossibly tiny hand with her fingertip.

"She looks a bit like a potato," Deacon said with a smile, his heart breaking. His little girl's lips turned down into the cutest frown. And she started wailing. "The cutest potato I've ever seen," he rushed, abandoning the flowers on the foot of the bed and dropping into the empty chair. "Don't cry. *Shhhh. Shhh* . . . I didn't mean it." The moment he touched her cheek, she fell silent. At first she peered up at him, then she turned toward his fingers. A tiny pink tongue darted from between bow-shaped lips. "She's cranky like her mother, I see."

"I think she's hungry." Vivienne started unbuttoning her hideous pink nightdress.

"Oh, right." Reluctantly, he turned his head away. "Do you want me to leave?" He didn't want to go. But this wasn't about him.

"Why would you leave?" Vivienne gestured toward their

daughter. "It's not like you haven't seen them before. Now stop staring and take off her onesie."

"Really?"

Vivienne's brow furrowed as she nodded. "Yes, really."

How did a person pick up a baby? Deacon's hands felt massive and clumsy as he unwrapped the blanket. He cursed silently when he saw the tiny buttons running the length of the pink-and-white one-piece.

Not buttons.

Snaps.

Whoever invented snaps was a bloody genius.

His daughter's skin was softer than anything he had ever felt before, her legs so thin and wrinkly. His arms felt empty the moment he handed her over.

Vivienne cradled their daughter in the crook of her arm as she unhooked the strap on her bra. How did she know exactly what to do? Women were something else.

"You really remember me?" Deacon asked.

"Of course I do," she snorted, rolling her eyes.

He had been terrified that when she got the injection, it wouldn't work. It had worked for the other forgetful, but HOOK had stolen all of his optimism.

He sank onto the chair beside the bed and watched in fascination as his wife smiled down at their now quiet child.

"I'm sorry I didn't let you in the room," Vivienne whispered.

Emotion caught in Deacon's throat as he nodded. He knew Vivienne had been going through hell, and not being able to help her through it had nearly killed him. But he couldn't allow himself to get down about it now. "Are you feeling all right? Is there anything I can get you? Is there—"

"Deacon? I'm fine. Just talk to me. Tell me what I've missed."

Everything Vivienne had missed, Deacon had missed as well. He hadn't left Ohio since he was discharged from the hospital in Virginia. "They're still deciding whether or not to go public. No one is swaying. Peter still hasn't made a decision and keeps giving lame excuses as to why he refuses to weigh in. And Lee's going to marry my Mum."

The wedding was in a month. Deacon wasn't thrilled about it, but he hadn't seen his mother smile this much since before his father had passed away, so he figured it was a good thing. Not like there was anything he could do about it anyway.

Vivienne adjusted their little one as she leaned back against the pillows. She looked terribly uncomfortable. He shot to his feet and propped the pillows around her so she could relax. With a smile playing on her lips, her free hand smoothed down his stubbled cheek. He wanted to kiss her so badly.

Being around her but not able to touch her had driven him mad.

"I like this," she said, rubbing her thumb over his chin. "It suits you."

Deacon averted his gaze as he pulled away. He didn't want to talk about anything that would lead them down a dark and dreary path. He needed sunshine and rainbows and unicorns and tiny babies in pink blankets.

"Although," she said with a small laugh, dropping her hand to idly stroke their baby's wild hair, "I'm pretty glad I didn't grow one when Dr. Carey gave me the injection."

HOOK was gone, but Deacon was relieved Vivienne would be safe for eternity. Well, not eternity-eternity. Eternity-ish. Not that he'd be there to see it.

"Have you chosen a name?" he asked, desperate to change the subject. Every time he had asked her what she was going to call her baby, she had given him a different answer.

"I think we should call her Angela. Angela Anne Ashford."

Angela for Deacon's grandmother. Anne for Vivienne's mother. "It's perfect."

"Are you sure? Because if you hate it, we can call her something else."

"Absolutely not. It suits her."

Vivienne's lips lifted into a contented smile. Angela squirmed away, milk dribbling down her chin. She looked like she was sound asleep.

"Would you like to hold her while I go shower?"

"Is that even a question?" Deacon removed his jacket and reached for the sleeping bundle.

Vivienne clamped a hand around his wrist, freezing him in place. "Let me see your arm."

Shit.

How could he have forgotten about the unsightly black marks highlighting his veins? Deacon had worn the jacket for that very reason. "Go have your shower, Vivienne."

Her response was to roll up the sleeve of her night dress and show him her arm.

Her veins were black too.

"I thought . . . " His words trailed off as he searched her expression for some other explanation than the one swirling through his mind. If she had gotten the injection manufactured in Harrow, she shouldn't have those lines. "You let them neutralize you?"

Vivienne nodded. "I told you I was going to."

"But . . . how? When?" She had only just remembered him.

"Apparently, I called Dr. Carey back in July and told her that I didn't want the vaccine. I wanted HOOK's poison. She said she tried to talk me out of it, but I was adamant. Doesn't sound like me at all, right?"

Deacon didn't want to smile, because his wife was grounded and she was going to get old and die, but *dammit* . . . they were going to do it together.

355

"I wanted to love you forever," he said with a laugh, touching his forehead against hers, "but I'll settle for one lifetime."

Vivienne drew him close and pressed her lips to his. "You and me."

Deacon smiled. "You and me."

EPILOGUE

"Yes. I understand. Thank you." Deacon ended the call and turned to Vivienne. His wide eyes and stunned expression left her heart sinking.

"Well? What did he say?" The fact that Alex had called Deacon was strange enough. The two were finally on speaking terms, but Alex *never* called.

Deacon shook his head slowly. "Jasper found it."

"Found *what*?"

"A way to activate dormant genes."

Vivienne was afraid to hope. "Does that mean he can fix us too?"

A V formed between Deacon's dark eyebrows, and a smile played on his lips. "I wasn't aware we were broken."

"Shut up. You know what I mean." If they could activate dormant genes, maybe that meant they could activate genes that had been neutralized as well. She and Deacon would be able to fly again. They could live for a long, long time. They could be around to watch Angela grow up and meet their grandchildren and great-grandchildren and maybe even great-great grandchildren.

"We can go in for an injection next week. Apparently it worked on Lee."

Oh my gosh. Oh my gosh. OH MY GOSH.

Vivienne squealed and threw herself at her husband. His hands came around her, and she could taste the relief in his kiss.

"Quiet on the set!" the director shouted, shooting a glare at the two of them.

Vivienne had completely forgotten where they were. She muttered an apology but didn't let Deacon go.

It had been a year since their miraculous escape from HOOK, and NBC4 Washington was doing a three-part special on the whole ordeal. They had interviewed Jasper Hooke two days ago.

Vivienne and Deacon had given their testimony yesterday. They'd had to memorize a script written by Paul Mitter and approved by Leadership. It was basically the same information they had given to the police when they were interviewed after the incident.

Peter was being hailed as a hero. In order to give Jasper an alibi, Peter had taken credit for calling the police and saving Deacon and Vivienne.

"We can celebrate when we get home." Deacon's whisper sent chills down her spine. He released his hold, and they moved to a free space behind the cameras to watch Peter's interview.

The station had opted to film outside the former HOOK facility—which Peter now owned, and Jasper operated.

The interviewer, a pretty dark-haired woman named Sarah McBride, took a drink from her bottle of water before handing it to the assistant putting some last-minute touches on her hair and makeup.

The director called for quiet on the set one last time.

Deacon squeezed Vivienne's hand. She was so full of adrenaline and happy thoughts that if she'd had an active Nevergene, she would've been flying.

"I'm Sarah McBride, coming to you live with an exclusive story one year after the harrowing events that took place in Virginia. Two teens were being held captive by The Humanitarian Organization for Order and Knowledge, a medical research facility outside of Winchester. I'm here now with one of the heroes from the event, Peter . . . " She narrowed her eyes at the teleprompter. "Peter *Parker*. Is your name really Peter Parker?"

Peter grinned. "It is today, Sarah."

"Whose idea was it to let him on the tele?" Deacon muttered, shaking his head and rubbing his temples.

Vivienne stifled a laugh.

"Right. Peter Parker. You're called a hero."

"The men and women who coordinated the rescue, and the doctors and nurses who saved Deacon, are the real heroes," Peter said with a shrug. "All I did was make a call."

The woman's sculpted eyebrows came together. "Still, for someone so young, you were very brave."

"Young? I'm almost two hundred years old."

"What's he doing?" Vivienne whispered, panic settling in her stomach. He was supposed to say he was twenty-nine. Hadn't he read the script?

Deacon shrugged and shook his head.

"It appears that, in addition to being a hero, Peter Parker is also a comedian," Sarah said, her smile strained.

Peter's composure slipped, and he started laughing. "I'm so sorry," he said when he caught his breath, clutching his stomach. "You should see your face right now."

"You are aware this is live, right?"

"Oh, I'm perfectly aware." He wiped tears from his eyes and started fiddling with the mic attached to his black button-down shirt.

Sarah McBride narrowed her eyes at Peter. "Do you mind telling us what's so funny?" she said with forced lightness.

"My name isn't Peter Parker."

She picked up her notes from her lap and shuffled through the pages. "Then what is your name?"

"Peter Pan."

Her smile looked like it was going to shatter. "Are you saying your parents named you Peter Pan?"

"To be honest, it was such a long time ago, I'm not exactly sure what my parents named me."

"Shit." Deacon tensed. "He's taking off his mic."

"I can see that," Vivienne snapped. She wasn't blind.

Peter removed his mic, then collected the cord and pulled the battery pack from where it was tucked in the back of his dark jeans. He set them all on the table between himself and the interviewer.

"But *why* is he taking off his mic?" she asked.

A smile broke across Deacon's face. "I think he's casting the deciding vote."

"Is this some sort of . . . joke?" Sarah asked, forcing a laugh and flipping through her notes like she was searching for a lifeline.

"No, it's not a joke, Sarah. It's the truth." Peter stood and walked toward the camera, a goofy grin on his face. "I'm Peter Pan."

Then he shot into the sky.

ACKNOWLEDGMENTS

To each and every member of The PANdom, those of you who fell in love with this sci-fi twist on a classic fairy tale and told their friends, family, IG followers, and everyone they knew about these books, I thank you. I know people say this a lot, but without you, this trilogy wouldn't have happened. (And it certainly wouldn't have been a success.) I appreciate every mention, tag, DM, and review. You made me excited to continue this story instead of letting the project fall by the wayside.

I'd like to give a specific shoutout to the #DamesforDeacon and #Isthisakissingbook girls, who have welcomed me into their Bookstagram community and have championed this story from the beginning. You girls have made my day on so many occasions. Thank you.

To Elle Beaumont at Midnight Tide Publishing: thank you for being the perfect home for The PAN Trilogy. It's been such a pleasure publishing with you. And to my fellow MTP authors: thank you for being such a brilliant support system.

To my editor, Meg Dailey: I know I've said it a million times, but you are a GODDESS. Your notes and asides kept me going, you helped me polish this story to its full potential, and you always seem to know how to make the story better. It's like your superpower. I'm lucky to have you on my team.

To my beta reader, Barbara Kloss: thank you for lending your skill and insight and enthusiasm to make this one epic conclusion.

I want to thank Candace Robinson, Miriam Sincell Burton, and Megan Paulk for helping me out with ARCs and being my go-to cheerleaders when I needed that extra push to keep going.

To Jimmy, my husband: you're great. (There. I said it.) You took on the bulk of the housework, giving me time to make some pretty tight deadlines. Thanks also to my children who have been patient with me, and my in-laws who have been a huge help babysitting when I needed extra time. To my mom: you're my number one supporter, even when things on the page get a little "racy." To my sister Megan: you're a big reason I finished this book so quickly. You kept bugging me for more stuff to read. And to my sister Dani, who has helped me get through some hard days by listening to me whine and complain on more than one occasion. God gave me the best family.

Finally, I want to thank the characters that have lived inside my head for the last eight years. Instead of saying goodbye, let's say, It's been fun. And maybe someday I'll see you again.

ABOUT THE AUTHOR

Jenny grew up in Oakland, Maryland and currently lives in County Tipperary, Ireland with her lilting husband and two tyrannical children. Her love of reading blossomed the summer after graduating high school, when she borrowed a paperback romance from her mother during the annual family beach vacation.

You can find Jenny across social media @authorjenny-hickman or follow her author journey via her newsletter at www.jennyhickman.com

ALSO BY JENNY

The PAN Trilogy
The P.A.N.
The H.O.O.K.
The C.R.O.C.

MORE BOOKS YOU'LL LOVE

If you enjoyed this story, please consider leaving a review!
Then check out more books from Midnight Tide
Publishing!

Emmie and the Tudor King by Natalie Murray

One moment, Emmie is writing her high school history paper; the next, she is lost in 16th century England, where she meets a dreamy Tudor king who vacillates from kissing her to ordering her execution.

Able to travel back to her own time but intensely drawn to King Nick and the mysterious death of his sister, Emmie finds herself solving the murder of a young princess and unraveling court secrets while trying to keep her head on her shoulders, literally.

With everything to lose, Emmie will come to face her biggest battle of all: How to cheat the path of history and keep her irresistible king, or lose him—and her heart—forever.

Available Now

Clouded by Envy by Candace Robinson

Sometimes the very thing you wish for, is your undoing...

Brenik has always been envious of his twin sister, Bray. Everything always came naturally to Bray, even after crossing through a portal from their fae world, while Brenik spent his time in her shadow. So, when Brenik discovers a way to get what he has always desired--to become human-- he takes it. However, the gift turns out to be a curse that alters him in ways he never saw coming.

Bray can't help but be concerned for her brother, more so when he vanishes. While waiting for Brenik to return, she meets two brothers who realize she is not the least bit human. Her dark bat-like wings are proof of that. But some- how, an aching bond forms between Bray and the older brother, Wes.

When Bray reunites with Brenik, she finds an overpow- ering need for blood stirring deep within him. If Bray doesn't help Brenik put an end to his curse, it will not only damage those who get close to him, but it could also destroy whatever is blooming between her and Wes.

Available Now

9 781953 238290